"A TERRIFYING RIDE . . .

No one is better at the literary equivalent of a road movie
than Thomas Perry, and *Blood Money* shows perfectly
all his many strengths. . . . A terrific, pell-mell book."
—*Minneapolis Star-Tribune*

"A delicious treat . . . Perry has a knack for creating
memorable characters, but where he really shines is in
his breathlessly paced and beautifully streamlined plots."
—*The Seattle Times*

"Jane Whitefield [is] a sleuth with the most original
occupation in mystery fiction—she makes people in
trouble disappear. . . . Her methods are ingenious, and
Perry's writing is as sharp as a sushi knife."
—*Los Angeles Times*

"[This series] just keeps getting better. . . . Perry has
created a very strong and likable protagonist who
continues to evolve as a human being. An interesting
plot backed by good writing, intriguing characters, and
realistic dialogue makes *Blood Money* a winner."
—*San Francisco Examiner*

Please turn the page for more reviews. . . .

Also by Thomas Perry

THE BUTCHER'S BOY
METZGER'S DOG
BIG FISH
ISLAND
SLEEPING DOGS
VANISHING ACT
DANCE FOR THE DEAD
SHADOW WOMAN
THE FACE-CHANGERS
DEATH BENEFITS
PURSUIT
DEAD AIM
NIGHTLIFE
SILENCE

BLOOD MONEY

Thomas Perry

BALLANTINE BOOKS • NEW YORK

A Ballantine Book
Published by The Random House Publishing Group

Published in the United States by Ballantine Books, an imprint of The Random House Publishing Group, a division of Random House, Inc., New York, and simultaneously in Canada by Random House of Canada Limited, Toronto.

www.ballantinebooks.com

ISBN 0-8041-1541-9

This edition published by arrangement with Random House, Inc.

Manufactured in the United States of America

First Ballantine Books Edition: May 2002

OPM   9   8   7   6   5   4   3

To Jo, Alix, and Isabel

Their Great Men, both Sachems and Captains, are generally poorer than the common People, for they affect to give away and distribute all the Presents or Plunder they get in their Treaties or War, so as to leave nothing to themselves. If they should once be suspected of Selfishness, they would grow mean in the opinion of their Country-men, and would consequently loose [*sic*] their Authority.

—Cadwallader Colden, *The History of the Five Indian Nations Depending on the Province of New-York in America*, 1727.

There were still moments when the old life seemed to be on the verge of returning—there would be something out of place near the vanishing point of her sight or in the periphery. A bit of the past seemed to materialize for an instant, just long enough to catch Jane's eye and cause her to remember it, then recede again to become indistinguishable from the soft, familiar landscape. Sometimes it would be no more than a sound—a spring-loaded metallic click-scrape noise that turned out to be a door bolt slipping into its receptacle, but could have been the slide of a pistol cycling to snap the first round into the chamber.

Usually it would be a man who made her uneasy. A few times it had been men in crowds who had resembled other men from other times. Once it was only a stranger in a deserted mall parking structure who happened to be walking in the wrong place for too many steps—a bit behind Jane and to her right, where she would be most vulnerable to attack. The old habits of mind emerged again in a reflex. As she prepared her body to make the sudden dodge, her ears listened to his footsteps to detect a change in his position. Her eyes scanned the area around her to record its features—the shapes of parked cars she could put between them, small pools of bright light on the pavement to avoid, the railing she could roll over to drop to the next level down without running for the stairs. Then, as each of the others had done, this man changed his course, unaware that he had startled her, and walked off in another direction. Usually it had been men. Today, it was just a young girl.

From a distance, the girl looked about fourteen: the thin, stringy blond hair that kept getting in her eyes; the narrow hips and bony chest; the clothes she wore that were a little too tight and too short, but made Jane wonder about her mother rather than about her. The girl first appeared on the Seneca reservation, and that was the first sign. She was too blond to be somebody's cousin from Cattaraugus or Allegany, and too young to work for the government, and Jane couldn't see any obvious explanation of how she had gotten there.

It was twelve miles from the Tonawanda reservation to the house in Amherst where Jane and Carey lived. Since Jane had begun to construct her new life she had spent more and more time on the reservation. First, she had visited friends and relatives, then let the friends talk her into going with them to meetings about tribal issues. At one of them she had volunteered to work in an after-school program to teach the old language to kids who had not learned it. All of them knew some words and phrases, and a few could make sentences, so the classes were easy and pleasant.

Jane had held her walks three times a week for over a year on the day when she first noticed the girl. Jane had waited on the high wooden front porch of Billy and Violet Peterson's house under the tall hemlock and watched for the school buses. When enough of the children had gathered, Jane had gone inside with them and talked. The simple, inevitable logic of languages was appealing and satisfying to her students: "ah-ga-weh" is mine, "ho-weh" is his, "go-weh" is hers, "ung-gwa-weh" is ours, "swa-weh" is yours, "ho-nau-weh" is theirs.

But a language carried implications and assumptions that had to be explained. There was a history even in its lapses and absences. A modern Seneca conversation was filled with borrowed words for the things that filled the children's houses—computers, television sets, microwave ovens.

Jane found herself taking the group out to walk the roads and fields and woods of the reservation to talk about the world. Whatever scurried across the path ahead of them or hung in the sky above or shaded them with its branches she could talk about without words from new languages.

Most of the time, if Jane saw a teenaged girl watching, she would wait until the girl's curiosity led her close enough, then invite her to join the walk. This girl appeared at the edge of a distant stand of sycamores, then disappeared. Jane saw her five times that day, but the girl never came closer. Jane couldn't help knowing at each moment the route the girl must be taking, and where she would appear next. That was part of what Jane had spent years training her mind to do. When she had seen the girl twice, she could follow the rest of her progress with as little conscious effort as a hunter needed to track the trajectory of a pheasant.

Jane asked her little band of linguists who the girl was, but each of them waited patiently for someone else to answer. Jane said, "If she comes to join us, I want everybody to make her feel welcome."

But she didn't. The last time was when Jane got into her car at the Petersons' house. Jane considered driving a quarter mile, then quietly making her way back through the woods on foot to come up beside her for a talk. Jane lowered her head and pretended to search for something in her purse while she kept her eye on the rearview mirror. The girl was coming out of hiding to talk to a couple of Jane's students. Now that she could see her clearly, Jane began to feel a vague sense of discomfort.

There was a haggard, feral look around the eyes, and a set to the thin lips. It was a small-featured, precocious look that reminded Jane of the undercover policewomen they sent into high schools to impersonate students. Jane started her car and slowly pulled out onto the highway. If the girl was just a girl—maybe a friend of one of the kids on the reservation— then probably she would overcome her shyness by Monday. If she wasn't, then Jane had accomplished what she had needed to: she had memorized the face.

Almost certainly, this was just another time when Jane's old reflexes had been triggered by something innocuous. She glanced at her watch. She would have just enough time to

make a few calls for the hospital fund drive and then get
ready for dinner.

Jane finished setting the dining room table, then walked back
into the kitchen to wash the crystal wine glasses by hand. She
had noticed that there were water spots on them. If Carey had
been here, she would have said it was because the last time
they had been put away, she and Carey had both been suf-
fering from the ill effects of having used them the night before. They only had wine with dinner on special occasions,
and special occasions always ended the same way in this
house. The wine glasses would end up somewhere in the bedroom, and the dishes would be left for morning.

As Jane rinsed the two glasses and reached for the towel,
she saw in her memory her mother making the same motion
in the small house in Deganawida. Her mother had probably
been the happiest woman Jane had ever met. She had also
been a fraud. She had decided at the age of twenty—or
twenty-two, as Jane had corrected her after her death—who
she wanted most in the world to be, and then spent the rest of
her life impersonating that woman. It had been a very sophisticated, wise thing to do, and what had prompted her to do it
had been the same five or six years that had given her the
sophistication.

Jane had grown up knowing little about her mother that
was true. Her mother had been an expert at cheerful evasion,
and when Jane would ask insistent questions, she was capable
of lying with tenacity and consistency. What was true was
that Jane's mother had somehow turned up in New York at the
age of sixteen alone. The next five or six years were what she
never spoke about. Jane had learned a little after she had
grown up. Her mother had spent those years in the company
of men who had money to share because they took it, and
who, without thinking of it, offered her a certain safety because they inspired fear. At the end of the time, in a display
of the preternatural cunning that people who live on the mar-
gins develop as a substitute for everything else, she had re-
invented herself.

She had met Henry Whitefield, a worker in structural steel who traveled the country with a crew of men—three Mohawks and a couple of Onondagas from Grand River, and two other Senecas. Now that Jane was a grown woman, she knew that their chance meeting had been contrived. Her father, Henry Whitefield, had been too perfect a counter to the men her mother had decided to desert. He was tall, with skin like a copper penny and eyes like obsidian. He was scrupulously honest—even blunt—but most of all, he was manifestly not a man who could be dissuaded by any conceivable threat of harm. Men who walked on steel girders twenty-five floors above the street in uncertain winds were unlikely to be intimidated by anything they met on the ground. The fact that he traveled in the company of a whole crew of similar men would have reassured her too: she would have misinterpreted it at first, because it looked like the way her old companions behaved. But she had been a woman with acute instincts, and she had probably sensed that the misinterpretation was not entirely wrong: if he were in danger, the others would circle around him.

They were both long dead now, but they were not absent. They had taken up residence behind Jane's eyelids. Jane's mother had re-invented herself as Mrs. Henry Whitefield and lived the next eleven years in blissful imposture. She was the sort of wife who always looked as though she had just changed her clothes and fixed her makeup. She was the sort of mother who had time for everything and overdid the birthdays and indulgences. And she had tended Jane as though she were training her to rule a small kingdom.

Before Jane was born, her mother became conservative in dress and manner like other children's mothers, but it didn't disguise either the reasons why she had gotten into her troubles or why she had survived them. Henry Whitefield's best friend, Jake Reinert, who still lived next door to the old house in Deganawida, had once said to Jane that her mother had been "the single best-looking female human being not only to live in Deganawida," but, he had insisted, "the best-looking ever to pass through it by a nonflying conveyance."

Then he had added wistfully, "It's a shame you didn't get more of her . . . disposition."

During the horrible summer, six years after her father was killed, when her mother was dying of cancer, there had been a frantic period of talk. Her mother would palm her medicine and fight the pain so she could talk to her for hours at a time. She had been doing something she admitted was laughable— trying to tell her daughter everything she would need to know from the age of nineteen to the age of forty.

Their conversations were full of things almost said: "After I met Henry I was never unhappy another day of my life." For years afterward, Jane wondered at the foolishness of it, but she sensed that she had heard only part of it. Her mother had not told Jane that happiness was not something she had waited for, but something she had decided.

Jane had carried the things her mother had said and done as though they were statements in another language, then slowly, one by one, she had realized that she understood them. In a way, she knew, she was emulating her mother. She had spent the early part of her adult life doing something that was dangerous—always illegal, and on the occasions when she made a wrong turn or a wrong guess, punctuated with bright flashes of violence. She had been a guide. People whose lives were in danger had found their way to her—first a young man she knew, and after that, a woman who simply knew someone she knew, and, later, strangers. She had moved them to other places, given them other names, and taught them how to live other lives. Then one day, she had agreed to become Mrs. McKinnon, and begun to make Jane Whitefield the last of the fugitives to disappear.

Since then she had devoted herself, just as her mother had, to being the woman she wanted to be. For the past two years, she had refused to allow herself to fall asleep at night without being able to say to herself, "This was a good day. I'm glad I didn't waste it." She was not ashamed of her premeditation. When Carey got home, she was going to demonstrate that her mother's wisdom had not been lost on her. Carey didn't have to go to the hospital tomorrow until

evening rounds, and she had decided she was going to keep
him up for most of the night. She went upstairs and began to
fill the tub for her bath.

Over the rush of water, she thought she heard something.
She turned off the faucet. Was it the phone? Then she identified it: the doorbell. She looked down at the front steps from
the upstairs window, and saw the girl. Jane didn't have time
to list all of the reasons why seeing her here caused a sick,
breathless sensation in her stomach. As she hurried down
the stairs to the front foyer, she let one reason stand for all.
This wasn't something a shy young girl would ever do.

Jane swung the door open and assumed a false smile.
"Hello," she said. "Didn't I see you at the reservation?"

"I . . ." the girl began, but it seemed that she had started
wrong. "Can I come in for a minute?"

Jane stepped aside, took a careful look at the street beyond her in both directions, and found it empty. The purpose
of the visit wasn't to get inside and open Jane's door to men
who were here to harm her. Whatever threat the girl was
bringing didn't take that form.

Jane scrutinized her as the two walked into the living
room. There were no weapons, and no purse to hold a microphone. There was the skirt that was fitted to hug hips that
were too narrow, the halter top that left bare a flat stomach
and bony lower ribs but was there to hide almost nothing,
the blond hair that had begun to look dirty. Jane said, "I'll
bet you're thirsty. What can I give you to drink?"

She surprised Jane by saying, "I just didn't want to stand
out there while I asked you."

"Asked me what?"

The girl took a deep breath, and Jane could hear a quiver
in it. "I'm sorry to come like this, but I. . . . You never seem
to be alone. I talked to some of the kids out there, and they
said your name used to be Jane Whitefield. Did it?"

Jane concentrated on making her breathing smooth and
even. This was the first time since she had married Carey
McKinnon that anyone had come to this house looking for

Jane Whitefield. If the girl was asking, then she already knew. "Yes," she said. "And what's your name?"

"I'm Rita Shelford. If I've got the wrong person, I don't know what I'll do." She looked around her at the big living room of the old house, and Jane could see it through her eyes. Jane had to resist a sudden impulse to make excuses for it. The heavy, shining pieces of antique furniture were there because Carey's ancestors had been accumulating them since the 1790s, probably with as little awareness as he showed about such things. The enormous stone fireplace had been put there not out of pretension, but because that was the way to warm a house in those days.

Jane tried to help the girl, but warily. "I think you've got a problem?"

The girl nodded.

"Come on," said Jane. "Let's go into the kitchen and we can talk while I make some lemonade or something." Jane stood and led her by the route down the hall so she wouldn't be alarmed by the elaborate preparations Jane had made in the dining room. Each step on the wooden floor sounded to Jane's ears like a hammer.

Jane entered the kitchen, where cooking smells and steaming pots made her feel as though her impersonation of an ordinary doctor's wife was stronger. She had to be careful. She stood by the sink, where the sunlight streamed in behind her, and studied the girl's face as she sat at the kitchen table. She had been right that the girl was older close up. Jane turned and cut lemons at the counter, then put them into the squeezer and watched the juice collect in the bottom. "How old are you?"

"Eighteen."

Jane remained undecided. In certain circumstances, a sixteen-year-old would say she was eighteen. In others, a twenty-two-year-old might. "Who told you to look for me?"

"Celia. She said you would remember her." She looked hopeful. "Or somebody named Terry."

"Celia Fulham?" It didn't seem possible. Maybe Celia

had moved north, or maybe Jane had detected the lie easily. "Where did you meet her?"

"Florida."

Jane was frustrated to hear the right answer because it didn't settle anything. Celia Fulham was a social worker in northern Florida. Jane had met her seven or eight years ago, when the mess that had been a child's life came to Celia's attention. The child's name had been Terrell James Arbogast, and at the end of that there had been a Roman numeral . . . had it been IV? It had been bestowed on him with the unintentional irony that always seemed to stick to people like his parents. When Celia had met them, they were being hunted by the sheriff, not for the frauds they had committed in selling bogus cases of Chanel No. 5 in a parking lot, but because they had not paid him his customary fee for fleecing the locals. Taking the boy into the system would not have made him safe but turned him into a hostage.

Celia Fulham had hidden the family in her own house, and begun to track down a rumor she had heard a year earlier at a workshop in Atlanta. The rumor was that in those instances when the system simply had no way of protecting a child or removing him from an environment that was about to kill him, the system wasn't necessarily his last chance. There was a woman who could make people disappear. "You came all the way up here from Florida," said Jane. "And Celia told you my address."

"No," said the girl. "She told me an address in Deganawida. I went there and rang the bell, but nobody was there. But she said that if you moved or something, they would know at the reservation."

It was another frustrating answer. Celia Fulham had been part Seminole, and had asked Jane if she had Indian blood. Jane had broken an inflexible rule against letting people know anything about her personal life. Jane measured the water and sugar by eye and tasted the mixture, then added the ice and handed the lemonade to the girl. She had expected to be able to distract the girl with it so she could study her, but the girl took a sip without taking her eyes off Jane. "You don't believe me," she announced.

"Sure I do," said Jane. "There is no way that you could have learned that Celia knew me unless Celia told you." The girl had really seen Celia, but that didn't mean Celia was right about her. There had to be some other way, some sensible solution that Celia simply hadn't thought of. Jane wanted to say, "I'm not Jane Whitefield anymore. People who are about to die don't come to me anymore and ask me to make them vanish. I can't leave my husband and take on your problem. I made a promise." Maybe if she knew more, she could figure out a way to help this child without risking her own chance for a new life. "What made you go to Celia?"

The girl said, "I went to her because she was nice to me once a few years ago, when my mother had a fight with her boyfriend and the police came. Celia said that if I was in trouble I should come back."

When Jane heard the word "mother," she felt a half-second of hope—that's right, she's a kid, so there's a mother—but the rest of the sentence dampened it. "Where are your parents now?"

"My father . . . I don't know about him. He was just another boyfriend, and he took off when I was a baby. My mother, she had some trouble a couple of years ago and . . ." The girl shrugged placidly. "You know. She's a doper."

So much for the mother. "How long has she been in jail?"

"A year and a half, about, counting the trial. They won't make her do the whole five."

"What about you? Who has been taking care of you?"

The girl shrugged again. "My mother lied to them and said I had an aunt that was taking care of me. I asked her to, and it was the least she could do after something stupid like that: set me free. Otherwise, they lock you up in a county home, or they farm you out to foster parents, who lock you up at their house, and I wasn't the one who did anything to get locked up. So I bought some ID from a guy I used to watch in a park selling driver's licenses and Social Security cards to Central Americans who came to pick fruit. I went all the way to Tampa to search for jobs, so the ID didn't look too familiar."

Jane kept probing, listening for some statement that had to be a lie. "What was the job?"

"Hotel maid. You work pretty hard, but it was just cleaning and making beds, and I knew how to do that much."

Jane said, "All right, Rita. Let's get to your problem. Exactly what kind of trouble are you in?"

"It's hard to say."

"You mean you don't know, or just that it's hard for you to tell me?"

"I don't really know. I was working at the hotel. There was this man who stayed there a lot. He was nice. Kind of handsome for an old guy, and funny. His name is Danny."

"How old?"

"At least thirty." She saw Jane's eyes begin to look as though she'd heard the story before, and said hastily, "It's not that kind of trouble. Danny never touched me. He had a girlfriend. She never even pretended she wasn't married. The first time I saw her she had a wedding ring on, with a great big diamond. He would meet her at the hotel about once a week around lunch time, and they would do it for about an hour. Then she would slip out the back entrance and go to a parking ramp a block away where she put her car. Fancy."

"The car?"

"The car too, but mostly her. Very expensive clothes, a lot of jewelry, big hair. The car was a cream-colored Mercedes convertible. Danny was there on some kind of business, and for the rest of the day, other men would come to his room, some with briefcases and some with nothing, but all kind of . . . not quite clean, you know? Like they didn't get a shower that day, just put on their clothes and combed their hair."

"And?"

"Danny knew that I knew what was going on. One day I'm on his hall when she leaves in a hurry, practically running. He came into a room I was cleaning and gave me twenty bucks to give his room a quick clean-up first. The man who was going to be there in about fifteen minutes was this woman's husband."

"He told you that?"

She smiled and shook her head. "No. He kind of gave me a sheep-face grin, like I was the one who caught him at something. A few minutes later I couldn't help knowing. It was the car. The man drove up to the front of the hotel with a car so the valet would park it, and it was the same one the girlfriend had used the week before. Anyway, I had just cleaned the room, got rid of everything that had her lipstick on it or smelled like her perfume." She frowned. "It was a good thing, too. Her husband was scary. He was maybe sixty, and he wasn't big, but he had eyes like one of those turtles at the zoo they tell you is four hundred years old—and how they found that out, I'd like to know. I mean, who was there? But you get the picture about him. He had three guys with him. Two came in a different car, but they were all wrong. You know how you can see somebody and something inside you says, This isn't normal? The three were all young—late twenties or thirties—and they were just wrong. They wore suits, but they didn't look like men who wear suits. They were all big, like weight lifters, and the suits looked like they all bought them in the same store on the same day, and it was yesterday. You see men like that, but not usually three of them."

"So what happened?"

"Nothing. They came and left in about a half hour. My friend Danny came out looking like he just got to the end of a tightrope, and smiled at me again. Next time he came to town, he offered me a job."

"What kind of job?"

"It was the same thing—cleaning. He offered me three times what I was getting at the hotel. There was this house in the Keys, and I was supposed to clean it. That's all."

Jane sighed. "And it turned out there was more to the job than cleaning."

"No," said Rita. "That was it."

Jane decided not to make more guesses aloud. Maybe this Danny just figured that if he could bribe her to keep his secret, the husband could bribe her to reveal it.

Rita said, "It was a beautiful house, on the ocean. The one who lived there was a nice old man. I was there for a year. It was great."

"When did it stop being great?"

"Three days ago. The old man went away for a little trip. My friend Danny took him to the airport at four in the morning. I figured this was a great chance to show off, so I spent the whole day giving the house a real cleaning. There's nothing in that place that can be polished or waxed or shined that wasn't that day. I didn't stop until about nine at night. I took a shower and fell asleep as soon as I was off my feet. The next thing I know, there are eight or nine big guys. They come into the house in the middle of the night—not like burglars. They were talking loud and stomping around like they were in a big hurry. For a second or two, I thought it must be firemen coming in because I left something plugged in and started a fire. Then three of them come into my room. They look wrong, like the ones at the hotel. They haul me out of bed. One starts asking me all kinds of questions— where the old man kept this, or that. I don't know any of the answers. When they figure that out and go down the hall, I go straight to the closet and start packing. One of them comes in again, and when he sees the suitcase, he flips it over on the bed and says I'm not leaving. I'm going with them."

"Did he say where?"

"He said, 'To see Mr. Delfina.' "

Jane's jaw tightened. "Do you know who that is?"

"No. But it sounded like I was supposed to. You know: Mister."

Jane stopped listening, but the girl didn't notice. "So I left the suitcase there on the bed where they could see it, and left my clothes and everything, and I put my money and ID and my mother's picture and stuff in my jacket pockets. After daybreak, most of them left. There were only three of them searching the closets and the attic, and one in the back yard. I went out the sliding door off the patio on the side, went over the wall, and walked to the bus stop . . ."

Jane watched the girl's lips move, and she knew she should be listening, or should tell the girl to stop because she would have to hear it all. The girl didn't know that she was thinking about the husband she loved so deeply, and that her eyes weren't focused on the kitchen window because she was concentrating on the story. She was looking at it because she was getting used to the idea that she might never see it again. The girl didn't know that she had said the only word that had needed to be said: Delfina.

After a moment, Jane turned and switched off the burners on the stove and closed the window, then walked through the house checking the others. When she came back the girl was standing beside the table, her skinny arms now crossed on her chest so each hand gripped the opposite elbow as though she were protecting herself from the cold. Jane said, "Does anyone besides Celia Fulham know you came here?"

"No," said the girl. "I never heard of you before yesterday, and I didn't get off the bus until I got to Celia."

"What about after that? Where did you sleep last night?"

"A hotel." She reached into her pocket, pulled out a pack of matches, and handed it to Jane. "I kept those so I'd know my way home."

Jane's eyebrows knitted as she looked at the matchbook. The girl had called it home, and it was probably as much of a home as anywhere. Jane knew the hotel, and it wasn't the sort of place she had expected. It wasn't a cheap, obscure cluster of wooden buildings on a little-used highway. It was a big, respectable hotel. Jane returned the matchbook. "I know where it is. What name did you use to rent the room?"

"My name?" It was a question.

Jane needed to be sure. "You used your own name. Rita Shelford."

"Well, almost. My mother called me Anita, and that's what it says on my birth certificate. Her name is Ann, and she decided I was like a miniature her. Really dumb, huh?"

She didn't detect a reaction from Jane. "So that's what my credit card says too."

Jane hid her uneasiness. "Have you checked out yet?"

"No," said Rita. "I had to have some place to sleep in case I didn't find you. And I brought some stuff with me that I didn't want to carry around, because I might lose it."

"Is it important?"

The girl hesitated, confused.

"Let me explain," said Jane. "If it's anything that money can replace, or that you can live without, it's not important. If finding it will tell someone who you are and where you went next, it's very important."

The girl looked down at her feet, then at Jane. "It's important."

Jane picked up her purse from the little cloakroom off the kitchen and checked to be sure her keys were in it. "Let's go get it and check you out."

"Now?" The girl had sensed the urgency.

"Now," said Jane. She stopped to scribble a note on the pad stuck to the refrigerator where she had written shopping lists. "Something came up. Dinner's ready on the stove. Just heat it. I'll call you later. Love, Jane." She considered writing "Don't worry," then put the note as it was on the dining room table. It was hard to imagine how lying to Carey would make it any easier for him to accept what she was going to have to tell him.

2

Rita sat in the front seat beside Jane and let the rush of air blow over the half-open window to cool her. She wanted to feel as though it was over now, and she was safe. The tall, thin, black-haired woman beside her seemed to do everything with a kind of quiet competence. Whenever Rita noticed the cold blue eyes turned toward her, she saw no doubt or indecision, nor any hint of that sloppy, apologetic look her mother had that showed her that a decision had been made and Rita wasn't going to like it. But Rita saw no softness in them either, and that was probably not good news. She supposed that, once again, it was wrong to think that anything might be going well. On the balance, she judged that the appropriate thing to do was cry, but the air and motion and having her feet off the pavement felt too much like progress to be anything but good.

Jane took the bridge over the Niagara and drove across a flat island so big that Rita needed to remind herself that an island was what it was, then another bridge, and Rita began to recognize the outskirts of Niagara Falls.

Jane drove to the hotel, but Rita didn't feel the seat belt pulling against her to signal that the car was slowing down. "That's it," she said. "You're going past it."

"I know," said Jane quietly. "I like to get a look at a parking lot before I drive into it, and I don't like that one. There's only one way out, and I don't want to get stuck if we have a problem. We'll park on the street." Jane turned the next corner onto a smaller street that had a few souvenir shops and a liquor store, and stopped the car.

She turned to Rita. "Now we'll walk in. If you see anyone inside that you remember from Florida, don't look into his eyes, and don't nudge me. Just tell me in a normal voice and keep walking at the same speed. We'll go right through to another exit and make a run for the car."

"Okay. What if I don't see anybody?"

"We'll go to your room, get what you left, and go down to check out. The way we do that is—"

"I used to work in a hotel," she interrupted. "I know how to check out." Jane could hear a slightly offended tone. "Anyway, it seems like standing around at the front desk will just give people more chance to notice me."

"I know," said Jane. "But I'm hoping nobody learns you're here in time to see you. When you checked in, you used your credit card. Usually they take an impression of it and file it. They don't actually notify the credit card company of the charge until you check out. So we'll transfer the bill to one of my cards."

"Why?" Now she was sure she should be offended. "I told you I have money. I work."

"It's not about money," said Jane. "You don't seem to know why Frank Delfina wants you. But I know that the easiest way he has to find you is to request a credit check on you every hour or so and look for new charges. Yours is in your own name, mine isn't."

"Oh," said Rita. Her mouth was a little o.

Jane walked with her to the hotel entrance, chatting cheerfully about nothing, but kept her eyes moving, glancing ahead to detect someone waiting for Rita, then watching Rita's face for the expression to change from tension to alarm.

As they entered the lobby, Jane's eyes scanned the loitering places—the armchairs along the side walls, the entrance to the bar, and the gift shop. She turned suddenly toward the gift shop. "Just a second," she said.

"What's wrong?" Rita whispered.

"Nothing," said Jane. She went into the shop and pretended to study the souvenirs and supplies for a moment while Rita stood beside her, but she was using the time to watch the lobby through the glass. Finally she went to the counter, picked up a newspaper from the pile, and bought it. As they returned to the lobby Jane said, "If somebody I didn't see had been watching from outside, he would have followed us in. This looks like a good time. We'll check you out and then go up. Here. Hold this." She handed Rita the newspaper and went to the counter.

Jane gave the clerk her Kathleen Hobbs credit card, asked her to charge the bill to it, and checked Rita out while Rita stood beside her, staring at the newspaper.

They walked toward the elevator, and Jane could tell Rita wanted to say something, but she whispered, "Wait."

When the elevator bell rang, they stepped inside, Jane pushed the close door button, and they were alone. "What floor?"

"Fifth," said Rita. She was staring at the newspaper, her eyes wide. She held it up anxiously. "This is it!" she said. "That's the house!"

"What?"

Rita pushed the newspaper in front of Jane. "It's a picture of the house where I lived."

It was a photograph of a sprawling one-story house with a tile roof and stucco sides above the beach in Florida. There was an extremely high wall, and inside it a few tall coconut palms. But the words printed above it were bold: LIFE AND DEATH OF A LEGEND. The caption beneath said, "The secluded Florida compound Bernie 'the Elephant' Lupus called home for decades."

Jane muttered, "Great. Just great," as she took the newspaper. Her eyes fought through the unnecessary verbiage and plucked out phrases. "Murdered in Detroit . . . shot down outside the airport." Aloud she said, "Is that the old man you worked for? Bernie Lupus?"

"Bernie," Rita said. "I never knew his last name. They all called him Bernie. Why is the house in the paper? Do they think I did something wrong?"

"It's not about you. It's about him. He . . . died."

"Oh, no," Rita said sadly. "He was such a sweet old

man . . ." Then she looked distracted, puzzled. "Why is it in the papers here?"

"He was famous."

Jane stood in silence as the elevator rose. Everything was clear, but it didn't help, because each bit of information led to a dozen questions that each led to a dozen more, and none of the answers seemed to matter. If Bernie "the Elephant" Lupus had been shot, when had it happened? The girl had been on the road for a day and a half, and spent most of today trying to get close to Jane. That meant the shooting had taken place two days ago. Why hadn't Jane heard of it instantly? She answered the question herself. She had not turned on the television news last night, because she and Carey had gone out to dinner after his hospital rounds, and had come home late. And now, because she had spent two years trying to distance herself from people who cared about this kind of news, there was no longer anyone who might call and tell her.

Bernie Lupus was the private banking system of the bent-nosed and bull-necked. He had supposedly been hiding Mafia money for fifty years. Jane had no clear idea what he even looked like. She glanced at the article inside the paper and saw there was no photograph of him. She had seen mug shots from the 1940s in a magazine once—a young man in profile and full-face with his hair slicked straight back from a large forehead, with sharp, alert eyes that glowed with the light from the flashbulb like a dog's. After that, it seemed that the only photographs of him had been taken from enormous distances with telephoto lenses, dark and grainy images of a sport coat and baggy pants hanging from a short, bony body below a bald head and a face half covered by sunglasses.

There had been rumors that had grown into accepted parts of the story. He was protected. He was never glimpsed without a couple of bodyguards, but Jane had always thought their job must have been easy. He had no need or, apparently, desire to step outside the ten-foot walls around the yard of his house in Florida. It was said that the reason he couldn't be taken out by a sniper from a building near his house was that every building on the streets surrounding his had been quietly bought by one of the families he served, and was kept occupied by people who could be trusted to watch his back.

It was also said that the secret of his success was that he never wrote anything down. Jane knew it was true that there had been federal raids on his house—always referred to in the newspapers as a "compound"—at intervals since the late 1970s, but no incriminating paper had been found. The myth was that he had developed a system of codes and mnemonic devices during a prison sentence to remember the accounts where he had hidden vast sums of money. That was always given as the explanation for the name Bernie the Elephant.

Jane had to assume that some of what was said was intentionally fabricated, and some was just the normal accretion of nonsense to anyone who is known to exist but seldom seen. Until now, the stories seemed to have served Bernie well. They had protected him from all of the people who were most active in the killing business—his clients. If one of the families killed him, they would not only lose whatever money of theirs was hidden in his famous memory, but they would bring down on themselves the simultaneous vengeance of all the other families.

She glanced at the girl. She still could not have stated precisely what kind of trouble the girl was in now, but she had the distinct impression that in the last sixty seconds it had grown.

The elevator stopped on the fifth floor and Jane stepped in front of Rita to look into the hallway before she moved forward to let her out where she could be seen. The door closed behind them and Jane said, "Give me your room key." She took the key and handed Rita the keys to her car. She pointed at a door below an exit sign. "Go into that stairwell and wait for me. If it's safe, I'll come and get you. If you hear a commotion, run. Go down the stairs and use a side door to the parking lot. Head for the street. At that point the car will be yours. Consider this my will."

The girl looked pale, but she obeyed.

Jane took the key and made two turns along the hallway to find the room. She approached the door carefully and quietly, then put her ear to the door and listened. If someone was waiting inside for the girl to return, there should be some sound—footsteps, a creak of a bed—but she heard nothing. Maybe the girl's luck was better than it seemed. Jane pushed the key into the lock quietly, waited for a few seconds, then swung the door open.

There were two men sitting at the table by the window. Jane called, "Maid service, excuse me," and pulled the door shut. Jane slipped to the side of the door, put her back to the wall, and waited. If they didn't make a rush for her in the next ten seconds, she would be okay. If they did, she would try to land a kick and a jab and then dash for the staircase.

As she waited, she studied the image her mind had retained of the two men at the table. One had been big, dark-haired, and thirtyish. He'd had his coat off and his tie loosened. The other had been much smaller, wearing suspenders over his white shirt. What had they been doing? Of course. Cards. There had been a deck of cards on the table, and each had been holding a hand with a lot of cards in it—too many to be anything but rummy. What else had been on the table? Nothing. There had been no guns where she could see them, no money, no pad for keeping score.

Jane's sense of pace told her that enough time had elapsed, and she began to walk away from the door. There were several ways through this, and she just had to choose the right one. Waiting for them to leave seemed to be a bad idea. She could tell a bellman she was having trouble with her key and bring him back to open the door, then profess shock that someone was in her—Anita's—room. But she couldn't be sure this time that the men would feign embarrassment, put on their coats, and hurry to get out of sight. Now that she knew this had something to do with the death of Bernie Lupus, the stakes were much, much higher. They might very well kill her and the bellman, pile the bodies in the closet, and sit down again to wait for the girl.

Jane knew that the sensible course of action was to go

downstairs, hand in the key, and explain to Rita that nothing she could have left was worth dying for. She did not dismiss the possibility of lying—telling the girl she had retrieved her things and taken them to the car before she had come back for her. Jane had never hesitated to lie to runners when their lives depended on their being kept docile and obedient. All she would have to do is let a bit more time elapse to make the story credible, then get the girl into the car and onto the Thruway. Jane could get her two hundred miles from here before she had to tell her that her belongings weren't in the trunk.

As Jane walked toward the stairwell, she felt a slight twinge. She wasn't sure she should leave the two men behind without finding out anything about them. Since the ones who had searched Bernie Lupus's house three nights ago had worked for Frank Delfina, this pair probably did too. Jane had no way to be sure of even that, and she wasn't certain whether it mattered. What did matter was finding out what they knew, so she could go about making their information obsolete.

Men who planned to hang around a hotel waiting for a girl to show up couldn't have arrived expecting to camp out in her room. They couldn't know in advance whether they could get in. They would have needed to rent a room for themselves on the same hallway, so they would know when she arrived. Without a room, they would have no plausible reason for being on this hallway at all.

As she walked, she found herself eliminating rooms that she passed. Three had PLEASE MAKE UP room signs hanging from their doorknobs. She sensed that men here to kidnap somebody would want privacy, not maid service. As she went on she heard voices behind one door and a television set behind another. There was one door that was open, and when Jane passed she could see that the bedclothes were rumpled, so she guessed someone must have just left to check out. There was one door on the hall that had the PRIVACY PLEASE side of the sign on the knob. Jane knocked on the door quietly, listened, then knocked again. After a moment she decided to take the chance.

She took her pocketknife out of her purse, opened it, and slipped it between the jamb and the door to feel for the bolt. She could tell the shape was going to make it difficult, but if those two men had gotten into Rita's room, she might be able to get into theirs. The bolt was thick, rounded, and flat on the end, so she wouldn't be able to slide a credit card behind it and ease it out of the receptacle.

Jane searched her purse until she found the necklace. It consisted of small beads strung on a silver wire. She would have to try it. She cut the wire at the clasp and dumped the beads into her purse. She took the twelve-inch length of wire and bent the end into a hook, then inserted it into the crack over the bolt between the door and the jamb until the end came back below the bolt. She used the knife blade to guide the end of the loop into the receptacle that held the bolt. She kept pushing the wire until she had gotten it in as far as possible, removed the knife, then slowly pushed the two loose ends of the wire back and forth, trying to work the loop to the end of the bolt. When it felt as though it had reached the butt of the bolt, she twisted both loose ends around her forefingers and tugged hard. The bolt gave a click and snapped back into the lock.

Jane was inside. She closed the door behind her and looked around. There were two suitcases, one at the end of each bed, both unlatched. The girl had said she'd stuffed everything important into a jacket. Jane guessed that if the men had found it in her room, they would have taken it back here. There was no sign of the jacket, so Jane turned her attention to the suitcases. She had hoped there would be tags on them from an airline that would tell her where they had been, but there were none.

She opened the first one. It was filled with clothes that had to belong to the smaller, older man, but something struck her. They were all new, still in packages, with tags and pins stuck to them. Even the socks and underwear were new. There was nothing that could possibly belong to Rita. She moved to the second suitcase, and found another trove of clothes that had not been touched since they had come from the store. She looked at the collar of a shirt: neck 17, sleeve 36. That was definitely the bigger man.

There was nothing in this suitcase that could belong to Rita either. Jane moved to the wastebasket. It seemed to be full. She quickly picked out the first few pieces of trash she saw: road maps. There were maps of New York State, Pennsylvania, Ohio. That made sense, she supposed. The men had found their way here, and the way home was never as hard to plot. But then she looked deeper. There were other maps: the District of Columbia, northern Arizona, Colorado. Below them was a layer of travel brochures. She looked at the covers of the little folders and booklets. The first one that caught her eye was for Disneyland. There were brochures about Yellowstone National Park, Yosemite, Dinosaur National Monument. There was one about New Orleans, and others about Williamsburg, Virginia, and San Antonio.

Jane stood and moved toward the door. It was time to get the girl out of the stairwell and into the car. This was too much. She opened the door a crack, peered out into the hallway, and saw Rita.

The girl had already knocked on the door of her room, and the door was already opening. Jane pushed off with her back foot and broke into a run. The distance seemed to be just a bit too great. The girl stepped inside, and the door began to close behind her. Jane got her hand on the door just in time to keep it from clicking shut, and pushed it open.

She stepped in, closed it behind her, and stood still. The two men were standing now, the light still behind them so that they looked like silhouettes. The bigger man's stance—arms out from his sides and his feet planted at shoulder width—made him seem shocked and disturbed, but he made no attempt to reach for a weapon. The smaller man's face was difficult to read in the shadows. Now that he was standing, Jane could see that he was much older than he had seemed when he was seated. There was a stoop-shouldered, bent look to him.

Rita turned to look at Jane. "Jane. I thought you were in here, and I hadn't heard any noise, and—"

"I know," said Jane. "You thought it must be safe."

Rita waved her arm toward the two men. "Jane, this is—"

This time the old man interrupted. "Hello, there. I'm Rita's grandfather, Ben Shelford."

"No, you're not," said Jane evenly.

The old man seemed not to have heard her. "And this is my son, David." He nodded. "Rita's uncle."

"He's Danny," said Jane. The younger man's head swiveled to look at the older man in alarm.

The older man went on, unperturbed. "We sometimes call him that, but his real name is David."

Jane slowly shook her head. "You're Bernie Lupus."

The old man stepped closer, and Jane could see his small, pale eyes. He didn't seem angry. He looked intrigued. "How did you come to that?"

Jane said, "I happened to notice a few minutes ago that you were playing a card game that goes to five hundred without either paying for each hand or writing down the score. Then I went in your room, and looked at your clothes and your trash."

The old man said, "Ah," appreciatively. He nodded his head. "What did they tell you?" He sounded, not like a teacher exactly, but like an examiner, maybe a diagnostician.

Jane shrugged. "They told me that somebody staying in the room wanted to go all over the country being a tourist." She realized he was waiting for more. "Everybody wants to go somewhere. The only one who wants to go everywhere is somebody who's been locked up for a long time."

"Or a kid?" he suggested.

"Or a kid," she agreed. "There were no clothes in the suitcases for a child. What was in there were clothes that came straight from the store. Everybody likes to have new clothes, but nobody has nothing but new clothes unless he couldn't take anything at all when he left home."

The old man was quiet for only a moment. "You're an astute girl," he pronounced.

The younger man said to Rita, "Who is she?"

"Nobody you want to know," said Jane. "And just to make everybody feel more comfortable, it makes no difference to me whether he's alive or dead. My only interest in this is that his death put Rita in danger."

Hearing her name seemed to strike Rita as permission to join the conversation. "She makes people disappear," she said. "Somebody in Florida told me about her, and so I—"

Jane interrupted. "Get your things, Rita." She turned to the two men again. "I'm going to take her with me."

The old man stepped a tiny bit closer, then realized that Jane's body had become tense. He sat down on the bed. His stare was now attentive and intense. "She makes people disappear? Interesting."

Jane was watching the bigger man, preparing herself for the possibility that he might be about to move.

The old man said, "We're not going to stop you. That was pretty much what we had in mind, too."

Jane kept her eyes on Danny. "If you care about her, why didn't you do something for her?"

Bernie shrugged. "What could I do? My death was untimely. I wasn't prepared. Once I had heard about it, there was no way I could stop it. It was too late. Things were in motion, and people would really have gotten killed."

Danny looked disapproving, as though Bernie was making a damaging admission. He went to the window and looked out. Jane studied the old man. He looked tired and sad. "What do they want Rita for?" she asked. "What do I have to worry about?"

He held up a hand and shook his head. "I know those guys. I know how they think. Nothing is ever over. If somebody killed me, then they must have figured out in advance how to get the money I was holding. If the killers weren't that smart, then I must have left something around that would help the families get their money. If I didn't, then I must have told somebody where it was. If I didn't do that, then I must have slipped up once, or said something, or done something that somebody saw that will lead them to it.

Eventually, they'll want to talk to everybody—even the little girl who cleaned my house."

"So you decided to take a risk to find her?" Jane asked.

Bernie shrugged. "What else was I going to do?" His mouth pursed in a look of distaste. "Would you want to see this kid go have a long talk with Phil Langusto or Victor Catania? How about Salvatore Molinari?" His eyes widened. "How about Frank Delfina? She doesn't know any answers." He looked down and shook his head.

Danny spoke from the window. "Uh-oh. Bernie?"

"What is it?" asked Bernie. He stood and walked to the window, then followed Danny's gaze downward. "I knew I shouldn't have said the bastard's name out loud."

Jane took a step closer. "Who do you see?" Jane could see a white panel truck with the words "Trafalgar Square Flowers" painted in filigree script on the side. A door in the back opened and two delivery men emerged carrying big displays of flowers in baskets.

"It's one of Delfina's companies. I'll bet one of those flower baskets has got her name on it." He tugged Danny's arm and picked up his coat. "Watching them isn't going to be a good use of our time. Let's get going."

Bernie turned to Jane. "Maybe you'd better come out the back way with us. The reason they stopped there is so they can pull ahead to block the exit to the parking lot."

Jane shook her head. "No, thanks."

He pulled an envelope out of his coat pocket and handed it to Rita. "Then here's your severance pay, honey. It's enough to keep you out of sight for a while." He frowned at Jane. "Keep her alive."

Jane stepped to the door and opened it, but Rita lingered, and suddenly threw her arms around Bernie. "Thanks, Bernie."

The old man was so surprised he nearly toppled over. She released him, and said, "You too, Danny."

Danny said, "Good luck, kid. Stay out of trouble."

The four hurried out of the room and Jane headed toward

the stairwell, but Rita said to the men, "Our car isn't in the lot. Come with us." Jane winced.

Rita stopped walking and said to Jane, "Please. Can't we give them a ride?"

Jane said, "It's not a good idea."

"They offered to let us go with them," she reminded Jane. "And they came all the way here just to help me."

Jane said, "They got you into this mess in the first place."

"It's just a ride. Just far enough so they're away from here."

Jane saw the "L" above the elevator light up, then the "2." She sighed. "All right. Just hurry." As she slipped into the stairwell and started down, she was astounded at her own decision. Her only excuse was that she had witnessed the unthinkable several times in a few minutes.

She'd only had two minutes to get used to the idea that Bernie "the Elephant" Lupus had been murdered. Since then he had suddenly popped up from the grave to try to save his young cleaning lady from dying, handed her a pile of money that must have represented about twenty years' pay for cleaning a house, and offered to—of all things—help Jane Whitefield disappear. She wasn't sure that these new impressions were any more reliable than the news of Lupus's death, but she couldn't afford the time to sort them out while men who worked for Frank Delfina were coming up in the elevator.

Her ears were tuned to the sounds below her. She had seen two men carrying flowers. One was on his way up in the elevator, but it wasn't out of the question that the other might come up one of the stairwells. She had to hope it wasn't this stairwell. She heard no door opening below, so she kept moving, trying to keep the echoes of their own footsteps separate in her mind. Abruptly, it occurred to her that the footsteps on the stairs above her were wrong. She stopped and looked back. "Where's Danny?"

She saw Bernie's look of surprise, then sudden under-standing. He turned and began to climb back up, but Jane passed him, taking three steps at a time. "Keep going."

She reached the fifth-floor landing, quietly pushed the door open a couple of inches, and looked out. She saw Danny hurrying down the hallway toward her, carrying the two suitcases she had seen in the men's room. He had gone back for the luggage. She felt a horrible frustration with him. Nobody was here looking for him or for Bernie. There was nothing in their suitcases that could have made any difference: everything was still in its package.

It was only a second later that she saw the delivery man. He stepped out of Rita's room carrying the basket of flowers with his back toward her. She pushed the door open and took a step toward him, but there was no time. He reached inside the basket and produced a pistol with a silencer on the end. There was a soft, spitting noise as he shot Danny in the chest. He fired three more times as Danny fell. Jane heard the sound of one of the other stairwell doors opening down the hallway, and pulled her door closed.

She held her ear to the door until she heard the second man go past her, then pushed it open a crack. She heard their voices. "Danny Spoleto?" That one sounded surprised.

"What was I going to do—wrestle with him? Help me get him in the room, quick. He probably stole her credit card and used it to get here." She heard them dragging Danny's body, then one of them said, "Call and tell them to bring up the trunk they were going to use for the girl."

The door to Rita's room closed, and Jane could hear no more words. She closed the door to the stairwell and hurried downward. She found Rita and Bernie standing at the first-floor landing.

"Where is he?" asked Rita.

Jane met Bernie's eyes. "He had to go out another way." She could see that Bernie understood.

Bernie held the girl in the corner of his eye and said, "We had a plan for this kind of thing. He knows where to go." Then he looked at Jane, sadly.

Jane said, "Let's go." This time, when she went out into the first-floor hallway, she held the door open until the others had passed her. Then she led the way down the residential wing to a side entrance. She walked along the outer wall toward the back of the building, down the service driveway and across the street, then around the block to the car.

She unlocked the doors, then looked up and down the street while Bernie got into the back seat and Rita sat in front. Jane started the car and drove a block, then said, "I want to get on the Thruway, and the entrance is on the other side of the hotel. Lie down, both of you. Don't raise your heads until I tell you."

She drove past the hotel, and she could see that the florist's truck had already left. In the loading zone in front of the lobby, a big black Lincoln Town Car had stopped. A blond woman in a smooth beige suit was standing beside it, watching a man pull a large trunk from the back of the car. Jane had time to see the man tip it up on its wheels and push it toward the lobby. The woman pivoted on her high heels to follow, and Jane was past.

3

Jane drove along Lake Erie into the northwest corner of Pennsylvania, then on across the Ohio line. It was dark now, and she had watched the mirrors for three hours. There had been no car that had stayed in their wake more than a few minutes, no indication that they could have been followed. Rita had slouched in the front seat reading the newspaper Jane had given her at the hotel for a time, then fallen asleep. Every time Jane had glanced up at the mirror, she could see Bernie's sharp, pale eyes staring ahead at the road. She said, "Bernie?"

"Yeah, honey?"

"Do you know where you want me to drop you off?" Jane saw Rita stir and sit up. The voices had awakened her.

He said, "Someplace sort of on the small side. Not Cleveland or Cincinnati. How about Mansfield?"

"How do I get there?"

"How is he supposed to know?" said Rita. "The paper said he hasn't been out of the house in, like, twenty years."

"He knows," said Jane.

Bernie said, "Stay on 90 until just before Cleveland, and then take 271 south. Stay on it, and it'll change to 71. Keep going until you're right outside Mansfield, then switch to 30. It'll take us right into town."

Jane looked at Rita. "I found road maps in their trash at the hotel. That was what made me sure who it was."

"I don't understand," she said.

"I've been doing this for a long time, and I know how people running from trouble behave. A road map isn't big, it isn't heavy, and it isn't incriminating. So who would throw one away?"

Rita was silent, so Jane answered her own question. "A person who can look at it once and still have it later, in his memory. Bernie Lupus."

Rita sucked in a breath and turned to Bernie. "But you left them in the room. What if—"

The old man said, "Don't worry, kid. If the guys who are chasing you were as good as she is, we'd be riding in their car, not hers. Even if they played way over their heads and found the maps, what would they do with them? They'd spend two weeks looking for fingerprints on them that aren't there."

Rita seemed skeptical, but she was silent. Jane drove the dark highway, thinking. She couldn't get the sight of Danny's face out of her mind. He had been moving along the hallway in a quick, stiff-legged gait, his face only slightly touched by worry, like a man in an airport hurrying to catch a plane. When he had seen the man step out of the doorway, there had been no question he had recognized him. He had made no attempt to avert his eyes and walk past, just stopped and died.

She glanced at the old man in the back seat again. That

was what he was thinking about too. He stared into space, probably remembering some good qualities in the man that Jane would never know.

She thought backward from that moment and remembered the bath. She had been running the water for her bath, heard the doorbell, turned off the water. It seemed to her now that at that moment, the floor beneath her feet had simply given way and dropped her here. She thought about Carey. What must Carey be thinking? He would be sick with worry. She had to find a way to call him. "Bernie?"

"Yeah?"

"Is there a good place to make a stop up ahead?"

He considered for a moment. "There are some little towns. And there's a rest stop on 271 just after the exit for Richfield, if you can hold out that long."

Jane glanced at her watch and drove on in silence, keeping the car moving. At this hour, the rest of the traffic was moving fast, the pace set by the long-distance truckers who planned to drive all night, pushing the speed limit a little while they could.

When she reached the rest stop, she drifted past the small buildings that housed the rest rooms and the telephones before she began to search for a parking space. Near the entrance, everyone who pulled in would be glancing at all the spaces, and they would see her car. She wanted them to go past her car after the building, when they would be staring ahead at the ramp onto the highway, matching their acceleration to the speed of the traffic, and not noticing cars in the lot.

Jane glanced at Rita. The girl had fallen asleep again, and now she sat up and looked around her, dry-mouthed and blinking. "We're at a rest stop," said Jane. "The bathrooms are in that building, if you need one."

The girl got out without speaking and walked toward the building. Jane looked at Bernie. He said, "I suppose that's not such a bad idea."

Jane waited until both of them had started out, then locked the car and followed. She stopped at a telephone beside the first building, dug a handful of change out of her purse, and dialed the number of the house in Amherst.

His voice was tight and worried. "Hello?"

"Hi," said Jane. "It's me. I love you." It wasn't the first time that she had noticed that "I love you" was what you said when the rest of what you were going to say was bad.

"I love you too," said Carey. "What happened?"

Jane said, "It's hard to describe. I was getting ready for dinner, and this young girl came by. She had come from . . . a long distance to find me."

"So you dropped everything and took off without telling me." His voice wasn't angry. It was disappointed, as though a grim expectation about her had merely been confirmed. He had simply left off the word "again."

"I'm sorry. She had left some things in a hotel room, and I could tell that she hadn't made a serious attempt to keep people from finding out she was there—didn't know it was necessary, didn't even know how. I was trying to pick up her belongings and get out before anybody else showed up. I couldn't hang around waiting for you, or even send people around the hospital to hunt you down." She hesitated for a moment, then realized that she owed him the next admission. "I didn't even know what to say to you if I did."

"That brings us to my next question," he said. "Where is 'out'? Where are you?"

She thought for a moment. If anyone was listening to this conversation, they would already know where it had come from. "I'm in Ohio right now, but I'm just at a rest stop, and I'll be on the road again in a minute. I know this makes you angry and it hurts your feelings. I know I promised never to do this again. I swear I'm not doing this because I missed the old days, or that it's fun. I don't, and it isn't. I felt that I couldn't say no."

"I figured that out," he interrupted. "This call isn't exactly a surprise, you know. I've had a couple of hours to think about where you must have gone, and about what I should feel about it, what I should say. What it comes down to is this. When I said 'I love you' it wasn't just automatic, like 'How are you?' 'Fine, and how are you?' It's the truth. The decision is made. It's too late to talk you out of it, so all I can do now is figure out how to make this easier for you. I would like you back in one piece, and very soon."

Jane could feel tears beginning behind her eyes. "Every time I think I have you figured out, you always amaze me."

"I don't think I want to get into an amazement contest with you. Now, what can I do? Do you need me to send money, or—"

"No," she said. "Nothing. I don't need anything. I just called to tell you that I'm all right, and to say I'm sorry I had to do this. I probably won't be home for at least a couple of weeks, and I may not be able to call."

"A couple of weeks?"

"That's a guess," said Jane. "Her situation is a little vague, so I haven't figured out exactly what I'm going to have to do to get her out of it. It could be longer."

"You mean you did this without even knowing what her trouble is?" he asked.

Jane sighed. "I know who is looking for her. The rest doesn't really matter, because I know about him. I can't just let him have her."

"Who is he?"

"I can't talk about it anymore," she lied. "I'm in a public place, and I've got to get going in a second."

"You aren't saying it because it's a name people know, isn't it?" he said. He was too quick, too perceptive.

She took the phone from her ear, wanting to hang it up, but sure that he would know it had been intentional. "Yes," she said, her voice just above a whisper.

"If it's somebody like that, how can you possibly expect to—"

"I have to try."

"My God." Carey's voice was strained, incredulous. "It doesn't matter to you who wins, does it?"

"Of course it does," she said. "But it matters more that somebody try."

He was silent for a few seconds. She heard him draw in a deep breath and blow it out slowly. "I don't understand. Or maybe I do, and I just don't agree. I can't pretend that I do. Arguing about it isn't going to do any good, is it?"

"No," said Jane. "It isn't."

"I love you, and I'll be in the usual places waiting to hear from you. You already know that if I can do anything to help you, I will."

"Thanks, Carey," she said. "I promise that the second I can come home, I will. I love you. Got to go." She hung up.

As she walked to the ladies' room she felt guilty and sorry and, most of all, unsettled. What she had been doing from a year before they had met in college until the day they had married had always been hard to talk about. She had considered agreeing to marry him to be a promise to stop being a guide. But she had been away twice since then.

The first time it had been Pete Hatcher—a man she had hidden before she had made the promise. One night she had learned he'd been spotted, and was running again. She had considered him unfinished business, and she had gone off to make him disappear for good.

In the year after that, she and Carey had both gotten attached to the idea that making people disappear was just something she used to do when she was young and single. When they talked about the past, it was the shared past—things that had happened to both of them—or the distant past inhabited by parents, aunts, and uncles. But Richard Dahlman had changed that.

Dahlman was a doctor, the older surgeon who had taken Carey on as a novice and taught him. Jane had never met him until the night when he had turned up at Carey's hospital with a policeman's bullet in his shoulder. Jane had plucked Dahlman out of the hospital and kept him invisible while she had tried to sort out how a respected surgeon had gotten into that kind of trouble. She had done it because Carey had asked her to.

But apparently then, or in the months after that, something had quietly changed. It seemed that when Carey had asked her to make one more person disappear, he had forfeited—no, knowingly spent—his right to demand that she never do it again. She had heard it in his voice tonight, and she didn't like it.

While she was listening to the girl's story this afternoon, she had acknowledged that Carey would not be pleased. Then she had told herself that Carey would understand why this, too, was an exception. But to Carey, this had been merely the first instance to occur after he had given up his right to an opinion. Marriages were more fragile and complicated than she had ever imagined. Trouble came in quiet, unexpected ways. Things had to be said over and over again, all existing agreements renewed and clarified.

When Jane returned to the car, the girl was half-turned in the front seat and the old man was leaning forward in the back, while they talked. As soon as the girl saw Jane coming, they stopped and both stared straight ahead. Jane wasn't sure that she liked that, either. She got into the driver's seat, started the engine, and drove off onto the highway.

It took only a few minutes for the old man to speak. "You know, I think I'm going to need a car. Mansfield is big enough to have a couple of used-car lots. Suppose Rita comes in with me to buy one. I'm old, so nobody is shocked if I'm old-fashioned enough not to trust banks. I pay cash. Rita makes a big deal about what a crazy old coot I am—you know, like she's embarrassed—and the salesman sells it to me. That way I don't need a bank account with a name on it and all that."

Jane muttered, "If you have a valid driver's license, I assume it must be in your own name. Otherwise it might work."

"What might work better?" asked Bernie. "How about if we rent an apartment, you buy a car under a false name, wait for the ownership and registration to come in the mail, and sign the pink slip over? Would that be better?"

"You know it would," said Jane. "But I'm not staying in an apartment with you for a month while the state of Ohio gets around to mailing a lot of papers. I own this car—not in my real name, of course. We'll go to Mansfield. I'll sign the car over and Rita and I will be on our way."

"Oof," moaned Bernie.

Rita turned in her seat. "What's wrong?"

"Uh . . . nothing," said Bernie. "I guess I'm just tired." To Jane he said, "Keep going."

"I don't have much choice," she said. "There's not much point in stopping unless we come to a hospital."

"No," said Bernie. "I don't need a doctor, and if I did, the price of stopping would be a little steep. I'm just not used to the excitement, and I've been out a lot today. When we got to the hotel and Rita wasn't there, I went to see the Falls. Pretty spectacular." Jane expected him to be quiet, but he added, "The day I died we were in San Antonio, Texas. Before the credit report came telling us where to find Rita, I got to see the Alamo."

It was clear to Jane that he wanted to continue talking, but she was not sure whether he was trying to ignore some pain or keep her occupied. "What did you think of it?"

"All my life I've been hearing about it," he said. "But it's not much to look at. A crappy place to die. Don't you think so?"

"I'm not a believer in last stands," she said. "I'm a believer in running."

Bernie chuckled. "That comes with the high I.Q., I guess." He was quiet for only a few seconds. "I wanted to go to all of those places."

"You mean since you died?"

"No. I've wanted to see Disneyland, for instance. I've wanted to know what the fuss was about since they started building it in the fifties."

"Danny was going to take you to all those places?"

"Others, too. He was a good kid. He was scared shitless for this trip, but I kept him at it. We just got to Niagara Falls this morning."

When they reached the Mansfield city line, Bernie said, "Honey, I hate to be trouble, but I'd like it if you could stop at a motel around here. I got to rest."

Jane was careful not to pick the first one. She wasn't ready to trust Bernie the Elephant.

When the car came to a stop beside the third motel, Jane saw that Rita was sitting stiffly, pretending to stare straight ahead, but her eyes had sneaked to the corners of their sockets to see what Jane was going to do.

"Thanks, honey," said Bernie. "Get three rooms. If they see you two go into one with an old man, they're not going to respect you."

Jane reached across Rita to open the glove compartment and take an envelope out.

Bernie said, "What are you doing?"

"I'm signing the pink slip to the car." She put it back into the glove compartment and closed it. "This way, if my sanity returns in the middle of the night, Rita and I can get a cab without waking anybody up to say good-bye." She got out of the car, slammed the door, and walked toward the motel office.

4

Jane awoke, already aware of the sound. It was a man walking along the corridor. She heard him stop at her door, and she identified the disturbance that had brought her out of her sleep. The man had been trying to walk quietly. She rolled off the bed, picked up the heavy ashtray from the nightstand, stepped close to the door, and waited in the darkness.

She heard something go into the lock, then saw the door open until the chain caught it. A bent coat hanger snaked inside, hooked onto the last link of the chain, slid it to the end of its track, and removed it. The door opened a few more inches, and Jane saw him through the crack at the hinges.

"Hello, Bernie," she said quietly.

"Oh, there you are," said Bernie. "Can I come in?"

"It's a little late to ask for an invitation."

The old man stepped inside and closed the door, then flipped the light on, and quickly averted his eyes. "Sorry," he said.

Jane remembered, picked up the jeans and white blouse she had left at the foot of the bed, and slipped them on. "How did you learn to open a hotel door?"

He shrugged. "Oh, it's just an old trick from when I was young. I was so broke I couldn't afford hotels in those days, so once in a while I needed to use one without paying."

She shook her head. "Bernie, when they're unoccupied, the chain isn't fastened."

"That's a different trick. I thought you meant the lock. Motels like this don't give a shit about what happens to their customers. The doors are hollow and easy to kick down, so they put cheap locks on them to save the expense of replacing them."

Jane decided that she didn't really care why the old man had once broken into occupied hotel rooms: armed robbery, probably, but that had been long ago. "What do you want, Bernie?"

"Just friendly concern. I went out for a walk, and I happened to notice the light in the window. I thought I'd see why you were up."

"If there was a light, it wasn't in my window," she said. "Let's get beyond the preliminary lies and get to the big ones. You want me to take you to some safe haven."

"That would be nice," he agreed. "But I guess I'll have to figure out how to close out my own life."

"That's how you're seeing this?"

"How can it be anything else?" he asked. Then he said thoughtfully, "Did you hear how I got killed?"

Jane nodded. "I watched the television news before I went to bed. They said that a seventy-year-old woman died when you did. How did that happen?"

"She was the one who shot me." He looked sad. "I guess the excitement was too much for her heart. She died on the way to the hospital."

"You were supposed to be killed by an old woman?"

Bernie sighed. "It wasn't my idea, believe me." He looked

at her, and the pain in his eyes seemed genuine. "I loved her. Francesca Giannini." The eyes looked colder now, as though they were judging Jane. "People saw her near the end, and they probably saw this old lady with hard, sharp black eyes like a hawk, and wrinkled skin. They wouldn't have been able to imagine what she was like in the old days."

Jane could tell that Bernie was testing her: whether she was smart enough to know that she would be old too. She sat at the foot of the bed beside him.

Bernie said, "I met her at the Fontainebleau in Miami. She was twenty, I was twenty-two. In those days, mob sit-downs were different. They used to meet in places like that. It's hard to believe now, but they'd bring their wives, kids, dogs. Her father was Dominic Giannini. He brought her along, like it was a vacation. Looking back on it now, I think he probably did it because he was afraid to leave her home alone. Not that she was in danger or something—he had Detroit sewed up tight. He just knew that if he left her home, what he told her not to do was only talk."

Jane nodded. "I guess things like that don't change much."

"You have to understand what the problem was," said Bernie. "She was beautiful." Jane could see his eyes glaze over, and then he gave a little shake, as though coming back to the present was painful.

Jane was astonished. "You're not just remembering, are you? You're seeing it."

Bernie touched Jane's arm gently, as though he were a parent soothing and reassuring her. "That's part of it, too, you know. You don't just get to bring back what will make you happy. Once you've seen something, you're stuck with it. If I think about it, I can see her now. She isn't any different from the way she looked then. Where every long black hair was, every pore of that smooth white skin, whatever was reflected in those huge brown eyes at different times; even things I didn't notice at that moment—things in the room. There was a lace cover on the counter behind me, and the corner was folded up, just like this." He folded the edge of Jane's sheet to demonstrate. "There was a sand fly that was on its way to the window to get out."

Jane's throat was dry. She cleared it, and said, "It must be hard."

"Not in the same way as it used to be," said Bernie. "I told you we were at the Fontainebleau. The big guys were in a meeting in a suite upstairs with their *consiglieres*. Their *caporegima* were mostly in the bar by the pool keeping an eye on each other. There were a few soldiers, mostly older guys sitting in the hallways on those French chairs with the squiggly gold edges that nobody ever sits on, pretending to read newspapers. I saw her in the dining room. She looked right at me, not peeking and looking down, or any of that. She came to me and took me by the hand. We went for a long walk, and talked. All of a sudden she stopped, turned around, and started leading me back. I said, 'Do we have to go back now?' She said, 'I thought you'd like to see my room.' "

"You don't need to tell me this."

"Yes," he insisted. "I do. She locked the door and started taking off her clothes. It wasn't like she had any experience at it, just determination. This was something she was going to do. She got down to the skin in about five seconds—sort of a 'There. That's done' look on her face. Then she looked up at me for a minute. I'm still standing there with my mouth open. Finally she shrugged her shoulders and said, 'Tell me what to do.' Do you understand?"

Jane remembered. The event that you were warned about as most to be feared slowly became an obsession, until virginity was like carrying a handful of hot coals. "I think I do."

He nodded, and gazed at the rug for a moment. "That was how it happened. It wasn't one of those things where she just lays there with her eyes shut tight and tolerates it while you work your will on her. She wanted to do everything a man and a woman ever did together. She just didn't know how."

In spite of her resistance, Jane could feel it in her own memory. Of course that must always have been a part of it since time began—she remembered the fumbling and clumsiness because she hadn't been exactly positive about how things were supposed to happen, and had been so afraid that she might be awkward. She remembered the longing to have everything be beautiful and seamless, but it was impossible because she had been watching herself with a critical, unforgiving eye.

"I didn't know anything either," said Bernie. "In those days, at that age you were just a kid. But we learned, like everybody does. We sneaked off six more times. Every time the bosses would disappear into the suite upstairs, she would find me."

"What happened afterward?"

He sighed, and there was a rattly sound in his throat. "She said she was going to work it out with her father, and we would get married. I was a kid, and an outsider. I didn't know what a job that was going to be. See, I didn't really fit in. I was only there because I was working for the Augustinos in Pittsburgh."

"Doing what?"

"Not much. In my one conviction, I was in with Sal Augustino. We were the same age. They didn't have libraries and college courses and counselors. Radio wasn't allowed. There weren't many TVs anywhere, and there sure weren't any in that prison. What you had was a cell and a bunk. I used to do tricks to keep myself from going crazy—describe baseball games I'd seen, batter by batter, you know? I had read a few books, so once in a while I'd recite one out loud to them. When I got out, Sal told the family about me. They didn't know exactly what to do with me, but they put me on the payroll. I was a city housing inspector. I had to show up bright and early every Friday for five minutes to get my pay."

"I take it that wasn't impressive enough for her father."

"Worse than that," he said. "At those big meets there were lots of people around, so a lot of little side deals got made."

"What kind of deals?"

He sadly shook his head. "You have to understand. These were—are—people for whom everything is for sale. The only issue is price."

Jane said, "He arranged a marriage for his daughter?"

"No," said Bernie. "Two things were decided that week. The

first was the reason the Augustinos brought me along. They sold me."

"Sold you? Like a baseball player?"

"Yeah, it was a lot like that. They wanted something from the Langustos in New York. You got to remember what happened after Capone. They got him for tax evasion, and everybody realized that was the easy way to get all of them. I had been keeping the books for the Augustinos in my head, moving money around and keeping track of it. If having a lot of money you can't explain is a crime, you have to hide it. The Augustinos didn't have that much, so it didn't take a lot of time. But the New York families had a lot. I was supposed to go live in New York under the care of the Langustos. The Langustos had worked out a side deal in advance. I would start keeping track of money for all five families in New York. That way, all of them had some protection from the government, and they all had a stake in protecting me."

"When I heard of you I always wondered how that came about," said Jane. "I mean, these people don't seem to trust each other very often."

"It was a special time," he said. "Some of these guys hated each other, but the idea of going to jail just for having money was new, and it was killing them. And the New York families had been breathing down each other's necks for thirty years by then. I was a way to protect their money from each other, too."

"And you agreed to the arrangement."

"Who asked me?" said Bernie. "What happened was that my friend Sal got called upstairs. When he came back down, I'd barely made it back from meeting Francesca in her room. I was almost into the bar before I noticed I'd forgotten to tuck my shirttail in my pants. Sal hugs me and says, 'Bernie, I just got the best news in the world about you. You're going to be an important man, and you deserve it.' " The old man sat silent for a moment. "I told him, 'Sal, I met a girl. I can't go to New York.' He said, 'Bring her with you.' I told him who she was. I told him all of it. He looked sick. After about a minute, he says, 'You're my friend, and I'll try to help you. If she really loves you, then no father is going to stand in the way. Just go to New York and I'll call you when I've got it arranged.' I told him, 'I can't go to New York.' He said, 'Bernie, if you're in New York, you're an important man. You'll have money, respect.' He could see I wasn't getting it, so finally he said, 'If you're with the five families, he can't kill you.' "

"And you said yes."

"I went to her and asked her what to do," he said. "She told me that Sal was absolutely right. She said I had to go to New York, so she could help Sal work it out with her father. That night I got on a train with Carmine Langusto and eight guys."

"I take it her father didn't go for it," said Jane.

"I'll never know," said Bernie. "I said there were at least two side deals arranged that week in Florida. That was the second one. She and her father and his guys went back to Detroit. About two days later, he comes out of a restaurant and gets his head blown off in the street."

Now Jane was moving into familiar territory. She had heard stories like it a hundred times. "Who did it?"

"I'm not sure even now. There was a story around then that some guys in Chicago wanted to break away and take charge in Detroit. Maybe it was them. If it was, it backfired. They never got to set foot in Detroit."

"What stopped them?"

"It was way over my head. It was a Commission thing. They met in New York while I was there, but by the time I heard about it, it was over. The family in Detroit—what we used to call the Giannini family—was going to stay put. The new don there would be some local guy I'd never heard of, named Ogliaro. And he would hold the family together by marrying the old don's daughter. Period."

"They arranged the marriage without her consent?"

Bernie's eyes squinted at her as though the light was hurting them. "That week in Florida, the cards got reshuffled, and we were all holding new hands. It was 1947, and this is a twenty-year-old girl who is pregnant. I didn't know it, but she did. She is also the last remaining daughter in the direct line of men who have been in power in that city for three generations. If she holds out on the off chance of marrying me, the people who killed her father are going to take everything he had. They're going to kill people who were loyal to him. And if anybody knows she's carrying the heir apparent, she's probably first."

Jane struggled to take it all in. The name Ogliaro meant something to her. Bernie had said "heir apparent." If there was a child, could it have been Vincent Ogliaro? He would be about the right age. She remembered reading about a conviction a couple of years ago, and some sort of a federal sentence. Jane needed to fight the feeling of sympathy that had been growing in her. She used the only method she had. "She didn't just go along with it, did she?"

He looked down at the carpet again. "No. She arranged it. She thought of it and got some old guys to go to the Commission with it. I don't even know if she had Ogliaro's consent in advance or not. It doesn't matter. He had to do what they said, just like I did."

"Why him?"

"He was the perfect choice, exactly the sort of man that everybody would accept. He was a brute, with an animal's face and an animal's constitution, and the kind of cunning that some animals have."

"What do you mean?"

"He started out by cleaning house. Everybody who might be a problem got killed. He built on what was left and went on from there. He was never foolish enough to get in on anything outside his own territory, but he protected the city line like it was made of his own skin. There are people who say that she had something to do with that—that it was too smart for him." He added unconvincingly, "But I don't believe that."

Jane had listened to the description and had already decided that the woman must have done it. She shrugged. "Then don't. Did you ever see her again?"

"A few times."

"How?"

"In those days, a lot of women with money used to go to New York twice a year to buy clothes: fall and spring. They'd take the train and go on a shopping spree. A few times I could meet her in her hotel. Then it got too dangerous."

"Ogliaro suspected?"

His face showed distaste and contempt. "Ogliaro wouldn't have cared. It wasn't a marriage. They both went into it with their eyes open. She made him powerful and rich, and he made her and the boy safe. There wasn't any love. No, the problem was me."

"You?" Jane was distracted. He had said "the boy." She was almost sure she knew who the boy was.

"Years were going by. I was handling money for the New York families, and it was training my memory. They started bringing in more families, as a favor."

"Detroit, too?"

"Never Detroit. Ogliaro couldn't stand it. He knew he couldn't do anything about what had already happened, but he wasn't going to leave any of his money with me. But by the mid-fifties there were the New York families, Pittsburgh, Boston, two New Jersey families, one of the Chicago families, New Orleans. The ones in Los Angeles were connected to families in the East, so they were part of the package. The only person who knew where any of it was invested was me. You can see the problem."

"They wouldn't let you out of their sight," said Jane.

"In the fifties there were a couple of wars. They were afraid somebody would clip me just to cause trouble. Then it was the big uproar caused by the wars. Citizens had found bodies lying around, so the government had to start making noise about the Mafia—holding hearings, doing raids. People started to worry about me getting picked up. They moved me out of New York and set me up in a house in Florida."

"So you couldn't go to New York anymore."

"She couldn't either. It was the sixties by then, and women weren't doing that anymore. A department store in Detroit had the same clothes as one in New York. Then a bad period started. From the late sixties on, you couldn't trust your telephone or go talk to somebody outdoors without getting your picture taken. The FBI raided my house six times, and each time I got hauled in for forty-eight hours so they could ask me questions while the families were crying real tears and wringing their hands. In 1978 my house burned down."

"Arson?"

"Yeah," he said. "I know, because I did it myself. I hadn't seen her in fourteen years. I talked them into taking me to Chicago while it was being rebuilt so I could be closer to her. I slipped my bodyguards once and spent the night in a hotel with her. That was the last time. A new house got built, only this time it was in the Keys. While my house was going up, they built houses all around it."

"So those stories are true? The whole neighborhood is Mafia?"

"I don't know what you heard, but here's what's true. There are three streets on each side. They built the houses and put people in them. The houses aren't all occupied all the time, but some are. There are places on the island where you can see a boat coming from miles away in any direction, and there's only one bridge. It was all for me."

"Didn't her husband die right around then?"

"Yeah," he said. "That was why I had to see her. To propose."

"Marriage? After thirty years?"

"What do you want from me? I couldn't make the calendar go backwards. It was the first realistic chance I had."

"She turned you down."

He nodded. "I figured if anybody would understand that, it would be another woman. I sure didn't."

"It was the boy, wasn't it? If her husband was dead, then her son was going to be the boss. Your son."

"That's just about the way she said it. Vincent was practically a kid, late twenties, when Ogliaro died. She was afraid that without her at his elbow to tell him what was what, he couldn't do it. It would be like setting the baby on the ground while the wild dogs circled him. She couldn't bring him with her to Florida to live with me. She said that would be like castrating him."

"What about later, after he was established?" she said carefully. "He seems to have had an aptitude for it."

"Then it was too late. People were already watching him, worrying that he might get too strong. If his mother came to live with me, then the families who gave me their money would decide he was trying to get his hands on it. They would have killed him." He shook his head. "That was our son. He was what she traded our lives for."

Jane was quiet for a few seconds. "I'm sorry," she said. "It's a sad story."

She thought about the woman. This was her story, not Bernie's. She tested it. "And your son—Vincent—he arranged for your death?"

He shook his head. "How could he? He's in prison. You knew that, didn't you?"

Jane nodded. "I remember seeing it in the papers."

"She did it. She did all of it. All I knew about it was that if I could get that particular flight to Detroit that day, and come outside for some air, she would handle the rest. I see her, she fires a gun at me. I fall down. She gets hustled into a car and away. About six big guys all crowd around me. One takes my picture, then slips a coat on me and a wig on my head. Another lies down in my place. Another squirts blood all over the place with a plastic bottle. One takes my fingerprints. An ambulance shows up, they lift this guy into it and drive away. A couple of these guys take me into the airport with them, and push me onto a plane, where Danny is waiting for me."

"That's a lot of people," said Jane.

"One of them works in the coroner's office, a couple more are cops. Danny didn't know anything about the others, but they were all people she had on the hook. He said she paid them all, but none of them would tell anyway, because they'd have to say they were in on it."

"So now you're dead."

"I'm dead," he agreed. "Only it didn't work, because she's dead too. All those years. All the waiting and wishing, and then this. She has a heart attack. When the hell did women start having heart attacks?"

There were tears streaming down his face. She could see they were coming from his tear ducts, but that meant nothing. There were no actors and few women who couldn't cry any time they wanted to. What caught her attention were the lines on his face. As she studied them, she understood something that had distracted her since she had met him. The expressions she had seen on his face didn't match the lines. He would say something cheerful and the voice didn't match the words, and then he would smile, and the face would appear to wrinkle across the lines. The expression on his face at this moment made the lines and creases fit perfectly. There was only one expression his face had assumed habitually. For fifty years, he had been in anguish. He was old now. The skin on his temple was getting a thin, almost transparent look, like vellum, so she could see the veins.

She said, "She didn't choose this time because it was good for her, or for Vincent, did she?"

"No," he said. In his watery blue eyes was the worst agony of all. It seemed to contain within it all of the pain he had felt for fifty years. But she was sure that there was something new, too. "I was beginning to forget things."

5

Jane looked at him a moment longer. She began to feel that her pity was what was giving him pain now, like the weight of a soothing hand on a burn. She turned away, walked to the other side of the room, and began to rearrange the magazines.

"You're still a kid. Maybe my telling you this will help you out."

"What do you mean?"

"That's a very strange little skill you've developed. Rita was telling me about it. Somebody is in trouble, you come along, and—poof!—he vanishes." Jane turned to look at him, and the sad eyes were on her. "I had a strange little skill too."

"It's not a business," Jane said. "I wasn't trying to get rich."

"I know, I know," said the old man. "I wasn't either. I did it because my friend Sal Augustino asked me to. I could save a friend from going to jail. I did it because there was no way not to. But it wasn't over. You do a favor, it doesn't make you paid up. It just proves you can do it."

Jane was beginning to feel uncomfortable. He seemed to be able to intuit what had happened to her.

Bernie went on. "But pretty soon, it wasn't just a favor for Sal. It was friends of Sal's I never knew existed. That's how they talk, you know. If the person is just some guy, they call him 'my friend so-and-so.' If he's a made mafioso, they say 'our friend.'"

"What about you?" she asked. "How did you get introduced?"

"Me?" He looked shocked. "I wasn't even Italian—ineligible by accident of birth. My parents were Polish. Besides, you think they needed to give me a blood oath to convince me I'd get killed if I talked?"

"So you were a mercenary."

"Haven't you been listening to me? What the hell did I need with money? I couldn't leave the house to buy a loaf of bread. In the forties I got salaries for phony jobs. Even then, all I could do was invest it. After that, people gave me presents once in a while, that's all."

Jane's breath caught in her throat. She had never taken money for her services. When someone had insisted, she had answered, "A year from now, or maybe two, when you're living your new life and haven't felt afraid for a while, think back on the way you felt tonight. Then, if you still feel like it, send me a present." She waited a few seconds, then tried to simulate idle curiosity. "What kind of presents?"

"All kinds. Mostly money. But I couldn't keep it lying around, any more than I could leave their money lying around. So I invested it, and kept the account numbers in my head. In the sixties, I flat refused to take even the presents. They were dangerous. I was handling a lot of money for these people. If they knew that I had millions of dollars of my own, what would it mean to them? Where could it have come from except out of their pockets? Even if they somehow got the records from my brokers, and found out I had invested it before they were born, they would have assumed I had stolen it from their fathers or grandfathers."

Jane said, "When did you realize you were forgetting things?"

"About a year ago," he said. "It was a new experience for me, so at first I wasn't sure that was what it was. I would try to take an inventory, and my mind would feel . . . tired. I could kind of see the words and numbers like before, but it was an effort to pick one out."

"Do they know?"

"No," he said. "I figure I've lost maybe five or ten percent of what was in here." He pointed at his head. "Most of the investments have gone up that much in the past six months. There was never any reason to tell anybody. What got them nervous was that I was getting old. They started talking about computers."

"You were going to be replaced?"

"A little delegation came to me and we had a talk. They were polite and sympathetic and careful the way those guys never are except when they're conning somebody. They had it all figured out. Everything in my head could fit on a three-and-a-half-inch disk."

"Having a disk like that could be a dangerous thing."

"There are ways around that. The world is full of expert consultants. There's a system that the government uses called 'strong encryption.' Nobody else is supposed to, but a lot of people know how. Each code is different, so if the FBI gets the disk, they still can't read it. And nothing gets lost, because you can make copies: hide one under a penguin's nest at the South Pole, shove one up a camel's ass in Saudi Arabia, tape one in a kid's lunch box in Peoria. They even explained how my memory would get into the computer."

"How?"

"I would start writing things down, one page at a time. Then I hand the computer guy the paper. He types it in and encodes it. Another guy shreds the paper, and another guy burns the shreds. There would be two other guys with nothing to do but watch to be sure nobody pockets a paper with an account number on it and burns an empty sheet."

Jane raised an eyebrow. "It sounds a bit ornate for them."

"This will show you the mentality. The shredder and burner are going to be guys they bring in specially from other countries—one from Central Europe and one from Asia, because they use different alphabets and can't read letters in English. They won't know where they are, or who the rest of us are. The phones will be cut off, and everybody stays until the job is done. When it's over, they'll be strip-searched to be sure they take nothing with them, given brand-new clothes, and shipped home, where there's nobody they could tell who would know what they were talking about. I figure probably when it comes down to it, these two are not going to make it all the way. Once the precautions get elaborate enough, one of the guards is going to say, 'Oh, what the hell,' and pull the trigger. The computer guy, I suspect, has problems too. These families are never again going to let themselves get into the position of having a big chunk of their money in one guy's brain. There will be another disk that holds the program for decoding the encryption."

"And you?"

"What do you think?" He smiled wearily. "Dead. I looked into their eyes, and I could see they didn't know it yet. They didn't know themselves well enough; these are not introspective people. They thought they were making a generous deal with me, and they would stick to it. I would stay on in Florida doing nothing forever. What they didn't know was that the minute the money was on the disk, I would change. All of a sudden they would notice that I was so old and sick that it would be a favor to put me out of my misery."

"So she saved you."

He nodded. "She knew."

Jane took a deep breath and let it out slowly as she contemplated the old man. She was tired. She knew what was coming and she knew that she would have to let it come before she could move on. "You came here to make a proposal. You've taken half the night working your way up to it."

"I wanted to understand you first, and to let you know who it was making the proposal."

"You had better say it now, so I can say no and go to sleep."

"I'm a ruined person, used up. I didn't get this way because I made the wrong decisions, but because I didn't make any decisions. The woman I loved all my life just killed herself to show me that she cared. And I have our son on my mind now. He's a problem."

"A problem . . . for you?"

The old man looked at the carpet. "I don't know what I expected. His mother . . . I'm sure she did what she knew, and couldn't do anything else."

Jane felt sorry for him. Bernie might have been able to bring back a photographic image of Francesca Giannini's lovely black hair and radiant skin, but he seemed never to have let himself think about who she was. The son must have made it impossible for him not to know. A child was what he learned to be at his mother's knee, and from a distance, Vincent Ogliaro seemed to have grown up to be exactly like the men Bernie Lupus had worked for.

Jane said carefully, "He makes you sad, doesn't he?"

"I want . . ." He started again. "Vincent is like one of those lion cubs that stupid people bring home, and don't know what to do with when they grow up. It's not the lion's fault. He is what he is. He can't choose to be a canary. His mother trying to save me put him in a terrible position."

"I'll bet," said Jane. "Do they know his mother was the one who killed you?"

"I don't think so," he said. "She was too smart for that. She set up one of those 'shots from the crowd' things. She was in a spot that the airport surveillance cameras couldn't pick up. Vincent has been inside on that postal-fraud conviction for three years, and won't get out for a couple more. Everybody knows he could have arranged something like a hit from a cell, but if he's inside he can't take the money and run. The fact that his mother died from it will make most people think it's impossible he had anything to do with it. And why would he?"

"Does anybody else know you're his father?"

Bernie winced. "I'm not his father. The one who was there every day was his father—Mickey Ogliaro. I'm a man he never met. The one who took his mother's virginity in a hotel in Miami when she was too young to know any better, and got her to kill herself when she was old."

Jane said, "Bernie, what do you want?"

"He's all I have left. I have to provide for him. If I could give him all the mob's money, I would do it. But how can I? If a man like Vincent suddenly appears on the horizon with more money than most states have, what happens? There's no good way to have that kind of money all at once. He would set off all the trip wires the government has set up to catch un-taxed money. And what would he do if he had it?"

"I don't know."

"I do, because he's no different from the others. He'd try to make himself boss of bosses. He would get himself killed."

"What do you want?"

"Save my son."

"What does saving him mean?"

The old man stood up and went to the door. "It means fig-uring something out."

Jane watched him disappear, then heard his footsteps re-ceding down the hallway. She sat still for ten minutes, thinking about what she had heard, her eyes turned, unfocused, toward the clock beside the bed. Slowly, she remembered that the red numbers on the digital display meant something. It was late, and she had to sleep. She turned off the lights and lay on the bed.

For a few minutes, her mind was agitated with strange images, things that had been waiting in the back of her memory to jar and clash and keep her from sleep. She fought them by concentrating on Carey. She pictured him in the living room of the house, just going off to work. This time he was a little late—the digital clock said so—and his long legs took the distance across the carpet in fewer steps than he could have in real life, when she was awake. He stopped and smiled at her, then closed the door, and Jane passed into deeper sleep.

Suddenly, her breath caught in her throat. The water. She had left the bathtub running. How could she have been so stupid? Jane ran up the stairs to the second-floor landing. She could feel the smooth, curved wood of the railing on the palm of her hand as she grasped it to make the turn up the hallway. She rushed into the bathroom and reached for the faucet, but it was already turned off. The water was high in the tub, but it was still and glassy.

She gazed down into it, and she realized that the white she was seeing wasn't the bottom of the tub. The water was cloudy, and it seemed to extend downward for a long distance. She touched it with her hand, and she found she could make a swirl in it, like smoke, but it was still not clear. She reached deeper to dispel the illusion, but she couldn't feel the bottom of the tub. Jane sank to her knees and leaned downward. She submerged her arm to the elbow, then the bicep, and finally to the shoulder, but the bottom wasn't there.

Her fingers brushed against something, and she jerked back and withdrew her arm. She rose to her feet and backed away. She could tell that the thing she had touched had been coming up, and that it was big. In a moment she could make out the shape rising from the depths. It wasn't merely floating to the surface, but somehow forming, coalescing as it rose closer, the chalky white particles adhering into the body of a man.

First the nose, then the forehead and cheekbones, the eye sockets still filled with the milky liquid came up, and then the head tilted and the shoulders emerged. His hair was blackening, the long strands on the sides slicked back by moisture and gravity, and he blinked to clear his eyes. He stood up, the white water pouring out of the sleeves and down from the bottom of his sport coat.

"Danny?" said Jane. "Why?"

His shoulders gave a twitch, and he reached to tug at his cuffs, the left one first, just as he had when he had put on his coat in the hotel room. He reached up to his collar and lifted his chin to adjust the necktie. She could see the four ugly holes in his shirt, where the bullets had hit. He stared at her. "You saw me die. I'm part of you now."

Jane's eyes stung with sadness and regret. She had not been able to do anything but watch, and hide. "I'm so sorry, Danny. I've been telling you that at least once an hour since it happened. Did you hear me?"

He shrugged. "Who was listening? When you're dead it doesn't matter what anybody says about it. You're just dead. I don't feel anymore. I slipped up, so I'm meat. You know that's the way it works. You live until you make a mistake."

"Why are you here, Danny?" asked Jane.

"It's your turn now," Danny said.

"I'm going to die?"

Danny shrugged. "Maybe. It's what you're for."

"That's it?"

"Somebody falls, and somebody else steps into the line to take his place. I'm down, and your turn has started already." His dark eyes assumed a concerned look. "Don't let them make their move before you're ready."

"But I don't even know what's going on."

He scowled. "Don't give me that crap. You know the only thing that matters. The world is a place where good and evil fight. It's no different from what your father and his father taught you: Hawenneyu the right-handed twin creates, and Hanegoategeh the left-handed twin destroys. Everything that happens is part of their fighting."

"What am I supposed to do?"

"Better than you've been doing," he said contemptuously.

"Until now you've been running these little errands—taking some loser to a safe place. Just moving pieces around on the board. Tonight you're close to something very big."

"What is it?"

He sighed. "What is this? Have you been asleep all day? Does the name 'Bernie' ring a bell? You know—the old man in the room down the hall from you with a brain full of money?" As he spoke, Danny took his index finger and poked at one of the holes in his shirt. "Tomorrow he could look like this, and Frank Delfina will already be putting the money into play."

"Money? That's what's important?"

"Everything is important to the brothers because they use it as a weapon. Hawenneyu makes a little boy. Hanegoategeh gives him a virus. Hawenneyu strengthens his body to give him immunity, and Hanegoategeh makes the virus mutate into a plague and sends the boy off to kill eighty thousand people. Hawenneyu has made sure one of the eighty thousand is a man who would have started a war and killed eighty million."

"But you haven't told me what I'm supposed to do."

"Look at the configurations and make a choice." His voice was quick and urgent. "Do something before things change again."

"I don't know enough, can't see enough all at once to know what's happening," she said. She hit on a simple strategy, a way of sorting it out. "Is Bernie telling the truth?"

Danny looked at her without appearing to have heard. "Money is a weapon," he repeated, and Jane awoke.

6

At dawn, Bernie Lupus opened his eyes. A ray of sunlight had entered the dark hotel room. He knew that much. It took him a moment to see the figure standing beside the curtain. "What? What's going on?" he whispered.

"I came to talk while Rita is still asleep," Jane said. "I don't think it would do her much good to hear us talk."

Bernie put on his glasses, looked around the room, then took them off again. He eased himself out of bed, wearing a pair of boxer shorts and an undershirt. He picked up his clothes and walked stiffly into the bathroom.

When he emerged, he said, "Let's go for a walk."

She kept her steps at Bernie's pace. The stiffness seemed to leave him gradually as he moved his limbs. When they reached the door that led to the parking lot, his strides had grown longer, and he stood straighter. Jane walked with him away from the motel toward a little plaza where the stores seemed to be closed. The morning sun glinted off the windows with such strength that his face was lighted by the glow. He said, "It's going to be a hot day here."

"The car is air-conditioned."

He squinted at her. "Who's going to be driving it?"

She said, "That depends on what we say now."

"So you've been thinking about it."

She returned his squint. "I'm always thinking. That's why I'm not dead. What about you? How are you planning to stay alive—on the money you're holding for the families?"

Bernie shook his head. "I wouldn't touch it with somebody else's hand. I told you, I have money of my own from the old

58

days." He looked at her in amusement. "Danny bought me a couple of nice suits, but I never even tried them on. I always wear this coat. Here, feel it."

Jane touched his arm, and felt a thick padding. She squeezed it, and recognized the crinkle. "Cash?"

Bernie nodded. "I had a couple hundred thousand lying around the house one time, so I started sewing hundreds into the lining, just in case. I brought some more in envelopes for expenses."

"Is it enough to last you for the rest of your life?"

"I sure as hell hope not."

"I mean if nothing happens to you."

He held the hem of his coat out a few inches. "Feel this."

Jane touched the hem, and felt hard, round pellets between her thumb and forefinger. "What am I feeling?"

"Diamonds. They're all more than two carats and less than five, all flawless. None of them are hot, either. I had somebody buy them years ago in Amsterdam, right after they were cut."

"You can't sell diamonds on any street corner."

"No, but they're worth the effort. I've seen women no bigger than you carry a few million bucks on them without working up a sweat. And I got a few million more in my head. I used to deposit it in accounts under the name Milton Weinstein. I can get all I want by writing checks against it . . . if I can keep remembering the account numbers."

"Tell me more about your memory problem."

He walked in silence for a few steps. "It's not bad yet, but it's like a fire. You look at it and say, 'Hey, it's a little fire.' But they grow. I'm still about ninety percent. Bits of the other ten keep coming back. I get little flashes, and if I'm quick I can read parts. The mind is a weird little mechanism. You'd think that what's gotten cloudy would be the old stuff—sheets of paper I saw sixty years ago, wouldn't you? But it isn't. It's only the most recent stuff."

"That's too bad. The ones who gave you money sixty years ago won't be coming to ask you to account for nickels."

"I should have expected it," he said. "When my grand-father got old, he used to tell me stories about when he was a kid in Poland. After seventy years, he could tell you the weather on some particular day, the flowers that grew along this muddy road where he walked, exactly what people said to him, and what they were wearing. But he couldn't tell you what he had for lunch an hour ago. What gets erased is short-term memory."

"Have you added up how much you still remember?"

He shook his head. "It would be a full-time job to keep track. When you're hiding money, you've got to put it in a lot of different places. If a government accountant sees a hundred thousand someplace, he keeps looking down the list. If he sees a hundred million, he says, 'Let's find out who this guy is.' Pretty early on I had to start putting some in for-eign countries, real estate, precious metals. It must be ten billion by now, but it could be twenty."

"Billion? With a B?"

"Yeah. It would be worse, except that even in the old days I only saw a small part of the take. These guys liked to have most of their money where they could reach it. And I lost customers, too. There were fathers who trusted me, and sons who didn't. The amounts got bigger each year, but they were a smaller and smaller part of gross receipts." He paused. "You must have come up with a counterproposal."

"Not exactly," she answered.

"Why not?"

"My interest in this is Rita," said Jane. "You're an unex-pected complication."

He nodded. "I never thought of myself that way. I guess I'd better get used to it, though, now that Danny's dead. Keeping me out of sight would have been a good deal for him. He would have been a very rich man." He turned his head a little and held her in the corner of his eye. "Tell me what you're thinking."

"I think I can take Rita to a safe place and teach her to live quietly for long enough so they don't find her. I can't guarantee that I can keep you from being found, but I can make it very difficult." She looked at him to judge his reaction. "I think I can arrange something that will help your son without making him too strong."

"You want something in return," he said. "What is it?"

She walked on. "I wouldn't be here if I didn't have a general idea that appeals to me. I'll tell you what's on my mind. I've always been careful to stay out of the Mafia's way. There's never been any question that if I ever happened to attract their notice, there wouldn't be anything left of me. And I never had any illusion that I could do them noticeable harm, so I never thought of how to go about it. One of the families you've been helping happens to be looking for people I've made disappear in the past few years. I won't say who, and I won't say which family. It occurred to me that I would like it if the families were weaker. My friends would be that much safer. And I would be too."

"So you want to hurt the Mafia. How?"

"I want you to take all of their money and donate it to charities."

"What?"

"That's my price."

"That's your price? Ten billion dollars?" He grinned at her, but his expression slowly changed. "You're serious, aren't you? You don't want any, you just want to give it away? I didn't think anybody would be able to hear what I had to say last night, then go to sleep and not wake up thinking about being rich."

"You wanted a way to help Vincent without giving him enough to get himself killed. It happens to coincide with what I want: I don't want any of the rest of them to have it either."

Bernie laughed, looked at her, then laughed again, a high, rheumy hoot that ended in a cough.

"I guess that means no," said Jane. She held out the keys to the car. "You'd better take these now, because I've got a plane to catch."

Bernie drew his hands back and stuck them into his pockets. "I didn't turn down your deal. Just let me think for a minute. This isn't the first time I've thought about it, either. Once in a while I would say to myself, 'What I ought to do is screw these guys and give it all away.' But it's not easy. It's a tough thing to do with that much money. It means dreaming up lots of tricks."

"I saw somebody do something like it once," said Jane. "I know how hard it is."

"And you have a way to take care of Vincent?"

"We can offer him a way to be comfortable for the rest of his life without taking any risks. Whether he agrees or not is up to him. It's the best I can do . . . or at least, the most I'm willing to do."

"It would have to come from my money," he said. "Nothing from them."

"Of course," said Jane.

Bernie walked along for a few seconds, thinking. Finally, he shrugged. "It's probably the best either of us can do."

"You'll consider it?"

"You think I've got to go through a pile of other offers before I decide?" he asked. "I'll do it."

"Good," said Jane.

"You don't sound as though you mean it," said Bernie. "Honey, I think you've got to open up just a little more."

She looked at him. "It's what I think should happen. It's not what I want to do. It takes time, and it's dangerous."

"Ice cream," announced Bernie.

"What?"

"Homemade ice cream. You got to crank a machine to get it, it's got raw eggs so it's the biggest source of food poisoning. It's full of fat and sugar, so it'll give you strokes and heart attacks. If you eat it too fast, you can actually freeze some nerve in your head and go blind." He smiled. "Tastes good, though."

Jane smiled back at him. "Tastes very good."

They turned around and walked back toward the motel. As they came into the hallway, Bernie touched her arm. "Wait. Have you figured out what we do with Rita?"

"That's something I've wondered about since you turned up," said Jane. "What's your interest in her?"

Bernie looked down at the carpet. "I guess it's another crummy thing that happens when you get old. When your body gets soft and weak, your mind does the same thing. You get sentimental about whatever it is that makes people alive. Some skinny little kid who moves quick and doesn't seem to be affected by gravity is a kind of miracle. She has so much of it that she kind of throws it off around her like heat and light. It kind of kept me going." He gazed at Jane as though he had not seen her before. "You don't have any idea what I'm talking about, do you?"

"I'm not sure."

"Do you know anything about her?"

Jane gave her head a little shake. "She told me some of her story. I knew I didn't have time for more of it if I was going to get her out of there."

Bernie said, "She's not as delicate as she looks. Just the opposite—sort of like a little animal. A raccoon, maybe. Ever try to keep one out of your garden?"

"I'm a big-city girl," Jane lied. "I buy my vegetables frozen."

"I had a bodyguard years ago, right after they built my place. He was right from Sicily, and they thought he'd be good because he didn't know anything. He planted a bunch of grape vines, I guess because he was homesick. But the place was right where a raccoon used to live. The new house doesn't faze her. She wants those grapes. You put in a fence, she climbs it. You put up a bit of wire on top, she shimmies through. You electrify it, she climbs a big tree nearby and drops into the middle of the vineyard, then digs under to get out. If you put in a moat, she swims it. You stay up all night watching for her, then the second you doze off she's back. There's a maddening persistence there, but it's not stupidity. She just puts up with what she has to, because she's going to survive, no matter what. She's going to keep coming at you until you get tired and go away, or you put a bullet into her.

Seeing her die would be a shameful thing. Besides, she's the best friend I've had since Sal Augustino."

It took Jane a second to identify the moment when the raccoon had transformed back into Rita. "Friend?"

"I know," said Bernie. "It sounds pathetic in a man my age. Living like I did is lonely. She used to take the time to talk to me. Nobody else did. Once in a while when things were slow, I'd get her to play a game of cards. I could tell she wasn't much interested in cards: too much sitting still for a person like her, I guess, and too much thinking about something that's pointless. I guess she was lonely too. We'd kind of look out for each other when there were other people around. And she got to go out—you know, shopping for groceries and so on. So I'd use her for my eyes and ears. She'd come back and describe everything she saw and heard out there. Seeing her was like getting a visitor in jail. Until you've been there, you don't know what that is."

"I understand," said Jane.

"So what do we do with her? Before we do anything that's probably going to bring the roof down on our heads, we've got to—"

The door beside Bernie's opened suddenly, and Rita glared at them. "Where have you two been?"

Jane stepped inside and pulled Rita with her. When Bernie had entered, he closed the door behind him. "What are you doing up at this hour?" he asked.

"Looking for you," said Rita.

"We went for a little walk," Jane said. "Don't worry. If we were going to abandon you or something, we wouldn't be here. Bernie wouldn't have followed you all the way from Florida, and I wouldn't have driven half the night to get you here."

Rita gave her a sullen look. "I fell asleep and everything changed, didn't it? Now it's you and Bernie. What are you going to do with me?"

Jane said, "What I had planned to do all along. I'm going to get you some very good identification that says you're somebody else. Then I'm going to find you a safe, pleasant

place to live and try to teach you to be that other person.
When I'm satisfied that you've learned enough to stay alive,
I'm going to leave."

Rita looked at the floor, then back up at her. "I . . . I'm
sorry. I'd rather go with Bernie."

"What?"

She looked at Jane apologetically. "I'm sorry. I came to
you and begged you to help me. And I know there's a way
you do these things, because Celia told me. I have to do
everything you say, as soon as you say it and not even ask
any questions. Now you've gone to a lot of trouble and taken
me all the way here. But I don't want to go off by myself and
hide somewhere. I'd rather go wherever Bernie's going."

Bernie looked amazed, and even a little frightened. "Wait,
kid. Who invited you? I just didn't want you on your own
without any money. But you won't be on your own. Jane
will help you."

The girl's eyes were beginning to well up. "Please,
Bernie. I worked for you for a year. You know I won't be any
trouble. I can help you a lot."

Jane looked at Bernie, waiting. He said, "I'll tell you the
truth. I've always tried to seem like this nice old man, but
that's not what I am. The reason I lived in that house is that I
worked for the Mafia. I was hiding money for them. They
don't get money from some nice clean enterprise. It came
from things like lending somebody's father a few bucks so
they can make him pay ten times that in interest, or they'll
break his legs. Or from taking girls younger than you and
forcing them to have sex with twenty strangers a day. You
told me your mother was locked up for drugs. There's a
good chance the money from bringing it in came to me."

"You sound like I'm five years old," said Rita. "You didn't
do any of those things, any more than I did. You couldn't
have left if you tried."

Bernie looked at Jane in desperation, so Jane said, "You
saw what happened when they heard Bernie was killed. They
seem to be tearing the country apart looking for anybody

who might know anything. Right now, the only one I know about is you."

"They're not looking for Bernie, because he's dead. And he's smarter than they are. It said in the paper he was. If he doesn't get caught, neither do I." She said to Bernie in a pleading voice, "This isn't her problem. It's our problem. She's this nice woman, and we're just going to get her killed."

Jane said, "I'm afraid you don't know everything . . ."

"I know enough."

Bernie said, "Danny isn't going to meet me somewhere. They caught him in your hotel and killed him."

She closed her eyes to hold the tears back. "Then you're the only friends I have left. I want to go with you. I can help with what you're doing."

"What is he doing?" asked Jane.

"Not him. Both of you. You're going to take all the money he hid for the Mafia."

"Why would you think that?" asked Bernie.

"Because you hate them. That's why you pretended to die. I watched you sometimes when those men came to the house. And I watched you looking out the window at them when they left. You hate them."

Bernie looked at Jane, his eyebrows raised.

Jane took in a deep breath and sighed. "I guess when you know enough to get yourself killed, it won't make things any worse if you have the story straight. Yes. We've decided to try to retrieve all the money he was holding in his head for the families. What we want to do is steal it and donate it to charities."

Rita's body straightened and her head bobbed backward as though something had jumped up at her. "Get real." She waited for Jane or Bernie to say something, then cocked her head. "All of it?"

"Every penny, if we can."

Rita glared at her, then let her eyes move to Bernie, then back to Jane, as though she was still waiting for one of them to reveal that it was a joke. Very slowly, her eyes widened,

and her lips curled up at the corners. "It's kind of funny."
After a pause, she said softly, "Okay."

"What do you mean, 'Okay'?"

"I'm in. I'll help. Maybe it'll pay them back just a little bit for Danny."

"You don't seem to understand what this means."

Rita's smile lingered on her lips, but her eyes were still wet from the tears. "I understand enough."

"I'm not sure you do," said Bernie. "I'm holding money that belongs to twelve families. Not little ones, either. Right now they think I'm dead, and they hate me for dying. They can't wait to die too, so they can go track me through hell to kill me again. If they ever get one whiff of a suspicion that I'm alive and gave away their money, they'll go crazy. There will be hundreds of guys out looking for me every day. They'll still be looking when nobody's seen me for forty years and I'd have to be a hundred and fifteen years old. Then they'll quit. You know what will happen then?"

"What?" said Rita.

"They'll start looking harder for you."

"I'll be fifty-eight," said Rita. "And I'll know that I at least did something to them before they got me."

Jane stood closer and looked into Rita's eyes. "We've told you what we're going to do. What you're going to do hasn't changed. You're going to a place far away where you can pass as a different person."

"What am I supposed to do there? What's the use of it?"

"Who knows?" said Jane. "Maybe so that when we're dead, there will be somebody alive who knows what we were trying to do."

7

Frank Delfina opened the big steamer trunk and gazed down into it at Danny Spoleto's body. It had been jammed into the trunk with the knees nearly to the chest and the arms folded. The neck had needed to be twisted a bit so the head would fit into one corner. The face was aimed upward at the light hanging from the ceiling of the garage. The door to the florist's work room was open, and the thick, sweet smells of jasmine and gardenia clashed and competed with the oil and gasoline of the fleet of delivery vans.

Delfina craned his neck so his head was aligned with the face of Danny Spoleto. He stared into the dead eyes for a minute, then walked to the other side of the trunk. "This is one dumb son of a bitch," he muttered. He gave the trunk lid a kick so it snapped shut. Then he turned his attention to the two men who had delivered the trunk. "Is the hotel room completely cleaned up? No blood or anything?"

"Yes sir," said Strozza. "We got him into the bathtub before there was much blood, and we gave the floor a quick job ourselves before we left. John and Irene got there about two minutes later. After they got him in the trunk they went over everything with cleanser and disinfectant."

"And you're sure there was nothing in the room and nothing in the luggage?"

"He had two small suitcases. Nothing in there but clothes he had just bought—shirts in those plastic packages, and pants with the tags still on them. Irene even sliced open all the linings in the suitcases. He didn't seem to own any paper."

Delfina glanced down at the body. "You searched him too?"

Strozza nodded. "All he had was his wallet and car keys."

Delfina said, "I guess there's no reason to hold on to the body, then. Go bury it."

Strozza and his partner squatted to tip the trunk up onto the dolly, then wheeled the trunk up the ramp of their truck and secured it to the back wall. "We'll take it out to the seed farm. There's a field they're getting ready to plant with begonias in a couple of days."

"Don't be lazy: make it deep."

When the two men had closed the tailgate and climbed into their truck, Caporetto pressed the thumb button beside the garage door and opened it so they could drive out, then closed it. Delfina was in a sour mood, but he gained some comfort from seeing his men moving, doing things efficiently, paying attention. He said to Caporetto, "As soon as those guys come back, put them on a plane to L.A. Call Billy and tell him to find them something to do."

"Sure, Frank."

As an afterthought, Delfina added, "Make sure it's nothing important."

Delfina caught a look of mild surprise on Caporetto's face. He shrugged. "I know Spoleto wasn't what they expected to find, but they should have done better than this. You notice they didn't even find a gun on him. They saw him and panicked. It would have been nice to have that guy in a small room someplace where I could have a long talk with him."

Caporetto nodded, but his face revealed a slight discomfort. "I still don't understand what he was doing there."

"I don't know yet where he fits exactly," said Delfina. "But I plan to."

Caporetto said, "You think he just stole her credit card from Bernie's house and charged everything to her so we wouldn't know he was traveling?"

Delfina looked at him in disappointment. "That's what Strozza thinks. But you heard him. They found his wallet. If he'd had her credit card, you would have heard about it. So where did it go?"

Caporetto shrugged. "I don't know."

"He never had it. The girl made the charges herself."

"Then it was both of them? He was the one who got the girl the job as Bernie's housekeeper, right? Maybe he used her to find out where Bernie put the money—had her pull receipts or something from the trash for a year or so. Then he somehow lured Bernie to Detroit, popped him, and took off to collect the money. That would explain why they came all the way up to New York. That's where the big banks and brokers and all that are."

Delfina said, "New York City, not Niagara Falls. But it's something like that."

Caporetto's excitement slowly grew. "Yeah," he said. "Got to be. Danny Spoleto was supposed to be this ladies' man, right? He didn't look like any great shakes stuffed in a box, but I heard he had to fight them off. So he gets this green kid—she's what, eighteen?—and charms her like a snake. All she has to do is hang around Bernie's house, sweep the floor once a day, and keep her eyes open when she empties the trash can. When she's found enough, Spoleto pops Bernie, meets the girl, and cashes in all the accounts she's located for him."

Delfina smiled indulgently, but his customary look of stony intensity returned. He shook his head.

"Why not?" asked Caporetto.

"It's a good story. I like it. But let me tell you about Danny Spoleto. He started out ten years ago in New York. He had a cousin who was made, and the cousin asked the Langustos if they could find something for him. Since the old days, the Langusto family was supposed to take care of Bernie. Maybe it meant something fifty years ago, but since then, it's been kind of nominal, like the Swiss guards at the Vatican. They still supplied bodyguards, on a regular rotation. So they sent him down to Florida to take some other guy's place. He didn't get on Bernie's nerves, so they left him there for a few years. Then they made him one of their bagmen. He would deliver money to Florida for them—most of it not even in cash—and Bernie would make it disappear. Bernie may have sent him on a few errands, too, but that was it. This was not a guy in training to enter the world of high finance. It was a guy who had to wait six or seven years before anybody would promote him to delivery boy."

"What about the girl? Maybe she was smarter than she looked. Maybe she was the one who came on to Spoleto, knowing that he could get her into that house."

"I thought of that, but she didn't know in advance what was going to happen to Bernie."

"She didn't?"

"When our guys got to the house that night, it was about four hours after Bernie got shot. She wasn't gone. She was still in bed."

"Then what do you want her for?"

Delfina brought his lower lip over the upper one, then down again in a little shrug. "I think she can't help but know something. She saw people come and go. Maybe they wouldn't mean anything to her, but they would to me. But what she knows for sure is what happened before Bernie left for Detroit. It wasn't normal. For years, Bernie barely went outside. I think somebody called him, or sent him a ticket or something, and I'd like to know who."

"Why not Danny Spoleto? If he was a bagman, he must have brought briefcases full of money and stuff into the house—all for Bernie's eyes only."

"Maybe," said Delfina. "But we just caught him when he didn't expect us. The guys searched him, searched the bags, searched the room. They didn't find anything that showed he had access to serious money. Bernie the Elephant might have carried a hundred account numbers in his head, but you can't tell me this bodyguard did. So even if he had something to do with setting Bernie up, he didn't end up with any way of getting at the money."

"The girl? Nobody searched her. She might be carrying it for him."

"That's as good a reason as any to look for her."

"She's all we've got," Caporetto agreed.

"Except that we don't have her anymore," Delfina reminded him. "We've got her picture, right?"

"Yeah. When they hired her, they told her it was for a work permit. She didn't know any better."

"Okay," said Delfina. "Here's what we do. First thing is, nobody in this family knows anything about Danny Spoleto. As far as the other families know, we didn't find him, and we didn't kill him, and it never occurred to us to look for a girl. Second, I want a full-court press on finding her fast. As of right now, nobody has anything to do but find her. Get the picture copied, and make it look like one of those mailers they send out: 'Girl missing from her home since June twenty-third,' and give a phone number that's got nothing to do with us."

"Okay," said Caporetto.

"And what else do we know about her? Where's she from? What family has she got?"

"She grew up in northern Florida. The only relative she's got is her mother. Her name is Ann Shelford, and she's doing five in Florida State Penitentiary at Starke."

"For what?"

"Peddling meth," he said. "Turns out it was ours, actually. Just a coincidence. Some of that stuff from the lab in California."

Delfina nodded. "Find a couple of people inside that we can use. I want her watched. I want somebody reading her mail, listening to her phone calls. I want somebody at her elbow all the time."

Caporetto nodded. "We're already working on it. As soon as the girl disappeared, that was the best guess as to where she was going first." He added, "We're still looking for boyfriends or just girls she used to hang out with, but nothing has come up yet." He waited for a moment for what Delfina was going to say next, but he got the familiar cold stare that always made him feel as though Delfina were a machine that had suddenly turned itself off. He hurried to the door of the garage and slipped out.

Delfina went out through the work room and shut the door. He picked up a bouquet of roses lying on the table, then moved through the shop carrying them. He paused in the darkened room and looked out the front window, up and down the street. He hated the inside of the florist business. The cutting rooms always smelled like the biggest funeral in the world was in progress. He had not been in this building in three years, and would never have come except that it was the only safe place he owned in Niagara Falls. After a moment he was satisfied that there was nobody in a car watching the door. He slipped out and locked the door behind him.

As he walked off carrying the roses, he breathed in and out rapidly and deeply, then forced a cough to clear his lungs of pollen and perfume. He looked around again to be sure he wasn't under surveillance, dropped the flowers into a trash can, then got into the car he had rented and drove off alone toward his hotel. In the silence, he had time to think.

In the settlement after the failed coup twelve years ago, Castiglione had been forced into exile in Arizona, and his holdings had been crudely split up. Tommy DeLuca had gotten the Castiglione territory that amounted to half of Chicago, and Frank Delfina had gotten all the far-flung enterprises, the feelers that Castiglione had been extending outward for years before he made his failed attempt to gobble up his rivals. People still talked about the inequality of the partition: DeLuca had inherited an only slightly diminished empire, and Delfina had gotten an illusion—laughable assets like a flower business in Niagara Falls, a few radio stations in places like Omaha and Reno, a bakery in California. The partition had satisfied the coalition of families that had assembled against Castiglione: no single man would retain the power to harm them.

What nobody seemed to have known was that DeLuca had won the right to preside over a dying carcass. The old neighborhood-based mob that controlled city blocks and paid off the cops in the precinct and depended on enterprises like bookmaking on sports and moving stolen TV sets was dying before he and DeLuca were born. What DeLuca had inherited was the tentative loyalty of three hundred men with rap sheets who needed to be fed and kept occupied, and the attention of a variety of state and federal agencies that had been invented in the last generation for the sole purpose of harassing the publicity-cursed Chicago families.

Delfina had left Chicago within two days of the Commission's ruling and begun to learn. He had taken a lesson from conglomerates, and begun to slowly, quietly, build the enterprises he had. He didn't buy out his competitors. He starved them to death, then bought up their facilities and customer lists for practically nothing. He studied the suppliers and services his businesses used, induced them to borrow money so they could expand and meet his companies' needs, then canceled the contracts. In a year he could buy them for the price of their loans.

The distance between his various businesses had made other people assume there was no way he could do anything with them. The distance had been full of advantages. He could move anything—money, people, contraband—from Niagara Falls to Reno, or Omaha to Los Angeles in trucks registered to corporations. When they got there, he could make even the trucks disappear into the fleets of other businesses. He could transfer profits from one company to another: declare income in states that had no income tax, report sales where there was no sales tax, or sell things to himself at a loss and write off the loss. He could do anything the big corporations did.

He had begun early to construct a culture that would separate his men from the old attachments to particular neighborhoods and the families that had run them for generations. What he had been given to work with was a small cadre of displaced Castiglione soldiers like Caporetto. If he had dispensed with them at the beginning, he knew, he would not have lasted a month. He had needed to find a new way to use them.

He paid them extravagantly, gave them praise and assurances, then split them up and sent them to regions as far apart as possible. He let them recruit new, younger men and assigned the trainees as overseers of his businesses. He rotated the young men regularly from one part of the country to another, the way major corporations did. They never stayed settled long enough in a single city to be tied to it. Within a year or two they knew all the cities well enough to navigate them comfortably, and by the end of the second cycle, they were experts. Each of them had spent some time working for all of Delfina's underbosses, and their loyalty was to the only constant he permitted them: Delfina.

For Delfina, the scattered and diverse nature of his holdings provided various forms of security. He could count on the predictable, quasi-legitimate profits of his visible companies to pay his people. If one industry or region hit hard times, the others could subsidize Delfina's stake in it until times changed.

Delfina was part of a new world, but he knew he was not invulnerable to the one he had come from, so he looked for new models of physical security. He had read in the newspapers about the habits of foreign potentates, and studied them. It seemed to him that the most ingenious self-protectors were men like Qaddafi and Hussein. They could have surrounded themselves with thousands of troops and lived in hardened bunkers, but that would have made them bigger targets. What worked for them was a combination of anonymity and mobility. Delfina imitated them. He had no permanent residence. Instead he shuttled about the country, showed up unannounced at each of his businesses in turn, stayed for an hour or a month, and moved on.

As he drove through the dark streets toward the river, the steamy night air noticeably cooled, and big drops of summer rain splashed on his windshield. He turned on his wipers and slowed down. He thought about the two men going out to bury Danny Spoleto, then shrugged them off. They deserved a little discomfort, and the rain would hide any disturbance in the soil. By this time tomorrow they would be in California. They wouldn't see rain again until November.

He wondered what his life would be like in November. By then he would have had time to get used to having Bernie Lupus's money, and would have begun to put it to use. All of those cities that he had conscientiously, prudently bypassed in his endless commuting—New York, Chicago, New Orleans, Philadelphia, Cleveland, Pittsburgh—would probably already be his. People like DeLuca, John Augustino, Al Castananza, the Langusto brothers, and Molinari would just be more underbosses he would have to visit now and then. It was almost inevitable. Bernie the Elephant had spent fifty years collecting their money and salting it away and making it grow, and now it was ready for Delfina to take. When he had it, those men would lose control of their own soldiers. The guys who had been making peanuts shaking down mom-and-pop grocery stores for their local bosses would make quiet inquiries to see if there was anything they could do for Delfina. And when that happened, the bosses would come too. He would use the money to attract their allegiance, or finance their retirement, or buy their deaths.

8

As Jane drove along the highway into Illinois, Bernie's patience seemed to be slipping away. Finally, he asked, "Where are we going?"

"Chicago."

Bernie said, "I don't know about Chicago. If Delfina's started looking for her, the others will be too. There are people in Chicago who have seen her."

"Really?" asked Jane. "Who?"

"Tommy DeLuca used to send a bagman down about once a month."

Jane said, "That's one out of three million. You can wait for me outside Chicago in case he happens to be at the bank. I have some things in a safe-deposit box there that I'll need."

"Look, I don't know what it is, but—"

"Forged IDs that I can work over to fit the two of you."

Bernie seemed unable to think of a suitable argument, so he sat in disapproving silence. After a few minutes, Rita said, "Anybody mind if I play the radio?" as she turned it on and punched buttons to flood the car with a rhythmic noise punctuated by a man's voice chanting incomprehensible words. She turned down the volume to keep it from irritating Jane and Bernie.

Jane glanced at Rita. She was chewing gum in time with the music and rocking slightly as she listened. There was a peculiar innocence to the expression, and Jane wondered if kids still had those conversations she remembered about what the lyrics actually were. They must, she decided. "How about you?" she asked. "Are you afraid of Chicago?"

"Nope," said Rita distractedly. "I'm afraid of the places I've been already. Are you sure the music is okay?"

Bernie answered hastily, "It's fine, kid." Jane could tell he was lying. "The silence was getting on our nerves."

Jane told them no more until she had stopped and rented two rooms at a hotel in Frankfort. She brought Bernie and Rita inside the first of the two rooms, put the DO NOT DISTURB sign on the door, sorted through her purse at the table, and handed each of them a key.

"Here are your keys. I'm going to be gone for a while."

Rita asked, "Can I go with you?"

"I didn't mean an hour or two," said Jane. "It should be a few days."

Rita looked uncomfortable. "You're leaving us here?"

Jane looked around her. "It's a nice enough hotel. If you do as I say, you'll be fine. Don't go out. Order your meals from room service. When the waiter comes, take the tray at the door, sign the bill, and send him off."

"What's this about?" asked Rita. "Where are you going?"

"First I'm going to my safe-deposit box, then I'm going to shop for a place that's safer than this one."

"How do we even know you're going to come back?"

"You don't." She let Rita get used to the idea, then walked

toward the door. "If I'm not back in a week, check out. Rita, you'll have to do it, I'm afraid. The credit card is in the name Katherine Sanders. It's on the dresser with the receipt. Make your way to Decatur and check in at the Marriott."

"You going to meet us there?" asked Bernie.

"If I miss you here, I will. If I'm not there within a week after that, something happened to me. Go to a quiet town somewhere and do your best to make it on your own."

On the fifth day at eleven in the morning, Jane returned to the hotel. She found Bernie sitting on the bed where she had left him, and Rita curled up in a chair in front of the television set. The set was tuned to a music video station, where a girl who didn't seem much older than Rita was wearing something that looked like the top of an unflattering suit and the bottom of a bikini, and angrily singing words that she emphasized by pointing fingers with inch-long nails at the camera.

Rita said, "Do you think that's a real tattoo?"

Bernie answered, "Looks real to me. But I don't remember it from her last album."

Jane closed the door, and they both looked at her in alarm. Rita recovered, then pretended it had not happened. "Oh, hi," she said coolly, and turned her attention back to the screen.

Bernie stood up. "Well?"

"I've already paid the bill and checked us out. I just have to drop your keys at the desk." She accepted the two keys and turned to go. "The car is in the third row from the north end of the building."

When Jane joined Rita and Bernie in the car and they were on the highway, Bernie asked, "Did you find what you were looking for?"

"I think I did," she said. "It's a little far, but it seems right."

"Just how far?" he asked.

"New Mexico. You'll have a couple of days on the road to think about it."

"Where in New Mexico?"

"Santa Fe. Or, just outside it, really. I found a house. It's small, but it's got two stories. That's something that runners don't always think about in advance, but it's worth trying for. You can make it very difficult for anybody to get to you while you're sleeping. It's on a sparsely populated road, set back about two hundred feet on a little rise, so you can see people coming from a long way off. The country around it is mostly low brush and rocks."

Bernie squinted doubtfully. "I don't know about Santa Fe."

"Have you been to Santa Fe?" asked Jane patiently.

"No, but it's famous. People know about it."

Jane smiled. "That's right. People go there on vacations. Other people live there for part of the year, and might rent a different house each time. All of it means that strangers don't rate a second look—even strangers carrying a lot of cash."

"It also means a lot of pairs of eyes pass through town. What if one of them is—"

"Who?" she interrupted. "You must know a lot about the people who would recognize your face. When they travel, do any of them go to Santa Fe?"

He looked away and said grudgingly, "I never heard of any. But they might stop on the way to Las Vegas or Hawaii or someplace."

"Santa Fe doesn't have a major airport. Most people who want to get there fly into Albuquerque and drive the last sixty miles. It's not on the way to anywhere else except Taos."

"But what goes on there?" asked Rita. "What do people do?"

"Nothing we have to worry about. It's the state capital, but states in the Southwest don't take much governing—lots of land, not many people."

"But what about him?" asked Rita protectively. "He's got to be happy."

Bernie said, "I'll be happy just to get out of the damned car."

But for the next two days, he would suddenly stir and a question would come from nowhere. "What am I supposed to be doing there?"

"You're pretty much what you really are. You worked for a large company for fifty years, then retired. You've been living in Florida but didn't like it, so you moved. You shouldn't have any trouble learning all about some legitimate business. Just read a book and you'll be able to recite it. But you should still avoid specific questions about it. If somebody asks, talk about the people from those days. That's all they're interested in anyway: people stories."

They arrived in Santa Fe in the evening. The route Jane chose through the city was calculated to give her two passengers a good impression. She drove in on Federal Place, past the post office and the Federal Courthouse, then down Lincoln Avenue between the Museum of Fine Arts and the Palace of the Governors, skirted the seventeenth-century Plaza, where they could see the lighted shops and restaurants, then went along East San Francisco Street to Saint Francis Cathedral.

Before she turned right to reach Canyon Road, she was sure she had given Rita and Bernie enough of a taste of the place to reassure them a little. It wasn't the sort of city they were used to, where enormous corporations elbowed their forty-story steel-and-glass towers onto the main streets. But it wasn't a desert outpost with one stop light and a gas station either.

She kept up a running commentary as she drove. "The Plaza is a great place, but it would be best to go in the evening."

"Why?" asked Rita.

"Cameras. Most of the time, the picture ends up in a family album in Dubuque, Iowa. But if it gets blown up on the cover of *Travel & Leisure*, Bernie's face could be on a lot of newsstands. There are a dozen restaurants on all sides of the Plaza. Just go down any of these smaller streets leading away from it." Then she added, "But the places that will be safest are the ones that don't interest tourists: grocery stores, dry cleaners, and so on. Any time you find yourself surrounded by Navajo rugs, silver jewelry, or Zuni pots, be alert and get ready to move on."

She drove out on Canyon Road for four miles, then turned up a gravel drive between two wooden posts. She turned around the house, pushed a remote control to open the garage, and pulled the car into it.

Bernie looked glum as he got out of the car and stretched.

Jane stood close to him and whispered, "Go out, walk about two hundred feet that way, and then watch me from there. If somebody is in there waiting to blow my head off, go to the riverbank and follow it back into town. Don't try to walk on the road."

"Jesus, honey," he whispered. "If you're not sure, then what are we doing here?"

"I do it because this is the way the game is played. You take all of the precautions the first time. Right now I need to see that the house is the way I left it, and I can't do it if you two are making footprints and moving things. So go."

She exerted light pressure on his shoulder and watched him take a couple of steps, then stop. But Rita quickly took his hand and led him off into the darkness.

Before Jane had settled on this house, she had been careful to visit it at night as well as in daylight. There were no street lamps, no neighbors close enough to throw light on the surrounding land. That gave her control. If she needed to light the yard up, she could do it from a switch inside the house. If it was time to run, she could get Rita and Bernie out in darkness.

Jane took a flashlight out of the car and bent low as she walked the long way around the house to the front door, studying the ground. Three times she knelt close to the dirt and switched the flashlight on, but none of the variations on the surface were footprints. As Jane moved silently beside the house she passed close to each window to be sure the glass was intact, the latch still closed, and the layer of windblown dust still on the sill. By the time she had reached the front door she was reasonably sure nobody had been here.

She used her key to open the door, stepped inside, and turned on the light. Before she had left, she had poured some talcum powder into the palm of her hand and blown it over the hardwood floor inside the entrance, so it formed a thin, nearly invisible film. She bent and examined it, but it had not been disturbed.

Jane wandered through the house turning on lights and searching for other signs. The five drawers she had left slightly open had not been opened and reclosed. None of the carpets she had vacuumed to raise the pile had been pushed down by shoes. She went to the front door and stood in the lighted space for a moment, waved the others in, then closed the door to keep the light from illuminating them.

When Rita and Bernie came inside, they found Jane spreading a blanket on a couch in the living room. She said, "The upstairs is yours. There are two bedrooms up there, each with its own bath."

"This is nicer than I thought it would be," said Rita. That didn't sound good to her, so she amended it. "It's really nice." She looked at Bernie.

Bernie had been gazing at the stairs, but he seemed to take the cue. "Yeah, nice," he said. "You shouldn't sleep down here. Take my room."

Rita looked at Jane and decided she must have made another mistake. "We could share a bed. I don't snore or anything."

"No thanks," Jane answered. "I want to be down here, and I want Bernie to get settled and begin getting used to the place."

Rita started up the stairs, but Bernie stood and glared down at Jane for a moment. "You're keeping watch, aren't you?"

Jane sighed wearily. "If you hear a loud noise, don't come looking for me. Turn off the light on your way up."

9

In the morning, Rita tried out the shower, and found it much better than she had hoped. For the past few days she had been in bad hotels, where the shower always produced a misty trickle, and that made her feel big and dumb, like a cow standing in the rain. She dressed and ventured to the top of the stairs to look down.

Jane was sitting on the couch with a cup of coffee. She didn't look up and notice Rita: her eyes had been fixed on the spot where Rita stood before she arrived to fill it.

"Good morning," said Rita.

"Good morning. The coffee is on the counter, and the cups are in the cupboard above it."

"I don't drink coffee," said Rita. Her tone made it sound as though she suspected she should.

"There's orange juice, if you like that, cereal, milk, eggs, bacon, and a few other things."

Rita walked into the kitchen. A short time later Jane heard Bernie upstairs, then waited until he was downstairs before she repeated the instructions. He mumbled, "Thanks," and went into the kitchen.

After twenty minutes, Rita and Bernie came into the living room looking more alert. Bernie glanced around him. "I was expecting this place to be empty. Where did all this furniture and food and stuff come from?"

"Everything in the house is here because I picked it and brought it here. I went to the real estate office that was handling the place and got the key. I looked it over and signed a three-year lease. I drove down to Albuquerque and spent an afternoon picking out furniture from a used-furniture store so it would look as though it had been moved from somewhere, then had it delivered to a storage warehouse. The next day I had a moving company truck it all up here and put it into the house. The appliances came from three different stores down there. The pots and pans, dishes, sheets, and blankets I bought here. Nothing I did should raise any eyebrows."

"Whose name is the lease in?"

"Renee Moore and Peter Moore. I'm Renee. You're Peter." She walked into the coat closet, turned around, and reached above the door. She took down a large manila envelope that had been taped there. She brought it into the kitchen, emptied it on the table, and sat down.

"What's that?" asked Rita.

"Bernie's birth certificate."

"I suppose you went out reading gravestones for this one?" asked Bernie, as he studied the paper.

"The police figured that one out a while ago, so it doesn't work very well anymore. This one's not a forgery. A man I knew used to work in the county clerk's office in Franklin County, Pennsylvania. He added about fifty names to the records and sold me their birth certificates a few years ago. I couldn't get the age perfect—I don't have that many left—but your birth is officially registered. You're sixty-seven."

Bernie nodded and set the certificate aside.

"Here is your driver's license," said Jane. "It's real too. I had a man use the birth certificate to apply and take the driving test. It's from New Jersey, because they don't require a photograph. You can take it to the Motor Vehicles office in town and trade it in for a New Mexico one."

"Today?" asked Rita.

Jane shook her head. "We have other things to do first. This one will be good for a long time, and the longer he waits, the less dangerous it will be." She set an American Express card, a Visa, and a MasterCard on the table in front of Bernie. "Over the years, I grew Mr. Moore some credit. The limits aren't high, but you won't need much."

Bernie said, "Anything else?"

Jane said, "Social Security card. That's fake."

"Who gives a—"

"Bernie . . ." Rita cautioned.

"Sorry," he muttered. "Is that it?"

"Not quite," said Jane. "Here's your DD-214."

"What's that?"

"It's an honorable discharge from the army. It's a fake. There's a company that advertises in magazines. If you lost your discharge papers, they'll sell you what they call a 'Deluxe Memento Replica, Suitable for Framing.' This doesn't do anything for you except help build a deeper cover." She was coming close to the bottom of the pile. "I have other things like that too. They don't have any legal status, but everybody has a few: auto club membership, library card, and so on. You carry them around in your wallet, and it helps make Peter Moore a person, not a flat picture of a person."

She left the rest of the cards and papers on the table and stood up. She swung the refrigerator door open. "There's enough food in this house to live on for a week or two. The freezer is stuffed, and the cupboards are full of canned goods."

She walked to the kitchen door. "Keep the doors locked and bolted, of course," she said. "I put an extra dead bolt into the floor, so you have to bend over to free it. That way nobody can just break the glass and let himself in."

They followed her back into the living room. She stopped at the couch where she had slept, and lifted the telephone so they could hear the dial tone. "I ordered phone service because everybody has a phone. Obviously you won't get much use out of it for now."

She led the way up the stairs. "I put all the clothes and things into this room." She opened the top drawer of the dresser. "I bought clip-on sunglasses to go over your glasses if you have to go out."

Bernie slipped them over his glasses and glanced in the mirror. "Not much of a disguise."

Jane said, "They're not looking for you. You're dead. If you get spotted, it will be because the wrong person happens to be here and gets a very good look at you close up. You can't completely avoid that possibility, but you can make it a bit less likely." She reached into the drawer again. "Hats. People here wear hats in the summer because the sun is fierce, and in the winter because it's cold."

She opened two more drawers. "Clothes. I got them in stores in Santa Fe, so you'll fade in a little better."

"You know what size I am?" asked Bernie.

"I searched your luggage in Niagara Falls," said Jane. She moved into the bathroom. "I see you found the toothbrushes and things."

Jane left the bathroom and went down the stairs. "Now for your money."

"What about it?" asked Bernie.

Jane walked back into the kitchen and opened a drawer.

"I've opened a joint checking account. The names are Peter James Moore and Renee Moore. You do have to keep the checking account supplied. You can deposit up to a thousand or so in cash now and then without anyone noticing. You can convert a few thousand in cash into traveler's checks, or money orders, and deposit those. Just don't transfer any money from any old accounts, or write yourself any checks. That will be one of the things they're looking for."

Rita looked at the checkbook. "There's already ten thousand in the account. How did you do that?"

"By check."

"Whose check?"

"None of your business. Just use checks when you need to, for mailing in bills and things. You can buy almost anything small with cash."

"I understand all of this stuff," said Bernie. "I knew it before you were born."

"Sorry," Jane said. "The last thing is the car. You get the one in the garage. I had already signed the pink slip, so I signed the other half and transferred it to myself—Renee Moore—so I could get New Mexico plates. You just sign the line below as Peter Moore."

"What happened to our deal?" asked Bernie. "When are we going to get started?"

"Soon."

"I just want to remind you, we've got a little time problem," said Bernie. "At a lousy six and a half percent, we'd be making two million a day. We're making more. It's like crabgrass. If you want to get rid of it, the sooner you get started, the less there is."

Jane felt the beginning of a headache. "I know that," she said patiently.

"We're safe, right? You did it already. This place is great. It's comfortable, but nothing about it says 'money.' The town is not too big, not too small. I don't think God knows where we are. Now what's the holdup?"

Jane sighed. Her eyes rested on Rita for a moment.

"No," said Rita.

"I'm afraid it's time," Jane said. She turned to Bernie. "Get used to the place. If you're up to it, begin writing down the information we'll need to retrieve the money. When I get back, we'll need all of it."

Jane picked up her purse and walked to the kitchen door. "Come on, Rita," she said.

Rita hesitated. She looked at Jane, then looked at Bernie, her eyes desperate and pleading. "I haven't been a problem, have I?"

"No," said Jane. "That isn't the—"

"And you shouldn't leave Bernie here alone," she interrupted. "People need company. What if he falls down and breaks his hip or something?"

"Then I'll crawl outside so the vultures can clean my carcass beyond recognition," Bernie snapped. "Look, kid. You're wasting our time."

Rita sighed. "I'll go get my stuff." She turned and walked heavily up the stairs.

Jane and Bernie sat in the kitchen, their eyes fixed on each other. "Well?" asked Jane. "What am I supposed to do?"

"I didn't say a word," said Bernie. "I can be sorry to see her go without letting her do something stupid, can't I?"

They heard Rita's footsteps on the stairs, and fell silent. When she came into the kitchen she was carrying her thin blue jacket with the bulging pockets. She went to Bernie, put her arms around him, released him, and stepped back. "I have to ask just one more—"

Bernie put his finger over her lips. "Don't bother, kid. Anybody who stays in this house with me is probably going to die. So what's the right thing to do? Get out of it."

In a moment, Rita was in the rental car sitting beside Jane, watching the clumps of dry, spiky desert plants slide past her window. Here and there a tree—or what passed for a tree in this part of the country—jutted upward in the distance. Jane drove her into the city, then south on the big highway toward the interstate.

"Why are you doing this?" asked Rita. "Why do you want to ditch me?"

Jane considered for a moment, trying to find the way that she could say it that would mean anything to this girl, a person who knew so little but had seen so much so young. "It's the only thing I know how to accomplish that makes any sense. A person like you—someone who hasn't done anything to deserve it—is in danger. I know how to take her to a place where nobody wants to hurt her."

"You're just dumping me," said Rita. "You want to get back to Bernie and his money."

Jane let the jab go past her, then diverted it a little. "That's not precisely what's happening," she said. "When you came to me you asked for something reasonable. You wanted to stay alive. It's something I thought I could give you, so I agreed. But you have to stick with what you asked for."

"Things have changed since then. Bernie being alive changed everything. You act like I'm a child. People my age have kids, fight wars."

"Sorry," said Jane. "I'm not much in favor of them doing either."

"I'm not afraid, you know."

"I noticed that, and it worries me. A little bit of the self-preservation instinct wouldn't be out of place in a girl your age."

"I can help. I can shop and do whatever else has to be done outside, so you and Bernie can be invisible. I can cook and clean and do chores, so you and Bernie don't have to. I'm really good at not being noticed."

"Good," said Jane. "Then you'll be even safer in San Diego, where nobody's even looking."

"San Diego?" asked Rita in distaste. "I don't know anything about San Diego."

"It's pleasant, and it's big. It's one of the fastest-growing cities in the country, so there are lots of newcomers, particularly young ones. It has no winter, which is something you've never experienced and would certainly hate, and it's on the ocean, which is what you're used to."

"Please," said Rita. "Don't do this to me again."

Jane watched her eyes fill with tears. "Again?"

Rita said, "It's what people always do to me. For as long as I can remember, my mother was always doing this. She would get me into the car by telling me we were going someplace nice. Then, when we got there, I'd find out it was just me that was going there. She would stop just long enough to go into some other room alone with the woman who lived there— some friend of hers—and talk her into keeping me for a day, and she would leave. Sometimes she would be gone longer than she'd expected, or at least longer than she'd told the woman, and I could tell. The woman would start to look at me funny, like it was me that lied to her. When I got older, my mother couldn't do that anymore. I would just get home from school and find that she was gone. Usually a couple of days later she would be back. On the good times, she would just be nervous and depressed and nasty. But about once a year, she'd bring home a new boyfriend. I would come home and see the front door open and the windows, and I'd be so happy. But then I'd come up the walk and I'd hear her voice inside, and I would know that she couldn't be talking to herself."

"That's . . . I'm sorry," said Jane. "But this isn't the same. That's over."

"No," said Rita. "It's not over. It's always like this. The world just goes on, and everybody's so busy, doing things together, and I'm always the one that's alone on the outside, wondering about it. I can't ever get in, and I can't do anything to get included. I used to look at the people my mother spent her time with—laughing at what they said—and I'd think, 'I'm funnier than that.' I'd watch her look at them and smile, and I'd think, 'But they're all ugly, and this one's mean, and that one stole from you. Why don't you want to be with me?' "

Jane said carefully, "I'm sure she did want to. Your mother had a drug problem, and that seems to be a full-time occupation. It doesn't leave much time or energy for things like raising children. But you've made it this far, and you've done some difficult things since then, and that proves to me that you survived it. There's no reason you can't have a terrific life from now on, if you'll just let it happen."

"It's not going to happen," said Rita. "There's something about me—something missing. I didn't tell you everything, because I wanted to make myself sound better than I was. When I went to Tampa, it wasn't some brave new start. I went because I knew a boy from school who was there. I didn't find myself a job. He asked them to hire me. I didn't even find my own place to live. He just took me in, because he had an old couch in his apartment."

"I take it he wasn't a boyfriend?"

Rita looked down at her lap. "I thought it meant something, like he wanted to be with me. I kind of worked myself up and got all nervous wondering when something was going to happen. But he never felt that way at all. It was just that he was a busboy, and the rent cost so much that he couldn't afford a car, so he needed a roommate to help pay. After a couple of months he had enough for a down payment on an old car, and he found a girlfriend. I came home from the hotel one day, and he had already moved her in. Her stuff was all over the place so you could barely walk, and she was in the bathroom, using my hair dryer."

"Did you get annoyed?" Jane realized that Rita wasn't interested in indirection. "Jealous?"

"I just felt lost. I didn't know what to do, or where to go. I didn't want to be alone. I didn't leave. It was awful. I knew they wanted me to go, but I didn't know how. It was like being a ghost. They were alive, but I wasn't. They would look at each other, talk to each other, but hardly ever to me. It wasn't even like they were being mean. It was like I wasn't even there. It started to affect me. Every day, I felt a little weaker, a little less real. They were always . . . touching each other, and I hated that the most, because they wouldn't do that in front of anyone."

"How did it end?"

"Danny offered me the job in the Keys."

Jane's mind was jerked back into practical matters. "Did you tell them where you were going?"

"Sort of, but not exactly," said Rita. Then she added, "I lied. What I did was, I bought some stuff from the grocery store while they were at work. It took most of the money I had left from my paycheck. I made this really nice dinner, with a cake. I bought a card—a blank one with a picture of a red Lamborghini on it, because I knew he liked cars. Inside I wrote this thank-you note, you know, for letting me stay here, and helping me get a job and everything? Then I left and met Danny at the parking garage near the hotel."

"Good," said Jane. "Then there are no extra people who know more than they should. What exactly did the note say?"

"I said in the note that I had met an older guy who was taking me to live with him in the Keys."

Jane said, "I think you can be forgiven."

"It was a lie."

"You may be confessing to the wrong priest," said Jane. "I've told a few myself."

"I said a little bit more."

"What was it?"

Rita said, "I left the note right by the cake where they'd both see it at the same time. He used to get off work at the hotel and then pick her up from her job, so they came in together. I knew he would read it first, because he always went straight to the refrigerator, but she would see him read it. The way I said it was that I was sorry to dump him, but I had met somebody else. I did it so that he would be stuck. He wouldn't want her to read that. He couldn't throw it in the garbage, because if he did, she would dig in and find it as soon as he turned his back. He couldn't hide it, because then she would think he was trying to save it. If he tore it up, she would know he didn't want her to read it, so she'd really be sure to dig out the pieces and put them together. See what I mean?"

Jane gazed at Rita with new interest. "I wonder what he decided. Do you suppose he ate it?"

Rita frowned at her, then abruptly giggled. "I don't know." Then she frowned again. "It was a mean thing to do. It was just pure meanness."

Jane smiled. "What made you do it?"

"I didn't start out to. I guess it was being in the store buying their dinner. I just kept thinking about how all they would ever buy was beer and pizza, or they'd eat out on the way home from work, and I would eat alone. I would buy regular food at the grocery store, and when I went to look for it in the refrigerator it was gone, or at least opened and partly eaten. Then I thought about how I was still paying half the rent even though there were two of them now. And they got the bed, while I was out on this couch with broken springs, and I couldn't even go to sleep sometimes because they worked in the evening and sat on it to watch television. And a lot of other times it would be worse, because they would be in the bed and I could hear them until it was just about time for me to get up, because I worked early in the morning."

Jane said, "Okay. You shouldn't have done it, even though they probably deserved it. But it doesn't matter anyway, because that was in another life. That wasn't you."

Rita gaped at Jane in disbelief. "Of course it was me."

Jane shook her head. "I'll say this another way. Rita Shelford's life is like a book, and you just read the last page and closed the back cover. It's over. You can't go back in and fix anything to make it a prettier story. Starting now, you're in the next life. In this one, you don't just have a new future, you have a new past, too. You're Diane Arthur, and you've always been Diane Arthur, so you have to make up what's happened to Diane Arthur until now, and it will be the only truth."

"Why can't Diane Arthur stay with you and Bernie?"

Jane winced. "Why would you want to?"

"I didn't tell you what it was like to work at his house. The house was big, so they had a nice maid's room. It had its own bathroom and a window that looked out on the part of the back yard by the fence where nobody but me ever went. The job wasn't hard. Bernie didn't go out and get muddy shoes and walk on the carpet. And we liked each other."

"What do you mean?"

"I would try to clean the places where he wasn't, and then stay in the kitchen cooking, or at least be out of the living area. But a few times a day we would run into each other. He would drink a cup of coffee, and then bring it in himself and put it in the sink. He'd see me and say, 'How's it going, kid?'

If I was doing something big, like waxing this huge floor in the living room, he'd say, 'It's too hot to do that today. Why don't you take a load off? Nobody sees how shiny that is but me.' "

Jane noticed that Rita had a good ear. The voice she gave Bernie was unmistakably his. "That's not exactly a close relationship."

"But it is," Rita insisted. "Don't you see? There were all these other men. There were the two who were always around, younger ones like Danny, but not nice. I don't know what to call them . . ."

"Bodyguards."

"I guess so. They never talked to me. It was like being a ghost again. And whenever they talked to each other, it was ugly: fuckin' this, and fuckin' that, like the word didn't mean anything at all, just a sound. And the others, the ones who came about once a month, they were worse. They always acted as though they didn't trust anybody, even to be alive. If I walked through a room while they were in it, they would whirl around and glare at me."

"They were probably bagmen. They had good reasons to be jumpy."

"They were the enemy. Bernie and I were on one side, and they were on the other. They didn't seem to like him any better than they liked me. It was almost as though we were prisoners in our own house."

"You were," said Jane. "You just didn't know it because you didn't try to leave."

"But we did know it, sort of. That was how we got to be friends."

"He said that too—called you his friend," said Jane. "It's kind of unusual to see two people so different who feel that way."

"He's a special person. He doesn't seem to look down on you just for being young. He can tell you things—all kinds of things—that you wouldn't find out unless you were as old as he is and remembered everything. I used to get him to play cards with me, just so he'd tell me stories. He's so good at games that it doesn't use up enough of his attention, so he talks and talks. And he remembers so much that it's just like a movie, only you can stop it whenever you want, and he'll show you another part that you're curious about, or go back and let you see everything about one of the people, only it's all true." She chuckled at the memory of it. "Pretty true, anyway. And I could tell him things, too, and never worry that he would embarrass me, or tell anyone else. I would get him to go out in the yard with me, like he was taking exercise, and he would listen as long as I wanted, and never give me his opinion unless I asked for it."

Rita sat in silence for a long time, thinking. "He doesn't want to act like it in front of you, but he's the best friend I ever had. Look at the risk he took to find me. How many people would do that?"

"In his profession? Not many," said Jane.

"Bernie doesn't have a profession," said Rita. "He has a good memory. That's what's so horrible about those people. They watch you to see what they can take away." She fell suddenly silent.

"Did they harm you?" asked Jane.

"You mean did they make me have sex with them, don't you?"

"I guess that's what I mean," said Jane.

"They didn't. Most of them acted like I wasn't human. One of them—one of the bodyguards—started talking to me, and I would see him staring at me sometimes. He would ask me questions, like whether I had a boyfriend, and stuff. I could tell he was thinking about it."

"What did you say?"

"I told him about living with the boy from home in Tampa, only I added some things."

"Like what?"

"That after I left I heard he had AIDS, so I was a little worried because I got tired so easily. After that he didn't talk to me much."

Jane said nothing, but she began to feel more optimistic.

Rita had an instinct for trouble and an ability to think quickly. Some runners had lived for a long time on less than that.

"I never told Bernie. I didn't want to worry him." She sighed. "I miss him."

"I understand."

"Then we can go back now?"

"No," said Jane.

10

Jane took the key out of her purse and unlocked the door of the apartment, then waited for Rita to push the door inward and enter. When Rita was inside, Jane walked to the refrigerator, opened a can of cola and handed it to her, then sat down to wait.

It was like moving a cat from one house to another. The trick was to put butter on the cat's forepaws. While the cat licked it off, her keen senses would be working, assuring her with every second that the new place was not worse than the old, and was certainly superior to being in a moving car. By the time the butter was gone, she would have given the place her tentative approval.

Jane watched Rita sipping her cola as she walked the living room, examined the kitchen, then climbed the stairs to explore the bedroom. She heard her push aside the blinds in the upper window, and after a few seconds heard the blinds clack against the sill as she released them.

Rita came halfway down the stairs and sat, still sipping. "What am I supposed to say? You already rented it."

"It's not a lifetime lease," Jane announced. "Unless you make a mistake. I was here a couple of years ago, and I remembered it as the sort of place for you. The manager told me there are young women in the other apartments in the building right now, most of them older than you, but not by much. You won't stand out. There are no obvious attractions in the vicinity for people who might be aware that you're worth money, or how to cash in: no prostitutes, no street drug sales, no bar scene. The draw is the view of the ocean, which you know, since I heard you move the blinds to look at it."

"But who am I supposed to be?"

Jane said, "You're Diane Arthur. You're a young woman who just moved in. You're looking for a job, but at least for the present, you're picky, so you won't do much except circle ads in the paper. If you talk to your neighbors, don't exaggerate. You graduated from high school, but you haven't decided what to do with yourself yet. You're eighteen, not twenty-five. You're not an heiress traveling incognito, or an Australian tennis champion recovering from a failed love affair."

"So I'm supposed to stay dull."

"Not dull, just not unusual enough to get in trouble. You want to be the sort of newcomer who doesn't make a great topic of conversation. When people mention you, you're cute, pleasant, funny. You don't cause any phones to ring. You stay hidden without appearing to be hiding."

"But what do I do? How do I spend my time?"

"In my experience, if you don't get found within the first month, your chances go way up. So for the first month, you do very little. You arrange your furniture, look at magazines, watch the local news on TV. You read the newspapers to get to know San Diego. If there's a stabbing every third night in some neighborhood, then you'll know enough to stay away from it. Start to form a picture of the city in your mind."

"And after a month?"

"Then you start going out, but cautiously. You can go to the university, where you won't stand out, but anyone likely to be looking for you will. You can go to the beach, if you stay close to groups of women your age. You can go to a movie, if it's an early showing in the right part of town." Jane glanced at her watch. "I've got to go out and do some errands."

Rita stood and started up the stairs. "I'll be ready in a minute."

"I said I was going out, not we. I'll be back around dark."

When Jane returned, Rita wasn't visible, but Jane could hear music coming from the bedroom upstairs. Jane was putting away groceries when Rita appeared. "Hi," she said.

Jane glanced at her and returned to her work. "Hi."

"I hate this place."

"Oh? Why?"

"Because it's not mine. I didn't do it."

Jane looked at the can in her hand, set it on the counter, and leaned against the wall with her arms crossed. "It's always like this."

"It is?"

"It's not much fun to be a runner. First you have to give up whoever you were—your job, your friends, even your name. Then you have to hand over your freedom. You have to let a total stranger tell you what to do, how to act, where to live. Some of the people I've taken out over the years have felt worse about it than you do. They were quite a bit older, and were used to ordering other people around—making decisions for them. All I can tell you is what I told them."

"What did you tell them?"

"It's temporary. I'm temporary. I'm pretty good at one small, narrow function. I put big blank spaces between the place where you were last recognized and the place where you end up. I stay long enough to be sure it's the right place, and to help you fit in quietly. Then, one morning, you'll wake up and I'll be packed and ready to leave. After that, you'll be the one making all of the decisions. And you have a lot of advantages most of my other runners didn't have."

"Like what?"

"You're young. You're not a company president who's going to start cleaning hotel rooms. You're a hotel maid who might end up as a company president. That's a distinction that's bigger than you can imagine. And time will help."

"What good is it?"

"You're an eighteen-year-old who's a late maturer. In a year, you'll look very different. In five, you could be a different person. You're just at the age when society starts paying attention to you—caring about your identity. You won't start out with a long history—credit, work, education, and so on—but neither does any other eighteen-year-old girl. Your history will be as solid as most of theirs, even to an expert. In three years, nobody in the world will be able to pick it apart, because it won't be fake. All of the things I made up will be backed up by a real record: real years of driving with that license and using those credit cards and paying the bills with that bank account."

"You've thought of everything, haven't you?"

"No," said Jane. "I've thought of everything that has come up before, and everything that I know is likely to come up this time. That's what I do. You can never think of everything. But you have a lot of advantages. The whole structure of society ensures that forty-year-old criminals don't have much access to eighteen-year-old girls. You're the perfect runner."

"I don't want to be the perfect runner. I don't want to be a runner at all."

"What do you want to be—dead?"

"No," said Rita. She began to pace, agitated and angry. "I told you what I want. I want to be somebody who does things, not somebody who goes where people tell her, just to keep breathing. This is my chance to do something that matters, and I'm hiding."

"What would you do?"

"Fight them."

Jane stared at the floor and shook her head sadly. "I admire you. Really, I do. What you're thinking isn't wrong. It's just not a strategy that can work this time. You can't fight these people just by saying you're not afraid and standing your ground. They would happily scoop you up and torture you to death while they asked you questions about Bernie that you can't answer. If you were to fight them, here's how you would go about it. We would drive to the local FBI office. There's sure to be one in San Diego. You would tell them you want to testify against the people you met at Bernie's. Let's pretend you're there now."

"All right."

"I'm the FBI agent. Tell me their names."

"I don't know."

"Tell me the crimes you saw them commit."

"Money laundering. Hiding money from the government, and not paying taxes on it." Rita seemed proud of herself.

"What money? Did you see any money?"

"Well, no. But I saw them. And I know that's what they were doing at Bernie's."

"So does the FBI, probably, but they didn't catch them at it, and neither did you. Thank you very much for your help, Miss Shelford. Don't call us, we'll call you."

"You're saying they won't believe me?"

"Do you remember the day I met you? I asked you a lot of questions that probably didn't make much sense to you at the time. As soon as I heard the name Delfina, I was hoping that you had seen something or found some evidence. But you never saw him, and didn't even know who he was. You're not lying, but you're not a witness to anything."

"I was there when they broke in and searched Bernie's house."

"Eight or nine nameless men you'd never seen before were in the house, probably with a key. That's not even good evidence of breaking and entering, even if they didn't all have alibis, which they certainly will, if anybody ever asks."

"They tried to keep me from leaving."

"Not hard enough to make it a crime."

"They said they were taking me to Mr. Delfina."

"Which proves nothing, because they didn't do it." Jane sighed. "Enough. The only way to fight them is to let the cops do it for you. If you haven't got any evidence, you run."

"But you're not running."

"I plan to. I'm just delaying it long enough to take away some of their motivation for chasing us. The second the money is gone, I'll be running as hard as anyone."

Rita stared at her for a few seconds, then turned, went upstairs, and quietly closed the door.

After midnight, Jane went to the door and heard soft, even

breathing. She quietly opened the door and walked to the side of Rita's bed. On the sheet around Rita, arranged against her sides from her armpits to her thighs, were a clutter of objects.

There was a small coin purse that had been thickened by a few folded bills. There was a dog-eared, smudged envelope with a flap that had come open to reveal part of an official paper with scrollwork around it like birth certificates and diplomas had. The cheap blue windbreaker Rita had retrieved from the hotel in Niagara Falls was folded neatly and placed with the other things, and there was a photograph in a plastic frame. Jane knelt by the bed to look at it.

It was a picture of Rita at the age of about twelve, sitting on a white beach bordered by palm trees, and above her, a blond woman who must be her mother. The mother had been in the process of walking away, then had half-turned to look when the photographer had called to her. She seemed no more than thirty, but her eyes were squinted into the sun to reveal the beginning of a collection of crow's-feet beside the blue eyes. At first Jane thought there was a smudge on the picture, but then she saw it was part of a tattoo of a rose. The petals began just above the waistband of the bikini and extended downward, so the process of getting it must have been less an embellishment than a relationship.

Jane slowly retreated without waking Rita and closed the door. As she walked toward the stairway, she told herself that this was just because of Rita's recent troubles, but she could tell that was not true. She knew that the girl must have slept like this always, placing her few, pitiful treasures around her body so they could not be taken from her in the night.

11

Jane brought the clothes into Rita's room and began laying each hanger on the bed without speaking. She held Rita's face in the corner of her eye. At first Rita appeared unaware, then indifferent, then intrigued. Jane laid the fourth outfit across the bed and went into the hallway to get the fifth, then returned to find Rita slowly running her hand along the crease of a new pair of pants.

Rita quickly withdrew her hand, then conceded, "I always wished that I was the kind of person who had clothes like this."

"It doesn't take anything important," said Jane. "Courage, intelligence, even taste. If you don't know what to buy, go to the best store in town, then pick out a clerk who looks terrific. She'll tell you. All you need is enough money to feed the cash register."

"Am I supposed to be rich?"

Jane said, "Not rich. Just a single working woman who's too young to care about saving, and has nothing to spend it on but herself, like the rest of the girls in this complex."

Rita's eyes stayed on the clothes, but they had a soft focus. "At the hotel, I would sometimes look."

"Look at what?"

"I would be cleaning a room, and it would be late enough so the people weren't just downstairs having breakfast, so I figured they'd be gone at least until lunch. I would open a suitcase and look at everything inside. Not to take anything, just to look."

"Did you see anything interesting?"

"Rich people are old-fashioned. They don't want to own anything that's plastic, unless it's the kind that looks like ivory. Or maybe it was ivory. I probably wouldn't know. Everything is leather, wool, silk, silver, wood. I would look at it, especially the clothes, and wonder about the women who owned it. When people travel, they always have a lot of new clothes. I would find something, and half the time the tags would still be on it." She looked up at Jane in wonder. "I remember one time it was just a pair of jeans, and I saw the price and swallowed my gum. They cost more than I took home in a week. Just jeans." She frowned, and her shoulders crept up as though she were preparing to endure a blow. "I got caught once."

"Somebody came back while you were in her suitcase?"

"Not that. It was my boss, the housekeeping supervisor. She was real cold and nasty at first. But I asked her to search my pockets, my cart, everything so she would know I didn't take anything. So she did. Then she kind of took my arm and gave me a little smile. She said she used to do the same thing. But she made me promise never to do it again. She said that after you looked in a hundred, they were all pretty much the same stuff as the first one, and if you got caught you'd get fired and go to jail."

"Did that cure you of it?"

"Not completely, but I forced myself just to look at the clothes while the women were wearing them. I still liked clothes, but I never thought I would ever have anything like these." She petted a sweater as though it were alive.

Jane said, "I did buy clothes that were more expensive than average. That was because I'm trying to make a change. Anyone looking for an eighteen-year-old runaway maid will expect her to have less money—to sleep in bus stations and carry her things in a backpack. So we take a step in the other direction. We give you an apartment that costs more than you used to make, and dress you better. Nothing here will draw attention to you, it just puts you into a cubbyhole where they're not looking." She walked toward the door. "I know it's kind of a pain, but try them on for me, will you? Let me know if I need to exchange anything."

Jane went downstairs to the kitchen and made a simple dinner of salad and capellini marinara while she waited.

When she was sure that the smells had risen and penetrated the second floor, she heard Rita coming down the stairs. Rita stopped in the doorway and watched Jane for a few seconds, then set the table. She said, "I don't know how to thank you for the clothes. They're the best clothes anybody I know has."

"Do they fit?"

Rita shrugged. "Close enough. They're all a little on the loose side, but I can take them in a little."

Jane stopped stirring and poured the pasta into a strainer in the sink, then put down the pot. "Do the waistbands fit, and the pant legs fall to the right place?"

"Yeah," said Rita.

"Then they're probably the way they're designed to be."

"It's not exactly my style."

"I hope not, or I've wasted a lot of time and effort," said Jane. "I'm trying to make changes. Examine anything that's a habit, anything you could say that about—that it's your style—and lose it if you can."

"That's how you hide? Do everything the opposite of what you like?"

Jane assembled the plates of food and carried them to the table. "Identity is a slippery concept. We think that any time anyone sees our faces, they know us. They'll be able to pick us out of a crowd forever. Sometimes that's true, but other times it's not. The person who sees you forms a picture of you in his memory. In a way, it's more than a picture. It's like a movie. It includes our bodies, our posture, the way we walk, our faces showing the whole sequence of expressions we had when they saw us, our voices, and whatever else came to their attention. What we have to do is manipulate it, and a lot can be accomplished without doing much."

"Doing much?" Rita was suspicious.

"Here's a simple example. Private detectives spend a lot of time following people. They don't want to be noticed. One of the tricks they use is to carry a few hats in their cars on the passenger seat. After they've followed somebody for a time, they put a hat on. A little later, they'll take it off, and maybe put another one on."

"That works? You're telling me people are that stupid?"

"Not if they're paying attention. But most of the time, they're not. They might happen to look behind them and see the man. No big deal. He's just one of many elements—people, objects, cars, birds, buildings. There's no reason to consciously single him out for attention or thought unless he's too close. The next time they happen to look is the one that counts. If they see him a second time, then he's the only element that hasn't been replaced. He's following them. But if they happen to look and see that this time there's a man with a hat on, he's not the same man. What the detective is trying to do is keep them from bringing the whole issue up to the level of conscious thought. That's all I'm trying to do for you. If we change some of the things about you that stand out, then any person who doesn't have an extremely clear idea of who he's looking for might not notice you. Probably what each searcher will have is a photograph. He'll look at lots of girls, trying to find the one who matches it. It's likely he won't even notice that you do, because you don't match it *exactly*."

"It doesn't sound like it can work," said Rita.

"It's not a sure thing," said Jane. "But there are easy ways to make yourself safer, and there are hard ways. This is one of the easy ways." Jane prepared herself, then said, "I bought some hair dye."

Rita's hand went involuntarily to her shoulder, and began fiddling with one of the long strands. Her eyes lowered to see it. "My hair?" she asked doubtfully.

"It's the easiest part of you to notice from a distance. It's something people can see even better when you're looking away from them. They're looking for blond hair, so we'd make it brown. I've picked out a chestnut color that would go well with your light skin. It would take some getting used to, but in the end I think you'd like it." She paused. "We could do it tonight, before people around here get a look at you."

Rita looked down at her plate and returned to her dinner.

Jane waited for a few minutes, then said, "You can take a day or two to think about it if you want."

"No," she said. "I'll do it. I'm just waiting to hear what else is wrong with me."

"Nothing. We're not correcting things, just changing them. You're thin, and you wear your clothes tight. So I bought styles that are worn loose. They have vertical lines: sweaters and blouses that hang shoulder to hip, and pants that hang hip to ankle. There's no disguising the fact that you're thin, but we change your silhouette. They also make you look older and more sophisticated." Jane hated herself for using those arguments, even though they were true.

"I like them. Don't get me wrong. I like them a lot. I just don't usually dress that way. They're all one look, like they were made for a particular person I don't know."

"You have special requirements right now. There are lots of pants. I bought the right pair of shoes for each outfit. 'Right' doesn't just mean they don't clash. It means there are no high heels, no stacked heels, not even any slip-ons. If something goes wrong, your only chance will be to run."

Rita kept eating methodically. She seemed to be listening, but she was not ready to divulge what she was thinking.

Jane finished her dinner, got up, and went around the corner of the counter to bring back two more big shopping bags. She caught Rita staring. "Accessories," she explained. She lifted an eyeglass case and opened it. "These are photo-sensitive lenses with no prescription. When you're in the sun they're as dark as most sunglasses, but when you're inside, they're nearly clear."

"Sunglasses?" Rita put them on and studied Jane's face for a reaction.

"Perfect. You look good in glasses, and they change the shape of your face a bit. Wear them when you're out." She picked out a small silver box and opened it.

Rita's eyes widened, and she kept her eyes on Jane as though she didn't dare look. "Jewelry?"

"People wear it, so if you never do, you're different. You don't want to be different."

Rita stared at the necklace and earrings on their cotton bed. "They're so beautiful."

"Glad you approve," said Jane. She lifted the necklace out, put it around Rita's neck, and clasped it. "You'll notice the chain is very thin. That's because if a man is trying to grab you, sometimes he'll get his fingers around a necklace and pull. This one will break, and you'll be gone."

"But the stone . . . it looks real."

"That's another part of the image. You're a woman like the ones in the hotel. You don't want anything that's not real. But this is a peridot, and they're cheap. This one's the size of your thumbnail and it cost a couple of hundred dollars. It adds to your cover. Your papers say you were born in August, and it's your birthstone."

Rita carefully lifted the earrings to her ears.

"Those too," said Jane. "If somebody spots you, don't forget to take them off."

Rita stared at Jane sullenly. "You try to make everything sound practical and cold, like some kind of trick. But you're giving me presents. Why are you pretending?"

Jane avoided her eyes. "I didn't say you couldn't enjoy them, I'm just teaching you things." She pulled out the next jeweler's box and opened it with a click. "Here's something else. Most people wear watches."

Rita took the watch off its holder. "What a great watch!" She put it on and held out her arm to gaze at it, then looked at Jane. "It's all so . . . pretty, so much better than anything I've ever had before."

"I'm glad. But if you lose any of it, or have to duck out without stopping for it, don't give any of it a second thought. Never compromise your safety for things." She added, "If it bothers you, let me know afterward and I'll replace them."

Rita looked confused. Her eyes were glistening. "Why would you do all of this for me?"

"I admit that I might have overdone things a little this time, because we could both use a bit of pleasure right now. But the idea is always the same. A shopping trip takes a day, and it doesn't involve risking my life or yours."

"But why are you doing any of it—anything at all?"

"Because it works. And I do like you. There's no reason to lie about that. But I also have calculated, practical reasons for everything I do. If you look different, you're harder to spot. If you're happy, you won't do anything foolish to make yourself happy. But if you're found, then I'm in danger too."

Rita's face looked suddenly brittle. "I would never tell them anything."

Jane said only, "Thanks." There was no reason to go into all of the reasons why feeling that way wasn't sufficient. She reached into the other shopping bag. "I got you a new purse."

It was a large black leather shoulder bag with a thick strap. Rita took it into her hands and felt the soft, smooth leather, then reached inside and took out the tissue paper that the manufacturer had stuffed inside to make it hold its shape.

Jane could read her mind as she ran her hands along the inner surfaces and measured each of the big compartments. She was checking to verify that it would hold the small collection of treasures that she arranged around her body at night.

Suddenly Rita stood up, threw her arms around Jane, and hugged her. Rita's head rested on Jane's shoulder, and she swayed almost imperceptibly from side to side, as though she were rocking in her mother's arms.

The next day, Jane brought home the car. She parked it close to the apartment, went inside, and led Rita to the window. "That's yours," she said.

"Mine?"

"You can't live here without a car. It's a Honda Accord, because it has the right look and price for your new personality. They sell over three hundred thousand of them a year, and I doubt if the owners can tell one year from another. The temporary registration is in the glove compartment, and the final one will come in the mail." She handed Rita the keys.

"Can I try it?"

"You'll have to," said Jane. "I left my rented one near the dealer's lot, so I need a ride back. After that, park it in your space in the lot."

Jane studied Rita's driving habits with the critical eye of a licensing examiner. She was relieved. Rita was competent, and she was cautious enough to keep Jane from having nightmares, but she wasn't timid. Jane followed Rita home, and detected no uncertainty in Rita's ability to remember the route.

When they were home, Jane said, "Leave the car there for now. You'll have to drive it a little about once a week to charge the battery and keep oil on the moving parts. Keep the tank full."

She sat at the kitchen table, took a road map out of her purse, and unfolded it. "When you drive the car, there's something else you can do. I've marked a couple of routes. Study them."

Rita leaned over her and looked. "They're pretty complicated."

"When you've memorized them, take the car out and drive them over and over. Practice until you could do it fast at midnight with your headlights off. Then destroy the map."

"They don't seem to go anywhere."

"They go out of town. They take you out in ways that most people wouldn't expect you to know, and a person from out of town would have a hard time following. There are lots of twists and turns and, in each one, a place where you backtrack."

"Why?"

"Most people who are running drive straight to the nearest freeway entrance ramp and push the pedal to the floor. That's a bad idea. These routes take you past a few entrances for freeways going in different directions, then send you off instead on roads that aren't as well known, but where you can go nearly as fast. At rush hours, the freeways jam up, but these roads don't, so they're actually faster."

"I guess I meant why am I doing this now? Did you see somebody following us?"

"No. You take all the precautions at the beginning, so if

you see anything suspicious, you don't have to waste time making plans. You see it, and you go."

"Out of town. What then?"

Jane said, "Find me again, and I'll help you start over."

"I get a lifetime guarantee?"

"My lifetime," said Jane. "That's not so good. I've been doing this a long time. Every time I do it again—probably every time I leave my house—the odds against my coming back get worse. You don't have to remember all my tricks if you just remember the attitude. Be premeditated. Always know what your response will be if something happens. The plan doesn't have to be perfect if you move instantly, without hesitation."

Jane got up several times each night, stood at the upper window, and stared out across the lot and along the nearby streets to satisfy herself that there was nothing worrisome that went on after dark. A few times she went out and walked the neighborhood to search for signs she had missed. The only unusual activity she detected was other tenants of the building coming home late from parties or dates.

During the days she worked at the details of Rita's life. She bought car insurance as Diane Arthur's mother, then opened a checking account and a savings account for her, subscribed to magazines so she would receive mail, activated the telephone. One morning, Rita awoke to find Jane sitting at the kitchen table with her car keys beside her coffee cup.

"Are you going out again?" asked Rita.

"It's time."

"Oh," said Rita. She kept looking at her hands as though she had just noticed them and didn't know what to do with them. "It's not that I don't want you to go. I want to go too."

Jane shook her head. "We've been through this."

"I know," said Rita.

Jane stood and hugged Rita. "The best thing for you to do is stay here and build a life for yourself. You have all the pieces. Put them together."

"I want to do something."

"Someday, when someone else needs it, help them."

Rita nodded. Jane walked to the door, took a look back, and said, "Good luck." Then she stepped out, locked the door behind herself, and walked to her car. She drove around the neighborhood one more time, looking for a sign that her leaving had interested someone. If nothing else she did worked out, this part had to. When she was sure that she had missed nothing, she drove toward the airport.

12

Jane drove to the San Diego airport, bought a ticket for Miami with a plane change at Dallas–Fort Worth, and sat down to wait. Airports were the worst places for her. There were security people watching for lunatics and terrorists, as well as federal, state, and local police watching for a long list of fugitives and a shorter list of men and women who had done so many things that it was worth official time and money just to know where they were at any given moment. There were customs and DEA officers watching for contraband, and immigration cops watching for people with false identification.

She was confident about the identification she had picked up from her safe-deposit box in Chicago because it was real. Once, six years ago, she had helped a little girl disappear from Ohio. There were three people who had known she had done it—the girl, Jane, and a social worker from Children's Services.

The woman had been frantic with worry, so Jane had needed to explain to her all of the steps in advance: the way she would slip the girl out of town, how she would get her across the country, even where the girl's new birth certificate had come from. She had told her about the man in Franklin County, Pennsylvania, who had invented people and registered their births.

Later, when it was over, Jane had come back to tell her the little girl was safe. The social worker had begged Jane to accept money. Jane had said, "Send me a present," then forgotten what she had said until a few months later, when the present had arrived. It had been the birth certificate of a woman named Donna Parker. The social worker had a friend in the county clerk's office. About once a year for the five years since, the woman would send other presents. Sometimes the certificates were for girls, sometimes for boys, sometimes for men or women. But Jane had already begun to cultivate Donna Parker. She had applied for a driver's license and Social Security card under that name, obtained credit cards, and then a passport.

Jane kept her head down, pretending to read a magazine until her flight to Dallas–Fort Worth was announced. She boarded with the crowd, then closed her eyes and tried to relax through the flight. The wait for the second flight was shorter, and she felt a temporary relief, but as soon as the plane landed in Miami, the feeling that she was being watched grew more oppressive. Jane had long been aware that no airport was a good place for her.

Jane checked the television screens above the concourse to find out which gate her next flight would be departing from, then walked to it. She still had a half hour before her flight was ready for boarding, and she had a feeling that the waiting area here was too exposed. It was midway along the concourse, and the seats all faced the open floor, where she could be seen by hundreds of people walking back and forth. She kept going until she reached the gate at the end of the concourse, where the traffic was much thinner, found a seat, and stared out over the darkened runways.

The woman's voice on the loudspeaker announced Jane's flight to Tortola in the British Virgin Islands. She stood up and walked toward her gate. She did not feel foolish for having walked a few hundred extra feet. It had used up some of the time, and had cost her nothing.

She was nearly to her gate when she saw the man. He was sitting in one of the seats that faced the open walkway, holding a newspaper in his lap and watching the passengers disappear into the boarding tunnel across the concourse. He didn't show any sign of getting up to join them, and he made no move to see anyone off. He looked at each of them in turn, then returned to his newspaper.

Jane turned to the right and walked up to a little cluster of pay telephones placed in a hexagon. She took a phone off the hook and kept her eyes on the man. She was sure she recognized him. He was one of the men who had been hunting Nancy Carmody a few years ago. There had been a moment, after Jane had gotten Nancy into a car, when the three men had been running to keep them from driving off. Jane had stood still for five or six seconds with the car door open, looking at their faces as they ran toward her. She had done it because Nancy Carmody's life might be in jeopardy if she was unable to recognize the faces the next time she saw them.

The next time had not come until now. This man was definitely one of the three. He had worked for Frank Delfina, so tonight, he was probably in the airport watching for Rita. But that was not a problem, because Rita was safe in San Diego. The problem was that if Jane had seen this man's face so clearly that day, how could he not have seen hers? He was sitting in a seat between Jane and her departure gate. She studied the area behind him, to see if there was any way she could slip past, but there was not. There was a wall that screened the side of his waiting area, and trying to get around it would bring her within ten feet of him.

She heard the announcement repeated. "Passengers on TWA Flight 6645 to Tortola, please report to the boarding area." Maybe she could slip past him if she could insert herself into the middle of a crowd. She looked behind her to see if there were any large groups of passengers coming in her direction. There were not. She had prevented that by going to the most sparsely populated corner of the airport. She looked back toward the man.

He watched the last of the passengers disappear into the tunnel to board the flight across the concourse, looked down at his newspaper, and sighed. He stood up, stepped to the nearest trash can, and stuffed the newspaper inside. Then he looked up the concourse and began to walk.

Jane hung up her telephone and stepped slowly, warily after him. She watched him walk into the wide entrance of a store that sold magazines, books, and newspapers. As he turned to face the big magazine rack along the wall, she hurried past him to her gate. There were only a few passengers ahead of her at the doorway. She kept her eyes straight ahead while she waited, and when her turn came she handed the airline man her ticket and walked quickly into the tunnel with the others.

It was only after she was in her seat and the hatch had closed that she was finally able to breathe normally. She pushed the man to the back of her mind and tried to think about what she was going to say.

It was after midnight when Jane walked beside the long seven-foot wrought-iron fence and stopped at the high ornamental gate. She pressed the intercom button on the left gatepost and waited. She had expected to have to ring many times, but a woman's voice said, "I'm sorry, but we don't receive visitors at this time of the evening."

Jane said, "Please tell George that my name is Jane, and I need to speak to him now."

"Mr. Hawkes has retired." The voice had an edge to it now that was more than annoyance. There was a tightness in the throat that sounded a bit like jealousy. Servants might get irritated, they might be self-important and officious, but they didn't get jealous.

"I'm sorry to come to your house so late," said Jane. That was a good start—"your" house. "But my business really is urgent." She hoped that the use of the word "business" might help dispel the tension.

This time it was his voice. "Jane?"

"Yes, George?"

The intercom cut off, there was a beeping sound, and the gate swung inward. Jane started walking up the long, curving cobblestone driveway. She could see the tile roof of the huge three-story white villa beyond a distant stand of trees. A bright light went on at a spot that she judged must be the front entrance.

Jane followed the driveway across the middle of a flat lawn the size of a golf course fairway, then between tall, umbrella-shaped trees with flowers blooming among the leaves that she could smell but not quite make out, through a zone of short, bushy citrus trees, and then into the open again. When she could see the lighted entrance, she smiled. There were a couple of twisty baroque pillars that looked as though they had been stolen from Saint Peter's in Rome, and between them, a pair of doors that were a full two stories high. One of them had a man-size door cut into the bottom of it, and that was what was open.

George stepped out wearing white shorts, a pair of sandals, and a striped T-shirt. His merely human size and the childlike clothes he wore made him look ridiculous next to the imposing building he lived in. The little figure began to walk toward her quickly, the sandals slapping on the cobblestones. Jane thought of Richard Dahlman's comment on the place. "It was the sort of villa you would expect to find on the Mediterranean, but wouldn't." Dahlman had been summoned here in the middle of the night, led here by a waitress from his hotel because Dahlman was a surgeon and George was in pain. He had taken out George's appendix at the local hospital. Since Dahlman wouldn't accept money, George had insisted on giving him the name and address of a woman who could make him disappear if he should ever have the need.

George saw Jane emerge from the little forest and began to trot awkwardly toward her. Finally, he stepped out of his sandals and went the rest of the way barefoot. He stopped abruptly in front of her. "Jane!" he said. "I can't believe it!" He hugged her, then held her at arm's length to look at her in the dim light from his doorway. "Come inside. Is anybody chasing you, or did you get out clean?"

"Nobody's chasing me," said Jane. She was already looking over his shoulder for the woman whose voice she had heard. She saw the face in an upper window—a brown, perfect oval, with large black eyes. It turned and disappeared from the window. Jane moved her eyes to the next window and caught a glimpse of a tall, thin shape clothed in a gauzy white nightgown as it passed by. "As far as I know, I'm not being chased, followed, hunted, or watched . . . until now."

George feigned disappointment. "Oh, I was hoping to return the favor you did me."

Jane said, "You've been well—other than the appendix?"

"You know about that?" He frowned. "Then the doctor did get himself in trouble. I knew it. American doctors and lawyers are down here all the time hiding money from the IRS. I told him that someday he might have a problem. He wouldn't believe me."

"He's all right now."

George Hawkes looked at Jane affectionately. "I feel wonderful, since you asked. I feel like I'm in the story about the lion and the mouse. The lion spares the mouse, and later the mouse gnaws the net so the lion can go free." He bared his teeth and gnawed feverishly. "Ngyah-ngyah-ngyah."

Jane looked at him through half-lidded eyes.

He said, "You've been here for thirty seconds, and already you've made my night."

"I think there was somebody else upstairs who wanted that job," said Jane. "Who is she?"

"Clara?" His smile returned. "She's my wife. Local girl."

"She's very pretty."

"Spectacular," said George. "You should see the kids that woman produces . . . of course, you will, when they wake up."

"George," said Jane. "I'm afraid I won't be here that long. I came this way because I needed to talk to you with no chance of being overheard or having a call traced."

He turned to contemplate Jane's face in the light. "I

thought you weren't in trouble." He began to pull her toward the house, but she resisted.

"I'm not yet. This is business, and I need to keep it secret. I'd like to be on a plane for home before daylight." She stared at him. "I'm sure that if you've lived up to the agreement we made, your wife hasn't heard this kind of conversation before."

When she had met him, George Hawkes had not been his name. He had been a travel agent for money, who specialized in sending it on complicated world tours. He had just managed to leave his building in Los Angeles as the police were coming in the front door, and he had done it masterfully: he had brought with him a suitcase full of his clients' cash and some enormous checks made out to their Los Angeles company. George's clients had misinterpreted his escape as an attempt to rob them, and he had come to Jane. She had negotiated a treaty. Under its terms, the clients' capital would complete its round trip, with George's regular percentage deducted. George would go out of business, so they wouldn't worry about his being caught and trading them for a light sentence. They, in return, would never do him harm, search for him, or mention his existence to a third party.

George said, "She doesn't know where the money came from. She thinks I was the heir to the Wright brothers' fortune."

"There's a Wright brothers' fortune?"

"How could there not be?"

"I don't know," said Jane. "I can do this quickly. I just need a name."

"A name of what?"

"I need a person who can make some unusual financial transactions for a friend of mine."

George squinted. "Unusual means illegal. I understand that. But I think I need to narrow it down a bit."

Jane shrugged. "It has to be somebody who knows his way around, but can also get lawyers and bankers and brokers to cooperate in some moves that might make them curi-

ous. In other words, it has to be somebody I can trust absolutely, but nobody else can trust, even a little."

"What are you paying?"

Jane shrugged again. "I don't know what the going rate
is. He would have to devote himself to this for a few weeks,
and at the end of it, he never heard of me or my partner."

"How much money are you moving?"

"About ten billion dollars."

George stared at her in silence for a moment. "Ten billion. You have it already?"

She said, "We know where it is. Nobody else does."

She watched George's eyes narrow. They burned into her
for a few seconds, then turned up toward the window of his
house where Jane had seen his wife. He shook his head, and
it grew into a shiver. "It's better if you don't tell me where it
came from. I can't afford to know that kind of thing anymore." He sighed, as though he were saying good-bye to
something. "It doesn't matter anyway. The answer would be
the same. Henry Ziegler, CPA."

"Henry Ziegler," she repeated. "I take it he's somebody
you dealt with in the old days?"

He shook his head. "I was never big enough to be worth
his time and trouble, but he was a friend, so he helped me
out a few times." He amended it. "More than a few times."

Jane couldn't help looking away from George's face at his
house. It was bigger than the high school she had gone to in
Deganawida, New York. The walk she had taken from his
front gate had been longer than the distance from the end of
the track to the girls' locker room. "That gives me a new
worry. There will be some men who start getting very dangerous the second that the money starts appearing. If he's
that big, they might know him."

"That's the way it is when you handle money, love," said
George. "The more there is, the more people there are who
have an interest in it. But Henry Ziegler is discreet. Even if
he passes on the deal, he'll never mention it."

"What is he, anyway?"

"The reason you never heard of him is the same reason he

never heard of you: he's no more interested in getting famous than you are. He's an accountant. When I met him
twenty-five years ago, he was going to law school at night
and handling small accounts in the daytime. He wasn't doing it so he could go argue cases, it was so he couldn't be
called on to testify against any of his clients. So he's a
lawyer, too."

"Who are his clients?"

"He once told me there are about a hundred. I was one of
his first, and he doesn't forget the people who knew him
when times weren't so good. I've known him all this time,
but I can't name any of the others. I just know who they
are."

"Who?"

George looked up through the clear black sky at the stars.
"How do I describe them? Picture this: the *Mayflower* arrives and eighty people step on Plymouth Rock, jump down
and kiss the ground—the land of religious freedom! This
gives the next guy off the ship a chance to pick their pockets
while they're bent over. He uses the money to buy rum and
guns to sell to the Indians. He uses the profits from that to
buy a ship so he can get into the slave trade. Four hundred
years later, the descendants of this guy are still around. Have
they changed? They dress better and have bigger houses.
They've got a few more last names, because the daughters
married too—mostly to people just like them. These are the
people who got in at the head of the line. If you wanted to
build a railroad, have a war, or buy up land and put suburbs
on it, they had the capital. Henry's clients aren't the current
crop of computer geeks from California or discount-chain
rubes from the South, people who love to read their names
in the papers. Henry's clients don't like to be visible, except
when it suits them. That's what Henry does these days."

"You mean he handles their money?"

"Not just their money, but everything that can be done
with money. And he keeps it quiet. Say some foolish citizen
sues the family. Does Henry grease this citizen's palm? No.
He knows the senior partner of the law firm representing

this citizen. This lawyer is the fund-raising chairman for the symphony orchestra. He quietly gives the committee a big donation. The law firm advises the client to settle cheap. If the case gets to court, the citizen's lawyer certainly doesn't say everything about the other side that he might have. Or, maybe the family has a teenaged son who needs help getting into the right college. Henry goes in politely and has a talk with someone on the board of trustees, someone who knows the family name and might even be distantly related—these people inbreed like chinchillas. He has a talk about new buildings and endowments. If it's a tough case, he might bring a check with him."

"How did he help you?"

George shrugged. "He just steered a little business my way. Somebody in one of these families died unexpectedly: he was about forty. Henry needed to make some money disappear from the dead guy's accounts and get spread to relations before the death got reported. Otherwise there would have been a huge inheritance tax. Another time, he needed to have some money come out of nowhere and land in a politician's pocket."

"I don't suppose Henry Ziegler's got an ad in the Yellow Pages. How do I get in touch with him?"

George said, "If you're as hot as you deserve to be, don't try. He'll meet you somewhere tomorrow night."

"Where?"

"Can you get to L.A.?"

"All right."

"He stays at the Bel-Air Hotel. He's there now. I'll tell him to expect you."

Jane hugged George Hawkes. "Thanks, George." She looked at her watch. "I've got a plane to catch." She took a step backward. She looked up at the windows of the house, but saw no sign of the woman. "If I were you, I'd go in now. The longer you're out here with me, the worse it will be for you. You can rest easy, though. No matter how this goes, I'll probably never see you again."

George raised his head to stare up at the stars. "Life is a lot weirder than that." He looked at her again. "You need a ride?"

She shook her head. "People see cars. They don't see one more tourist out for a walk, and pedestrians don't have to wear license plates." She turned away and moved down the long driveway toward the gate. After a few steps, Hawkes could see only the dark shape of her shadow against his lawn. As soon as she was out of the light from the house, he could not see her at all.

13

Jane's flight brought her into Miami in the early morning, when she was reasonably sure the watcher she had seen last night would be home asleep, but she found that he had been replaced. The crowds were thin and she could pick out other watchers. There were three men in tight T-shirts along the wall who paid little attention to the arrival of her flight but were very interested in all departures. Their behavior added a bit to her fears for Rita. If Rita had not gotten out of Florida already, this was the airport she would have been most likely to use.

This generation of wiseguys—the ones now in their twenties and thirties—seemed bent on dressing badly. Their fathers had worn suits like salesmen when everyone else had been in jeans and sweatshirts, so they had been easier to pick out. Jane noticed four police officers in the next waiting area. There were two men who wore windbreakers that hid their equipment, and two women who had identical taste in purses. Theirs were made by a company named Galco and they consisted of two compartments designed to surround a center pocket that held a gun.

Jane moved downstairs to buy a ticket to Los Angeles, then went into a ladies' room to arrange her hair and change clothes before the flight. The pressure had increased over the past few days, and she wasn't sure why. It looked as though the authorities had noticed the increased Mafia presence in airports and decided to place a few more cops nearby to find out what was up, and then the Mafia had reinforced its complement to spread the police thinner. It was getting to be more dangerous to fly.

When Jane reached Los Angeles, the numbers seemed to have increased again in a few hours. She rented a car at the airport under the name Valerie Campbell and drove it to Beverly Hills to do some shopping. When she had what she needed, she approached the Hotel Bel-Air by a long and circuitous route, then watched the parking lot for fifteen minutes before she went in to register for the night.

It was evening when she picked up the telephone in her room and asked the operator to ring Mr. Ziegler's room. He answered, "Yeah."

She said, "A mutual friend—"

"He talked to me," Ziegler interrupted. "Meet me on the bridge in front where the swans are."

Jane walked out of her room, down the narrow pathway through the garden, and across the margin beside the tables under the trellis where people were eating dinner. There was a certain absurdity to this spot. She had noticed on another visit to the hotel that the terra-cotta tiles under the patio were artificially heated from beneath. She had set her purse down, and when she had picked it up, the bottom had been warm. A few of the diners looked up as she crossed the little courtyard, but none of the eyes lingered on her for more than a moment.

She was dressed in a black linen dress that she had bought this afternoon, so she could have sat down at any table and looked enough like the other women to be the sister who always arrived late—or the daughter, at some tables. She turned left at the end of the path and came out on the little arched bridge over the pond.

There were still cars pulling up at the end of the bridge. Valet parking attendants got out and expensively dressed guests got in and drove off to claim their reserved tables at other restaurants in other parts of town. Jane stood apart from the other guests and stared over the railing. Two swans were still down there, gliding gracefully across the surface of the water toward the curtain of high reeds that separated them from the parking lot.

"You Jane?" The voice was low and gravelly, with a harsh, edgy quality to it, like a stage whisper.

It carried so clearly that she raised her head and scanned the doorway and the edge of the parking lot before she nodded.

"Me Henry." He was short and dapper, his suit beautifully tailored to disguise a chubby torso. He seemed to be in his fifties, but his wavy hair had grayed and thinned enough that he could be sixty. He said, "Come on," and turned back toward the hotel. She followed him through the arch, then up a maze of paths to the doorway of a bungalow with an enclosed garden. He opened the door and let her enter first.

The suite was larger and a bit more lavish than hers, and it had a big couch and a full desk with a fax machine. Open on the desk was a laptop computer that he had not turned off. The display glowed bright sky blue with a rainbow pie chart in the corner and a few lines of print. She noticed the proportions were changing constantly.

He said, "I sweep my rooms for bugs, and put a scrambler on the telephone as soon as I check in." He gestured at the couch and, when Jane was seated, dragged a straight-backed chair up to sit across from her. "George told me just enough about you so I could place you in the universe. I suppose he did the same about me."

"Yes," said Jane.

"We have the same problem," said Ziegler. "With both of us here, the feds could seal the exits and set fire to the hotel with all those rich bastards still in it, and still come out ahead after the lawsuits." His eyes never moved from her face. He was studying her. "What's the business you're bringing me?"

Jane took a deep breath, then said carefully, "There are two of us. We have control of about ten billion dollars."

"What do you mean you have control of it?"

"We're the only ones who know where it is and can get our hands on it. It's in lots of different places under a lot of different names: domestic and foreign stocks and bonds, bank accounts, real estate, precious metals, cash. It's been built up over a period of about fifty years."

Ziegler shrugged. "Anything that's been invested for more than ten years is safe. If there was going to be trouble with it, the trouble would have come right away. There are a lot of ways to launder money, and you stumbled on the best: time. If you came to me for expert advice, here it is: you don't need advice."

"We want to give it all to charities."

His left eyebrow went up. "Seriously."

Jane held her eyes on Ziegler's. After a few heartbeats, his expression changed. He looked more alarmed than puzzled. She supposed she must have undermined his sense of how people behaved. Part of her was pleased, but she had to keep him from taking the next step, which was to silently declare her insane and begin to speed up her departure. "That's why we came to you," she said. "We could try to leave it where it is forever. Probably some of the inactive accounts would be confiscated by the authorities. But it's likely that others would be tracked down and claimed by people we don't want to have it."

He squinted, as though he were trying to block out what she was saying and hear something else. "Why don't you want it?"

Jane said, "A lot of reasons—some practical, some not."

"Give me a few practical reasons."

Jane frowned. "Given enough time, these people may be able to trace some of the money. If they trace it to a charity, they'll be out of luck. If they trace it to a person, that person will be out of luck. You said George told you something about me, so you know I have other reasons not to show a high profile. If I have billions of dollars, I'm not going to be invisible anymore."

"What about your partner?"

"He has good reasons to stay invisible too. The money is poison."

Henry Ziegler had his elbows on the arms of the chair, and he rested his chin on his fists as he stared at her thoughtfully. "So you want nothing out of this. You're just sitting on ten billion dollars and figure it might as well go to good causes."

"That's about right." She paused. "All of it except for your fee—I'm counting on you to identify enough money that's very old and cold to make helping us worth your risk. You can pay yourself whatever is fair."

He studied her more closely. "What do you think that is?"

"I don't know," she said. "I don't want to make this sound easy, or safe. The people we're up against are about the worst enemies you could have. They're already looking for anyone who might know the slightest thing about the money. If we make a mistake, the danger won't ever go away."

He said, "I respect that. I agree that we should be very careful not to con each other. You and your partner have somehow gotten your hands on the money that Bernie the Elephant was holding for the Mafia."

Jane hesitated. There was no uncertainty in his expression. "It's that obvious?"

He shrugged modestly. "I'm probably more up on these things than most people. At least I hope I am." He leaned forward and spoke in an avuncular tone. "There's always a certain amount of big money floating. Right now there are a few other chunks that big that could show up any day. But it's not money you could have gotten your hands on. It's from treasuries and central banks, and the people who have it also have armies and intelligence services to keep an eye on it."

Jane asked, "Well, what do you think about this chunk?"

He held up his hands in a gesture meant to announce the

obvious. "If you have money, charities will take it. We'll have to be very careful about it, and do some preparation." He stood up and paced the room. "It's an interesting problem." He stopped and asked, "I assume you want it all to move in a short period, so the Mafia doesn't have time to figure out what it is, or where it came from—just hit them in the face with it?"

"I think so," said Jane. "If we give them time to find the address of some building while we're still in it, we're dead."

"It's going to be interesting," he said, and resumed his pacing, then stopped again. "And you don't have any special charities in mind?"

Jane shook her head. "I'd like them to be legitimate. There's no sense in moving money from one set of crooks to another. Beyond that, no."

"Don't get me wrong," he said. "You wouldn't have much choice beyond that." He sat down beside her. "Let me tell you what ten billion dollars is. There are roughly forty thousand foundations in the country right now—some for charity, some for art, science, and so on. Ten billion dollars is what all of them put together give away in a year. No matter what we do, this is going to hit the papers—front page. The best we can hope for is that when it does, it's at the end of the year as a statistic: 'Charities Report a Good Year for Giving.' "

Jane's brows knitted. "How do we do that?"

"We spread it thin enough, package each donation small enough so it doesn't make a big splash by itself." He waved a hand. "And we use a few tricks."

"What sorts of tricks?"

He grinned. "For ten billion? Everything we can think of." He turned his wrist to look at his watch. "I'm going to make some calls and clear my schedule for the next couple of weeks. I'll have a few ideas for you by morning."

Jane recognized her dismissal. She stood. "Please give some thought to the size of your fee. I'll have to clear it with my partner."

He turned to look at her slyly. "If I said it was ten percent—

a billion dollars to move ten billion—would you be sure I was cheating you?"

"No."

"Then I'll do it for the goodwill."

"What goodwill?"

"That means I have reasons too, some practical, some impractical. Be here at five o'clock in the morning."

It was still dark at five a.m. when Jane stepped quietly along the path and knocked on Ziegler's door. He swung the door open quickly and closed it after her. She noticed that he was wearing the pants from the suit he'd had on the night before and had his white shirt open at the collar and the sleeves rolled up.

Jane said, "You haven't slept, have you?"

He picked up a piece of paper from the corner of the desk. "Here's the plan. Phase one: we set up twenty private foundations. I've already faxed orders to twenty law firms in different parts of the country to start cutting the papers, but to leave the names blank until I call them in."

"What does that do?"

"It sets up an impersonal vehicle. If a big donation check says Joe Smith, 101 Maple Street, charities want to know who that is. If the check is from a law firm representing the Smith Foundation, they think they know, so they don't look. It's not going to be listed anywhere until next year's *Foundation Directory* comes out. By then it's gone." He went on. "Then we select a couple of hundred community foundations. You know what those are?"

"Not even vaguely."

"They're foundations that already exist for the benefit of some city, county, or state. People donate to them, and they make a budget and give the money to charities. For us, it takes the sting of newness off, mixes our money with other people's, and puts another barrier of paper between the real contributor and the charity."

He looked down his list. "We're also setting up twenty corporate foundations of our own. This does roughly the same thing. The corporations are closely held, with maybe one or two imaginary people owning all the stock. The donation comes from Abadabba Tool and Die Foundation, not a person. If the name and the donation amount get printed on a list somewhere, nobody knows anything. Since they never heard of Abadabba Tool and Die, they don't know if it's tiny or huge, or if this is a lot of money for them or peanuts. I've already got people printing out articles of incorporation, and after that we'll cut papers for the foundations."

"This is beginning to sound like a lot of paper."

"A blizzard of it, and it's all meaningless. If it didn't have to be complicated, you wouldn't need me. I'm also setting up twenty public foundations. A public foundation is one that can legally solicit donations from the public."

"Why would we solicit donations from the public?"

"We don't. But judging from where the money came from, there's bound to be some that smells like dead fish—too suspicious to slip to a real foundation directly. We run it through one of our public foundations to clean it, then the foundation gives it to a charity. The report of where it came from might set off alarms at the IRS, but who cares? The worst they can do is shut down the foundation, which will already be shut down. They can't put anybody at the foundation in jail, because they're not responsible for where the money came from, only where it goes. Since they don't exist, they're not in much jeopardy anyway."

"I have no way of knowing how much of the money is suspicious," said Jane.

Henry Ziegler set down his paper and shook his head. "Probably not much. Bernie Lupus was a genius of a sort that ordinary people will never be able to appreciate, because you have to know so much just to imagine what he was doing. It's possible that every dime has been washed, dried, fluffed, and folded so perfectly that it's unrecognizable. But there's a problem with trusting a murdered man. We know he made at least one mistake, and it was a big one."

Jane felt a little uncomfortable, but she said, "I agree: let's take as many precautions as we can."

Ziegler picked up another piece of paper from the desk. "There will be some money that looks like some old guy's fortune. That's money that Bernie the Elephant invested fifty years ago in some bogus name and left to mature. This is good. All we need is a will for each account leaving it to some charity and a death certificate. We mail one copy to the bank and one to the charity and let them work out the details. They're good at that, and it takes time, which is good for us."

Jane let out a breath in a silent whistle. "This is pretty impressive."

"I'm not anywhere near done."

"I still have a question that's on my mind."

"Let's get through this first," he said. "The next tier of donations goes to the giant charities: United Way, Red Cross, Catholic Charities, United Jewish Appeal, UNICEF, March of Dimes, CARE, Salvation Army, and so on. They're like big clearing houses. Whatever our imaginary people give gets mixed into a big pot. They give it away and account for it later. Then we go to the next level down."

"What's that?"

"Slightly smaller charities that specialize. Mostly it's 'Name That Disease': National Cancer Society, Muscular Dystrophy, Alzheimer's Association, AIDS, et cetera. We've got enough to swamp all of them, and they're still big enough to swallow a few million without blinking. Then we go down another level to the relief agencies and single institutions: homeless shelters, battered women's shelters, hospices, orphanages. You get the idea."

"That's it, right?" she asked.

He shook his head. "Not even close. We'll actually run out of charities at some point. A lot of these places are going to freak out if they get a check for more than a hundred thousand, and we'll have to give each of them more than that."

"What do we do?"

"Branch out. We give money to a lot of causes that aren't charities but get donations now and then. Some universities will have to get funds for scholarships named after made-up people. We give some to Indian reservations." He looked at her sharply. "Did I see a funny look on your face? Some of the poorest people in the country live on reservations. We make out a check to the tribal council, such and such reservation, right? They decide what to spend it on to help their own community. They may or may not report it to anybody, because it doesn't happen very often."

"It wasn't an objection," said Jane. "I think it's a great idea. I guess I'm surprised that you're . . . that you've figured out so much."

"Moving money is a talent," he said. "Knowing how to do it is like being the world's greatest nose-picker. Most of the time, people would rather you didn't.

"Anyway," he went on, "if you've been paying attention, you get the idea. We capture the biggest sums by putting them into our sixty foundations. We use the giant charities to sop up the next chunk, and move down from there. We'll have to pay attention to the size of each gift, so some charity won't choke on it and reach for the phone to call a press conference. If we still have money left at the end of it, we can start mailing checks to symphony orchestras and museums and arts councils and so on."

"I still have a question."

Ziegler put down his sheet of paper and met her gaze. "I know. Why don't I want to take any money myself. The same reasons you don't. I don't really need it enough to die for it."

"What about the impractical reasons? You could have said no, and been in no danger."

He smiled sadly. "Bernie Lupus. I wasn't exaggerating about what he must have been like. With a mind like that, he could have done anything. He could have been a great scientist or something. It's one of the biggest wastes I ever heard of. It's as if Einstein spent his whole life disconnecting smoke detectors in airplanes so he could have a cigarette, or rigging pay phones to get free calls. I guess I see this as a chance to change Bernie the Elephant's life after the fact. If I had listened to your pitch and said no, then Bernie Lupus was just one more dead guy who made the Mafia richer. If I said yes, then it's a whole different story. Everything Bernie did for fifty years amounts to suckering the worst people in the country into doing good."

"And you?"

"Me?" Ziegler smiled. "Maybe if I run into him in hell, he'll tell me how he did it."

Jane was silent for a moment, then decided. "You'll get to meet him tonight."

Ziegler's mouth dropped open. "Is he alive?" asked Ziegler. "Or am I going to be dead?"

"The first," said Jane. "Maybe the second too. We'll do our best to avoid that, though. Are you ready to travel?"

14

There were still lights visible behind the upstairs window blinds when Jane drove around the last curve. She stopped the car along the road and walked the rest of the way in the darkness, then stepped into the pool of light on the porch and rang the doorbell. She listened for the sound of footsteps on the stairs, and when she heard them they were wrong: too light, too quick for Bernie. Jane slipped to the side of the house and waited. The door swung open, and out on the porch stepped Rita Shelford.

Jane hurried to the porch, dragged Rita inside, closed the door, and bolted it. She leaned against the door and stared at Rita in silence.

Rita struggled to hold her eyes on Jane's, then tried to avert them, but found that she could not. She took a breath and said, "I . . . decided . . ."

Jane interrupted. "You decided. I guess that's all anyone has to hear. I showed you your best chance to survive, and that's all I could do. You never pretended that it was what you wanted, so I suppose I shouldn't have been surprised."

"I'm sorry," Rita said firmly, "but—"

"No, you're not," Jane said quietly. "Not yet, anyway. But things are in motion now, and I can't stop to drag you back across two states and make you stay there. I hope that at the end of this, you still think you made the right choice. Either way, you're in."

Rita stepped forward and grasped Jane's hands. "Thank you. I'll help you, honest. I'll—"

"Where is it?" Jane interrupted.

"Where's what?"

"The gun."

Rita gaped at her, but said nothing.

"I plan to be here after the lights are out, and I don't feel like tripping over a shotgun. That's what it is, isn't it?"

Rita opened the small broom cupboard behind her. Between the mop and the broom was a short-barreled Winchester Defender. She started to close the door again, but Jane stepped past her and held it open. She bent down to the trigger guard of the shotgun and pushed on the safety so the red line went in. "Is there a shell in the chamber? I didn't hear you pump it."

Rita said, "I don't know. I never saw one close up before. Bernie made me take him to garage sales until he found one."

She sighed. He had done the smart thing, of course. Being smart was what had gotten him into trouble and kept him there.

She stepped back toward the door and turned the dead bolt. "I'm going out to bring in a guest, so be on your best behavior, whatever that is."

Rita's face was a mask of fright. "A guest? Oh, God. Look at me." She gestured in despair at her tank top, shorts, and bare feet. She began to run her fingers through her recently dyed brown hair to straighten it. "What kind of guest? Who?"

Jane said, "You look fine. Your hair looks great. I still like that color, by the way. His name is Henry Ziegler. He already knows about Bernie."

"What's he doing here?" she asked suspiciously.

"We can't get rid of ten billion dollars by sitting here writing thousand-dollar checks. We could do it until our arms dropped off, and we'd attract attention in time to die with nearly all of it still in the accounts. We need help, and he's a specialist."

"I just wish you could have . . . like, warned me."

"I didn't know you were here."

"Oh . . . yeah," said Rita.

Jane slipped out past her, then returned a minute later with Henry Ziegler. Jane watched the man and the girl assess each other from a distance of eight feet, like two strange dogs. After three seconds, the short, dapper Ziegler suddenly grinned, stepped up to Rita, gave her hand a quick shake, and said, "I'm Henry."

"Rita," said the girl, looking at his hand instead of his face.

"Very good," said Ziegler. He looked around brightly. "Nice place. I was afraid it would be more of a hideout, and less of a house." As he walked around the kitchen, Rita was two steps behind him, watching him suspiciously. But Jane could see that Ziegler was counting electrical outlets. He seemed to be pleased. He turned to Rita. "Can you type?"

Rita gaped at him, dumbfounded.

Jane stepped closer and volunteered, "I can."

Rita seemed to recover from a reverie. "I can type." She addressed Jane. "I took a computer class in school."

"Excellent," said Ziegler. He turned to Jane. "We'll need to get to a computer store first thing in the morning." He began to pace. "We'll need two PCs, two laser printers. A fax machine, some supplies. High-quality paper to print our own letterheads, envelopes, a hell of a lot of stamps. I'll write everything down tonight." He stopped and looked at Jane. "When do I get to meet Bernie?"

"I guess it's now," said Jane. "Bernie?"

The old man stepped into the doorway from the dining room. "Yeah, it's me. It's hard to sneak around much when you're hard of hearing. Who are you?"

"This is Henry Ziegler," said Jane. "I asked him to help us move the money."

Henry Ziegler stepped forward and held out his hand. Bernie gave it a perfunctory shake and dropped it. He spoke to Jane. "Are you keeping us safe, or just collecting more of us to kill?"

Rita said, "She's doing the right thing, Bernie. If you never heard of him, it's got to be the best thing about him. And if he's done anything like this once, it's one more time than we have."

Jane noticed Bernie's expression and decided it must be a mirror of her own.

Bernie shrugged. "Yeah, you're probably right." He said to Ziegler, "You know what happens if you screw it up?"

"There's not much point in worrying about it," Ziegler answered. "If we didn't all think it could be done, we wouldn't be here, would we?"

"I would, but you could look at it that way if you want," Bernie said. "I'm just putting everything up front." He gestured toward Jane. "A woman like that comes to talk to you, and pretty soon you think you're better than you are, and the crocodiles have lost all their teeth. I can tell you they haven't."

"I'm just hoping we can keep them from waking up until after we've drained the swamp."

"Sleep," said Bernie. "That's a good idea. I'll see you in the morning." He walked out of the kitchen, and Jane heard his footsteps going slowly and deliberately up the staircase.

"Take me to the Eldorado Hotel on West San Francisco Street," said Ziegler. "I've got to do some faxes and E-mail tonight."

A few minutes later, Jane brought Ziegler to the lighted front of the big hotel and cut the engine. "You don't have to stop," he said. "They're expecting me. Can you pick me up at seven?"

"I'll be here," said Jane. As he took his leather suitcase from the back of the car, Jane added, "See if you can lose the fancy clothes. You're not in New York."

At seven the next morning he was standing outside with a cup of coffee in one hand and an attaché case in the other. He got into the car beside her. "Drive to Albuquerque. We'll do our shopping now."

Jane looked at him, then pulled out into the street. He appeared exactly the way she had hoped he would, like a man who was used to wearing tailored suits but had come to New Mexico on a vacation. The jeans and comfortable khaki shirt looked as new as they were. She had known he had no choice but to buy everything in the hotel shop, and the effect was perfect. He looked like a man who might walk into a store and buy a lot of computer gear on impulse.

As they approached the outskirts of Albuquerque, she said, "Do we know where we're going?"

Ziegler handed her a list of stores and addresses. "I went through the Albuquerque Yellow Pages last night, so we can make this quick." Jane drove from store to store, and watched Ziegler move up and down the aisles with another of his lists. He bought computers, modems, printers, reams of business stationery that was thick and textured, boxes of envelopes: so many purchases that he and Jane had trouble fitting them in the trunk of the car and had to pile them in the back seat. When the car was full, Jane stopped at a Dumpster behind an office building that had a huge FOR LEASE sign. She said, "We've got to make some space." They took the computer equipment out of the enormous boxes and styrofoam padding and threw the packaging away to make more room.

They drove back to Santa Fe at one, and Ziegler went to work converting the dining room of the house to an office. He appeared to have thought of everything. He had included surge suppressors on extension cords that he ran into electrical outlets in the living room and kitchen. As he worked, he talked to Jane. "We're going to have things on the hard disks while we work, and that's a risk. If anything happens, don't think you can smash the computer with a hammer and that's going to do it. A computer is just a plastic box. You have to take the disk out and destroy it—put it in a fire, or break it in pieces. There are people who make a living retrieving data from disks that supposedly got erased. See? Undo these screws and slip it out with the drive."

In late afternoon, he plugged his laptop computer into one of the printers and began to print out the stored information he had received from all over the country while he was in the hotels in Beverly Hills and Santa Fe. An hour later he was ready. He said, "Bring in the others."

When Jane brought Bernie and Rita into the dining room, Bernie looked at Ziegler with distaste. "Computers. I hate computers."

Ziegler was imperturbable. "That's okay, Bernie. They're for these two." He handed Rita a long list of addresses. "You start out by typing in this list of names and addresses so they fit the grid on your screen. When you're done, call me and I'll show you how to print it out on labels." He grasped Jane's arm and led her to the other computer. "You start by writing a dozen form letters. You know what we're after. You address it to the blank charity, blank street, blank city. The blank foundation is giving them blank dollars to continue their fine work. Or Mr. blank is. His check is enclosed. Or Mr. blank died, and left it to the charity. Keep all of them vague and simple, so we can fill in names and use each one fifty times." Finally, he turned to Bernie. "You and I will get started on writing down where all this money is."

Bernie smirked. "She's ahead of you. She's had me working on it for a few days." He walked to the sideboard near the head of the dining table and took out a spiral notebook. He handed it to Ziegler. "That's a start."

Jane stood at Ziegler's elbow and watched him leaf through the pages. They were all covered with handwritten names, account numbers, names of banks and brokers, even the dates when Bernie had made the investments. Jane saw that the first fifteen pages were all in the 1940s. Ziegler said quietly, "I don't think I ever really believed this. I had heard about it, but it didn't seem possible." When he reached the end, he went back to the beginning and started through the notebook again. He said, "How much more to go?"

Bernie answered, "I can't say. That's the Langusto family."

"That's how you remembered it—by family?"

"Of course it is," said Bernie. "You think I could put it all together in a jumble up here and have them tell me how much of it was theirs? They were thieves, for Christ's sake."

Ziegler finished his second perusal, set the book on the table, and tapped some keys on his laptop computer, then glanced up at Jane. "Over two billion," he said.

She understood. It was far more than she had expected, more than Bernie had estimated. "I guess we should get started," she said. She sat at the computer and began to type.

"I'm working on the Augustinos now," Bernie announced.

"That's great, Bernie," said Jane. "It's a terrific start. Let us know when you have it." She struggled against a growing sense of futility. Across the table from her, Rita began with childlike concentration, slowly clicking away at the keys, muttering "Shit" every few seconds, then going back and correcting a single character. After ten minutes of it, Jane walked around the table and looked over Rita's shoulder.

She said gently, "Don't worry about mistakes. Make them and fix them as well as you can. No matter how bad we are at this, we're not going to get fired and replaced."

Rita stared at her mournfully, then returned to her work. After an hour, Jane noticed that the clicking of her keyboard sounded more even, and the expletives became rarer. Jane, Ziegler, and Rita worked at the computers for the next five hours, while Bernie sat in a chair in the living room writing in his next notebook. Now and then, one of them would stand up to walk around, or just stretch and sit down again. The talk was only occasional, low, and addressed to one person. At nine, Jane announced, "We're going to need dinner. I'll see about making something."

Ziegler said, "No. Just write down what you like to eat. I'll call in an order at the restaurant in the hotel and have them deliver it to my suite. We all need a break, and I can send some faxes from there. It's safer."

Jane said, "I'm not taking these two into a hotel. It's too dangerous for them."

Ziegler took in a breath to argue, but Bernie said, "Listen to her, kid. You're a specialist. I'm a specialist. So is she."

"She's also our best typist," said Ziegler. "I'll go order the food and send my messages while they're getting it ready. You can all keep at it until I come back." He typed a command and the printer beside him began to slowly extrude printed sheets as he walked toward the door.

Ziegler returned an hour and a half later carrying a pair of shopping bags filled with boxes, and unpacked them in the kitchen. "I didn't know who liked what, so I bought a bit of everything: steak, lobster, fish, chicken, pasta, red and white wine."

Rita came out to look at the containers as Ziegler unpacked them. She seemed uncomfortable. "I used to see food like this at the hotel," she said to nobody in particular.

Jane touched her arm. "Enjoy it. But if you're not used to things like lobster drowned in butter, you might want to go easy on it the first time."

Bernie said, "She means don't eat anything bigger than your head."

Jane picked up a plate and moved to the kitchen table with the others, then sat next to Henry Ziegler. "How are we doing?"

"Do you have that last batch of names I gave you filled in on the form letters?"

"They're printed, stuffed in envelopes, and stamped," she said.

"Then we should have a billion dollars ready to mail by this time tomorrow."

"Aren't you forgetting something?" asked Bernie.

"What?"

"Checks," said Bernie. "We don't have checks."

Ziegler smiled. "I'll have some ready by the time you go to bed, and the rest in the morning. I have a format in my computer for checks. I type in the account numbers and addresses and names, and they come off the printer. A lot of companies do it. If you use the right paper, it looks as good as any other check, and we have the right paper. I'm afraid you'll have to sign them, though. They'll compare your signature with the samples you signed when you put the money in."

"If I don't get writer's cramp from putting all this crap on paper."

"If you want to dictate it, we'll take it down for you," said Jane.

"I'll let you know if I have a problem," said Bernie. "I finished the Augustinos a while ago. I started on the Molinaris, the sons of bitches."

Jane rinsed her plate in the sink, withdrew into the dining room, and went back to work alone. After a time the others, one by one, returned to their places, but Jane sank deeper into her own thoughts.

She remembered a day a couple of years in the past. She had managed to get Mary Perkins out of the farmhouse where she had been held, and she was running with her. She had needed to get the injured woman indoors and out of sight for a few days while she regained enough of her strength to move on. Jane had stopped in Oklahoma on the single patch of old reservation that remained and knocked on the door of the trailer where Martha McCutcheon lived. Martha was a clan mother, and Jane had met her once.

It had been impossible to hide the fact that Mary Perkins had been tortured—repeatedly beaten, raped, and starved—so Martha had taken Jane outside into the bare, flat fields behind the trailer and demanded to be told everything. Because Jane had known that those sharp old eyes had seen a lot in seventy-five years and had been horrified but not frightened, she had told the truth. Martha had said, "What's a Nundawaono girl got to do with that kind of business?"

"It's what I do," Jane had answered. "Fugitives come to me and I guide them out of the world."

"Why?"

"Because if I didn't, they would give me bad dreams."

And Martha had said, "I'll bet a lot of them do anyway." The words came back now, but they came in her own voice.

Jane tried to think about what she was doing. She concentrated on the charities. There were a lot of resonant names, and she knew intellectually that each one represented thousands of people who were hungry or sick or desperate. But she could not force the charities to fill the space that the truth fit in.

Maybe what had induced her to concoct this scheme was that she had needed a reason to do what Bernie had asked her to. She had known that she could not tell herself that Bernie "the Elephant" Lupus was an innocent victim, so she had thought up a price he would have to pay for her services.

But what was Jane McKinnon doing offering her services at any price? She had been trying to keep herself from thinking about Carey, but here he was again. She had not just been happy with Carey, but also happy about Carey—happy that he loved her above all others, happy to spend time with him, happy to be Mrs. McKinnon. She found herself gazing through the doorway at the telephone in the living room.

She forced herself to look at her computer screen. This time she had to be more cautious than ever. If she made a mistake or simply ran out of luck, there must be no way that the trail could lead to Carey. Delfina had traced Rita as far as Niagara Falls, and that was uncomfortably close to home. If something went wrong in this house, it was likely that someone would obtain a list of the telephone calls that had been made.

It was better if she didn't try to explain to Carey what she was doing, anyway. It would worry him, confuse him, and offer him no comfort. She had already warned him that she might not be able to call for a long time, and that would have to stand until she had some reason to believe the danger was over.

Carey would get by. She had joked to him that he was a low-maintenance husband, but it had not exactly been a joke. He had already grown up and become a successful surgeon before he had convinced her to marry him. There had been no need for her to provide any of the usual contributions: money, work, even patience. She had moved into the big old stone house in Amherst built on land an ancestor of his had bought from her ancestors in the 1790s. McKinnons had expanded and remodeled it so many times that it had needed no modification to accommodate the marriage.

Carey was like the house: he had been built and improved, and the mistakes had been corrected before she had arrived. He had reached his final form. He was self-reliant and his mind was fully occupied. Carey was a person who knew what his days were going to be from now until he was too old to do anything. No matter how extravagantly Jane wanted to give, there was not even time for him to accept. He left for the surgical wing of the hospital at six-thirty each morning, and returned after his last rounds at eight in the evening. If Jane came to the hospital to have lunch with him, the doctors and nurses he saw every day would come in and join them at the table. In a clannish town like Buffalo, most people couldn't conceive of a husband and wife wanting to sit alone at lunch, unless they were having a fight.

Jane detected an odd tone in her thoughts. What she had been thinking was not exactly false, but it had started to sound like a too elaborate collection of excuses. It didn't explain why Jane had not gone home the minute Rita was out of sight, or why she was in a house in New Mexico with this strange assortment of people, engaged in this peculiar scheme.

Jane kept typing and printing while, one by one, the others left the dining room. First Bernie got up and climbed the stairs. Then it was Rita. An hour later, even Henry Ziegler stood and closed his laptop computer.

Jane said casually, "Henry, how long do you think it's going to take?"

Ziegler shrugged. "It's up to Bernie, really. It just depends on how much he remembers and writes down."

"The minute you see the end coming, let me know."

15

J ane awoke suddenly in the dark. She unwrapped herself from the blanket and sat up on the couch in the living room. A light shone from the crack under the swinging door to the dining room. She listened. The muted, steady clacking of computer keys was punctuated by the rhythmic sound of the printer cycling to roll out pages. She held her watch to her face, and moved it to the side to catch a little moonlight and determine that it was three A.M., then walked to the door and pushed it open.

The rheostat that controlled the dining room chandelier had been turned low, but the light still irritated her eyes. Henry Ziegler's face was bathed in the eerie phosphorescence of the display on his computer screen. She said quietly, "You never sleep, do you?"

Ziegler started in his chair, then saw Jane and slumped, his shoulders rounding as he took a few breaths to calm himself. "You startled me," he said. "Sorry if I woke you up. I thought I'd use the time to get the next part of this done. The papers for the corporate foundations I set up are starting to arrive at the hotel in piles."

"I didn't ask what you were doing," she said. "I asked about sleep."

"Don't be silly," he said, but his eyes returned to his computer screen before he said it.

Jane persisted. "I was with you at night in Beverly Hills, then met you the next morning to find you had already done a day's work. The same thing happened at the hotel downtown after we got here. Now you're at it again. Is it drugs?"

141

Henry raised his eyes to her and shook his head. "It's probably a disease, but I don't know what kind. I never told a doctor, but it hasn't killed me yet."

"How long have you been this way?"

"I don't know. I think since I was born. My mother always told everybody what a colicky baby I was. From the time I can remember, I would lie in bed on one side until I got stiff and sore, then roll over onto the other until the same thing happened. Around dawn I would doze off for a couple of hours. One night when I was about eight, I got up. The next night I went to sleep right away and woke up after a couple of hours. The next night, the same. It's been that way ever since."

Jane's sleep-dulled brain moved through several thoughts. She remembered George Hawkes saying that twenty-five years ago, when Ziegler had just started as an accountant, he had gone to law school at night. It had not occurred to her that it had been all night. She also had a dim memory of reading somewhere that Napoleon had slept about as little as Ziegler. "Well, I guess I'm awake too," she muttered. "I may as well put in a few hours." She sat at her computer and flipped the switch, then watched the screen light up and run its self-test sequence. "What's next?"

Henry held up a few sheets of paper so she could see the top one. "Write me a form letter for each of these corporate foundations. The number beside each one is the amount they have to give away. Pick a few charities off the list on this other sheet for each one, print the letters, sign them with the name of the president. Then stack them in a pile over here. When I'm done with this, I'll go through the stack and cut the checks. When Rita gets up, she can print the labels and stuff, stamp and stack the envelopes."

"Got it," said Jane. She set to work. After one day, she was already getting used to the work, and it went more quickly. It was like a game. The big charities got a million or more. The small ones got three or four hundred thousand dollars. The surnames of the corporate officers were all common and familiar, ones that she or Ziegler had taken from telephone directories and given first names and initials at random. Jane signed some with obscuring flourishes, some with illegible squiggles. She had been forging documents for over a decade, and she was good at making signatures that looked real.

By the time she had gone down the list of corporate foundations, Rita was up and working beside her, chewing bubble gum and popping it every few minutes. Jane worked eight hours, then showered and went out to buy another carload of supplies in Albuquerque. This time she went to different stores, but the extra time it took her to find them was bought back by the fact that she knew precisely what she needed. She used credit cards in three different names to pay for them, returned to the house at four with take-out dinners, then worked from five until eleven.

The next day, Jane wrote more letters and filled out checks to universities. Some were donations from corporations, some from foundations, and some from imaginary people with common surnames that allowed Jane to imply a connection without specifying whether they were alumni or parents or grandparents of students.

On the day after that, Jane gave money to tribal councils on Indian reservations. There was a secret pleasure to this day's work. She had always tried to keep her ancestry to herself while she was working. The only exceptions had been two occasions when she'd had no place to hide a runner except on a reservation and the single admission to Celia Fulham, the social worker in Florida. The secrecy was one of a thousand precautions that she had practiced until they were habitual. If one of her enemies considered her an American woman of unknown ethnicity, he would have to find her among a hundred and fifty million others. If he knew she was on a tribal enrollment list, he could eliminate about a hundred and forty-nine million. As Jane wrote the letters, she found herself straining to make the numbers as large as she could, and three or four times she caught herself making them too large. The reason for big checks was that reservations were starved for money. But the reason she couldn't make the checks even bigger was that reservations were starved for money. Huge donations of suspicious provenance would shriek for attention.

For the next two days, Jane devoted her time to grants for homeless shelters, soup kitchens, and relief organizations that helped the poor and hungry in cities. The day after that went to training and rehabilitation facilities for the handicapped, the undereducated, and the displaced.

A whole day and night were devoted to hospitals. There were thousands of them, and dozens seemed to have identical names. But hospitals were relatively safe recipients for the odd bits—money that cleared the accounts of an individual or foundation—because they were used to receiving donations of all sizes. Her fund-raising for Carey's hospital had taught her exactly how the letters should look.

Jane awoke each morning before dawn wondering whether this would be the final day, but each time she would find the insomniac Henry Ziegler up, printing out the lists of imaginary people who were going to be that day's donors. In the evening, Bernie would hand Ziegler his latest spiral notebook, and Ziegler would leaf through twenty or thirty pages at dinner, all of them crammed with new accounts and locations that had spilled from Bernie's prodigious memory. Each time the contents of a notebook had been transferred into the computers, Jane would take the pages to the fireplace and burn them.

There was a whole day and night of scholarships. Any organization listed in the *Foundation Directory* that gave scholarships got a large donation earmarked for its permanent endowment. There were two days of donations to institutions that cared for orphans and unwanted children. Jane was astounded at how many there were. She spent two days on nonprofit homes and relief agencies for the elderly, and there was even a half day for animals.

Jane had begun the work with a cold, composed determination, but as the days went by, she began to feel a dreamlike disorientation. She had tried to keep up with Ziegler, but the lack of sleep was wearing down her certainty, and she began to work from habit. The walls of the garage and the bedrooms upstairs were now lined with boxes of bundled and sealed envelopes, and the living room closets were filling up with the overflow.

One morning when she joined Ziegler in the dining room, he was typing in a series of Web addresses. He would complete one, then wait a few seconds, then nod to himself happily.

"What's that?" asked Jane.

"I'm looking over our shoulder," he answered. "Before any check gets into the mail, I want to be sure the money got into the account first. If a check bounces, we're not going to be around to cover it. Mr. Hagedorn and Mrs. Fuller aren't going to answer their mail."

"How does it look so far?"

"No mistakes, no problems with any of the big stuff: the hundred and ninety-two foundations, the fifty-six corporations, and the big trust accounts we set up are all solvent. Now all we've got to do is make payday before all these checks get stale and each of these accounts grows too much."

"Oh, that's right," said Jane. "I've been so busy I haven't thought about that lately. What can we do about the profits that keep coming in?"

"Zilch," he answered. "There's no way to clear off a billion without leaving a few million in uncredited interest that will come in later. It might be what saves us. It takes a bit of time before the federal and state governments realize we're not going to file tax returns, and the clock doesn't start until next April. Foundations owe a one percent federal excise tax. The government wants it, but if the account still exists, they don't get too alarmed. These crumbs and leftovers will probably buy us a year or two after that before the feds start looking for us in any way that matters. After five years, it becomes an unclaimed account. The state confiscates it, pays the feds off, and keeps the rest."

"It's like leaving an unfinished drink on the table," said Jane. "The waiter thinks you're coming back."

"Right," said Ziegler. "I hope giving it to them doesn't bother you."

"I'm not a big fan of governments," said Jane. "But I like them better than gangsters. Wait. If we run out of charities, can we just slip some to governments?"

"Don't even say it," said Ziegler. "We've got to do everything the way people expect us to. Governments don't like gifts. They like to snatch the money away from you."

"Then let them," she said. "What's for today?"

"Problem assets."

"What does that mean?"

"Bernie has been giving us clean, easy money as fast as we could spend it. But there are other things. He bought some land."

"What's the problem?"

"By definition, land is not something you can move from place to place, and you certainly can't disguise it as something else. Converting it to cash isn't easy. We can't advertise it. Even if we found buyers in some yet-to-be invented quiet way, we can't hang around for sixty-day escrows to close on a hundred and twenty pieces of property all over the country. And of course, the original deeds and papers are not at Bernie's fingertips."

"That shouldn't matter. The sales must be recorded in county courthouses. He remembers the names, doesn't he?"

"He's Bernie the Elephant. He remembers the dates, prices, and map numbers."

"Maybe we could put the land in the wills of dead people."

Henry Ziegler squinted for a moment. "Not bad. We can leave it to organizations that can use it or sell it themselves."

"What are the other problem assets?"

"He bought foreign bonds and stocks in foreign identities. It's taken me a few hours to work my way through all of them, but I think I'm finished. I put in sell orders, with direct deposit to local banks. Then I requested that taxes be withheld by the banks before the money is sent to accounts in the U.S. That should take care of it. Then there's the art."

"Bernie bought art?"

"Afraid so," said Ziegler. "Paintings. Mostly it was in the

forties and fifties. It was expensive stuff then, so I shudder to think what it's worth now."

Jane frowned. "I can't see Bernie buying paintings."

"He went through art dealers in Europe—used them as brokers. It's been done a lot. You can get one canvas that's two feet wide, one foot high, and one inch thick, and you've stored five or six million. And finding an art dealer who doesn't mind that the money is dirty is not exactly a head scratcher. If you say 'tax dodge' above a whisper, we'll have six or seven of them lined up at the door, and two of them will know where you can get a Vermeer or a Titian that hasn't been seen since the Allies bombed Dresden."

"Where are the paintings?"

"In a vault. I can't see us showing up at Sotheby's to sell them off."

Jane remembered the trips Bernie had made to meet Francesca Ogliaro in New York. "Is the vault in New York?"

"Yes," said Ziegler. "And some of the paintings are stolen. When a painting by a major artist that's been sitting in a vault for two generations hits the auction block, there are going to be TV cameras. Big players from all over the world will show up to bid. We've got about twenty of those. What we ought to do is burn them."

"Do we know for sure that some are stolen?"

"Bernie thinks seven or eight, so it's probably more."

"Good," said Jane. "We might be able to use that. Are there papers somewhere to show that different people bought them?"

"No," said Ziegler. "He called himself Andrew Hewitt, set himself up with a few dealers, so the name had clout. They brought the deals to him. The dealers are all gone now— mostly dead."

"Forget the dealers," said Jane. "Even if they were alive, they wouldn't come forward to say they sold stolen paintings."

"It doesn't get rid of the merchandise. There's no way to avoid the publicity."

"So let's decide what we want it to be," said Jane. "The fact that he bought all of them under the name Andrew Hewitt gives us a chance."

"People are going to want to know all about Andrew Hewitt—where he got his money, where he lived, what he was like," Henry said. "We can't invent a person like him on short notice and expect he'll stand up to the kind of scrutiny he'll get. They'll know it's an alias."

"Then what we need is a real person to put behind the alias. Can you get probate records on your computer?"

"Sure," he said.

"Good. Find a person—man or woman—who left an art collection to a museum."

"There must be hundreds," he said. "Thousands."

"Then be picky. We want one who doesn't mention any other heirs in the papers. And look for signs that there was a lot of money. If possible, the person died some time ago, so the air will be clear."

"I don't see how this helps."

"Andrew Hewitt was an alias this real art collector used to buy paintings. Who can quarrel with that? It's true. When the collector died—which the collector we find did—the museums were supposed to get all the paintings, including the ones in the vault. Only he waited too long to tell anybody about them, because some were stolen."

"But how do we spring the news? Who tells them?"

"Here's the best we can do. As long as one of the paintings is stolen, there's a reason for anyone who knew of it to want to be anonymous. The art collector had a friend who knew. The friend will write an anonymous letter to the museum today, explaining everything. He's old now, and for umpteen years the secret has been weighing on him. He wants to get it off his chest. The museum will notify the authorities in New York, who will get a warrant to open the vault. The seven or eight will go back where they belong. The ones Bernie bought legitimately will go to the museum. The whole process might take years, but it will get sorted out."

Ziegler gazed at her appreciatively. "It's not bad. We don't have to worry about faking an old document, because it's just this old person writing an anonymous letter now—like he happened to have the missing codicil to his friend's will."

"Right," said Jane. "But don't you think we should hold off on the assets that have a bizarre side until we've gotten rid of the easy stuff? Why fool around with this when we still have stocks and bonds and things?"

Ziegler nodded as he typed some codes into his computer. "I agree." He stopped and smiled at her. "I think we're going to hit that point at about eight tonight." He waited. "You hear what I said? We've written checks for fourteen point three billion dollars."

"That's why you were checking all those accounts when I came in?" said Jane. Her eyes had a glazed, faraway look. "It's almost over?"

Ziegler nodded. "Bernie ran dry last night."

16

Jane drove to Albuquerque the next morning and bought a Polaroid camera and four large soft-sided duffel bags with wheels on the bottoms. Then she stopped at a mailing service to buy thirty collapsed cardboard mailing cartons, labels, and tape. When she returned to Santa Fe she put Rita to work sorting envelopes by the zip codes of their return addresses, and bundling them. Bernie assembled and taped the mailing cartons. When they took a break, Jane posed each of them against the one remaining white wall that was bare, and took their pictures.

Rita watched hers slowly developing and becoming brighter. "That's so ugly," she said.

"It's for spare identity papers—licenses and things," said

Jane. "If they're not unflattering they don't look real." But
she relented and took three more.

Jane spent much of the rest of the day at pay telephones
making reservations. By the time she was back at the house,
the living room walls were lined with tall stacks of boxes. All
evening she and Rita filled the boxes, taped, and labeled
them. At eleven, Jane made her way down an empty aisle she
had left and settled onto the couch to sleep.

For the first time in weeks, Jane didn't awaken when Henry
Ziegler began to work. It was dawn when she walked into the
dining room to find him at his computer, scrolling down a
long list of numbers and names. He looked up.

Jane asked, "How is it going?"

"Great," he said. "It's going great. Bernie is amazing. Not
one account I transferred money to has problems. I've been
through every transfer once, and I'm just checking one more
time. He didn't memorize balances—why should he? But he
had a pretty good idea what was where. The signatures he put
on the withdrawals all got through. We're not going to have
any rubber checks."

"You wanted to know how he did it," said Jane. "That's
how. He's not remembering numbers. He's looking at the
image of a piece of paper he once saw. He just copies it." She
snapped her fingers. "Oh, one more thing. You did the Weinstein papers?"

"Transfers for the insurance premium were done last
night. All he has to do is sign." He looked toward the living
room, where the boxes were piled. "Have you figured out how
we get all these letters in the mail?"

"We start in two days," she said. "Want to see your
itinerary?"

"Sure."

Jane found her notes at the other end of the table. "You fly
from Albuquerque to Houston. You'll have two big rolling
duffel bags full of letters, which is what one person can handle
by himself. You'll check them at the airport. No letters go into
your carry-on bag. We don't want the security people going
through anything and seeing them. When you get to Houston,

mail the first pack of letters. Then you fly to St. Louis and mail
the second set. The third is Miami. In Miami I rented you a car.
You drive north: Atlanta, Charleston, Raleigh, Richmond,
Washington. There will be a second shipment of letters waiting
at your hotel in Washington, so you can refill your duffel bags.
You rest up, or whatever it is that you do, overnight, then keep
heading north. Stop in Baltimore, Wilmington, Philadelphia, a
couple of stops in New Jersey, a couple of stops north of New
York City. You turn east and make some stops in Connecticut
and Massachusetts, and end in Boston. That's your home base,
isn't it?"

"That's right," said Ziegler. "But that leaves us with an
awful lot of territory."

"I'm leaving at the same time—actually a little earlier. I've
got a flight to San Diego with a stop in Phoenix, so I can drop
the Arizona letters. In San Diego I have a rental car waiting,
so I drive north up the coast—L.A., Santa Barbara, San Francisco, and all stops in between. Then I fly to Seattle with a
stop in Portland. By then, my bags will be empty, so I'm
mailing more boxes to the hotel there. I fly to Minneapolis,
rent another car, and drive the Midwest—Milwaukee, Des
Moines, Kansas City, Chicago. I'll get my second mailing in
Chicago, rent another car, and head east through Cincinnati,
Cleveland, Pittsburgh, New York. Then I fly back here with a
stop in Dallas. We should both be finished in about a week."

Henry Ziegler stared down at his computer again, then
back at Jane. He said apologetically, "I've been so wrapped
up in setting this up—the mechanics of it—that I'm having
trouble believing it's almost over."

"I know," said Jane. "I keep going over everything to see if
we've forgotten something."

"Now are you ready to tell me what you did it for?"

Jane looked down at Ziegler's computer screen instead of
his eyes. It occurred to her that this was part of what computers were for. "Sure," she said. "I've come up with a lot of
reasons since we started, and they're all pretty sly. That's what
I am, you know."

"I noticed that."

"And all of the reasons sound okay when you say them to somebody else. I wanted to be sure the money never got to people who want me dead. I thought that maybe, if the money is really, verifiably gone, then it would give them a reason to stop looking for Rita. I wanted to help Bernie keep his son out of trouble. A lot of the time, while we were writing letters and signing checks, I would get pleasure thinking about some charity that had helped someone I know, and how much good a lot of money would do. But when I say the reasons to myself, they sound like excuses somebody made up to account for something she was going to do already."

"They do?"

"Yes," she said. "There are too many of them. The charities weren't the first thing I thought about. I thought of them because I once saw somebody loot a trust fund and make it look as though they were giving it all to charities. I noticed that it was hard to sort out afterward. It took the auditors a month or so to even trace how it had been done. I also noticed that when they had, it didn't bring the money back."

"That's what I've liked about it since I first heard the idea," said Ziegler. "Charities are all watched and audited. The IRS knows what they take in and every dime they spend. The IRS knows what each contributor gives, because he's going to deduct it on his tax return. They think that's all there is to know."

"How about you?" asked Jane. "Have you figured out why you did it?"

"I think I know more than I did the first night," Ziegler answered. "Charities are nice, but I never risked my life for them before, so I hardly think that can be what I'm doing now. I think it must be because I want to be a player—to be near the light and the fire. The side you're on isn't up to you. It's who you are. The only choice you have is to be in the place where big things are going on, or be someplace else."

Jane hesitated for a moment. It sounded too readily understandable, maybe even familiar. "I'd better get to work," she said softly. She moved into the living room and began arranging packets of envelopes and packing them in the four big duffel bags.

Jane squeezed her eyes closed and gritted her teeth. She wanted Carey. She wanted to be with him right now. She was tired of measuring her words. She wanted to talk, to tell her old friend everything, to find out what he thought.

As Jane stuffed the four big duffel bags with letters, she became aware that someone was behind her. She turned to see Bernie and Rita watching. Rita said, "Which one is mine?"

"What?"

"You got four bags. We each take one, right?"

"Wrong," said Jane. "Henry and I are going to mail the letters. I picked four bags because a person can handle two at a time."

"What are you talking about?" snapped Bernie. "You think I can't mail a letter?"

"It's not that you can't do it," said Jane. "It's that people might see you doing it."

"Nobody's looking for me," said Bernie.

"But if they see you, do you think they won't know who they're looking at?"

Rita scowled in frustration. "We did everything you asked for. We have a right to see this through. People are looking for me, but I dyed my hair, got new clothes . . . I've changed."

"You look terrific," said Jane. "But you don't look like a different person just yet." Finally, she stood up. She walked through the dining room and muttered to Ziegler, "Come in here." She walked into the kitchen, and the others followed her. They watched her open the cupboard and take four glasses down, bringing each one to the counter with a clack that made Ziegler wince. She took the newly opened bottle of white wine from the refrigerator, filled the glasses, and handed one to each of them.

Jane looked around her at each person in turn. Rita and Bernie stared at her stubbornly. Henry Ziegler just looked confused. Jane said, "Lady, gentlemen, and fellow philanthropists—and I mean all of those words sincerely—you have already accomplished the best thing you could have done with your lives if you had been born with the sense to start out with that in mind. You have given your all. Here's to you." She raised her glass and took a drink, then smacked it down on the counter.

"That does not mean, however, that I have joined with you in a brave little democracy. The world works on deals. I still have one with each of you. You have kept your end, and I'm going to keep mine. At the end of this, we are all going to walk away and go live some more. You should know that I've been in a few airports since this started, and each time there have been a few more big, ugly men standing around to watch the gates and the baggage claims, looking very hard at each face they see.

"The instant the first batch of checks hits the mailbox, the situation is going to get worse. In a matter of weeks, or even hours, the people who thought that money was theirs are going to start feeling wounded and frantic. They're already looking hard for Rita. If they see Bernie's face, it will take them a whole half-second to get over their shock that he's alive, and another half-second to come after him. This means that Bernie and Rita are going to stay in this house, invisible, while Henry and I mail the letters. End of speech, end of discussion." She walked out of the room.

Rita stared after her for a moment, her eyes unfocused and thoughtful. Ziegler looked uncomfortably at Rita, then went back to his computer.

Bernie patted her shoulder. "I guess she's right," he said softly. "We'll just lay low. It'll only be for a while."

Rita said, "That's not what you said when this started. You said they'd keep looking for forty years."

Bernie chuckled. "If they do, so what? You're a kid. You can do that kind of time standing on your head. I just finished doing fifty." He waited for Rita to see the humor in it, but it seemed to be lost on her. He left her alone in the kitchen.

The next morning, the men helped Jane load her big suit-cases into the car. Jane took Rita's arm and pulled her aside for a moment. "If nothing goes wrong, I should be back in a week or so. You have everything you'll need, so don't show your face if you don't have to." Something in Rita's expression worried her. "Are you all right?"

Rita shrugged. "Bernie and I will take care of each other."

Jane hugged her and then got into the car. Bernie and Ziegler came close to her window. "Keep her safe until I get back," she said to Bernie. "And yourself, too."

Bernie answered, "What can happen—sunburn?"

Jane looked at Ziegler. "Good luck, Henry."

As Jane drove off, she glanced at the small pile of letters on the seat beside her. She took a deep breath and blew it out. As soon as she mailed those first letters in Albuquerque, it would begin.

17

Paul Di Titulo walked out of the bank building into a dull glow of hazy sunlight. Immediately the humidity settled on his neck and shoulders like a weight. He walked ten steps on the sidewalk and began to feel sweat beading on his forehead. The expensive climate-control system in the fourth-floor conference room of the bank had made him more vulnerable to conditions in real-life Cleveland, where invisible bits of grit settled on the starched collar of a white shirt, and the perfumy smell of half-burned diesel fuel tickled his nasal passages and made him wait for a sneeze that never came.

As he walked down the street toward his car, he tried to think of ways to determine whether he was spending his time pondering nothing. He could call other charities to inquire whether unexpectedly large donations had arrived lately. He could try to find out something about this Ronald Wilmont who had sent the check to the Five C's. If Wilmont was a legitimate donor to the Cleveland Coalition of Caring Corporations and Citizens, then probably there would be someone in town who knew him, or at least knew what connection he had with Cleveland. If he had been born here, then there would be a birth certificate on file in the courthouse. If he'd once had a business here, then there would be a record of a business license. The archives of the *Plain Dealer* would almost certainly contain some reference to him. The property-tax rolls might have a deed with his name on it. There had to be some reason why a person would hand four million bucks to Cleveland.

He decided he would have a couple of secretaries at his office start working on Ronald Wilmont today. Di Titulo had to take every step he could to either prove his own suspicion was a daydream or prove it wasn't before he started making noises.

Di Titulo knew he was one of many people who had been watching whatever parts of the financial landscape were visible to them for the last month. Everybody in the country had been waiting, and by now there had probably been a few false alarms. He was sure that a man who blew the whistle without sufficient evidence would suffer later in prestige. For years, whatever he said or did would be denigrated and discounted. Just because men like him used computers and gold-nibbed fountain pens instead of cracking skulls with baseball bats didn't mean that they were exempt from the standards of behavior that being part of La Cosa Nostra implied.

As Di Titulo thought about it, he wasn't even positive that if he blew the whistle now, he wouldn't be the first. Being first was dangerous, but it had all the rewards. His job in the Castananza family had been to build himself into a pillar of the community, insinuate himself into the local establishment as a prosperous, astute businessman and public-spirited citizen. Getting himself invited to join the board of directors of the Five C's had been a verification of how well he had accomplished it. He had no idea how well face men in other families

in other cities had done. He decided he was not being arro-
gant to suspect that few had done as well as he had. And now,
because of that success, he had received an odd bit of inside
information that might mean something.

Everybody in the country had been waiting for signs of unusual financial activity. If somebody had popped old Bernie
Lupus for personal reasons, so be it. But the world seldom
turned on things done for personal reasons. So the whole
LCN had been waiting quietly to see if money in accounts all
over the country was going to start sprouting wings and
heading to roost in one place.

The whole story of Bernie the Elephant, the version Di
Titulo had heard since he was a kid, had been that he never
wrote anything down. But not all stories were true, and almost
none of them stayed true forever. It was just possible that, as
he got old and weak, Bernie the Elephant had begun to make a
ledger. The series of coincidences surrounding Bernie's death
had been mostly shrugged off by the old dons who had known
him. People died at stupid times for stupid reasons, they said.
But if what Di Titulo had heard was true, then it was not so
easy to dismiss. He had heard that after Bernie died, his house
in Florida had been searched. Nobody had found any papers,
but they had also not found Danny Spoleto, one of his bodyguards. And when one of the families—he heard it was the
Langustos, from New York—sent people to Detroit to see
what the Ogliaro family there had to say, they had found that
the mother of the head of the family had died the same day.
Maybe she had been killed because she knew something.

The older generation had gotten very attached to Bernie
Lupus, before anyone had known any better. He had kept
some of their money safe from the government, and from one
another, for a long time. When one of them wanted a million
bucks for some emergency, Bernie would have it delivered.
They weren't considering all of the implications; they were
just glad they didn't have to hide their money under their beds
anymore. But some younger minds had been dwelling on
Bernie Lupus for the past few years. They were better at arithmetic than their parents had been, and, to the extent that LCN

had not wasted its money educating them and staking them in businesses, they were more sophisticated about money. A few of them had begun to consider the potential of Bernie the Elephant. He had been taking in money for about fifty years and, the story went, investing it.

If he had put just a million dollars in a bank account that first year at five percent, then it would have doubled every fourteen years. That would be twelve point seven million by now. And the old guys didn't seem to know that he almost certainly had not done that. The IRS would have taken its cut. More likely, he had spread it around in places where the tax bite had not been big and instantaneous. He had probably put a lot of it in home-state municipal bonds, where there were no taxes, gold, offshore banks, real estate, and stocks. That was the one that made Di Titulo's mouth water. Since 1929, long before Bernie had begun remembering things, the stock market had averaged ten percent a year. That one million would be a hundred and thirty million by now.

But the real attraction was a possibility that had been floating around since Bernie was young. What LCN really needed to do was move the money that came in from labor-intensive activities like gambling, prostitution, extortion, drugs, and so on into safe, reliable businesses. Everybody knew that. In fact, that was the goal to which Di Titulo owed his existence. But there was a bigger, more tantalizing possibility that had never come to pass. If the LCN families saved their profits, pooled their resources, and used the face men wisely, they could start owning major corporations. The story was that they had never been disciplined enough to save, were never trusting or trustworthy enough to pool anything. But what Di Titulo and a few others thought when they heard the stories of Bernie the Elephant was that maybe they had.

If he had bought in early enough and acquired enough shares at the beginning, then automatic reinvestment, stock splits, and stock in small companies that got taken over by big companies for more stock would have multiplied the money incredibly over fifty years. LCN might already be majority owners of General Motors, IBM, AT&T, General Electric, and Coca-Cola, and not ever suspect it. The stock could be in five hundred different names known only to Bernie Lupus.

It might all be wrong: Di Titulo had no way of knowing what Bernie Lupus had done with all that money. But if any of Di Titulo's assumptions were correct, then the whole half-century Bernie Lupus episode was one of those wacky ideas that could have worked. It was Hannibal pulling his end run across the Alps on elephants to take over Rome for Carthage. A couple thousand years later, Rome was like an enormous palace full of shiny cars and women wearing designer dresses, and it took an archaeologist to tell you where the hell Carthage used to be. People forgot that it could have been the other way around.

But maybe Paul Di Titulo had just happened to be looking in the window on the day they forgot to pull the shade down. He had studied the finances of the Five C's for years, in the hope that someday he might find a safe way to divert a portion of the money that came in. It was only a coincidence that he had been there to hear about the Wilmont donation. And it took astuteness and imagination to understand that money moving into a charity in Cleveland just might have something to do with the death of Bernie Lupus. Everybody had assumed that what would happen was a steady stream of money flowing into some guy's bank account. But Di Titulo knew that the sign might not be anything that obvious. It might be any unusual money moving anywhere. If somebody was liquidating big investments, he might very well need to dump a bit of it in charities. He might even do it to test a route for moving bigger money later—get a brokerage and a bank used to the idea that Ronald Wilmont was a zillionaire who wrote big checks.

Di Titulo could see his car parked another hundred feet away, and it made him feel pleased with himself. He loved the look of his brand-new Cadillac Eldorado. He had gotten an insane discount on it, because he had bought three GMC tractor-trailer rigs this month for his company. While he was at the lot, he had made a show of wishing he could afford a car

too. That was what worming your way into the little brother-
hood of above-the-surface business did for you.

He reached into his pocket for his keys and fingered the
remote-control unit on his key chain. It was one designed
for women who left their cars in dark parking garages. They
could pop the door locks and turn on the lights before they
got there. It was silly at noon on a respectable street in Cleveland on a hot summer day, but the sooner he was in the car
and the engine was running, the sooner the air-conditioning
would kick in.

Di Titulo gave a squeeze, and he felt as though someone
had thrown a bag of rocks against his chest. A puff of hot
wind seared his face and hands, tugged his coattails, and
threw his silk necktie over his shoulder. He found himself
lying down. His ears were ringing before he was aware that
there had been a sound, and in his vision a patch of green
floated in jerky puppet-jumps before the flash of the explosion emerged from his addled memory.

After a time Paul Di Titulo recovered enough to roll onto
his side and look down. His clothes weren't ripped or burned,
and he seemed to have feeling in his arms and legs. He didn't
entirely trust that sensation, though. There might be some
horrible pain that movement would trigger, so he moved his
arms carefully and pushed himself to a sitting position. He
watched the bright orange flames flickering up and down the
length of his new Eldorado.

Di Titulo watched the waves of heat rising to make the tall
buildings beyond them bend and wiggle, and understanding
came to him. He had picked a rotten time to spend six hundred thousand on new trucks, and a worse time to be seen
driving a Cadillac with the dealer's stickers still on it.

As he got to his feet, he felt a wetness on his chest, and he
looked down with alarm at the spots of blood that were appearing on his white shirt. In a second he realized that the
blood was coming from above. His nose was bleeding. He
touched it. It didn't seem to be broken. The moving air had
just slapped him in the face. But he gave himself over to a
moment of despair. Some family had decided that Paul Di

Titulo was involved in Bernie Lupus's death. It was a sign of
what mouth breathers some of these guys were, how impov-
erished their imaginations, how stunted their brains. Whoever had managed to get control of Bernie Lupus's money
wouldn't reveal his crime in the form of three new trucks and
a Cadillac. He would walk away from anything as paltry as Di
Titulo Trucking and not bother to lock the front door. He
would have more money than a small country, all nicely laun-
dered and salted away a generation ago.

Di Titulo turned and walked unsteadily away from the fiery,
blackening wreckage of his beautiful new car. He would find a
pay phone and call Al Castananza himself. This was what
bosses were for—to get the other bosses off your back. As he
walked, he decided to tell him the rest of it too. Let the Cas-
tananzas use their time and money to look into the donation.
This had already gotten too big and ugly.

18

Di Titulo sat in the airplane for over an hour beside Al Castananza listening to engine sounds. The second in command, Castananza's old friend Tony Saachi, had told Di
Titulo the rules while he was waiting in the car for the old
man to collect his things. He had said it impersonally, in an
even, genial tone. People like Di Titulo were not expected to
speak except to answer questions. They would go where
they were told and do as they were told, and, if all went well,
they would come home. If they said things in public, they
might not.

Di Titulo had asked, "Do you think it's really necessary for
me to come at all?"

Tony Saachi had smiled; his long spade-shaped teeth looked
ghastly and his face was a skull. "Al likes you. It's a favor."

"What kind of favor?"

"If he goes and you're here, then whoever blew up your car
takes another crack at you. These bomb things are embar-
rassing. I would guess this time maybe they'd throw a bag
over your head and run a chain saw through the bag. They
won't do anything if you're with Al."

Di Titulo stared at the headrest of the seat in front of him.
He heard Saachi's voice from a distance. "You should have
been with us in '87 when the Castiglione thing broke. Nearly
two hundred guys went, just like that, in one night."

He spent the flight with the earphones in his ears and the
sound turned off, considering the strangeness of fortune. He
could remember when he was a kid, thinking about the rich
and powerful people who seemed to him to actually run the
city. He used to picture them sitting around a big poker table
in a smoke-filled room like the ones where people said deals
were made. There would be the owner of the Indians, the
owner of the Browns, the mayor, a couple of presidents of big
companies that signed every third father's paycheck, and Big
Al Castananza. That was what the papers used to call him in
those days, before it had become more fashionable to use
quotation marks. Now they said Alphonse "Big Al" Castananza, 69: always his age, as though they were counting the
days until he died. Di Titulo had never been this close to him
before, so the celebrity still affected him. He leaned away
into the aisle to stay out of accidental competition for the
armrest between them, and after an hour, his spine felt as
though it had been rotated a full turn at the pelvis.

When the plane landed in Pittsburgh, he followed Castananza to a pay telephone and watched him not dial it. A man
wearing aviator glasses who looked a little like a pilot
stepped up and stood beside him, then ushered Castananza
along the concourse without ever looking at Di Titulo.

They took the elevator to the ground floor and stepped out
to the curb. A car with tinted glass pulled up at their feet and
they were in motion before Di Titulo noticed that the man had

not come with them. The driver never spoke, and didn't appear to look at the two men in the back seat. Di Titulo watched Castananza's face. As they passed under street lamps, a stripe of light would move down it and then leave it immersed in darkness again. Castananza's small eyes were directed forward in a sleepy gaze, as though he were unaware that anyone was looking. The jowls spilled over the rim of the stiff white collar, and his jaw was loose, not tight and working like Di Titulo's.

Several unwelcome hypotheses flickered to life in Di Titulo's mind. Maybe the old man wasn't looking at him because the purpose of the trip was to deliver him for execution. Maybe the old man's summons had been intended to bring them both for execution. No, the old man must know when an invitation was real and when it wasn't. But how could he know? Bosses were killed all the time.

Slowly, the conclusion began to seem inevitable. Castananza couldn't know. The small, unmoving eyes looked like the glass-bead eyes of a stuffed animal. He had been in this position for thirty-five years, and he had learned to live with it—no, learned to get along without actually living. He had known since the beginning that any time he stepped through a doorway, the muzzle might already be pointed at him, so he had killed off that part of his brain. Di Titulo began to sweat.

Di Titulo wondered what he himself looked like to observers. He might very well look like a bodyguard. What else could he be? They would take him down first, and he would never see it coming. He grasped for a hint of hope. Maybe he would never even feel it.

The car seemed to be slowing down, so he looked over the driver's shoulder as it pulled up to the curb. There seemed to be nothing around here—the parking lot of a plaza behind them, a row of unlighted store windows across the street, a trash can. Castananza got out, so Di Titulo got out and joined him on the sidewalk while the car pulled away. Castananza turned to look up the street, looked at his watch, then looked down the street, but he seemed to have no impulse to say anything.

The bus grew out of the darkness like an approaching locomotive. The only way that Di Titulo could even discern the shape was by forcing his mind to fill in the space between the bright headlights and the lighted marquee above the windshield that bore the single word CHARTER. The bus glided to the curb with a hiss, and Di Titulo tried to see inside, but the windows were smoked glass that looked opaque. The flat, featureless side of the bus was painted a glossy dark color that simply reflected distant street lamps but seemed to have no quality of its own. As he followed Castananza to the steps, he looked to his left three times, but still could not tell whether it was more gray, or green, or blue.

The door wheezed shut behind him, and the bus began immediately to accelerate while he was still wedged on the bottom step. The driver was another man like the one at the airport. He was in his thirties and had close-cropped hair and an unmemorable, expressionless pilot face. He ran up through the gears with precise, effortless motions that made him look like an automaton.

The bus reached cruising speed and it was easier to stand, so Castananza climbed the rest of the way to the aisle. Di Titulo stepped up after him. As his head came high enough to see over the first seat, he looked toward the back of the bus. There were about five rows of empty seats, but beyond them, at the rear of the bus, the normal seats ended and there were two long bench seats, like enormous couches, and a long table in the aisle. There were men sitting around it.

Castananza moved down the aisle to the back, and as he went farther, Di Titulo could see past him. There were a few faces he had seen before. There were the Langusto brothers, Phil and Joe. He recognized John Augustino, and a man named DeLuca from one of the Chicago families. There was one he knew everyone had seen, because it had been in magazines for thirty years. It was Giovanni "Chi-chi" Tasso of New Orleans. The man with him must be his son—what was his name?—Peter? Yes, Peter.

Castananza's approach was acknowledged with friendly mutterings: "Good to see you, Al," and "Mr. Castananza," from the younger ones. Castananza stopped at the head of the table and held himself steady by wrapping a beefy hand around the overhead bar. "This is our friend Paul Di Titulo," he said.

Some of the men seated around the table nodded vaguely at Di Titulo. A few others stared at him for a couple of heartbeats, not in greeting but as though they were memorizing his face. Castananza said pointedly, "He's like my left arm." Di Titulo's breath caught in his throat. It was a lie. But the others seemed to take no interest in him.

"What do you think of my bus?" It was John Augustino from Pittsburgh.

Castananza looked around himself critically, glanced in the direction of the bathroom door, fiddled with the drink holder in the seat beside him, then peered up at the television set built into the wall above the space where the back window should have been. He shrugged. "Seems like a nice bus. You make anything off it?"

"Business is just so-so. I bought five of them. I do pretty fair during the football season if the Steelers are doing good. Off-season, I do runs to Atlantic City. But five is too many. You want to think about buying one, you talk to me. I'll give it to you at cost."

Castananza answered, "If the Steelers get their ass kicked, I'll give you a call." A few of the men around the bus looked up with little smiles. "Then you'll give me one below cost."

Di Titulo felt a little better. The bus wasn't some weird, ghostly death ship. It was just part of a business. Di Titulo felt comfortable in the world of business. It was all simple, straightforward propositions and simple responses. Everybody's motive was the same, and how passionate it was could be measured in numbers.

Di Titulo felt the bus slowing down again, and he looked past the Langusto brothers at the lights outside the tinted windows. The bus came to a stop at the curb, the door opened, and Di Titulo held his breath.

The three men who climbed aboard were frightening. The first looked like a professional wrestler, with a flat, pushed-in nose and a mouth that seemed to begin just under his ears and stretch six inches in a horizontal line. The two young men who came after were wearing jeans and windbreakers like teenagers, and they scanned the bus and the street behind them like Secret Service men. Di Titulo had no trouble inducing a premonition of these two pivoting to spray the back of the bus with bullets, but they simply followed the big man as he walked back.

The wrestler stopped and his big frog mouth opened. He spoke politely to the older men. He said, "Chi-chi, Al, John, Joe, Phil." To the others he said, "Hi, guys." He stepped aside. "These are my cousins, Mitch and Steve Molinari."

The big man had to be Salvatore Molinari from New York. Di Titulo noted that the two young men were given the same unenthusiastic stare that he had received, but not Molinari. The bus was beginning to fill up with extremely important people. The gathering of these men was like the building up of an enormous electrical charge, and Di Titulo felt uneasy as the bus stopped again and again. It began to seem to him that the bus would burn up, or the universe would seek to equalize this intense concentration of power in a bolt of lightning that would incinerate him.

As the bus moved from stop to stop, the talk among the notables was idle banter with obscure references to subjects Di Titulo knew nothing about. He noticed that the younger men seldom spoke, but smiled or chuckled politely when the bosses did. Finally the bus began to build up speed in increments that could only indicate a sustained stretch of open road.

John Augustino stood up in the aisle at the end of the table and said, "I'd like to thank you all for coming. The bus is going to keep moving while we talk. That way nobody can do much overhearing with a directional mike. It's been swept for bugs, and we've got cars ahead and behind to watch for cops. If we can ever talk, now is the time." He paused and looked somber. "I know we all share regret at the death of Bernie the Elephant. I think now is the time to express regrets of my own. It was my father who brought

Bernie into our thing fifty years ago, and I apologize to each of you for what happened."

"Yeah, yeah." The bored, ironic tone shocked Di Titulo. He turned and saw that it was Victor Catania, from New York. "Bernie's dead, and you're sorry." Two or three of the younger men stiffened, their shoulders flexed down from their necks, and their hands suddenly looked very empty. But Catania paid no attention. He adopted a parody of Augustino's master-of-ceremonies tone. "And let me take this heartfelt opportunity to say I told you so. And I told Bernie so, too. I had computer experts, I had everything set. Everything he knew could have been on disks by now, but the old bastard thought he was immortal. First, he had to take time to get everybody's permission, he had to have time to collect his thoughts, he had to be sure everybody was happy."

"It wasn't his fault that he got shot, Victor," said DeLuca.

Catania rolled his eyes. "So he got shot. The man was seventy-two years old. If it wasn't that, it would have been a coronary." Di Titulo noticed that the slim, erect Catania had not taken wine like the others. He was drinking bottled water.

Molinari said, "He's dead, and when we're through talking, he'll still be dead. I could have gone across town to hear Catania say he told me so. I thought I got invited here because somebody had a plan."

It was Phil Langusto who spoke. "Let's get to that. From the beginning, we all assumed that nobody dropped the hammer on Bernie without thinking he had a way to get to that money."

The others considered the statement self-evident, so only a few nodded or mumbled affirmative words.

"And everybody was watching to see the minute when any big money got moved. We've had a lot of cooperation, a lot of tips. And today seems to be the day. Big money is moving." Langusto paused. "Only it ain't all moving in one direction."

"What the hell does that mean?" asked Catania.

"It's complicated," said Langusto. "My brother can probably explain it better."

Joe Langusto cleared his throat. "Here's what we've seen so far. Somebody, somehow, got a list of the accounts where our money was stashed. The accounts are being closed."

Catania interrupted. "If you know it's our accounts, why couldn't you take it first?"

"We didn't know," said Joe Langusto. "You got a guy inside a brokerage. He notices a sell order on a big account. It's been there since the fifties, and it's got nine million in it. Because he belongs to us, he runs a credit check on the account owner. Besides this nine million, this man has got nothing. He's got no record of charging anything, because he's never had any credit cards. He has no driver's license, no car registered to him. Pretty soon you realize you're looking at a man who never existed. But the money is already gone."

DeLuca said, "Nine million? That's not necessarily ours. It could be some civilian."

"We've found a lot of these guys over the past few days. The money goes to a bank, then to some strange place—a corporation, some nonprofit organization. We've been trying to hunt down the accounts, find out where the money is going from there. So far we're not up with it. My guys tell me it's the kind of thing where it takes months to follow the trail, and when you lose it at any point, you're done. We don't need anybody's help to do the tracing, but we're picking up odd things. Al, I think you found one."

"Yeah," said Castananza. "My guy Di Titulo found something." He looked at Di Titulo. "Tell them."

Di Titulo had been rankling at the little lecture. Listening to Joe Langusto was like listening to all the New Yorkers he had ever met. Everything there was bigger, better, and closer to the action. Everybody else was a yokel. And these bosses were worse. Catania, the Langustos, Molinari all spoke with the assurance that each of their families was big—four or five hundred instead of sixty or eighty—and there were five of them in one city. But when he heard his name, his resentment turned to fright.

He straightened. "I'm on the board of a charity in Cleveland. Today they got a donation of four million, which is about a year's goal. The money came from a man named Ronald Wilmont. I tried all afternoon to get information about him, but couldn't find any. I called a few other charities, and every one I called had gotten a big donation today from some person or group they never heard of."

"My dog had fifty fleas today," Catania announced. "So did all the other dogs in the neighborhood."

"I don't get it," said Molinari. "What the hell is going on?"

Catania smirked. "Nothing. Forget it. You got a year with big ups and downs in the stock and bond markets. The big ups, people make money. The big downs come because they sell. When they do, they got to pay taxes on the profits. So they take a charitable deduction."

DeLuca had been lost in thought. "I'm not so sure. Four million to some charity in Cleveland is nothing. You're right. But I got a little story too. I've got a construction company. My Chicago office got a call today from a guy who ferrets out jobs for me. The Red Cross has been talking about a new building for ten years. Today, they say they have the money in hand, and they're preparing specs. An hour later, I get a call about renovating an old building for a Boys and Girls Club."

"More fleas in Chicago," said Catania. "Look, I'm as sure as anybody that our money is going to start moving eventually. But when it does, it's not going to a charity in Cleveland."

Di Titulo took a chance and spoke. "May I say one more thing?"

Nobody responded, but Catania watched him with suppressed amusement.

"There are a lot of reasons why they might do something like this."

"Such as?" Catania looked eager. Di Titulo decided he was waiting to prove Di Titulo was an idiot—a small-town idiot.

"One is just what you said—the IRS. I don't know how much money Bernie the Elephant was holding, but this might be a way to launder it. You have fake people donate it to a fake foundation. The fake foundation hands five percent of it to a real charity. Maybe it pays ten percent to a phony management company that owns the building it doesn't occupy, ten to an advertising company that's supposed to bring in new donations, twenty-five percent to imaginary employees, fifty percent to fake charities. You end up with ninety-five percent of the money, because it never left your hands. The imaginary donor owes no taxes: he gave it all to charity. The foundation has met federal standards by a mile. They only have to give away five percent a year. The best part is, it's July. Nobody has to file any papers until next April."

The men in the bus were suddenly animated. Advisers and counselors whispered to bosses in muffled tones. Finally, Molinari began to scowl. "You know a hell of a lot about this stuff, don't you?"

Di Titulo's heart stopped for a moment, then began again at a quicker tempo. He could think of nothing to say.

Al Castananza shrugged his big shoulders to settle into his seat more comfortably. "That's one of the things I have on my mind. Somebody blew up Di Titulo's new Caddy today. I would like to say two things. The first is that nobody in my organization killed Bernie or moved any of the money. Killing my people doesn't help anybody." The men in the bus watched him in silence, as though stricken by a common paralysis. "The second is that if anybody wants to play with bombs, I got guys who can do that kind of work too." His eyes flicked to Catania and bored into him. "I got one who could drop the Empire State Building so the top hit Thirty-ninth Street."

Catania held up both hands and shook his head. "Hey! Al! I didn't do that."

"I did," muttered DeLuca. He focused his eyes on Castananza. "I apologize. I had a tip." The apology had nothing to do with Di Titulo.

The air in the bus seemed to retain a steamy quality, but some of the men squirmed and shuffled their feet, as though the tension was dispersing. There was a sudden, deep growl, and Di Titulo involuntarily followed it with his eyes. It had come from the big chest of Chi-chi Tasso. He was the oldest man in the bus, a massive lump of fat settled in the wide rear seat, and it had not been clear that he had been listening. He said, "That's why I'm here too. I lost a guy a week ago. It made me sick. This isn't the first time we started killing each other for nothing."

Augustino spoke. "You're right, Chi-chi. Let's not turn on each other. The one behind it is obvious. Bernie gets shot in Detroit, and this bagman, Danny Spoleto, who used to be his bodyguard, disappears. So does the maid at his house in Florida. I had two guys there the day after they left."

Tasso gave a deep laugh. "What good are they? You could have read it in the papers like I did."

Molinari said, "I had some guys waiting in Spoleto's old neighborhood. He never showed up."

Tasso muttered, "You two should get together and look for some new guys." There was a nervous chuckle in the bus.

Phil Langusto said, "Has somebody eliminated Vincent Ogliaro? I mean, this happened in Detroit, right?"

Catania smirked. "He's in jail."

Langusto snorted. "I know. And when you were in jail, you never ordered a hit, did you?"

Catania said, "His mother got killed in this thing. You think he set it up to kill his own mother?"

Langusto said, "I don't know. What the hell was she doing at the airport?"

Tasso cleared his throat. "Let me tell you something about Vincent Ogliaro." He looked at the men around him. "He does things himself—like his father. You're lucky his father isn't alive to hear this. Mickey Ogliaro would have taken your arm off and beat you to death with it."

"I don't think Ogliaro did it either," said Catania. "It has to be Danny Spoleto."

Tasso looked at Catania with pity, then spoke to the others. "Of all the dumb talk I've heard since I moved to New Orleans, this is right up there with 'The South will rise again.' Listen to what these guys are saying. All this money is moving here and there: you can barely follow it yourself. This kid was a bodyguard, a pair of eyes with a gun attached.

If Bernie got his throat cut and he had a million in cash lying around the house that ain't there anymore, you look for a bodyguard."

Catania was offended. "You say Phil's stupid to go after Ogliaro. I'm stupid to go after the bodyguard. Who do you think is moving all this money around?"

Tasso said, "I think Bernie found Jesus."

"I think Jesus found Bernie," snapped Catania.

"It's not a joke." Tasso's angry stare silenced the laughter. "You said before that Bernie was old enough to know that he was going to die even without a bullet. He sure as hell was. I think it's just possible that Bernie gave all our money away."

"He's dead, Chi-chi."

"He was perfectly capable of setting all this up in advance."

"And then what? Did he fly to Detroit and shoot himself six times?"

"I'm saying that you look around for who has our money and you come up with a bodyguard. You come up with Vincent Ogliaro, who is a tough son of a bitch, but no mastermind. You come up with Al's bookkeeper in Cleveland. You think a guy who just stole billions of dollars is going to buy himself a Cadillac?"

Di Titulo was stung, but this was not a good time to claim that he was more than a bookkeeper.

Tasso looked around him at the men on the bus. "The only one we know with absolute certainty could move this money around is the only one you don't think of: Bernie Lupus. He moved it around in the first place. He knew where all of it was, he knew what names he used when he put it there."

Phil Langusto's expression was so respectful that Di Titulo could see that the only thing behind it could be sarcasm. "Chi-chi," he said quietly. "I'm just not sure how Jesus is implicated."

Tasso shrugged his shoulders so his pendulous belly bounced. "You think I'm old and crazy. Maybe I am. I can tell you, after my triple bypass, I had a bout of that myself. They gave me the last rites a couple of times. I had a lot of strange thoughts in that intensive care unit. And Bernie—

who knows what might have been going through his head? Some weird holy-roller religion, maybe. What do we know? He was some kind of Polack."

"They're Catholics," said Molinari.

"The Pope is a Polack," DeLuca added helpfully.

"It doesn't matter," said Tasso. "I think that the only possibility I've heard that makes sense is that Bernie set this up before he died. Everybody's saying he must have written it down somewhere, or it couldn't be moving now. So am I. I don't know why he would. Maybe it was just that somebody pissed him off with some scheme like replacing him with a computer." His eyes passed across Catania and then to the others. "If we don't know where he put our own money, how does anybody else know?"

Phil Langusto shrugged. "That's what we've got to find out."

Suddenly, Molinari spoke. "Where's Frank Delfina?" Di Titulo saw several heads turn to face Molinari, but others were looking around the bus, as though they were searching for Delfina in vain. Molinari raised his eyebrows. "Well, shouldn't he be here?"

DeLuca drew himself up straight. "I'm here," he said. "I didn't think there was any reason to invite more of my guys than necessary."

Molinari's eyes shot to Tasso—not in puzzlement, Di Titulo saw, but in silent communication.

Tasso said, "That wasn't the deal the Commission set up, Tommy. He's not part of your family anymore. He should be here. Everybody should be here who laid off money with Bernie."

DeLuca could see that his response had put him in danger. He shrugged. "I didn't mean I told him not to come. Like you said, he's got his own family now. I just meant, I didn't invite him myself. This isn't my meeting."

Tasso turned to Langusto. "Did anybody invite him?"

Phil Langusto looked at his brother, then at John Augustino, then back at the rest of the men. "We'll check on it." He took a deep breath, to signal that he wanted to change the subject. "I think we're getting ahead of ourselves. We're trying to reach a conclusion, and we don't have to. All we've got to do is stop this before it goes any farther."

Joe Langusto said, "Nobody seems to know how much money it is. I remember our father telling us it was at least a billion dollars when we were kids. To be conservative, let's say it's five by now. If there's anything any of you can do in the next week or two that will bring in that much extra money, go ahead. What we'd like to do is get it back."

"How are we going to do that?" asked DeLuca.

"We turn up the heat. Do everything at once. We look for any sign that more money is on the move. If there's five billion, the really big stuff hasn't budged yet. We put people on tracing all of these charity donations that already showed up back to their source."

Al Castananza said, "This isn't any different from what we've been doing."

Joe Langusto answered, "We've got more to work with now. We don't ignore any theory, any possibility. Some people think Ogliaro is involved. So let's watch his guys. See who visits him, have people on his cell block keep an eye on him. He might be able to order a hit without anybody noticing, but he can't run money all over the place without attracting some attention."

Catania sighed in weary resignation.

Di Titulo kept him in the corner of his eye, but didn't let it be known that he was watching him.

Phil Langusto said, "Some people think that Danny Spoleto was involved. So let's look harder for him, too." Di Titulo watched him hold up a photograph that had been blown up from a snapshot. Di Titulo could see a clean-cut, athletic-looking man in his late twenties or early thirties. He was positive that he would not have recognized him again in five minutes.

Langusto continued, "There's the maid." He held up another photograph. "This is the shot we had taken of her when she came to work for Bernie." Di Titulo could see an enlarged shot of a girl with shoulder-length, stringy blond hair. She looked younger than his own daughter. She was just a child. He waited for somebody to say something—someone strong and powerful—but nobody interrupted Phil Langusto's monologue.

"We've got five thousand copies of each of these pictures. What we want to do is cover the country. We've already got guys in airports and a few hotels. What we'd like to do is have everybody out looking—every made guy, every stringer, every wanna-be."

Al Castananza frowned. "Are you thinking we're going to find the two of them together?"

Langusto shrugged. "Anything's possible, but some are more likely than others. I think that if somebody's mailing letters with checks in them, it ain't Vincent Ogliaro, and it sure as hell ain't the ghost of Bernie."

Di Titulo sat still as the bosses around him accepted stacks of pictures and their bodyguards and lieutenants and coat holders stowed them in flight bags and briefcases. Di Titulo had not felt motion sickness since he was a child, but he felt it now. He looked at the window across from his seat. He could see the dim shapes of trees slipping past and, far away, fixed lights that were no bigger than stars. It wasn't supposed to be like this.

19

Frank Delfina wondered whether he should have done something about Augustino's bus after all. He had listened to a plan that his lieutenants liked, but had rejected it. He had spent an hour in his Jersey City cannery listening to the route, hearing his guys tell him the details, and had even examined some of the equipment. The presentation had been impressive. They had shown him how the stop-stick worked. He could easily accept the idea that the device probably didn't look like anything when headlights shone on it at sixty miles an hour. When the guys waiting out of sight beyond the reach of the headlights pressed a button, a row of spikes popped up from the flat base and punctured all the tires. Then a picked team of men would swarm over the bus like ants on a dead carcass, blow the doors at both ends with explosives, toss in a couple of grenades, and spray the interior with MAC-10s until the blood in the aisles was up to their ankles.

He had listened politely and thoughtfully. It was probably the only time in a generation when that many heads of families had been in one small, enclosed space all at once. But something in the back of his mind had remained hungry and unsatisfied. The men in front of him were credible. He knew they were not likely to be hesitant in the execution, or likely to panic afterward and fail to slip back into the darkness and escape. All of them had dropped the hammer on people before. They exuded fitness and strength and competence. He just didn't trust military-style operations that required perfect timing and mechanical efficiency. Once in a while they worked for armies, but not always. If any detail of the plan went wrong, Delfina was dead. And creating devastation around him was not even what he wanted.

"No, I don't think so," he had said. "It's not for me."

They had all looked at him like dogs that had smelled rabbit and then heard the click of the clasp as the chain was snapped onto their collars.

It had reminded him that he was alone. He could get people like this to take risks for him, but he couldn't get them to grapple with the complexity, the subtlety of events. Each act set off a series of reactions, and each of the reactions caused some divergence in other sequences of events. Yes, he wanted to get his hands on the money Bernie the Elephant had hidden. Yes, if most of the other people who had a realistic chance of getting to it were dead, it would increase his chances. But no, he didn't want to do it.

A massacre would have brought on a period of anarchy across the whole country, and that was not good for anyone. A few thousand soldiers in a dozen cities would suddenly be cut adrift without leaders. Undoubtedly they would regroup and reconfigure, but not instantly, and not in predictable ways. Everywhere there would be internal fighting to determine who would take the places of the dead men, and Delfina could not exert influence to determine the winners. When the struggle was over, there would be a dozen new faces, or even three dozen—who could say that the big families wouldn't split?—for Delfina to try to deal with.

While the fighting was going on, the rivals who were always waiting on the fringe for the Mafia to weaken would be eagerly streaming into pieces of territory, making inroads into businesses everywhere. The value and security of the mob's holdings would be drastically eroded.

Delfina's family would be more vulnerable than anyone's. The others had fixed, solid ground that they could defend. His empire was a network of filaments extending vast distances, like a spider web. He didn't have collectors and bagmen, he moved money on the Internet. He depended on the slow, lumbering dinosaurs to keep his enterprises safe. When he sent five of his people to visit a business competitor in Cleveland, what he was doing was invoking in the competitor's imagination the hundred soldiers that Al Castananza had within a mile of that office, and who would never go away. The fact that Castananza had no knowledge of what Delfina was doing or interest in it was not something the competitor could know.

Delfina had held his hand. But now he squinted under the glare of the New Orleans sun and wondered. He drove along Iberville Street looking for the corner, then realized that he must have missed it at least a block back. He spotted a big old Buick pulling out of a parking space and decided to take it. He eased his rental car into the space, then sat still for a moment in the air-conditioned atmosphere while he checked his street map. Yes, it had to be about a block behind him. He glanced in the rearview mirror, and he could see the four-story building just as he remembered it. He had come from his hotel south of here this time. Last time he had approached it from the north, so he had been looking on the wrong side of the street.

He folded the map, turned off the engine, and got out of the car. The weight of the hot, humid air came down on him as he glanced at his watch and began to walk. He still had fifteen minutes, and that was good. Being late would have negated the effect he had constructed in coming alone and driving himself.

He walked into the yellowed marble lobby of the building and looked around for the elevator. There was only one, and it fit with the ornate, old-fashioned decoration of the place. There was a pair of shiny gold doors with a folding gate behind them and an elderly operator sitting on a high stool who pushed a lever to get you to the right, unmarked floor. The building had been a bank when Chi-chi Tasso was a child, and it still had that substantial, heavy look. Tasso had told him that he had owned it for a year before he noticed that the designs on the pillars and pressed into the plaster along the edge of the ceiling were copied from the filigrees and swirls on a one-dollar bill.

Delfina stepped into the elevator, and the white-haired operator said, "Top floor, sir?"

He nodded, and the man cranked his lever all the way down and jolted him upward. He could see the floors moving from floor to ceiling, first old brick and then a horizontal stripe of concrete and gold doors, then brick. The elevator came to a quick stop below the floor, and the man nudged it upward in little jerks until the concrete stripe was roughly the same level as the floor of the elevator, then pulled back the iron fence as the gold doors parted.

Delfina stepped out and walked along the shiny floor of the empty hallway. The door at the end swung open and a man in his thirties studied him with an expressionless face. "Hello, Mr. Delfina. Would you mind if I . . . ?"

Delfina held his arms up and let the man pat his shoulders, ribs, legs, then run his hands along his belt and the small of his back.

"Thank you, sir." He stepped aside and let Delfina walk into the next room. It was a reception area that had probably once contained a desk for a secretary, but now it was furnished with only a set of long couches along the walls, where six men sat smoking cigarettes and talking. They did not stir while Delfina walked to the open door, but when he had entered, one of them stood and closed the door behind him.

Tasso was sitting behind a big desk, his head wreathed in smoke from his cigarette, the sunlight that shot through the blinds illuminating some layers of it and leaving the others invisible. He half-stood to shake hands. "Frank," he said. "It's really nice of you to come all the way down here to see me. I'm sorry I couldn't meet you someplace, but it's hard as hell for me to travel now."

"It's okay, Chi-chi," said Delfina. "It's like a little vacation. My business never takes me down here, so—"

"It better not," said Tasso. His wide grin showed the way his teeth had come in at odd angles.

Delfina smiled. "I'll bet sometime you and I could do something together," he said. "It wouldn't have to be anything based in New Orleans."

Tasso nodded politely. "I've given it some thought," he said. "I always had you picked out as the smartest one of the guys coming up, but it's probably too late. I'm old, and the time when I could have done much for you is about over. You're established, and you probably know everything I know and a few things besides."

Delfina kept his smile unreadable and waited.

Tasso's wide, jowled face assumed a worried look. "The reason I wanted to talk to you is that I think I caught sight of a little problem the other night."

"Problem?" Delfina feigned a low-level alarm. "Another one. First it's Bernie Lupus, and now what?"

"Actually, we're still not past the Bernie Lupus problem. This is part of it. The other night, a bunch of us had a sit-down."

Delfina's low-level alarm appeared to intensify. "You did? You mean the Commission?"

"No," said Tasso, looking up at the ceiling. "Just the heads of families that had money that Bernie Lupus was holding for us." His eyes suddenly settled on Delfina. "I was kind of wondering why you weren't there."

Delfina said, "I wasn't invited. Nobody said anything to me."

Tasso muttered, "Well, that takes care of that question. But it does raise another issue, doesn't it? You had money with Bernie, didn't you?"

Delfina nodded solemnly. "Sure."

"Why?"

Suddenly the sharp little eyes were on him, but to Delfina it felt as though the big, thick fingers were poking his chest. "Why?" Delfina repeated.

"Yeah. By the time you had any, he was already getting old. The guys of his generation, like me, he bought us fifty years of security. Why would you hide money with him?"

Delfina said, "I'll tell you, because I know you'll keep this in confidence." He saw that Tasso didn't contradict him. "I had a couple of things in mind. When Castiglione was out, and DeLuca and I were supposed to split the family, think about my position."

"I know your position," said Tasso. "I helped invent it."

"DeLuca got the city. He could put money anywhere inside it. I would have had to carry it in a suitcase. I had to put it in places that were guaranteed for a while, until I could start using it. I didn't lay off much with Bernie, but some."

Tasso took a deep drag on his cigarette, then slowly blew the smoke out. "Bernie was guaranteed?"

"Sure he was. He had you and the others to protect him." His smile returned. "Is there any other way I could have had you all protecting my money?"

"Not that I know of." He looked at the cigarette as though he was reluctant to say good-bye to it, and then snuffed it out in his big glass ashtray. "I'm trying to protect you now."

Delfina could see that what he had said wasn't enough. "There was another thing. I didn't put money with Bernie for a lot of years, but Castiglione did. He was in it from the beginning, I heard."

"Practically," said Tasso. "In the beginning it was the Langustos. And the Augustinos were in it before it started, because they found him. Then the other New York families, then me and Castiglione and Castananza."

"That's a long time ago. When Castiglione was pushed out Tommy DeLuca and I were supposed to split everything."

Tasso nodded slowly. "There. Now I heard something that sounds like you thought of it. You figure you're entitled to the money Castiglione laid off with Bernie."

"Half of it, anyway," said Delfina. "That was money the family made. When the Commission took the family away from him and gave it to me and DeLuca, did they mean he could take the family's money to Arizona with him?"

"And that's why you put money with Bernie."

"Sure," said Delfina. "That way I kept up a relationship with Bernie. I thought if DeLuca kept bringing money to him, and I didn't, he would start to think of DeLuca as a straight one-for-one replacement for Castiglione. Then I lose out." He shook his head sadly. "Only we all waited too long to ask for the money. Now we all lose out."

Tasso shrugged. It looked like a sudden jump of his mountainous body. "It ain't over yet. That's why there was a meeting." He reached into his desk and pulled out the two flyers he had picked up on the bus. "This one is Danny Spoleto. Know him?"

"No."

"He came up in New York. He was Bernie's bodyguard for a while, then he was a bagman for a while. He went 'poof' the day Bernie died." He sighed. "Probably he heard about Bernie and heard people were looking for him at the same time, so he got scared. But they want to talk to him." He handed Delfina the picture of Rita Shelford. "This one is even less likely. She's just a kid, but she worked as a servant in Bernie's house."

"Did she disappear too?"

"That's what they tell me," said Tasso. "I'm not real hopeful that this is the way to find out who killed Bernie. But the Langustos and some of the others have been watching to see if big money started moving around, and they say it is.

They think somebody got a list Bernie kept, or something, and now they're washing the money. I'm giving it to you, for whatever it's worth, just so there's nothing everybody else knows that you don't know."

"Why?"

Tasso smiled in appreciation. "Now you're doing it. But I like things the way they are. I'm old. I'm not happy that Bernie died with some of my money stuck in his frontal lobe. And if anybody ends up with it, I'm going to go see them. I haven't skipped any meals. I don't need it. But I like things in balance." He glared at Delfina. "That's the lesson I learned from Castiglione," he said. "We let him get strong. We let him make side deals with some families in other places without telling the rest of us about it. He almost got too strong."

"Are you worried?"

"I move before I need to worry. That's why I'm telling you this. At the meeting Molinari asked why you weren't there. It sounded like he wondered if the reason was that you were the one who did Bernie."

"Me?" Delfina looked shocked.

"You're in a lot of places, and you're smart enough to know how to move money around if you had it. I think he's satisfied, but don't forget that the subject came up. If the money doesn't turn up, the idea could come back. You might want to at least make motions to help find these two."

"How did Molinari get satisfied?"

"That's the other thing you should know. Tommy DeLuca said, 'I didn't think I should bring more of my guys than necessary.' "

"The son of a bitch," said Delfina.

"Don't get mad," said Tasso. "You would have done the same thing if there was a chance to claim all the money Castiglione laid off instead of splitting it. Just keep it in mind, and you'll be okay. You weren't invited because DeLuca kept you out."

"I see," said Delfina. "If I know it, then it's neutralized, and you maintain balance."

"Not quite. You need to know one other thing," said Tasso.

"Molinari knew that Augustino had called the meeting, and that he did it because the Langusto brothers asked him to. If they told DeLuca but not you, then there could be a special relationship."

"You mean they'll back him if he says Castiglione's money goes to him?"

"Maybe. But now you know."

"Now I know. More balance."

"That's right. We could sit here and watch the heads of the families in Chicago and Pittsburgh making an alliance with one of the New York families. But it sounds a little familiar." He lit another cigarette. "That's all I have to say right now. Do what you want."

"Thanks, Chi-chi." He stood up. "If there's another meeting will you tell me?"

Tasso nodded. "I'm not going to sit here and watch everything get all screwed up."

Delfina went through the outer office and down in the elevator with the white-haired operator. It seemed to him that the temperature rose as he descended from floor to floor, until the lobby seemed like an oven. When the old man let him out, he closed the doors and the gate again. Delfina could see the little lights illuminating on the wall above the doors as he rose to the cooler floors.

Delfina walked to his car. He could barely touch the door handle without burning himself. He turned on the air-conditioning as high as it would go, rolled down the windows, and drove a few blocks before he closed them again.

When he reached his hotel room in the Vieux Carré, he saw that there was a fax waiting for him. He called Caporetto in Niagara Falls. "It's me."

"Sorry to bother you," said Caporetto, "but there's something new. We got a guy to pretend he was a cop and talk to the desk clerks at the hotel. The girl was really there. She checked in by herself, with her own credit card. Then, when she checked out, there was an older woman with her, who had them transfer the hotel bill to her card. But the girl had eaten in the restaurant and charged it to her card, not the room. That's why the charge stuck and we got it."

"What's the woman's name?"

"Kathleen Hobbs," said Caporetto.

"Did you run her?"

"Yeah. The card is real, but I think the woman may be a ringer. The card's about five years old, but it looks like she doesn't use it much. There's nothing recent, and nothing major on the credit report, either. No mortgage, no car payment, nothing bought on time."

"Of course she's a ringer. Would you have put that bill under your real name?"

"No."

Delfina began to pace his room, but the cord kept pulling him back to the desk. He looked down, and the flyers Tasso had given him were staring up at him. "Did you get her description?"

"Yeah. Tall—like five-nine—and thin—a hundred and twenty-five or thirty. Late twenties or early thirties and pretty, but not like a movie star. More like a dancer or something, lots of leg and kind of all elbows and sharp edges. Long black hair. Blue eyes."

Delfina said, "Get an artist, the way the cops do. Have him work with each of the clerks separately until they both agree you've got a perfect likeness. Then get it out as fast as you can. Fax it to all of our guys."

Delfina hung up and thought for a moment, then went to the folding stand by the wall and closed his suitcase. He just had time to catch his flight to San Diego.

20

Delfina stood on the right side of the fairway, ninety yards out from the flag. The eighteenth green was a perfectly smooth oval sloping downward toward him. He looked back across the fairway toward the other men in his foursome, then prepared to wait while they took their shots from farther out.

Jim Flaherty was the cause of this outing. Delfina watched him run his pudgy pink fingers through the red-blond wavy hair above his perpetual sunburn, then stare into his golf bag to select a club as though this were the Masters. Flaherty was a conscientious golfer, but barely a city councilman at all. A few miles south of here in the city hall, the council was meeting right now. Flaherty wasn't thinking about that. He was bent on digging his spiked shoes into the turf to get a better purchase for his swing.

Delfina knew that Flaherty had been born in a trailer park somewhere in a dry lake bed east of San Bernardino, but he had, as he put it, "bettered himself." That meant that the bribes and inside deals he had were beginning to add up. Delfina didn't resent his own investments in Flaherty, because Flaherty was sure to be around for a long time. He had shown a virtuosity in the weird language of local politics in this part of the country, which involved a wide vocabulary of coded statements about immigration of Mexicans and school prayer and a strong defense, all issues that local governments had nothing to do with. What Delfina did resent was that the inferiority complex about money that made him receptive also made him insist on talking business at places like golf courses and horse shows. Flaherty took a swing with what

185

looked to Delfina like a six- or seven-iron and landed on the green.

Delfina hated trudging around on a perfectly good day, sweating in the merciless southern California sunshine and even carrying his own golf bag, because neither he nor Flaherty could risk having a caddy overhear their conversation. He was glad that Flaherty was finally on the green, because it meant the ordeal was nearly over.

Delfina watched Mike Cirro, the young man he had brought with him on this trip. Cirro reached into his bag without appearing to consider one club superior to another, gripped it like a baseball bat, took a quick, choppy swing, and slapped the ball onto the hard, dry center of the fairway far in front of the green. But because he had hit it too hard with the wrong club, it bounced twice, rolled the last forty yards onto the green, and came to rest just above the cup.

Delfina shrugged and smiled at Flaherty, who seemed to be pondering questions of chance and the supernatural. Then they all waited for Pucci. He was the manager of the Parliament Park chain of grocery stores that Delfina owned, and Delfina was feeling good about him today. He had made Flaherty into a receptive listener by the second hole. At that point Flaherty could think of no reason why a supermarket couldn't be built in Old Town, offhand, but he would need to check with a lot of interests before he could propose a zoning variance. The checking stage had only lasted until the tenth hole, when Cirro had handed Flaherty the envelope full of hundreds. Pucci feigned indecision and called to Flaherty to ask what club he should use. Delfina couldn't hear the answer across the fairway, but whatever it was, Pucci nodded and hit the ball to the lower edge of the green.

Delfina had to be careful to keep Flaherty in a good mood until the game was over, or all of this butt-kissing would be wasted. He took his nine-iron and made a practice cut, then stared at the green. Next he gauged the distance to the sand trap in front of it, and expertly lofted his ball right into the center of it.

He good-naturedly shrugged his shoulders at Flaherty

and walked toward the trap. When he reached it, he studied the positions of his opponents' balls on the green. Flaherty had left himself a ten-foot putt. Flaherty was certainly good enough to make it, but Delfina decided not to bet anything important on it. He took a bad cut at his ball and made it thump into the dirt at the edge of the trap to roll back and stop at his feet. Then he took a second shot onto the green and watched the others. Flaherty sunk his ball, and so did Cirro, but Pucci wisely took two putts to hole out. Delfina read the green carefully, swung his putter, and put himself out of his misery.

Flaherty was standing above him on the green, preparing to gloat. "Very nicely done," he said.

"You're still the winner," said Delfina.

"Well, sure," said Flaherty. "I warned you guys you weren't going to stand a chance against Jimmy Flaherty on his home turf."

"You were right," said Delfina. His eyes leveled on the others, and they nodded and mumbled congratulations. He could tell that Pucci would have been more effusive, but he was as miserable and sweaty as Delfina. Cirro was young, and golf was an old man's game. He seemed to be somewhere outside of the proceedings, waiting for something to actually happen.

As Flaherty and Delfina walked off the green, Delfina said quietly, "Do you know when we can count on having the zoning variance? We'd like to break ground in the fall."

Flaherty winked. "I should have it for you in a week or two." It seemed to occur to him that somewhere, either far away or nearby, there might be a microphone. He said loftily, "It's always been my belief that a big part of my job was attracting business to the city—making it a friendly place to invest, and a good place to live and work."

But his oratory was wasted, because his audience was distracted. Delfina's glance around the nearby clubhouse grounds had shown him that two men were waiting for him. "There," he said. "Wouldn't you know it? I just get to the green, and there's a couple of accountants waiting for me." He caught

Pucci's eye. "Why don't you take Jim to the clubhouse for a drink? I'm the loser, so I'll buy." He shook Flaherty's hand. "Jim, it's been a pleasure."

He left Pucci and Flaherty standing on the frog hair at the top of the green and headed for the parking lot. Before his cleats touched pavement, the two men he had spotted were hurrying across the terrace to meet him. One was Al Mino, an old Castiglione soldier he had placed in Oakland to oversee northern California.

Mino said, "We can wait if you want to stop in the clubhouse, Frank."

Delfina said, "Who's this?" as though he were deferring his answer until he knew who he was talking to.

Mino said, "Oh, I'm sorry, Frank. This is our friend Sam Zinni. I thought you two knew each other. He came to me in Oakland a year ago. Before that he was in . . ."

"Illinois," said Zinni. "I worked for DelaCroce."

Delfina nodded. "I'm sorry, Sam. I thought you looked familiar, but I guess the damned sun is affecting me. Of course I remember you. The Maurice Black thing."

Zinni smiled. "That's right, Mr. Delfina."

"Frank," Delfina corrected him. "You've been around long enough to call me Frank, even if I don't know it. What's this about?"

Mino leaned closer. "That picture of the girl."

"You got a car?"

"Right over here."

Delfina turned to Cirro. "Mike, go put the clubs in your car and get me my shoes."

He opened the back door of Mino's car and sat with his feet out the open door until Cirro returned with his shoes, then put them on and tossed the golf shoes on the floor. "Okay, Al. Drive."

When the car had pulled out of the clubhouse lot he said, "What about the picture? Has somebody seen Rita Shelford?"

Mino said, "I didn't mean that girl. The other one. With the long black hair."

"What about her?"

"I recognized her," said Zinni. "It was from the Maurice Black thing. You remember, Black came into the Sporting Life. It was set up so Stolnick, the off-duty cop, was going to take him out to a car. He wouldn't go, so Stolnick stuck him in the hallway by the telephones. This waitress, Nancy Carmody, saw it and took off."

"You mean the picture looks like Nancy Carmody the waitress?"

Zinni shook his head. "No. It's this other woman that came along later."

"Another one?"

"Yeah," said Zinni. "We caught up with Nancy Carmody at a camp. It was a bunch of fancy cabins just over the Wisconsin border in Lake Geneva. There were three of us: Jimmy McCormick, who's supposed to be this all-star hit man from New Jersey, a buddy of his, and me to be sure the family is a satisfied customer. I tell the buddy to park down the road away from the place, send Jimmy through the woods to watch the cabin and make sure he likes everything, while I go make a phone call to DelaCroce and give him the news."

Delfina was getting impatient. "What happened?"

"I get back like ten minutes later. I get the word, which is what I expected. Kill her there, bury her in the woods, and come home. I find McCormick and his buddy in the woods by the cabin. They've never seen her before, so they want me to look. It's her. We can actually see her through the window. She's wearing a red blouse and jeans and bright white sneakers, like she must have bought them that day because all she had when she ran was city clothes."

Delfina knew he had to let Zinni tell it his own way, but he had just spent three hours walking across a reclaimed desert. "So?"

"So just when we're ready to go in, she comes out. It seems she's going for a walk in the woods. Okay, that's fine. McCormick goes after her. The buddy and I follow at a slower pace, so we don't sound like an army and scare her. We get a couple hundred feet down the path, and we hear a car starting. If she's gone for a walk, who's starting the car? We run back, and there's a woman wearing a red shirt behind the wheel as it heads down the gravel driveway. We run for McCormick. He says we made a mistake, because she's still up ahead. He decides to do her right away, and runs. We do too. And there she is, about a hundred yards ahead: red shirt, white sneakers.

"She comes out of the woods onto a road. We try to catch up with her and get it over with before somebody drives up and sees her. Sure enough, a car zooms past us, pulls up to her, and stops. It's Nancy Carmody's car, with Nancy Carmody behind the wheel, still wearing her red shirt. We sprint to get close. This other woman opens the door of the car and just stands there, like she's trying to get a good look at our faces. This doesn't bother us, because she's going to be dead too. But it also gives me a good look at her face. She gets in, slams the door, and takes off.

"We dash back to our car, and McCormick drives after them. We get maybe three miles before black smoke starts streaming out from under the hood, so you can barely see. McCormick jumps out and pops the hood. I get out too, but not because I want to put out a fire with my shirt. It's because I see big orange flames. When I get to the front I can see them coming from the engine block and melting the wire bundle that runs along the side. There's this white goop all over everything, and it burns high and hot."

Delfina's eyes were sharp as he stared at Zinni. "And you think the picture is the same woman—the one who slipped Nancy Carmody out?"

"I know it is," Zinni asserted. "It's her."

Delfina was silent for a few seconds. For six years he had kept Nancy Carmody in the back of his mind, and other, newer problems had piled in on top. It was clear to him that he had not heard the whole story at the time. When the waitress had not turned up, he'd had Stolnick executed, so the immediate danger she represented had passed. "You know anything about this woman?"

"She's got to be some kind of pro," said Mino.

Delfina sighed. To these guys, the process of thought was like carrying big rocks to a river to use as stepping-stones. They would drop one in, then have to turn around and go all the way back to find the next one, carry it out, and drop it. "We'll have to move fast."

"On what?"

"Al, call Oakland. Get your guys to call all our people in cities across the country. Have them make a lot of copies of that picture—say, a couple of thousand each. We've got to get them to all the families as fast as we can. Tell them Rita Shelford has been spotted, and this woman was with her. Nothing else. Got it?"

"Sure, but what does it mean?"

"It means that we have to find a phone booth."

Mino stopped the car at a gas station and got out to use one of the pay telephones along the fence where cars were parked waiting for service. After a second, Delfina's impatience goaded him out of the car to the telephone beside Mino's. He called his underbosses in Niagara Falls, Omaha, Los Angeles, and Boston and repeated his orders.

When he was back in Mino's car, he sat with his eyes on the roof above his head, trying to assess his position. He had given up some of the information he had that the other bosses didn't. That was bad. But they would finally be convinced that he was joining in the general hunt for Bernie's money, and that was, on the whole, good. Now he had to decide exactly what his position was going to be after they found this woman for him.

21

Jane awoke slowly, listening for the clacking of the keys on Ziegler's keyboard, then opened her eyes to look for the light under the door. When she found it, the crack of light wasn't where it was supposed to be. She sat up in bed and remembered. The light under the door was the hotel hallway. This was the Olympic Hotel, and it was in Seattle.

The five-hundred-mile trip up the Pacific coast from San Diego to San Francisco had taken her a full day. The only stops she had made had been near mailboxes and post offices, sometimes to drop a single envelope in a slot. She had stayed one night in San Francisco, then spent most of the next day flying to Portland and Seattle, mailing more letters.

So far, everything had gone exactly as she had planned. California was a tenth of the population of the country, so there had been many stops. Portland and Seattle were smaller, so on her last flight she had been able to fold one empty duffel bag and put it inside the other with the rest of the mail. She had used the name Wendy Stein to rent the car, then been Katherine Webster in San Francisco, and Diane Finley on the flight to Seattle. When she had arrived at the hotel, the boxes of new letters had been waiting for her.

She had taken two hours emptying the boxes and packing the letters in her two duffel bags in the proper order, so the first bundles would be at the top. Then she had flattened the cardboard boxes, torn the mailing stickers off them, and carried them to the Dumpster in the little enclosure behind the building. After that, she had tried to go to sleep, but couldn't. From the moment when she had dropped the first envelopes in Albuquerque, she had been aware that she had started the clock. It would take only a day or two before the first checks arrived at the offices of charities. She had tried to make those two days count, but now she was stopped. She had to wait until morning for her flight to Minneapolis to begin her run through the Midwest. It was only when the clock by the bed said two A.M. that she was able to assuage the feeling of nervous eagerness. The bags were ready, the tickets were in her purse on the table, and the reservations were confirmed for the rest of the trip. It was now five o'clock in the East, and she knew that while she slept, Henry Ziegler would already be in the car she had reserved for him, driving up the coast dropping envelopes in places like Orlando, Jacksonville, Savannah, Charleston. Even if the least likely of the possible disasters had already happened, and someone had connected the sudden dispersal of big money with Bernie Lupus, it was almost impossible that anyone would connect the event with Henry Ziegler. Probably no wiseguy had ever heard of him. And Henry would be traveling in the safest, most anonymous way, staying out of airports.

Jane slept for four hours, then woke up to discover that she had regained her strength and alertness. She called the desk downstairs to have a bellman pick up her two large bags and summon a taxi for Sea-Tac airport. She showered and dressed quickly and hurried down to settle her bill. In a few days it would be over.

At the airport, Jane dragged her two bags a few feet to the end of the line of passengers waiting to check their luggage at the curb. When the skycaps had taken them, she entered the terminal, walked through the row of metal detectors, and began to assess the crowds of people in the waiting areas. She was trying to pick out the two or three men who would be watching for Rita Shelford, but she saw immediately that things had changed. There seemed to be more of them than there had been in San Diego. The man near the end of the first aisle studying something in his briefcase was a strong candidate. He kept dipping his eyes to stare down at the open case, then looking up at people walking past him on the concourse.

At first she thought it was possible that he was a police officer of some kind, but she dismissed the thought. His shoes were too nice. Cops never forgot that they were likely to spend a lot of time on their feet before the end of the shift, and might even have to chase someone down who was younger and faster, then wrestle with him. They didn't like leather soles and pointed toes.

She knew the man couldn't be looking for her, but she was glad to get past him. A few minutes later her eyes settled on a man walking along ahead of her. He turned his head to the right, and Jane followed his eyes. He had looked directly at a man sitting in the waiting area. The man stood up and began to walk too.

Jane kept going at the same pace, stepped closer to the middle of the concourse, where people at the sides wouldn't get as good a look at her, and watched the two men work. She tried to figure out whether they had spotted someone who looked like Rita, but it was difficult to tell. Ahead of her there were lots of people of all sizes and shapes.

The first man stepped into the stream of people ahead, stopped abruptly in front of the one he suspected, and stared up at the sign hanging from the ceiling above his head that had an arrow and the words GATES 10–22. The second man stopped behind, hemming the victim in. He had his hand in his pocket, and in it, Jane knew, would be something he wasn't supposed to have in an airport—maybe a blade made of sharpened plastic. But when the man who had caused the jam pivoted awkwardly and took a close look into the face of the victim, he muttered an apology and stepped quickly aside.

The victim stepped off again, pulling her rolling suitcase by its extended handle. Jane hurried to catch up with the woman before the two men had time to circle back to their positions, where Jane would have to pass them.

Jane could see now that what the woman was carrying in her free hand was not an airline's envelope with tickets in it. She had a little packet of business-size envelopes with stamps on them. The woman veered to the side of the concourse and Jane adjusted her course a few degrees to watch her more closely. The woman stopped at a steel panel with several horizontal slots in it and the eagle logo of the U.S. Postal Service. She dropped the letters in a slot and turned to go back to some gate she had already passed. Jane studied the woman's face. First the woman's eyes were unfocused, merely aimed ahead so she could see where she was going. Then she noticed Jane, and her eyes shot to Jane's face: her hair, her eyes, then down at the floor. A slight smile played on her lips for a fraction of a second. She had seen the resemblance too.

Jane looked away and walked faster. Jane had seen a dozen women of almost the same general description since she had stepped onto the curb outside the terminal. Women of her age and size with dark hair—even coal-black hair—weren't unusual. It must have been the letters the woman had been carrying that had made her worth a closer look.

Jane felt a chill moving up from the base of her spine and settling in her shoulder blades. They knew already. The first letters couldn't have arrived more than two days ago. How could they have picked up the pattern already? It occurred to her that maybe Henry Ziegler wasn't safe. Maybe they had caught him somehow, and made him tell them everything. She forced herself to think about her immediate problem.

She stepped into the first ladies' room she came to and waited to let the two men come back up the concourse. She looked at her face in the mirror and was startled by the haunted look in her eyes. She composed her features, then tried to think. She opened her purse and began to freshen her makeup as the door opened and another woman walked past her.

The two men watching the departure gates could hardly be the only ones in the airport. She had never heard that Seattle was a place where organized crime had a big foothold, but Sea-Tac was a big airport, and they could easily have flown a few men in from some city where they were redundant. No, she thought, not easily. It didn't have to be easy: they were after billions of dollars.

Jane glanced at her watch. It was a half hour before flight time. She had to calm herself and consider her options. She had already checked her two big bags onto the flight to Minneapolis. If she walked away now, the airline would delay the flight and take the bags off. They never flew bags without a passenger anymore. Stopping the flight, with its implication of bombs and airplane crashes, would attract attention from panicky passengers. It might even draw some of the watchers, if only because watching airports was dull work. The airport security people would certainly open the two big duffel bags and find nothing but envelopes inside. She tried to give a size to that loss. There was no way of knowing exactly how much the checks in this load were worth, but it couldn't be less than a billion dollars a bag. Some of the corporate foundations Henry had invented had been given names that sounded like midwestern agricultural conglomerates, and they would be in this load. A number of the names of individual families had been designed to sound like old fortunes from automobile companies, railroads, and department stores. But the sums of money weren't the worst problem. Giving the FBI a few thousand of these checks to study and trace was unthinkable.

She couldn't walk away from her bags. She would have to get on the flight to Minneapolis to claim them. She could wait here in the ladies' room until the second boarding call, then make a determined walk to the gate to join the travelers crowding together to get aboard.

Jane looked at her hair. Wearing it long and loose was probably not the best she could do. She pulled it tight, braided it, then twisted the braid and pinned it up in back. She searched her purse for the pair of tinted glasses she had picked up for herself when she had bought Rita's and put them on. She heard the first call for the flight to Minneapolis, then touched up her lipstick and heard the second call.

She took one last look at herself, turned, and walked to the door. Jane swung the door open and stepped out into the alcove. There was a jolt as a big body bumped against hers and slammed her into a side wall. There was the sharp sting of a pointed object pressed against her spine, and a strong forearm around her neck. The voice was low and nervous, so close behind her left ear that she could feel the damp, hot breath. "You're going to walk with me. The reason is that I can push this blade between the disks of your spine before you could get a word out."

Jane felt him tighten his grip with his left arm and push the blade a little harder to scare her. She couldn't tell from the feel what shape it was, or what it was made of, but she could tell it was short—an inch or two—because part of the hand that held it seemed to be resting against the back of her jacket. It could be a sharpened key. It could even be a pocketknife, if it looked short and harmless enough to the security woman at the metal detectors.

"Now walk back toward the escalators."

Jane struggled to sort out the sensations. The pressure against her back was strong enough to pierce the skin, if her jacket had not been there for padding. The man was standing behind her now, but when they stepped out in the open, he would have to move slightly to the side, as though he had his arm around her—his left side, because he held the knife in his right hand. That was a weak position, good for slashing, but not for stabbing. He would have to lean toward her if he wanted to stab.

He pushed Jane forward and she heard him take a step to move ahead to her left side. Jane's next step was slightly to her left to reassure him that she was heading toward the exit, and to trigger the reflex in his feet to move that way faster to keep from tripping over her. As he began to lean to the left, Jane started her third step, dropped to the floor just to her right, and rolled. Her legs came up to her chest, then kicked out together.

The man did as she had hoped. He finished his step to the left, then lunged to the right with the knife. His weight shifted to his right foot, and he was off-balance. Jane's two-footed kick caught his right ankle and swept his leg out from under him. He hit the slippery floor hard on his right hip and shoulder. His first impulse was to roll to his belly and go after her, so his hand came up, and he remembered that the little knife was in it and that people must be looking. He awkwardly rose to his right elbow to slip the knife into the inner pocket of his jacket.

His eyes rolled to survey the area around him to determine whether anyone had seen the knife. He needed to take his eyes off Jane for an instant. If his peripheral vision detected that Jane was still moving, his mind interpreted it as an attempt to stand and run. But Jane was already bringing her left leg toward him, exerting the strong muscles at the back of the thigh and calf that the body used to push off when it ran. Her heel pounded into the bridge of his nose and snapped his head backward.

Strong hands grasped Jane and lifted her to her feet. People were muttering the useless words that Jane knew would make them feel foolish. "Are you okay?" "Did you trip?"

"I'm okay," she said. Then, more angrily, like a woman who resented the embarrassment, she added, "I wish people would watch where they're going." She was already moving toward the gate again. As she slipped into the river of people heading in the same direction, she ventured a last, irritated glance back. The man was still lying there. She couldn't tell whether he had lost consciousness or simply couldn't think of a way to shake off the people surrounding him and run after her without being caught. Then the crowd gathering around him blocked her view.

Jane hurried on. When she sensed she had gone a sufficient distance, she began to run, dodging slow walkers and heavily laden passengers. She made it to her gate just as one airline woman was putting a new flight number on the board behind the desk and the other was preparing to close the door to the boarding tunnel. She handed the woman her ticket, heard the door slam behind her, then rushed to take her seat.

Jane fastened her seat belt and willed the plane to move, and almost immediately, it did. She watched the terminal moving backward as the plane was towed away from it. She sat back, letting the fear and exertion wash over her now. She felt the light-headed, jittery weakness and the pounding of her heart for a full minute. But then the plane stopped and began to move forward. The pilot must have been trying to preserve his place in the takeoff order. His voice came over the speaker and confirmed her theory. A few minutes later the plane was lifting off at the end of the runway and Jane was already reaching out against the exaggerated gravity to take the telephone off the back of the seat in front of her.

22

As the plane passed above the Rocky Mountains, Jane tried again to think of ways to reassure herself. The man who had spotted her in the airport had not gotten up in time to see which gate she had run to. It must have been two hundred yards farther on, and she had made a turn where the concourse did, so she had been out of sight. That was an advantage, but it wasn't safety. The people he had been with were certainly capable of checking the departure list to find out what planes had taken off at about the time when she had disappeared. The pilot had been in a hurry to get his plane into position, so there must have been a number of flights at that time, but it would be easy to eliminate some of them—ones that had taken off from gates on the other end of the airport, or ones that had been delayed. She had to assume they knew she was on this plane. She had to believe they knew when and where the plane would land, and they would be calling ahead to put friends of theirs into her path.

Jane reviewed her preparations again and again as the plane moved over the immense, flat expanse of geometric patterns of green and tan toward the Mississippi. When the man in the seat beside her stood up to go into the rest room,

Jane used the moment alone. She collected three little pillows the airline had put in the overhead compartment and sat down. She watched and waited to see whether any of the passengers nearby had gotten curious. The young man across the aisle was asleep, lying back in his seat with his long legs in a tangle on the empty seat beside him. The others seemed not to have noticed her movement. She wrapped her jacket around the pillows and kept the bundle in her lap.

A few minutes later the man was back. Jane stood up in the aisle to let him duck and sidestep past her to his seat. Then she walked down the aisle toward the rear of the plane. She found one rest room with its little slot moved to say VACANT, so she stepped inside, locked the door, and began to experiment with the pillows in front of the tiny mirror. It took her several tries to get the pillows arranged and the elastic waistband of her skirt over the bottom one to hold them. Then she draped her loose silk blouse over the bulge. The pillows were tightly packed with some synthetic fiber that made them firm, so the visual effect was not bad. It might work, if she was careful not to bend at the waist or let the pillows slip to the side.

Jane worked on ways to hold her jacket to conceal the pillows until she had perfected that obscure skill too. Since the man she had kicked in the Seattle airport had probably described the way her hair had been braided and pinned, she loosened it. She found her nail scissors in her purse, but when she tried to cut her hair, she realized that it would take hours with the tiny tool.

She sensed that the plane was beginning to lose altitude, and there would not be enough time. She combed her hair out and made a ponytail. She took a scarf and tied it around the ponytail so it hung down over her hair. Her reflection in the mirror looked as though she had much more scarf than hair. Since the man at Sea-Tac had seen her tinted glasses, she took them off. She heard the female voice of a flight attendant over the speaker above her head. After the first few garbled words she recognized that it was an announcement that it was time for passengers to return to their seats and buckle up.

When the plane landed, Jane walked out with the same

weary, relieved look that she saw on the faces of the other passengers. In the tunnel she stayed as close as she could to a pair of men who were big enough to partially shield her from sight, put on her jacket, and let her belly show.

Jane ventured to the edge of the crowd long enough to scan the line of people along the wall for a man holding a sign that said DEBORAH. When she spotted him, she said, "Hi, that's me," and kept walking. He set off beside her, and she kept her face turned toward him, not looking in either direction. "I'm in a bit of a hurry. I've got to make a quick phone call and stop in the ladies' room. Could you please take my tags and claim my bags?"

The man eyed her belly. "I guess so," he said. "What are they?"

"Two big green duffel bags with wheels on the bottom." She tore the two tags off her ticket envelope and held them out. He looked at them without eagerness, so she decided to put an end to his reluctance. "They're heavy, so I can meet you down there and give you a hand."

"You don't have to do that," he said gruffly. "I can handle them myself. You can meet me at the car. It's in the short-term lot, space 217. Black Audi with tinted windows." The man set off, glancing down at the numbers on the receipts.

She was relieved that the call she had made to order a car had actually produced one. She had asked the long-distance operator for the number of the private limo service that was first in the alphabet. She had guessed that it would be one with four or five A's in a row at the beginning. In her experience, the ones who wanted business that badly weren't usually luxurious, but they were eager. Now all that remained was to make her way to the car. Keeping her eyes forward, she walked along with the crowd. She had gauged the costume carefully, trying not to overdo it. Doctors always told pregnant women not to fly after the eighth month, so she had seen very few late-term women in airports. She had tried for the seventh month—the belly big enough to be unmistakable, but arranged high and not so large as to make her unusual.

Jane spotted a pair of elderly people waiting by a counter.

The woman had an aluminum walker with wheels on it, and the man looked nearly as frail. Jane's ears picked up an electronic chirping sound far up the concourse, and she recognized an opportunity. She stepped closer and caught the attention of the woman behind the counter. "Do you suppose there's room for one more? I'm a little . . . tired. I don't want to be a lot of trouble, but—"

The woman smiled her professional smile. "No trouble," she said. "Do you have a carry-on bag?"

Jane shook her head. The electric cart chirped up to the counter and stopped with a sudden jolt. The tall, thin young man stepped down from the driver's seat and said, "Three?"

The woman at the counter nodded, and Jane helped the two old people into a bench seat, then sat beside the driver. The cart started with a jerk and picked up speed. The driver weaved in and out around groups of walking travelers, slowing down only when two groups would unexpectedly converge to close his pathway, then beeping his horn.

Jane's position beside him was not the one she would have chosen, but there had been no other. The cart moved along with a flashing orange light on a pole and the annoying chirp, so there was no hope of not being noticed. She half-turned in her seat to face the old couple, so her belly would be visible from the front of the cart and her face hidden. She tried to start a meaningless conversation. "Thank you very much for sharing your ride with me."

The old woman glared at her in such apparent disapproval that Jane suspected some kind of dementia. But the old man muttered in a surprisingly cold tone, "We don't own it. There's plenty of room."

Jane sensed that she was missing something, then surmised what it might be. "Something happens in airplanes. It makes my ankles and fingers swell up." She waved her hand above the seat where they could see it and added, "After the first flight I could hardly get my wedding ring off, so I didn't wear it on the way home."

Jane had been right. Both faces brightened. The old lady said, "Oh, that'll go away soon enough, but by then you'll be too busy to notice." The husband laughed. "But that doesn't last long either. They grow up and go off on their own, and you'll wonder where they went."

Jane saw a pair of watchers over his shoulder. They were walking on opposite sides of the concourse toward the gate she had just left. Now and then they would glance across the open space at each other to keep their courses parallel.

She tried to keep the old people's attention. "I'll bet that's what you're doing now, isn't it? Visiting a son or daughter."

"Wrong," said the old man. "We've been and come back. Been in Los Angeles for two weeks: enjoyed ourselves about as much as we can stand."

Jane sighed. "I know what you mean. It always feels good to be home."

"Do you live here?"

Jane said, "Yes," because there was no choice. If Minneapolis was a stop on the way to somewhere else, the next place would be a small town, and she couldn't take the chance that they might know it.

Jane saw the second set of watchers walking along like the first, only this time there were three. One was a tall, heavy-set man who forced oncoming travelers to part and go around him toward the others on the wings. As the three receded into the distance, she realized that the cart must have passed so close to him that she could have touched him.

"Whereabouts?" asked the old man.

Jane told him only the name of the street. It was the address of the apartment she had rented while she had watched Sid Freeman's house for a visit from the people who were trying to kill Richard Dahlman.

The man said, "I know where that is. Are you right above a lake?"

"Yes," said Jane. "There's a beautiful park right below our house, with ducks and squirrels and things." She lowered her eyes to her belly. "It'll be a good place to play."

The old lady was suddenly curious. "Did you live there when they had those murders last summer?"

"Hush," whispered the old man, as though Jane's belly might hear.

Jane nodded. "It was only a couple of blocks away. We didn't hear anything, though. We saw it on the news. My husband said, 'Hey, isn't that around here somewhere?' and sure enough, when they showed it, you could practically see our house."

Jane detected that an unwelcome dose of real feeling had slipped through her defenses unexpectedly. She could see Sid's body lying in what had once been the big house's library, the dirty carpet soaked with his blood. She saw that her accurate memory of the neighborhood had soothed the old couple. It occurred to her that she could have done the same performance in a lot of other cities. In each one there were streets she had seen more clearly than the people who lived there because she had studied them for danger, houses where she had hidden runners, and, in far too many of them, she could conjure from her memory sights that the cameras couldn't show on television.

The old man said, "They ever figure out what that was about?"

Jane shrugged. "If they did, nobody ever told me."

"Drugs," said the driver.

"Really?" asked the old man. "I didn't hear that."

"I didn't either," the driver answered. "But it's always that."

His certainty sounded so authoritative that neither of the two elderly passengers seemed to be able to think of anything to say in response, and Jane had no inclination to tell him what had really happened. For a few seconds the insistent chirp of his electric cart was the only sound. He drove past the metal detectors and swung recklessly to the door of the elevator. "End of the line," he called.

Jane stepped down and held the old lady's walker while the driver helped both old people off the rear seats. Jane felt the disconcerting sensation that her pillows were slipping. She brought her left arm across her waist and held them in place. "Thanks for the ride," she said to the driver, and "Nice meeting you" to the old couple; then she turned and hurried toward the escalator.

At the bottom she walked purposefully to the ladies' room, went into the farthest stall, and latched the door. She longed to abandon the disguise, but the limo driver she had sent after her luggage was expecting to see a pregnant woman at his car. She carefully rearranged the pillows and secured them once more with the waistband of her skirt, then lingered in front of the mirror to be sure the effect was right. She wondered why the costume was so distasteful to her, but the answer was waiting for her. It felt like bad luck. It made her suspect that she was playing with a force of the universe in order to obtain a small and transient advantage. She might, in some mysterious way, be making a trade that she had not intended. Maybe later, when she wanted desperately to look like this, it would be denied because she had unwittingly spent her chance.

She strode to the door, took a last look in the mirror, then stepped out quickly. Beyond the long row of glass doors she could see travelers of all descriptions moving along or stopping to stare up and down the street for cabs or shuttle buses. A couple of the men had the look that she did not want to see. They were apparently waiting for something that was going to approach along the street, but they seemed to have a lot of fidgety mannerisms that turned their eyes in the direction of the doors, the sidewalk, and the terminal.

Jane walked past the window where she could see the baggage area. She could see her driver waiting at the edge of a crowd where a flashing light was turning and bags had begun to slide down a chute to the stainless steel carousel that turned below. She walked on, out the door into the warm, humid air. She kept her eyes ahead and never let them rest on the faces that came into her line of sight. She had trained herself to use her peripheral vision to watch for changes in the expected cadence of motion—hands rising quickly, a steady walk changing to a run—and to use her ears to warn her of motion behind her.

She hurried to join a group of people waiting for the traffic

signal to change so they could cross to the short-term lot.
Once she was in the little herd, she knew she was safer. When
the light turned green she matched her pace to theirs so she
would keep them around her, but as soon as she reached the
lot, her protectors dispersed rapidly. She searched for space
217, and the worry she had felt in the airport began to fade.
She had gotten through the difficult part.

She walked a zigzag path through the long rows of closely
parked cars to shield herself from view. Each time she had to
cross an empty aisle, she would stop and look in both directions. She kept these glances casual, but she had to give herself time to survey the windows of parked cars. She was
certain that the physical caution and the slight awkwardness
that women felt during pregnancy would satisfy anyone who
noticed her. Whatever else was true about pregnancy, women
in their seventh month didn't seem to feel much like sprinting
to avoid speeding cars.

She found the space and looked at the car without approaching it immediately. If anyone had seen her from a distance, it
would be dangerous to have him know exactly which car represented her ride out of here. She walked slowly in a course
that kept her distance from it constant, but she was behind it
now. She looked at the terminal and saw the driver come out
of the baggage area, and that made her feel better.

She turned her eyes to the car again. It was almost new. The
afternoon sunlight shone on the gleaming black finish of the
trunk, and she saw her reflection. The reflection was wrong—
a little bit wavy, like a funhouse mirror. She moved closer, but
the impression didn't change. She stepped to the trunk and
ran her finger along the finish near the lock. There was a
slight depression around the lock, and there was a thin layer
of oil on the lock's surface. She walked close to the driver's
side and peered in. The odometer said three thousand miles.
It was possible that a gypsy cab might have had its trunk lock
punched in by a thief in the first few thousand miles and had it
replaced. She bent over to bring her eye close to the long,
shiny side surface of the car.

The finish on the upper parts was perfect, but the paint near the bottom of the doors was thicker and duller, as though it had been applied in one coat and not rubbed as thoroughly as the upper part. No new car came from the factory that way, and it was unlikely that a car that had been totaled and salvaged would have three thousand miles on the odometer. It was also unlikely that the insurance company that had paid off wouldn't have gotten the key to the trunk. She surreptitiously removed her pocketknife from her purse and scratched the finish near the bottom of the door. The undercoat was bright green. The car had been stolen and repainted.

Jane straightened and looked toward the terminal. The driver had just crossed the street, and he was entering the lot pulling her two duffel bags. She was fairly sure that he had not yet looked inside. The baggage area would not have been a good place to break the locks, and a slash in the fabric would be difficult to hide. She scanned the lot to see whether any of the driver's friends were visible yet. He would be confident that he could pick her up and take her somewhere without help, because she would go eagerly. But there had been so many watchers between her gate and the baggage area that he'd had numerous chances to tip them off. They would come because there was no reason not to. If she resisted, they would make it easy to overpower her quickly and quietly without killing her. Even the first man, the one in Sea-Tac airport, had figured out that he needed to take her alive.

As the driver approached the car, Jane kept her eyes on the terminal behind him. At last, she saw two men coming out of the exit together. They walked quickly to the crossing, one of them pounded the button mounted on the pole to change the signal, then they both ran across. She was sure. There was always a reason to run to a terminal, but almost never a reason to run toward the parking lot. She focused on the driver and gave him a false smile.

He came around to the trunk and let go of the bags. "Been waiting long?"

"Not at all," said Jane. "Did you have trouble with the bags?"

"No," he said. "They didn't even hold me up at the door to check the tags."

Jane watched him open the trunk and lift the first heavy duffel bag into it. As he bent down for the second, she looked over the trunk lid toward the two men. They were getting into a dark blue Chevrolet four rows away. She stared down at the driver as he began to lift the second bag. She devoted two seconds to contemplating him. He was feeling very clever and masterful right now. He had managed to get a lone woman who was running for her life to trust him. In a moment she would be in the back seat and he would be driving her some-place where a group of his friends would be gathering. They would torture her until she told them where the rest of the money was, and then kill her. Afterward, maybe tonight, he would laugh about it—probably be very funny describing how stupid she had been. She had called the limo service herself—picked that one. But the details made the story: how he had waited at the gate to be sure that the "Deborah" who had called for a ride was the right woman. Jane converted the dull anxiety of the past few hours, and the growing fear of the past few minutes, into hot rage. As the man leaned into the trunk with the second bag, she felt the adrenaline pump into her veins, then exploded into motion.

Jane brought the trunk lid down hard on the top of the man's head just as he was rising to meet it. His knees gave way and he fell across the duffel bag, then unsteadily backed out in a crouch.

Her hands gripped his head and pushed it down as her knee came up to meet it. He seemed stunned, unable to pop up, so she brought her knee up again, harder. This time he stood erect, but reeling, his nose bloody. He lunged toward her. She pivoted to throw her leg in front of his feet and got both hands onto the space between his shoulder blades to add her full strength to his momentum. His forehead smashed into the rear bumper, and blood began to run down his face from a cut above the hairline. Jane snatched the keys out of the trunk lock, slammed the lid, and stepped toward the driver's door.

As Jane moved past the man, he suddenly rose to his knees

and swung hard. His blow caught her in the stomach and the force of it threw her against the side of the car. The man's eyes shone through the slick of blood streaming down from the cut above his hairline, and there was a kind of glee in them, until he looked at her. Almost instantly, the brows knitted, and Jane could see he was puzzled. He had hit the pillows. The wide eyes blinked and the man's hand came up to wipe blood out of them. Jane leaned her weight against the side of the car and kicked the face upward. The man's head jerked back and caromed off the car beside his. Jane unlocked the door, slipped into the driver's seat, and hammered down the lock button.

As she started the car, she saw the man's hand grasp the door handle. She threw the car into reverse, and the hand slipped off. She stopped and put the car into forward gear, then drove toward the end of the aisle and turned right at the exit sign.

She had lost track of the two men in the blue Chevrolet. She looked in their direction, but the space was empty. Suddenly a flash of blue appeared directly behind her, filling her rearview mirror. She could see that the car was big and powerful and new. It was so close that she could make out the safety belts across the men's chests. As she started up the next aisle, the blue car tried to edge up beside her, and she understood the uncharacteristic concern with seat belts. They were going to try to push her into the line of cars and stop her.

The belts reminded her of something she knew about cars. She turned up the next aisle and accelerated, groping beside her for the seat-belt buckle. She drew it across her and clicked it in, tugged it to tighten the lap belt around her hips across the lower pillow, adjusted the chest belt so it lay flat between her breasts and across the upper pillow, then leaned back against the headrest to test the fit. At the end of the aisle she slowed just enough to make the turn, and looked for the exit ahead. There was a small kiosk where people presented tickets and paid. She reached into her purse to pull out a bill without looking at it as she accelerated up the side of the lot. She would have to do this before she was too close.

When she found the money, she slowed a bit. The blue

Chevrolet closed the distance quickly. When the Chevrolet had advanced to within twenty feet of her rear bumper and begun to coast, Jane stopped, threw the Audi into reverse, stomped on the accelerator, and leaned back into her seat with her head pressed against the headrest. She heard a little squeal as the driver of the blue car slammed on his brakes, but it was too late.

Jane's Audi slammed into the front of the blue Chevrolet with a loud bang. The impact jolted her, and she had a brief impression that everything in her body that was loose had moved: her internal organs, her brain, her blood. She glanced in the mirror as she threw the car into forward gear again.

She had set off the crash sensors in the blue car, and both airbags had burst out in front of the two men and punched them back into their seats. All she could see through their windshield were the two big, inflated bags, barely contained against the glass.

Jane accelerated again and glided up to the kiosk. She pushed the button on her door and the window slid down. The parking attendant was standing up from her stool, craning her neck to look out at the lot. Jane said, "Wow! Did you hear that noise? What was it?"

The woman seemed to return from a reverie. She shrugged and said, "Sounded like an accident."

Jane was already holding out a twenty-dollar bill. She spotted the parking ticket sticking out of the ashtray, so she snatched it and stuck it out the window with the money. The attendant accepted it, counted out fifteen in change, and tripped a switch to raise the barrier that blocked the exit. If the woman saw the damage to the rear of Jane's car as it drifted out past her, she apparently did not consider investigating accidents to be part of her job description. She was already back on her stool, looking the other way, while Jane accelerated up the street.

23

As Jane drove, she tried to calm herself enough to watch the rearview mirrors, maneuver through traffic as quickly as possible, and still devote most of her consciousness to the time beyond the next minute or two. She had to get rid of this car. It was stolen, and that meant it had probably been intended to be used for one occasion only and then dumped. The new paint job they had given it and whatever they had done to prevent the license plates from being spotted would have bought her some time, but the rear bumper and trunk were enough of a mess to attract attention. She couldn't park it and walk off down the street dragging her two duffel bags, and she couldn't stay in Minneapolis long enough to rent a clean, anonymous new car. Before she did anything else, she had to get out of town. She slipped the pillows out of her clothes and tossed them on the seat beside her, and after a few minutes she began to feel a bit less panicky.

Jane noticed a mailbox on a corner and remembered the letters. She had letters that needed Minneapolis postmarks. She stifled the impulse to go on, then turned into the parking lot of a restaurant, pulled in between two pickup trucks, and opened the trunk. She unlocked the two bags, found the one she would need first, and took out the letters. She forced herself to walk at a normal pace to the mailbox, put the letters inside, then walk back to the parking lot. As she unlocked the car, she heard behind her the sound of an engine accelerating slightly louder than the rest of the traffic. She turned her head in time to see the blue car speeding up the street in the direction she had been going, both men in the front seat staring intently at the road ahead. She felt her shoulders give an involuntary shiver. She got into the driver's seat, started the car, and drove off the other way.

She headed due south on Route 35, then left the interstate and turned east at Owatonna. When she reached Byron, she turned south on a rural road, then east again to the Rochester Municipal Airport. As she drove along the driveway to the long-term parking lot she studied the cars, the people waiting outside the terminal, and the road behind her. She saw nothing that frightened her, so she decided not to give something frightening time to arrive. She parked the car, walked to the terminal carrying one of her duffel bags and towing the other behind her, and stopped at the rental counter looking as though she had just stepped off a plane.

While she waited for the woman behind the counter to produce the forms and contracts, Jane studied the people around her. There seemed to be no watchers in this part of the airport. It was possible that any watchers here would have been sent to wait for her at the Minneapolis airport, but she had no impulse to go upstairs to the departure gates to test the theory.

Jane used the Katherine Webster credit card and driver's license to rent the car, then accepted the keys. In ten minutes she was outside again, driving down the street in a new dark green Pontiac with one of the duffel bags on the seat beside her. As soon as she saw a mailbox she mailed the Rochester letters, then drove off again.

Jane tried to appraise her situation. All of her care and her precautions had not prevented something from going wrong. People were looking for her, and they were looking in the right places. The seven days she had allotted to getting the mailing done was no longer a real number. She would have to forget numbers and concentrate on what she had to accomplish. The idea had been to mail each check from the place where it supposedly had been written, and to have all the checks arrive at their destinations within a few days of one another. The bosses would hear of the sudden boom in charitable giving when everyone else did, and probably not suspect what it meant. Even if they figured out that the money was theirs, by then it would be too late for them to do anything. The letters would already be at their destinations, the checks cashed, and the money safely deposited in the accounts of thousands of organizations all over the country.

Now things had changed. She had seen the intensity of the search building since she had flown to the Caribbean. Each time she had been in an airport there had seemed to be more big, tough-looking men standing around watching passengers arrive and depart. Jane had not anticipated that they would be doing anything but scrutinizing people for a resemblance to Rita.

In Sea-Tac airport they had not been looking only for Rita. The first two had been stalking a woman who fit Jane's general description, and who had been carrying a stack of business letters. The third man had ignored a thousand people and gone after Jane. The Mafia—or some part of it, anyway—knew that the money was being moved by mail, and that the way to stop it was by capturing a dark-haired woman.

Jane tried to imagine how they knew about her, but the possibilities were unlimited, and each one that occurred to her had something about it that didn't fit. If they had found the house in Santa Fe, and Bernie or Rita had talked, then they would know that the way to end the flow of money would be by using the records in the computers to stop payment on the checks. If they had noticed Henry somehow, then they would have made him block the transactions. They wouldn't need to find Jane.

She gave it up and tried to think about where she was now, and what she should do. Today was the third day. Jane had finished the mailings on the West Coast, picked up her second load of letters, and gotten out. Henry would be nearly up to Washington, D.C., by now, and then he would have his second set of letters in his bags and start dropping them off, hour by hour, as he moved north along the East Coast.

In most parts of the country, today's mail had already been delivered, so another burst of donations would hit the banks this afternoon. Whoever was watching transactions for the Mafia would have a lot to think about.

As Jane made her plans, certain decisions were inevitable. From now on, she would have to try very hard to stay away from airports. She would have to make a second, more thorough attempt to change her appearance.

She turned onto Interstate 90, and after seventy miles drove over the Mississippi into La Crosse, Wisconsin. All night she drove through the Wisconsin countryside, stopping only to mail letters—first only a mile from the bridge, then 143 miles farther east at Madison, then 54 miles on at Beloit. Then she drove the last 74 miles to Milwaukee.

Jane stopped at a hotel on West Highland Avenue that she judged to be equidistant from the Convention Center, Marquette University, and the Pabst Brewing Company. She brought her bags into her room, then went downstairs, moved her rental car to the other side of the lot, where she could see it from her window, and went to sleep.

In the morning, Jane bought the local newspapers from the gift shop in the hotel lobby and went back to her room to read them. There were no articles that indicated the sudden growth of generosity in the country had come to the attention of the *Sentinel* or the *Journal*. There were no wire-service reports of murders in Santa Fe, New Mexico, or stories about the East Coast that she could interpret as harm coming to Henry Ziegler. The meteorological reports even confirmed that he was having clear weather. It was not until she turned to the want ads that she saw something of interest.

"Public Auto Auction, Rain or Shine," ran the banner above the huge advertisement. "You Inspect the Vehicles Before the Auction!" As though to prove it, the smaller letters said, "Inspection, 10:00, Auction, Noon." Jane looked at the long list of car models, years, and prices, then realized that they were simply examples of past bargains: it was an auction, after all. Along the bottom, the ad said, "If you don't have cash we accept all major credit cards for purchase or as a down payment! EZ financing available. Serving Milwaukee since 1993."

Jane took a taxi to the address at the bottom of the page. She found herself on the edge of a big lot, where a few dozen customers, nearly all of them men, walked up and down staring at rows of cars of all makes and sizes. A few of the men had pads or pieces of paper on which they made notes. Jane concluded that they were involved in some aspect of the used-car business, because anybody who just wanted a cheap car probably wouldn't need to write anything down to remember the one he liked.

Jane picked one man out and watched him stalk the rows. His hands were clean, but they had a few stubborn black stains on them that he had not been able to scrub off, and the knuckles of the right hand had an angry red look she decided had come from rapping them on something while turning a wrench in a confined space. She made a point of being nearby each time he looked up from his pad. Finally, he said, "You looking for a car?"

"What else have they got?" said Jane with a smile.

"For yourself?"

"Uh-huh."

He pointed at a black rectangle that rose higher than the line of cars in the next row. "If you like SUVs, there's a '97 Ford Explorer over there with about eight thousand miles on it. She's a couple of years old, and the finish has a few scratches, so she won't go for what she's worth." He turned and pointed in the other direction at two gray shapes that Jane could barely see. "If you want to go fancy, they have a couple of Mercedes down there. One of them has a dent that you could fix for two hundred, and it'll knock a thousand or more off the price."

"I just need to get from point A to point B. Where do the cars come from?"

He shrugged. "Some get confiscated, some are regular repos."

Jane said, "I don't know if I want to end up with a car that belonged to a drug dealer or an axe murderer or something. What if he wants it back?"

The man smiled. "They're not usually that exciting. Usually it's just the plain old IRS."

"Thanks," she said, and walked off to look at the cars he had pointed out.

When the auction began, Jane joined the gaggle of people who followed the auctioneer along the rows. She watched the bidding while the first few cars were sold. There was a tall, thin man who stood a bit to the side of the auctioneer and watched the bidders. If the auctioneer was getting nowhere, he would turn toward the tall, thin man. He would give a bid, the auctioneer would say, "Sold," and walk on. Jane decided the man must be the loss stopper, who made sure that nothing went too low.

When the auctioneer reached the Ford Explorer, Jane waited to see the other bidders. There were a few ridiculously low bids, and then her new friend appeared at her shoulder and whispered, "Offer eight." Jane said, "Eight thousand." There were bids of eighty-one and eighty-two hundred. Jane waited until the auctioneer turned to the stop-loss man, then yelled, "Nine thousand." The auctioneer looked at the other bidders, then declared the car sold and walked on.

Before Jane's friend followed, he whispered, "Good deal."

Jane grinned, then went off to pay for her car. She gave the man in the little building her Diane Fierstein credit card, received her bill of sale, and drove her car off the lot to register it in the name Diane Fierstein.

The hair was much more complicated than buying a mere car. It took time to find the right salon, then to call for an appointment on short notice. She had to improvise a story about how she was flying to Houston for her sister's wedding tomorrow, and her regular hairdresser had solemnly promised an appointment, and then gotten into an accident and hurt her hand, and could you please, please. . . . After her performance, Jane went to a bookstore to leaf through magazines to find the right picture. At four-thirty, Jane was in a shop near the university handing the magazine to the stylist.

Jane knew that the way she felt in the stylist's chair was idiotic, and found that knowing didn't help at all. She had always liked her long black hair. It was a peculiar, personal link with who she really was. She liked it because when she looked at it, she could remember her father's voice telling her it was beautiful, and her mother brushing it, then holding her own auburn hair beside it and smiling. "To think I would ever have a little girl with this thick, gorgeous black hair," she would say. Jane had kept it long and made the effort to care for it, even in times of her life when she could make no argument for its practicality. Since she and Carey had been together, it had seemed to her to be mingled in some complicated way into their relationship. He had talked about it and run his fingers through it in a way that stood for all of the differences between men and women that made each mysterious and fascinating to the other.

The first long tresses fell on the sheet the stylist had pinned around her neck, and she had to fight the tears—to keep her eyes from closing because that would squeeze them out. But then, after a few minutes, the cutting was over. She still had to endure the hair dye and the wave, but those things had no meaning for her now, because the long black hair was not hers anymore.

Two hours later, she was staring at a woman in the mirror, reminding herself that this woman was the one she had chosen to be. She had short brown hair with a slight curl. The stylist had treated her eyebrows to match the hair, and they made the blue eyes she had inherited from her mother look bigger, but somehow less startling than they had been this morning. She looked like a mildly attractive thirty-year-old who was probably married, probably worked in some kind of office, but lived in the suburbs.

Jane quickly turned away from the mirror. She kept her body turned toward the front of the shop to give the stylist a huge tip while she detested her for her skill, then turned with feigned cheerfulness to go out the back door without looking in the mirrors again. She drove her new Ford Explorer to a big mall, and spent the late afternoon shopping.

In a department store, Jane bought a pair of plain gray soft-sided suitcases that matched the interior of the Explorer, then a supply of makeup, beginning with a foundation that was a shade or two lighter than her skin. Next she selected clothes.

When she had been seen in the airport she had been wearing a skirt and jacket she had bought in Beverly Hills and a silk blouse, so she worked to get away from that image. She bought clothes that a married suburban woman might wear while she was doing errands: lots of slacks, comfortable shoes, and oversized tops. She also bought jeans and running shoes, a baseball cap, a pair of designer sunglasses, and a couple of light summer jackets.

She ate dinner in a restaurant in the mall, then drove up the street to a big hardware chain, found her way to the automotive section, and bought big floor mats to match the carpet in the Explorer. She used them to cover her suitcases, and drove to the street behind her hotel and parked.

Before she had left the hotel this morning, she had put up the DO NOT DISTURB sign. On her way out, she had counted the number of doors from the room to the elevator, and established that hers was the fourth from the left end of the building on the third floor. She could see that the curtains were still open, and the dim lamp by the bed was still turned on. The only thing left to check was the car she had rented in Minnesota.

She walked along the street behind the hotel until she found a tall office building with a parking garage beside it. She used the stairs to climb to the fourth floor of the building, then went out the exit door to the upper level of the parking garage, stepped to the edge, and looked down.

The parking lot of the big hotel was filling up for the evening. Most of the curtains on the upper floors of the hotel were closed, but there were lights behind many of them, and some of the small, translucent windows of the bathrooms were lighted. People were beginning the ritual of getting showered and changed for dinner.

Jane studied the people she saw entering and leaving the hotel by the parking lot entrance. It was a weeknight in a city that wasn't particularly renowned as a tourist attraction, so Jane wasn't surprised that most of the guests looked as though they were returning from business meetings. Men and women were dressed in suits, and they carried things—

briefcases, folders, squarish cases that probably contained computers or samples. A van pulled up and a mixed group of six got out. They were all wearing jeans or casual khaki trousers, but they all had little orange buttons pinned to their chests, and they didn't divide into male-female pairs when they walked toward the entrance, so this too was business of some kind.

It took Jane another minute to identify the watchers. There were two men in a car at the end of the lot, and two more on the street beyond the parking lot, but she wasn't sure that what they were watching was her car. She waited to see one of them move, but they waited too.

She walked back into the office building and tried to assess what she had seen. She had run from Minneapolis to Rochester in a stolen car. It would not have been difficult for the ones in Minneapolis to learn that a stolen car had been found in the lot of the Rochester airport, or even to find it themselves. She had hoped that when they did, they would assume she had gone there to board an airplane.

If they knew she had not taken a flight out of Rochester, then they would guess that probably what she had done was rent a car. If a man came to the rental counter—maybe a man pretending to be a cop, and maybe just a man who had a plausible reason and a roll of money—he might have been able to find out what kind of car a particular woman had rented a few hours before. That was simple. But Rochester, Minnesota, was a distance from Milwaukee. Could they have seen her at the airport and followed her all this way? It didn't seem possible. Even if she had been spectacularly unobservant and not seen them, she had given them plenty of chances to grab her on lonely roads. Somebody in Milwaukee had probably been told to look for a green Pontiac with Minnesota plates, and found it here in the hotel parking lot.

The fact that they were not waiting for her in her room didn't prove anything. If what they wanted was to capture her, they would not want her in a busy hotel. She descended to the lobby of the office building, found a telephone booth, and studied the phone book. A minute later, she was talking to the local office of Victory Car Rentals.

"I've got a problem. I rented a car from your agency at the Rochester, Minnesota, airport, and drove it to Milwaukee. Now it won't start."

"What's it doing?" the man asked.

"What's it doing?" she repeated. "Nothing."

"I mean, when you turn the key, does the starter turn over, or does it just sit there?"

"It goes 'Errr, errr, errr,' then nothing happens."

"It's probably flooded. Turn everything off. Just let it sit for fifteen minutes and try again. It should be fine."

"I tried that."

"Oh," said the man. "Well, then this time, push the pedal all the way down and hold it there while you turn the key."

Jane sighed loudly. "I've done all of those things. I'm running late. I've already called a cab to take me to the airport, and I've got to go or I'll miss my plane. I've got a client waiting to pick me up at the other end. The car is at the Columbia Hotel on Highland. I'm going to leave the keys at the desk for you."

The man's voice sounded forlorn. "There's probably nothing wrong with the car, ma'am," he said. "Maybe you're jumping the gun."

"Since you work in Milwaukee and the car is from Minnesota, you have no way of knowing, do you? If you want the car, it's at the Columbia Hotel. My cab just pulled up outside, and I've got to go."

Jane hung up, walked out of the building, and circled two blocks to approach the hotel front entrance from the other direction. She waited up the street until the right moment came. A cab pulled up and let a man out. Jane timed her arrival at the entrance to coincide with the cab's departure, and fell into step with the man. "Beautiful evening, isn't it?" she said.

The man, a tall, gangling guy with big feet, a suitcase in one hand, and a useless raincoat draped over his other arm, was startled. He turned toward her quickly, then recovered. "Sure is," he said.

They reached the door at the same time, and while he was trying to move the suitcase to the other hand, she pulled the door open for him. They walked to the desk together. Jane used the time to search the lobby for watchers, but saw no candidates. The desk clerk looked at both of them attentively and held his hands poised over his computer.

Jane spoke before the man did. "I'm checking out. My name is Stevens. I have two bags in my room ready to go. Can you send somebody up for them?" She held out her key card.

The clerk summoned a bellman, then sent him off with the card while he computed Jane's bill. She handed him her Lisa Stevens credit card and signed, then said, "I'd like to leave these keys with you. A man from Victory Rentals will be here to pick up my car."

"Certainly," said the man. He accepted the keys, slipped a piece of paper onto the ring, and wrote something on it before he put them into a drawer. "Anything else we can do for you?"

"Can you please check to see if anyone has come to the desk to leave a message for me?"

He looked through a small pile of notes. "Nobody's been here, ma'am."

"That changes my plan a little," said Jane. "Can you hold my bags down here for a while? I'll be back for them later."

"We'd be happy to," he said. She could tell he was beginning to dread her next request.

"Thanks," she said, then hurried out the front door. She took a different route back to her spot on the parking structure. If there had been a watcher inside the hotel, she had not seen him. If he had found her room, he had not done it by pretending to leave a note and following someone upstairs to her door.

Jane returned to her post at the edge of the parking structure and looked down at the hotel lot. The two sets of men were still down there. As the time went by, she reviewed what she had said and done. She had tried to sound rushed, angry, and breathless to the man at the car rental, so with any luck he would stick to his theory that she had simply flooded the carburetor and gotten too flustered to know it.

It was an hour before she saw her expectation confirmed. A Pontiac that was the same year, model, and color as her rental car pulled into the parking lot and stopped near the door. A young man wearing a blue work shirt and jeans got out of the passenger seat and trotted into the hotel. Jane watched the men at the rear of the parking lot. They turned their heads to confer, but she couldn't tell whether the coincidence meant anything to them. The man at the wheel of the new Pontiac sat with his window open and his elbow on the door, looking gloomy. He was clearly the boss—probably the man she had talked to. The younger man came out, trotted to Jane's rental car, unlocked it, and sat in the driver's seat without closing the door. The two watchers conferred again. This time, their heads turned back and forth in jerky movements.

The young man started Jane's car. He half-stood, stuck his head over the roof, and waved at his boss in the identical Pontiac. The man looked even gloomier, gave a halfhearted wave back, and drove out of the lot. The young man adjusted the driver's seat in Jane's car, pulled his long legs in, shut the door, and drove off after him.

The two watchers were confused. They were upset. Jane held her breath and watched them for a few seconds, until they did what she had expected them to do. They started their car and drove up the row after Jane's car. They could not ignore the possibility that what the young man was doing was bringing the car to Jane. If that wasn't it, and she no longer needed her car, then she was gone. Maybe she had been gone for hours.

Jane waited and studied the second set of watchers. They either felt less hesitation, or had less time for it. If Jane's car was gone, and their colleagues had gone off after it, then they were parked in the street watching nothing. They swung away from the curb and went off after their companions.

Jane pivoted and ran. She reached the door, swung it open, and dashed to the elevator. When she emerged on the street she slowed her pace to a purposeful walk, but she arrived at her Explorer quickly, pulled it to the front entrance of the

hotel, opened the tailgate, and hurried into the building. The
bellman had already recognized her. He had the bags out of
the little storeroom beside the door, and he carried them to
the Explorer. She handed him a ten-dollar bill, slammed the
tailgate, and drove off.

Jane made the first right turn, then a left, and pulled over
beside the curb to study her rearview mirror. After three minutes, she was sure that nobody had managed to follow her.
She opened her bag, looked at her road map, and headed for
the entrance to Interstate 94 south.

For the first time since morning, she began to breathe more
easily. She had changed her appearance, traded cars, and later
on, when she had gotten tired of driving, she would fold up
the distinctive green duffel bags and keep the rest of the letters in the gray suitcases with the carpet over them. The night
was just beginning, and Wisconsin wasn't used up yet. She
still had to hit Racine and Kenosha.

24

J ane worked her way through the stops north of Chicago—
Waukegan, Lake Forest, Winnetka, Evanston—as the
night was showing signs of ending. The sky to the east was
lightening into a luminous gray that wasn't yet bright enough
to reveal the true colors of the dark houses or the parked cars,
and the trees were still black shadows against the sky. During
the night she had changed her itinerary. She had expected to
save Chicago for the end of her swing through the Midwest,
but she was very close now, driving a clean car that she had
come by honestly. She had cut and dyed her hair, bought
clothes that made her look like a different sort of person, and

helped the new image with a little makeup. She had decided that she had better face Chicago now.

She approached the city during the morning rush, with carloads of commuters in the lanes on both sides of her, crawling slowly toward jobs and schools. She spent the slow stretches looking at the cars and the faces of her neighbors. In a single mile she counted twenty-two cars that looked a lot like hers—high, oversized utility vehicles with the small heads and narrow shoulders of women behind their steering wheels, their little faces peering down from above at the traffic ahead. On this road, there was not even a shortage of Wisconsin license plates.

Jane drove along the lake until the road became Lake Shore Drive. She stopped at mailboxes near Loyola University and Wrigley Field, and then kept going toward the center of the city. She left Lake Shore Drive at North Michigan Avenue and made her way south to Van Buren, then turned right to drive to the big central post office. The service windows would not be open until eight-thirty, but she entered the building with one of her two suitcases and put all of the remaining Chicago letters into the slots.

She retraced her route on Van Buren and turned north on Franklin, then found a public parking lot near the Sears Tower, and parked her Explorer. As she walked up West Adams Street toward the Dirksen Building, she studied the other pedestrians. There were more of them at seven-thirty than she had expected, and there were a few—maybe one per block—who she felt deserved a bit of extra scrutiny. They had the thick-necked look of men who wouldn't be surprised to have to duck a punch, and noses or eyebrows that showed signs that they had not always perceived the need in time. She watched their eyes without appearing to, but saw no flicker of excitement appear in any of them. By the time each of them had moved out of her line of sight, she had exonerated them all. As the hour moved closer to nine o'clock, when many offices opened, she began to see more and more women.

Jane waited anxiously until nine, then walked up the street to the bank. It had only been open a few minutes, so most of the people waiting in line for the tellers were shopkeepers holding big cash pouches or check ledgers. Jane walked past them to the counter for the safe-deposit boxes, where there were no other customers. A few weeks ago, she had visited the safe-deposit box to take out the passport she kept here, and this time, the woman at the counter remembered her. "Hello again," she said as she handed Jane the card to sign. "I love your hair."

"Thanks." Jane followed her to the vault, where the woman climbed a stepladder, took Jane's key, and handed Jane the box.

Jane went into one of the cubicles and let the door lock behind her, then sat down at the little desk. Before she opened the box, she looked up and to the sides. This bank had never installed surveillance cameras in places where they could tape what went on in the cubicles, and neither had the other banks where Jane rented boxes. She didn't know whether there was some federal bank regulation that ensured privacy, or if it was merely that people who rented safe-deposit boxes objected. But she had averted danger a great many times by looking for things where they weren't supposed to be, so she looked.

She opened the box, returned the Donna Parker passport to its place, and selected three fresh identities from the supply she had stored there: Mary Corticelli, Karen Pappas, and Elizabeth Moody. She chose those three because the photographs on the driver's licenses had all been taken when she'd had her hair braided or drawn back in a ponytail, so even with her short hair, she was still incontestably the same person. The credit cards in those names were all at least two years old and unexpired, so she was not worried about having them refused. She put away all of the identities she had already used on this trip except Diane Fierstein, because that was the name she had used to buy the Explorer, and Renee Moore, who had rented the house in Santa Fe. When this was over, she would change the pictures on the Renee Moore documents and give the identity to Rita.

It took longer to go through the identities she had placed here for runners. If Peter and Renee Moore were never found, then Bernie and Rita would never need more identification than they already had. If they were found and had time to get out, it would be a good idea for both of them to have backup identities. There were birth certificates for people aged three to seventy, and a few blanks. There were full sets that included driver's licenses, Social Security cards, credit cards, and a few membership cards of the sort that she acquired to give the impression that an identity had depth. She pulled out the best of the sets for elderly men. The name was Michael Daily, and his birth certificate made him sixty-nine years old. It was one of the genuine documents for names that had been planted in the Cook County clerk's records by a woman who believed Jane would do something worthwhile with them. The picture on the license was a man who didn't look precisely like Bernie Lupus, but didn't look so very different either: bald head, glasses, a thin face. In an emergency, Bernie might be able to use it even before Jane substituted the photograph she had taken in New Mexico.

As she stared at the picture, she remembered the man. She had picked him up in an unemployment office in Gary, Indiana. He had agreed to be driven across the state line to Illinois to take the tests for a driver's license in exchange for three hundred dollars and a day's excursion. She had paid him five, because she had liked him, and another two hundred as a finder's fee, because he had introduced her to three other people who were willing to take the same excursion.

She leafed through the cards for young women. The selection was much broader and richer. She had almost decided to give Diane J. Rabel to Rita when she remembered another one. It was a license she had obtained when she had invented Michael Daily. This one was for Karen Daily. It had occurred to her that if she ever had an elderly runner, he might come with a younger companion. She had obtained identification for a younger female the following week, and named her Karen Daily. She hunted through the stack until she found her, and added her to the pack of identities.

Jane arranged the sets of papers and cards into little packets and slipped them into a slit she had cut in the lining of her purse, then looked at the metal box again. She decided that it would be wise to take an extra five thousand dollars with her. The move-in expenses in Santa Fe and buying the Explorer had seriously depleted her credit, and her cash supply was low. She took one thick bundle of hundreds out and slipped that into her purse too. Then she faced the last decision.

There was something at the bottom of this box, wrapped in a cloth. It had been here since the day when she had said good-bye to Bobby Ortiz six years ago. By then he had not been Bobby Ortiz for at least a month: he looked a bit different, he had a different name, and he was living quietly in Cincinnati, far from the troubles he had brought on himself in Modesto, California. She had not even known that he had it until the moment when she was about to leave. He had simply handed her a paper bag and said, "You told me that if I went with you I would have to leave everything from the old days. I kind of forgot something." When she had gotten into her car, she had opened the bag and confirmed what the weight of it had told her. Inside was a nine-millimeter Beretta Cougar with two extra magazines.

Jane had left the gun in the safe-deposit box all this time for an emergency, but she had known even then that the kind of emergency that could be solved by putting a hole in someone never came with that kind of warning. If she could see it coming, she could probably evade it.

There had been occasions when she had considered it necessary to carry a gun, but she had noticed that guns had an unexpected effect. People—even thoughtful people—behaved differently when they were armed. She had noticed that her eyes remained sharp, her mind alert, but what they were doing was studying and evaluating each change in the configuration of people and events to recognize the one when she would need to pull the gun from its hiding place and fire it. That became the only decision: the gun was suddenly the only strategy.

She decided that this occasion, too, was not right. Her survival depended on unpredictable movement and fading into the scenery. If she could finish the trip without being noticed, she had nothing to worry about, and if she couldn't, then stopping the car to produce a pistol was not likely to help.

She watched the bank teller slip the box back into its slot, then took her key and walked out of the bank. It was only nine-fifteen, but she felt more impatient than ever to be out of Chicago. She had not put enough distance behind her since her rental car had been traced to Milwaukee, and Chicago had a deep, ugly history of Mafia infestation.

She made her way back to the parking lot, pulled out her ticket, and watched the parking attendant run across the lot toward her. He was a young black man with his hair combed straight back on his head and a blue vest with a button on it that said, DON'T LAUGH. YOU COULD BE CRAZY TOO SOME DAY. He ducked into his little wooden shelter, hung the keys of the car he had just parked on his pegboard, then reached for Jane's keys just as a car pulled into the lot behind him and honked its horn.

When he involuntarily jerked his head to see who was honking the horn, his eyes widened for an instant, and then the lids came down again. "I'm sorry. Just be a second. Got to get that car right away." He trotted to the car and opened the door so the driver could get out. Jane stood by the wooden shelter and held the proceedings in the corner of her eye. The driver was a big man about forty years old, wearing a fawn-colored sport coat that was unbuttoned to make room for a premature paunch. He got out and stood for a moment to watch the parking attendant slip behind the wheel, drive the blue Lincoln Town Car twenty feet ahead, then back it up to swing into a space right behind the little shelter.

Jane could see that this was a place of honor: the spot closest to the sidewalk, where the attendant could bring it out in seconds. There was no chance that as the day got busier, another car would be parked in front of it. The attendant couldn't help having his eyes on it, because he had to pass it to dispense tickets or accept money. Jane watched only long enough to be sure that the attendant didn't go through the charade of burdening the big man with a ticket, then turned her head away so that even her profile would be hidden while the man walked off down the street. She ached to get out of here. Everything about the man smelled to her like Mafia.

As the attendant returned and reached for her keys on the pegboard, Jane's eyes fell on the inner wall of the little shelter. The attendant had a collection of pinups pasted to the wall. At the top were two portraits of women lounging on beds with blissful smiles. Beneath them, at eye level, were four snapshots. Two were of a fully dressed young black woman, and the third was of the same woman with the attendant. His wife? Girlfriend? Below the snapshots was an anomaly—a black-and-white drawing. Jane took a step closer. The woman had long, black hair like the others, but it wasn't his girlfriend. It was Jane. She could see writing beneath. "Five feet eight or nine, 130 pounds, pretty." Then, scrawled in pencil along the top, she saw a telephone number.

Jane reached into her purse, pulled out a ten-dollar bill, and stepped to the left side of the exit as the attendant pulled up. As he got out, she handed him the money without looking at him, muttered, "Thanks," and got into the car.

The attendant said, "It's only five."

She said, "Keep it," pushed the button to raise the tinted window, and drove out of the lot. She put three blocks behind her, then took last-minute turns at the next three corners, watching her mirror. She found the entrance to Interstate 90, drove north for ten minutes, and got off at North Avenue.

Jane drove west for a few blocks toward the strip mall. She was sure that she had not been followed, but the drawing still frightened her. It was a fairly good likeness—good enough for the man in the Seattle-Tacoma airport, anyway. She knew that she had just been seen by two men who had looked at the drawing, and neither had apparently recognized her, with her haircut and glasses. But the sheer reach of the families terrified her.

The little delay at the parking lot had reminded her of how completely the Mafia was built into people's everyday lives. Unless there was a fresh scandal, people didn't even think about them. Maybe they were involved in this business or that one, and their extortion added ten cents to the price of a product. But maybe that was just a rumor, and the increase was just because of a strike, or a rise in the price of raw materials. You were never going to find out, and you couldn't do anything about them any more than you could control the weather, so you bought the product at the new price and didn't waste any time thinking about it.

Jane drove past the little strip mall and studied it. The stores were still the same: the doughnut shop, the hair-and-nail salon, the small hardware store, the dry cleaner, the mailing service, and the ever-changing restaurant. This time, the restaurant was Chinese. Last time, it had been Cuban, and before that, barbecued ribs and chicken. There was something about the building's position on the planet that made each tenant open a restaurant and fail, always to be replaced by another tenant with a restaurant.

Jane was used to coming here once or twice a year to visit the rented mailbox of the Furnace Company and pay her bill. The Furnace Company was a genuine corporation she had formed eleven years ago. She was neither the sole owner nor the sole officer, but none of the others happened to be made of flesh. When the Furnace Company received mail, it was forwarded to another box in Buffalo.

The Furnace Company had been a useful entity. It allowed her to request credit checks and background information on people without raising eyebrows, gave her another mailing address with an extra layer of anonymity, and had given her a few easy ways of providing histories for runners. Sometimes she requested references or school records for employees of other companies, changed the names, and passed them on. Sometimes she had presented the Furnace Company as an executive-search service that had already checked all references.

Jane drove around the block and pulled into her favorite parking space on the little strip of asphalt. She stepped into the mailing service and waved to Dave, the owner.

"Hey, Mary!" he said. "About time you got here. What the hell did you do with your hair?"

"Why, did you want it?" she asked.

Dave rubbed his bald head thoughtfully. "Nah. Doesn't go with my body. You got a shipment back here."

She moved to the counter and watched as he walked to the corner of the back room. She could see the ten boxes bearing the labels she had made in Santa Fe. "Gee, that's good time. I didn't think they'd get here so soon."

"Not so fast," said Dave. "Forgetting something? I'm a businessman, not your relative."

"What do I owe you?"

"Fifteen a month for the box is 180, plus 205 for forwarding, that's what? Three eighty-five."

Jane pulled out four of the hundred-dollar bills from her visit to the bank. Then, on an impulse, she handed him two more. "Here's for the next year," she said. "In case I don't get here again . . . for a while."

He counted out her change, then pulled a sheet of paper from under the counter and gazed at it, then at Jane. "I was saving this for you, but it's not as good as I thought now that you cut your hair." He spun it around quickly, staring into her eyes for a reaction.

It was the same drawing Jane had seen at the parking lot. This time it said, "Woman missing since July 20. Large reward." She couldn't recall whether the telephone number was the same. Jane said, "Are you saying that looks like me?"

He looked at it again. "I thought you'd get a kick out of it."

" 'Large reward,' " Jane mused. "Maybe I should try to turn myself in and collect. Where did you get it—the police?"

He shrugged. "Some guy came in and stuck it on my bulletin board. He didn't hang around long enough to hear about how my board space ain't free. I mean, this isn't the post office. Am I wrong?"

"You know me," said Jane. "The world's most rabid capitalist. Hey, you mind if I take that picture?"

He handed it to her. "I saved it for you."

"Thanks. I've got to get a second opinion." She folded it into her purse and surveyed the bulletin board to see if there was another with a picture of Rita, but if there was, it had not stayed on the board.

He laughed. "You want a hand loading your mail?"

"It's the least you can do."

She got her keys out while Dave slipped his hand truck under the first five boxes, tipped it back on its wheels, and brought the boxes out the door.

He followed her to the Explorer and shoved the boxes into the back, then went inside again. When he returned with the last five, Jane was rearranging the first five in the aisle behind the front seat. "Thanks," she said.

"See you next time," said Dave.

As Jane drove off, she wondered whether she had paid him a year's rental in advance to be fair because she never intended to come back, or because it was beginning to look as though she would not live that long. She held the wheel with one hand and pulled out the portrait. If they had this picture, then she had made some terrible mistake.

25

"**W**hat the hell is this?" shouted Catania. "Will somebody please tell me?" He stood up so fast that his belt buckle hooked on the edge of the table and upset his glass of orange juice. The two men across the table from him watched the pulpy liquid soak the deck of cards, then moved their chairs back to watch it drip onto the floor near their feet. The floor of the Rivoli Social Club was very old wood, and over the years a lot of things had soaked into it, but neither of the men wanted orange juice stuck to the bottoms of their shoes.

Pescati glanced at the cards in his hand, then at the wet deck on the table, and tossed his cards beside it. "It could be just a story."

"Yeah?" said Catania. "What's the point of making up a story that proves you can't find your own ass with both hands? Or that some little chick kicked the shit out of you and took your car?" Catania began to pace. "This is unbelievable," he muttered. "It's got to be a joke." He stopped, grasped thin air with his hands, and shook it. "Has the whole universe suddenly gone crazy?"

"If it did happen, it's just one of those things," said Cotrano.

"One of what things?" The two men could see that Catania was working himself into a blind rage. Since his rage was not directed at them, they were not afraid. If they could be polite long enough to weather it, they would be all right. "What kind of things? Talking dogs? Pigs with wings? Lifetime guarantees?"

"He means it's just a temporary setback," said Mosso in a soothing voice from the other side of the room. "They said she surprised Langusto's guy in the Seattle airport. I suppose it's possible she did. What does it take to trip a guy in the middle of an airport, with a million people around? Even if he was in the mood, he couldn't exactly gut her and skin her in the middle of a crowd, could he?"

Catania was calming down. "He could have stopped her, or stopped the plane. This is billions of dollars."

The other men looked at Mosso expectantly. He took a deep breath and walked closer. "We've been thinking about this," he began. "If I'm wrong, tell me to shut up. But it doesn't seem to us that everything they told you on that bus is true."

"They hardly told me anything on the bus," snapped Catania. "You know what I learned? Tasso thinks it's Bernie's ghost, who is pissed off because I wanted him to empty his brain onto a computer disk. Molinari thinks it's Delfina, who happens to be boss of a family about the size of a pro football team, which makes him a good one to blame it on. The Langusto brothers think we shouldn't waste time making guesses. We've got to do the same things to stop them no matter who it is, and we'll find out when we find out."

"That's the one that strikes me as odd," said Mosso. He was four years older than Catania, and at sixty-three was beginning to look wise and distinguished, so he cultivated the impression. When Catania had been a small, skinny boy on the streets, Mosso had stepped into the role of protector and quiet adviser, and let Catania speak for him. He had always been uncomfortable when he was singled out for notice, but he had seen instantly that Catania craved attention as though it were sunlight. Whenever Mosso spoke, Catania's head would turn toward him and he would fall into unaccustomed silence.

"What's so odd?"

"The Langustos. They kind of took charge, didn't they?"

"They wish," said Catania contemptuously. "Joe has connections in brokerage houses and banks, so he was in a position to find things out. The Langustos were supposed to be responsible for Bernie all these years, so they should take on more of the headache. And Phil's the head of their family, that's all."

Mosso nodded, and sat in silence. Catania looked away and walked back to the table, picked up his empty juice glass, then glanced at Mosso, still sitting in mute immobility. His silence was beginning to feel loud. Catania put down his glass. "What?"

"The Langustos call a meeting," said Mosso. "They tell everybody what they ought to be looking for, but they also tell everybody what they shouldn't be looking for. And it sounds like an odd choice: who's doing it. Then this woman nobody knows supposedly shows up in Seattle and hammers a full-grown made guy. But who saw it besides him, and whose guy is this?"

"Langusto's," conceded Catania. "But that could just be odds. They've got more guys out looking than anybody else. They flew them all over the place. I figured it's better Phil Langusto pays those travel bills than me."

Mosso sat in silence. His silence was expanding again, and Catania began to feel it taking up space. Catania said, "Are you thinking that the Langusto family don't want us to find the money?"

"I don't want to say the Langustos are trying to get all that money for themselves. Maybe they wouldn't do that."

"Of course they would," said Catania. "I would, you would, anybody would."

Mosso shook his head and feigned bewilderment. "I'm not as smart as a lot of people: you, them. . . . But wouldn't a good way be to send everybody else to look in all directions except the one that will pay off?"

Catania's eyes began to burn. He nodded.

Mosso said, "This is like being in a card game where the dealer is a little too good. You don't know he's dealing from the bottom, because you didn't see it, but you can tell he could if he wanted to. So if he's not, why isn't he?"

"It's true. The Langustos might be trying to keep us all out of the way while they concentrate on finding the people who have the money and then shaking them down."

Mosso shrugged. "I'm too slow to figure out what they're doing. It could be that. It seems to me that if the Langustos have all these connections and they're so good at figuring it all out, why call a meeting? Why cut everybody else in? Are they doing it because they want to be fair and make sure each family gets what it laid off with Bernie? Why? How?"

Catania stared down at the soaked cards on the table. He seemed to be unable to find an answer.

Mosso held up both hands. "I'm not saying it's one thing or another. We came to you because you're our capo, and you're smarter than we are. We came to ask." Cotrano and Pescati stared at Mosso in undisguised admiration.

Catania said, "You came to tell me I've been walking around with my eyes closed."

Pescati was braver now. "No, Victor. It's just that to us, the whole thing smells a little ripe, you know? We're all supposed to spot any of this money moving, and report to Langusto's guy, Pompi—who, incidentally, would steal the dirt from your fingernails. I've known him for years. We're looking for a bodyguard and a maid. What happens if we find them? Do we bring them to the Langustos?"

Cotrano said quietly, "It's a little bit like Phil Langusto was the boss, and we all worked for him."

Catania's head snapped to face Cotrano.

Pescati said, "He means—"

"I know what he means," Catania interrupted. "He means what he says." Catania walked faster, turning when he came to the wall, walking to the end of the room, and spinning again. "The truth is, I don't know any more than you do about this. Maybe Bernie really did do what we all thought, and started writing down where he put the money. Maybe he even did it because I asked him to think about it. This could all be my fault. Maybe I got him to write it down, and now there really is somebody moving it around to wash it. But you're right. Phil Langusto is trying to control this. It might just be that he wants to sucker us all into helping look for these people, then get to the money first and say he never found it— or pay everybody a tenth of what we put in, and hide the rest. But it could be a hell of a lot worse than that."

"What are you thinking of?" asked Mosso.

Catania's eyes began to glow again. "Think back a few months. Suppose that, while the rest of us were worrying about what would happen if Bernie died, the Langustos were thinking about it another way."

"What way?"

"Everybody knew Bernie wouldn't live forever. The Langustos added up what they would lose if Bernie kicked off right away. It came to—I don't know—say, a billion dollars. It occurred to them that they might make bigger money if they killed him themselves."

"I'm lost," said Pescati.

Catania spoke quickly but patiently. "They kill Bernie. They get every family together who stood to lose money, and say, 'We've all got to look for the money together, because none of us can find it alone. Just for efficiency, report what you find to us and we'll tell everybody else.' People get used to talking to the Langustos instead of each other. Pretty soon the Langustos are telling everybody's people where to look for the money and who to call if they see anything. And they're deciding who gets to be cut in and who's cut out. I told you they didn't invite Frank Delfina to that meeting, right?" His mind seemed to take another turn that surprised him. He asked, "Who have we got out on this right now?"

Mosso pursed his lips and looked at the ceiling. "I guess it's about three hundred made guys out of town, and the ones who work on their crews. Figure a thousand, fifteen hundred."

"Suppose something happened right now—today, right here in New York? Say I need guys to line up along Thirty-ninth Street and protect this building from the Langustos? How many will show up?"

Cotrano frowned. "Jesus, Victor . . ."

"How many?"

"In twenty-four hours, everybody, with all their crews. In half an hour, I don't know. Maybe fifty, probably less. We kept the good earners at home, not the guns. We've even got some of them out running down bank accounts and addresses and stuff."

"Mixed right in with people from the other families, right? Molinari's guys, Langusto's guys . . ."

Pescati and Cotrano began to look increasingly uneasy. Even Mosso seemed uncomfortable.

"See what I mean?" said Catania. "It's like this was designed to sucker people like me. I figure, if I keep my guys at home and the rest of them find our money, are we going to get it? No. So I send my soldiers away, so I don't lose out. But what if that was the whole point? The families that go along with the program like they already work for the Langustos . . . well, pretty soon, they're going to find out that they do. But the ones the Langustos know will be trouble can be handled. Like me. Instead of having to face my four hundred guys with his four hundred and fifty, they just have to face the fifty guys we kept home because they were good at arithmetic, but not so good in an alley on a dark night."

"You think Phil Langusto is making his move like Castiglione did?" asked Mosso.

Catania shrugged. "I don't know. I thought from the beginning that if somebody killed Bernie the Elephant and got his hands on the money, the place we'd find it wasn't going to be the March of Dimes. The only thing I'm sure of now is that this is a hell of an easy way to take over another family." His eyes were sad and wistful as he stared down at the street outside the window of the Rivoli Social Club. "I wish I had thought of it myself."

26

As Jane drove west out of Chicago on Interstate 90, her constant glances into the rearview mirror and her careful appraisals of each car that appeared beside her gave her a chance to study the women that she was trying to impersonate. That one ahead and to the right had probably dropped somebody off in the city—a husband at work, a child at school—and she was driving her Land Rover back to the suburbs. Jane read the frame around the license plate: Valley Imports, Elk Grove Village. Jane pushed a bit harder on the accelerator to pull closer to the woman. The hair looked almost exactly like Jane's. A lot of women with babies cut their hair to keep little fingers from tangling in it. As Jane drew abreast of the woman, she could see a child strapped in a car seat behind her.

Jane pulled ahead. She had to keep looking for danger, not finding new ways of telling herself it was gone. She had verified that the changes she had made had lowered her profile—made her look like a million other women—and proving it to herself over and over was pointless. She was doing what she had decided to do, and she had known exactly what the risks would be before she had made the choice. There were lots of people who had been dazzled by the sums of money the Mafia took in, and had concocted some clever scheme to divert some of it. There were skimmers and embezzlers and hijackers and con men, young members of gangs who got into grown-up rackets without considering who had been making all that money before they were born. The graveyards of big cities were full of them.

The half disguise she had assumed was not bad, but it was best in situations like this: if all anyone could see were brief glances from a distance, she was difficult to distinguish from the people around her. At close quarters, she was still Jane. She spent a few seconds thinking her way through the rest of her original itinerary, and decided it was not good enough. They had her picture, they knew that she was mailing letters. The only way to fight them was to try to do it quickly.

Jane stopped at mailboxes in Hoffman Estates, Elgin, Rockford. From there she took 39 south until she came to a tollway rest stop just west of De Kalb. After she had mailed her letters she filled the gas tank, spent a few minutes rearranging her boxes of letters in the Explorer to bring the next ones up to the front, and went into the little store to buy a pile of road maps.

Then Jane began to drive. She kept moving across the long, straight highways, always just fast enough to cheat the speed limit a little but not enough to be pulled over by the highway patrol. She drove to Moline, crossed the bridge over the Mississippi into Iowa, and stopped in Davenport, Iowa City, Cedar Rapids. She turned west again on Route 30 and reached Ames at six, then went south to Des Moines. She didn't stop for dinner until she had approached the southern edge of the city.

She ate quickly, spent five minutes moving the next boxes of letters to the front of the Explorer, collapsed the empties and stuffed them into a Dumpster, then drove onto Interstate 35. She reached Kansas City after dark, and found a big central post office just west of the junction with Interstate 70. She was fairly confident that even the most thorough search

for her wouldn't include any surveillance of closed post offices, so she drove up, dropped her mail in the box outside,
and headed for the entrance to Interstate 70.

She stopped in Columbia, reached St. Louis just before
dawn, and slipped into the city just ahead of the wave of commuters. She made five stops on her way through St. Louis,
and as the traffic around her began to crowd and slow, she
got back on 70 and crossed the Mississippi again into East
St. Louis.

Jane's nervous energy was beginning to leave her after the
night of headlights on nearly empty highways. She considered her options. She didn't feel ready to settle into a hotel,
because it would take too much time, so she pulled off the big
highway, made her way back to the park with a little patch of
green grass and shady trees she had seen from the road,
parked the Explorer, climbed into the back seat, and slept.

When she awoke, it was to the sound of voices. She lay still
and listened for a second, then verified that they were the
voices of children. She raised her head and looked at the
clock on the dashboard. It was noon, and there were other
cars in the lot. As she got back into the driver's seat, she could
see that there were three families at the picnic tables, the parents laying out food and drinks, the children running around
in that aimless way they did after they had been confined in a
car—first chasing one another, then rushing back, then just
running. Jane backed out of her parking space and headed for
the interstate.

The noon sun was bright, the day was clear, and the stops
were far apart. She stopped at Vandalia and Effingham to
mail letters, then followed Interstate 70 into Indiana at four
o'clock.

She stopped just over the border at Terre Haute, then at In-
dianapolis, then Fort Wayne. She ate in a truck stop, where
she knew there would be little competition for the ladies'
room. She locked the door, washed herself as well as she
could, and worked on changing her appearance again.

It was great to be a young suburban matron driving her

SUV around during the daytime, but it wasn't daytime anymore. Tonight she wasn't going to be driving across long, sparsely populated stretches. She knew that in some of the areas where she was going tonight, suburban matrons were going to be scarce. She tucked her short hair up under her baseball cap, put her thin windbreaker on over a loose sweatshirt, and laced up her running shoes. She evaluated herself in the mirror. She didn't look like a man, precisely, but she was as tall as many men, and on a dark city street, her silhouette wouldn't scream out, "What am I doing here alone?" She slipped her wallet into her back pocket like a man, and wondered how they could stand the way that felt. But when she stepped back from the mirror far enough to see herself at full length, she was pleased. It disguised the female shape of her backside pretty well, if she kept the windbreaker down to her hips.

She walked out to the Explorer and drove off to pick up Interstate 69. She reached the Michigan border at nine, then stopped in Battle Creek, Lansing, and Flint, so it was after midnight when Jane abandoned Interstate 69 and turned onto Interstate 75 toward Detroit.

Jane was premeditated and methodical, because time mattered. At each stop she walked quickly with her head up and her eyes scanning, dropped off her mail, and hurried back to the vehicle. Each time she left a freeway, she memorized the exit she had used to leave it and drove back the same way to the entrance ramp. She spent the night making the circuit of the cities around Detroit.

Jane had driven all day and most of the night after nothing more than a nap on the back seat, and she was feeling exhausted and dirty. She had once hidden a runner in Ann Arbor, and tonight her memory of the city made it seem like a good place to stop for what remained of the night. The University of Michigan was about half the population, so in the summer it probably wouldn't be difficult to find a vacant place to sleep. Her Wisconsin license plates would not be a problem, because university towns were full of cars from other states.

Jane got off Interstate 94 at State Street and headed north toward the university campus. She found a mailbox after only two blocks, mailed her letters, and began to watch for the right sort of motel. As she crossed Huron Street, she saw one that seemed right. It consisted of a big building in front for the reception area and a restaurant and, behind it, several smaller buildings shielded somewhat from the noise of the highway, where people could park their cars outside their rooms.

Jane stopped in front of the main building and walked toward the lighted glass doors, where she could see a small lobby. She reached for the handle of the glass door and stood still. Just inside the door was a bulletin board. In the middle, among the advertisements for band concerts, dry-cleaning services, and restaurants, was the picture of Jane. This time the block letters above the telephone number said, GRADUATE STUDENT MISSING.

Jane turned on her heel, walked back to the Explorer, and drove out onto the street to continue north. When she reached Highway 23, she turned east again toward Detroit. When she stopped at an all-night station in Plymouth to fill the gas tank, she knew that there was only one solution to her problem. She had to go on.

Jane got back into the car and drove, but within fifteen minutes she regretted it. She had begun to sense a light-headed, vertiginous feeling that told her she wasn't going to be able to stay on the road much longer. Every time she turned her head to glance at the mirrors, she would see flashes of light, and images that almost had shapes but didn't have time to solidify before she blinked them away. The next stage would be when they acquired firm, unchanging out-lines, and that would mean she had fallen asleep and begun to dream.

She rubbed her eyes and slapped her cheeks hard, so they stung for a few seconds, and stared ahead at the long, dark highway. It was a short run down to Toledo, no more than sixty miles of straight, flat freeway, but it seemed endless to her now.

When she reached the outskirts of the city, she could see that the light was already beginning to change. The sun would be coming up above the other end of the lake in less than an hour, and she would be driving straight into the glare. She was going to have to find a place to rest. She watched the exits until she began to see tall buildings. When she saw a sign that said CONVENTION CENTER, she took the next exit and drove south on Monroe Street. The kind of place she wanted would be in the center of the city, where visitors came to do business and cars were parked underground or in parking structures. She found a big Holiday Inn near the convention center and parked two floors down in the garage beneath it. When she picked up one of her gray suitcases and prepared to go inside, she noticed that one of the boxes of mail was visible, with the letters in plain sight. She quickly covered her boxes of mail with the carpet, and locked the Explorer. She had just seen the proof that she had not stopped too soon. Her life depended on alertness and premeditation, and she had long ago lost her edge.

When Jane entered her room and locked the door, she gave herself permission to feel the two days of exhaustion. It took a great deal of discipline for her to carry her suitcase to the stand near the bed. She stripped off her clothes, turned down the bed covers, then felt an irritated, fussy reluctance to lie down between the clean white sheets. She had been on the road for days without a bath. Could it have been since Milwaukee? She walked into the bathroom, ran the shower, and scrubbed herself. Then she closed the drain and let the shower fill the tub. She lay back in the hot, soothing water for a time, listening to the silence. She let her head submerge, and felt her short hair floating around her ears, then lifted her face just above the surface with her eyes still closed.

Jane awoke with a start, and sat up. The water sloshed in a wave toward the end of the tub, then rolled back toward her. She had fallen asleep. She climbed out, used the big, fluffy towels to dry herself, then the hair dryer and comb on her hair. The short hair dried much more quickly than she had expected it to: maybe it wasn't so bad.

At last she climbed between the sheets, turned off the bed-side lamp, and closed her eyes. The images of the past two days crowded one another behind her eyelids: the lines on a long road coming into being just beyond the range of her headlights, already brightening and streaking toward her like projectiles.

Jane knew that she was in a dream, because the trees around her seemed to form in some instant just before she looked at them. They would change and move to arrange themselves in better order, like a crowd of soldiers falling into line.

Jane was running. She picked out the narrow trail between the trees, keeping her eyes high enough to see the next twenty feet so her mind would record the high spots and obstacles and plant each stride safely while her eyes focused ahead to see that much more of the trail. She used an enormous amount of concentration, because of the ones who were track-ing her.

Each stride had to be longer than the ones that they were taking, and the rhythm of her feet hitting the ground had to be more rapid than the pace they were making. They were far enough behind her so that she could not hear them, and they were back beyond seeing in the thick forest. She knew that every time the path curved, the trees would appear to close behind her.

The one concern she had was that the sun had gone down. The light that filtered through the leaves above her was not reaching the path in bright, moving shafts anymore, and it was getting difficult to keep up her speed. The dark would have been comforting if she could have simply crawled into the thick brush and hidden, but she could not. All she could do was keep moving.

Just as the darkness fell, she saw the woman. The woman had thick black hair that was not like Jane's, because it had a bit of a curl to it, and Jane's was long and straight. Her skin was smooth and creamy white, and she was wearing a white silk dress that Jane recognized. It had belonged to Jane's mother once, before Jane was born, and she had worn it for a photograph with Jane's father that still stood on the mantel. To Jane it stood for all old-fashioned dresses.

The woman was standing perfectly still in the middle of the path, looking directly at Jane. She turned and walked through the low plants to the right, and Jane knew she was supposed to follow. The woman stepped through a thick barrier of bushes, and Jane tried to step through after her, but the opening the woman had found was gone. Jane fought her way through, scratching her arms and legs on the branches that rustled and snapped.

Jane came out the other side and stopped. At first she thought she was in the large clearing she had been expecting: thickets didn't grow in the shade of the tall forest trees, but in places where the trees had fallen. The space was more than that. It was a lawn. There was a big swimming pool with water that glowed from submerged lights, then a row of tennis courts, and a big old hotel. Dim lights on the ground floor shone through French doors, and Jane could see men in dark suits and women in bright, thin summer dresses dancing. After she had noticed them, she began to hear the music, a faint, melodious sound of a band from the 1940s.

The woman was on the lawn, and Jane stepped closer to her. When she reached a distance of five feet, the woman turned and Jane stopped. "You're a ghost."

The woman shrugged. She was very young—little more than a teenager—and the quick, playful movement of her graceful body made Jane feel heavy and tired from her run. "I'm a woman, like you."

Jane suddenly knew her. "You're Francesca Giannini. You're Vincent Ogliaro's mother."

The woman smiled. "Not yet," she said. "Not for at least nine months." She half-turned and pointed at the building across the lawn. "Tonight, I'm only twenty. I'm upstairs there—the fifth floor, third window from the right."

"How—"

"I'm asleep, dreaming. My father brought me here on the train. He's up in the private banquet room with his friends and his enemies and a bunch of soldiers. The women and children are asleep."

"I'm in your dream, and you're in mine?"

Francesca Giannini said, "There are things you can't know, and things you can. Hawenneyu the right-handed twin makes things—women who are smooth and fresh and beautiful. Hanegoategeh the left-handed twin makes time count, so it wrinkles and bends us and takes our strength. Hawenneyu gives us love to replenish the world, so living in time won't matter to us. Hanegoategeh separates the lovers, so the love turns into pain."

"That's you," said Jane.

"Is it?" asked Francesca. "The brothers fight. One is right-handed and the other left-handed, like images in a mirror. Each anticipates what the other's next stratagem will be, and constructs the counterattack before it begins. The first can predict the counterstroke, and changes his tactic ever so slightly, or does the opposite. It's like reaching your right hand to the surface of the mirror: the left hand of your reflection rises to meet it. They've been fighting this way since the beginning of the world, so time folds, and things that happened fifty years ago and others that are happening now are the same instant: attack and counterattack conceived simultaneously."

Francesca Giannini paused, and her bright black eyes seemed to change subtly to be older, to grow cunning and predatory, the way Jane had imagined her. "You think I spent my life embracing Hanegoategeh, the left-handed. Maybe I was just Hawenneyu's trick on his brother. Maybe I was put here tonight"—she indicated the big, ornate hotel—"as a stratagem."

"Why? So Bernie Lupus would meet you, and fall in love? That's how he was—will be—trapped into spending his life hiding money for the Mafia."

Francesca shrugged. "Maybe that's what happened. And maybe the opposite. Maybe it was so Bernie would spend a lifetime collecting it, and then someone—I—would love him enough to set him loose alive with the money."

"How do I know?"

Francesca Giannini shook her head sadly. "All we can know is what you always knew. Everything that happens is part of the fighting."

"Which one did this?"

Francesca shrugged. "Hawenneyu makes a man who can remember everything he sees. Hanegoategeh makes him poor and hungry. Hawenneyu sees that he's taken in and fed by strangers. Hanegoategeh has already ensured that the strangers will be a tribe of cannibals. Hawenneyu gives one of the cannibals a young daughter." She held out her white dress and twirled for Jane.

Jane said, "So beautiful. A man who could never forget would—"

"Would never forget," interrupted Francesca. "I'm wearing this dress in my dream because I've already laid it out to wear when I wake up tomorrow. That's when Bernie and I will meet." She closed her eyes and took a deep breath, like a sigh of pleasure, then let it out. "Later on I'll age, as Hanegoategeh wanted. Maybe I'll do savage things, the way he wanted. But it was Hawenneyu that made Bernie so that he will remember me exactly this way forever."

"But what am I supposed to do?" asked Jane.

Francesca shrugged. "I'm just a twenty-year-old girl. I suppose you should do what you think is best."

"But this whole story—everything any of us has been doing—it's all yours: your son, your lover, your death, your friends, your enemies."

"I can only see the little spot on the earth my eyes can reach for the brief time when they're open. Maybe that's why you're here: because the story is longer than one woman's life. Maybe we were both part of Hawenneyu's trick to fool Hanegoategeh into collecting money for the poor and the sick. Maybe your whole trip was designed to keep you away from Carey, so he would work late and be at the hospital to operate on somebody and save his life. Maybe it was all so that Rita would be killed in one place instead of another. For all I know, it was just so you would transport the Ford Explorer from Milwaukee so it will be wherever you leave it.

But be careful. You're making mistakes, and time moves so fast."

Jane awoke, her heart beating in a frantic rhythm and her eyes wide. She looked around her, and it took her a second to remember why she was in a hotel room. She lay there for a minute deciphering the sounds in the hallway. When she had satisfied herself that the two sets of heavy male footsteps were just a bellman taking a new guest to a room near the end of the hall, she sat up and looked at the clock. It was two-thirty in the afternoon.

Jane showered and dressed in a good pair of slacks, a clean blouse and jacket. She had lunch in the hotel restaurant and thought about what she had done so far. Somehow, somewhere early in this, she had made a mistake. She had only been mailing letters for three days when the man in Seattle had tried to grab her. For all this time, she had put off thinking clearly about it.

From the moment when she had first noticed the large numbers of men watching the airports, she had been afraid that one of them would be someone who had seen her before. When the man had approached her in Seattle, he had seemed to step into her fear and give it a tangible form. She was willing to believe that he might recognize her even though he didn't look familiar to her. Later she had seen the drawings, and they had seemed to explain everything. But they didn't.

Jane had ignored the fact that the men in Seattle had been stalking another woman first. She had looked a little bit like Jane, but the biggest similarity was that she had been mailing letters. It was possible that one of the men had recognized Jane, and it was possible that by then they knew someone must be mailing letters to charities. But how could they have connected those two facts? Had something been wrong with the first batch of letters?

Jane took the elevator to the garage and opened the tailgate of the Explorer. She unzipped the first suitcase. She picked out a pile of letters with a rubber band around them. The return addresses were all in Ohio, and the zip codes were in sequence. No, she thought. If it were that kind of mistake—a letter put into a mailbox in the wrong state—it might not be noticed even by the charities, let alone come to the attention of criminals.

It could be something wrong with the letters themselves, but they weren't all alike. She had written most of them herself, and Henry had read all of them before they were sealed. Maybe one of the checks had told somebody something, but the only way she could think of to find out what it might be was to talk to Henry. And how would the families know so soon? It had to be something that an ordinary person could pick up at a glance. And a person like that—any outsider— would be unlikely to see anything but the envelope. She would just have to look at the envelopes again.

She began to flip through the stacks of letters, then set each one aside. Each had been stamped, each had a plausible return address bearing a zip code in sequence with the others near it, and each was addressed to some charity.

It was ten minutes before she found the letter with no return address. It was stuck among the letters to be mailed in Lancaster, Pennsylvania. At first, Jane considered letting it go, but she glanced at the address: Ann Shelford, FSP, Box 747, Starke, Florida 32081.

Jane put the rest of her stacks of letters into their suitcases. She calmly placed them in order to match her new itinerary, and zipped them up. She took the single letter, closed the tailgate, and got into the front seat. Then she opened the envelope.

The print style was the one Jane had stared at for a month, from the laser printer in Santa Fe. It had been slipped in with the letters Jane had picked up in Chicago, so that it wouldn't have a Santa Fe postmark.

"Dear Mama," it began. Jane felt a twinge of discomfort at what she was doing, and an enormous sadness. "Things are going pretty well for me now. I'm still living in the house out in the country with that friend I told you about." Jane's heart stopped for a second, then began to beat harder. She reminded herself that the "friend" must be Bernie. She could have told her mother about him as long as a year ago. Jane forced her eyes back to the letter.

"She and I have a lot in common, and we get along fine. We both like being outdoors, and traveling, and nice food. Now and then we drive into town and eat at a restaurant in a hotel called Eldorado. I've been trying to keep track of what I taste, and see if I can piece together the recipe. Maybe by the time I see you again, I'll be able to cook something fancy for you. I don't mean to make you jealous. She's sort of like a big sister, not like a mother or anything." Jane felt the sadness growing. Rita was a child, and she obviously had been lonely and scared, so she had created a fantasy complete with a Jane who was the way she wished Jane was. Jane's guilt was getting worse, too. She wasn't sure whether she had even told Rita yet, but she couldn't think of a way that Rita could see her mother again for the next few years.

"I hope things are going okay for you. I know jail can't be pleasant, but be patient, and maybe they'll let you out early. I can't come visit you like I used to, but I think about you and send you good thoughts. Well, I should get this into the envelope, because my friend is going out to mail some other things. I just wanted to write to you again right away, so I could tell you that things are better. I'm afraid my last letter might have made you feel worried."

Jane whispered, "I don't know, but it makes me feel worried." She tried to collect her thoughts, but it was difficult because there were too many questions. She drove the Explorer out to the street and kept going until she saw a pay telephone attached to the front of a convenience store.

Jane dialed the telephone number of the house in Santa Fe, then pumped quarters into the slot until she had matched the toll. The telephone rang once, twice, three times, and her mind formed a picture of Bernie and Rita. They would be standing in the living room with the telephone between them. One of them would reach down to pick it up, and the other would say, "No. Don't. Nobody knows we're here." "It could be Jane or Henry." "If she was going to call, she would have told us." "Maybe she didn't know." "It could be somebody making sure we're in the house so they can come and kill us."

The telephone rang fifteen times, but nobody picked it up. Jane closed her eyes and stood beside the building, thinking. They could be dead already, killed by people who had read Rita's first letter. When the telephone had rung twenty times, she hung up. Jane heard a click, and her quarters came tumbling down into the cup at the bottom of the telephone.

As she walked back to the Explorer, she realized that the decision had been made. If there was an earlier letter, probably it had been among the ones she had mailed in California or Arizona, or maybe the first batch that Henry had mailed. There was no question that the families would have someone in the Florida State Prison reading Ann Shelford's mail. Just one detail in the letter she had read—the name of the Eldorado Hotel—would be enough. There was no way to know what Rita had put in the earlier letter. If they were alive, she had to pull them out.

27

Jane drove the last miles to Santa Fe. She felt the weight of the travel and the time and the work. Whatever else happened, she told herself, the bulk of the money must be going where she had wanted it to. She had driven halfway across the country with the radio tuned to news stations, and she had heard nothing that could be interpreted as the death of Henry Ziegler. There had also been nothing to indicate that Bernie and Rita had been found. Maybe Rita's earlier letter had not revealed anything. Maybe the postmark on it had been enough to lead the hunters in the wrong direction. She couldn't count on those things, and it was unlikely that talking to Rita would reassure her.

She was confident that the Explorer still had not been identified. She could use the anonymity of the vehicle to check the town for signs. Santa Fe was small, and the places where people gathered on a summer evening weren't far apart. She drove up and down the streets near the big hotels that surrounded the plaza, then parked and walked. There were lots of pedestrians on the streets, but most of them were grouped in ways that didn't worry her. There were many couples—some with children and a few too old to be dangerous. The males who had no females attached to them were not the sort who raised the hairs on the back of her neck. The ones who were young, strong, and appeared to be searching seemed not to be looking for a resemblance, but a reception. Their eyes passed across her face with expressions that began as appraisal and then softened into something like hope, and finally subsided into disappointment when she deadened her own expression to look through them.

After her short walk she knew she should be reassured. If some hunting team had been close to finding the house, she probably would have noticed a few soldiers by now. Her walk through the public places in the city would have turned up at least two or three men who didn't move much and stared at everyone who passed.

It still would not do to drive up to the house without being sure it was safe. If she approached it on foot after dark, she would have some chance of seeing an enemy before he saw her. She parked the Explorer on Canyon Road on a block lined with art galleries that had been closed for the night, then locked it and walked. Jane could see that it would be dark soon, but she had no fear that she would forget the way to Bernie's house. She had made the trip on foot several times, and once she was a couple of miles from the city, the lights of the house would serve as a beacon.

As she crossed Apodaca Hill Road and moved into the brush and stunted trees on the far side, she felt better. If nothing had gone wrong, this would be no more than a pleasant evening stroll.

She strode quietly with her eyes ahead and her ears tuned to the sounds around her. Jane had never been uncomfortable walking in wild country alone. The dry terrain of New Mexico was still alien to her, but it had an unearthly beauty in the early evening, when the last remnants of sun-glow kept the sage and piñon visible and let her feel confident about where she placed her feet. As the minutes went by, the deepening of the shadows made her feel even better. She had learned a long time ago that—barring falls and getting lost— a human being's worst chance of harm on this continent was from other human beings.

As she walked, she picked out shapes and configurations of rocks and spiky plants that she remembered. Somewhere in her memory she carried a map of this area, and she began to navigate by it. She knew she would have to turn and walk a few paces to the left soon, because there was a dry arroyo coming up and that was the most gradual way down. She did it, then came up the other side. She knew there was a big piñon tree at about the eleven o'clock position from where she stood, and she walked to find it. The longer she walked, the clearer it all seemed.

She could see the house now, alone in the middle of the horizon. Everything looked reassuringly calm. The lights in the kitchen were on but the blinds closed, and there was a light on upstairs in the smaller bedroom. She wondered what they were doing. Probably they were having a late dinner or washing the dishes, and they had left a light on upstairs.

Jane walked more slowly and carefully. If someone was watching the house, she didn't want to trip over him in the dark. She bent low and tried to tell whether anyone else had passed this way recently, but in this light every indentation in the dirt could be a footprint, or could be nothing.

Then, ahead of her, she saw something, a strange, unexpected shape that she didn't remember. It was about two feet high and bushy, but it was too long and unvarying to be natural. She changed her course to move closer. She was only a few feet away when she made out the structure. There were posts—four of them—sticking up, and strung between them was a net. She walked around to the far side of it. The net had plants stuck in it, and a couple of large rocks along the bottom. She walked around it again. The ground on the side away from the house was smooth and flat, with a plastic tarp spread over it. She knelt down and ran her fingertips along the bare surface behind it. There were footprints on this side. They were long and deep, as though a big man, or maybe two, had stood here. It wasn't just kids building a fort.

It was a blind. Somebody had built a blind. But what would they be hunting from blinds here, in midsummer? She stepped onto the plastic tarp, knelt down behind the blind, and looked. There was a clear, unobstructed view of the house and of the trail she was about to take to the kitchen door. She judged the distance. It must be about two hundred yards. There was a wing along the left side of the blind, so she moved to that side and looked over it. This side of the blind had been put here to command a view of the first curve of the road. A car heading from Bernie's house toward town would come around the curve, then drive straight toward the blind for—what?—ten seconds, before the next curve began and the car went past.

Jane felt an urge to run for the house, but she held it in abeyance. She moved to the front of the blind and touched one of the plants that were stuck into the netting. It was beginning to feel spongy and dehydrated, so it had probably baked in the sun. She followed the stem to the cut, and felt a sticky, wet residue, so it had been cut within a day or two. She decided they must have built this blind after dark last night, when Bernie and Rita could not have seen them doing it. She stared at the blind. They must have planned to come back tonight after dark to occupy it. The sun had already been down a half hour. She let her eyes go unfocused and looked around her for other disturbances in the landscape. A hundred feet to her right she saw a group of big rocks she remembered from her other visits, but it looked different tonight.

She moved closer and saw that a couple of feet behind the

rocks was a darker shadow that kept fooling her eyes. Was there a tarp there too? She reached the spot and looked down. It wasn't a tarp. It was a hole . . . a foxhole? She dropped to her knees and stared into it, then saw a vague line in the shadows. She reached down for it and touched a smooth wooden handle. She grasped it and lifted it, and found that it was much longer than she had expected, at least four feet. It was a shovel. This wasn't a foxhole. Nobody could stand in a six-foot hole and still see over those rocks. She looked at the shovel. The spade end seemed to have an odd glow in the darkness.

She held it closer. It was covered with a bright white powder-fine dust. She used it to probe the hole, and heard a sound of paper rustling. She pushed the shovel lower to bring the paper object closer to the surface, where she could see it. The object was a big empty bag. She saw the word "Lime." She dropped the shovel and stepped back to measure the hole with her eyes. It was a grave.

Jane turned toward the house and broke into a run, dashing straight for the kitchen. When she reached the steps, she leapt up to the landing and pounded on the door.

She stepped back, so that when the porchlight came on she would be right in the middle of it, where Rita could see her, but the light didn't come on. Instead, the door opened and Bernie said, "Sorry, honey. This is the doorman's night out, and I didn't hear your car."

Jane stepped inside and pushed past him. "I left it in town. Where's Rita?"

Bernie opened the broom cupboard to put his shotgun away. "Upstairs. She said she was going to read. She's got the radio on, so I guess her eyes and ears are on separate circuits." He frowned. "Is something wrong?"

Jane hurried through the dining room past the computers, across the living room, checking that the windows were covered, then up the stairs. "Rita!" she called.

"Yeah?" The voice came from the back bedroom.

Jane stepped inside. Rita was lying on the bed with her bare

feet propped up on a pillow with bits of tissue jammed between her toes while the nail polish dried. There was a magazine opened facedown on the other pillow. She sat up quickly.
"What's going on?"

Jane turned off the radio by the bed. She took a deep
breath, then glanced down at Rita. The girl's eyes looked
frightened and childlike. Jane's urge to shout at her dispersed.
Jane sat on the bed beside her. "We've got a problem."

"What?"

Jane said gently, "I know you miss your mother. I don't
blame you for wanting her not to be worried. I never specifi-
cally said, 'Don't write any letters to your mother.' But I wish
now that I had."

"But I didn't tell her anything. I didn't say where I was, or
who you were, or say Bernie was alive, or anything."

"How many letters did you write?"

"Two. And they were to my mother, not anybody else.
What—I can't write to my mother in prison?"

Jane sighed. "The problem with prisons is that they're
filled with criminals. I think somebody read your letter. It had
to be the first one, because I read the second." Jane pointed
toward the window. "Out there somebody has set up a blind."

Jane heard Bernie move into the room behind her. "A blind
what?"

"A blind. Like a duck blind. A little camouflaged barrier
you hide behind to shoot something." She looked at Bernie,
then at Rita. "It's set up to give them a view of this house and
the road to town. It's fresh—maybe a day old. Was anybody
out there today?"

Rita said, "Not me." Bernie didn't answer, but the look on
his face indicated that the question was unnecessary.

Jane said patiently, "I mean did you *see* anybody out
there?"

"No," said Rita.

"Then it's probably pretty much what I thought. They were
getting ready for tonight." She glanced at her watch. "It
doesn't seem to make sense to plan to shoot somebody from a
distance when they're asleep. I think they'll come when they

expect to find us still awake and walking around in front of lighted windows."

"You always struck me as a smart girl," said Bernie, "but—"

"When did you go to bed last night?" Jane interrupted.

"I don't know," Bernie answered. "It wasn't this early."

"Eleven-thirty," said Rita. "I watched the eleven o'clock news."

"Then we've got two hours at the outside. Let's assume it's one hour." Jane bent over, picked up Rita's sneakers, and tossed them on the bed beside her. "Both of you get packed as quickly as you can. Don't bring anything you're not going to need badly, but don't forget things like money and the IDs I gave you."

Bernie went to his room and Jane could hear him opening and closing drawers. Rita put the suitcase Jane had bought her on the bed, then lifted armloads of clothes and tossed them inside. By the time Bernie returned, Rita had finished packing. She put on her shoes.

"All ready? Good," said Jane. She opened her jacket and handed Rita the packet she had prepared. "These are new IDs for you and Bernie. What you've got to do is get into your car and get out of here. Go east, not toward town. That's the way they seem to be expecting you to run."

Bernie said, "What about you?"

Jane looked at him in surprise. "I'll be safer without you. Henry said we have to take the hard disks out of the computers and destroy them. That will take me a few minutes. After that, I'll be on my way too."

As Jane headed for the doorway, she heard Bernie say to Rita, "I'll wait for you downstairs, kid." Jane reached the dining room and a moment later, Bernie was at her shoulder.

"How did they find us?"

Jane didn't look up from the computer. "I don't think I want to tell you."

"Rita got in touch with somebody, didn't she?"

Jane nodded. "Her mother."

Bernie looked sad, but he wasn't angry. "I'm sorry," he said.

Jane looked at him in surprise. "Sorry?"

"She's just a kid. Don't blame her. Her mother is all she ever had. I just wish that you weren't here for this. You didn't have to come back. That wasn't the deal."

"We'll all be out of here in a few minutes, before those guys get to their blind."

"I don't think that's the way it's going to happen," he said.

Jane moved the computer closer so she could see it better, and opened the cowling on the side. "A few yards from the blind they dug a six-foot hole with lime in the bottom. What do you suppose that was for?"

"I don't mean that," said Bernie. "That's probably what you think it is. But the plan isn't right. It might be what they'd do, but it's not what they'd want to do."

"What do they want to do?" asked Jane wearily.

"They want their money. They don't know I'm alive, so they're looking for Rita, and they're looking for anybody who's with Rita. Probably they want you alive, so they can find out what happened to their money." He paused. "This is not entirely good news, of course. Getting caught would be worse than being dead. But they won't just open up on you from a distance. It's not what they did when Tony Groppa hid his skim from the horse money, or the way they got Tippy Bono after he hijacked the Augustinos' bagman, or—"

"I thought you didn't know things like that." She opened her pocketknife and used it as a screwdriver.

Bernie held up his hands in a gesture of innocence. "Hey, they told me. These guys kill somebody, and it's a story to tell for years. The ones who didn't do it, they think about it too, want to know every detail."

"Suppose they think the money's already gone? They're above revenge?"

Bernie said, "They might send two guys with rifles to pop somebody they couldn't get close to, but what's stopping them here?"

Rita appeared in the doorway with her suitcase. "I think Bernie's right. Even if they want to kill us, wouldn't it be easier if we were asleep?"

Jane gave them an exaggerated version of a cheery smile

as she pulled out the last screw. "That would be great. That would give you even more of a head start. Why don't you two talk about it in the car? That way, risking my life to come and get you won't have been a waste of time." She bent down and used her knife to pry the disk drive out of the first computer and disconnect the wires. She muttered to herself, "At least this is easy. Thank you, Henry, wherever you are."

"We can't just go out there and drive off," said Bernie. "That's what I'm trying to tell you. If somebody knows we're here, they wouldn't just go away and come back later, like they would with a normal hit in the middle of a city. They have to be watching the road, so we can't get out."

Jane pulled out the second disk drive and put both of them into her jacket pockets. "I can't tell you how all this information makes me feel." She paused. "Because it would take longer than I'm going to be here." She walked toward the kitchen door.

"I wouldn't go out there," said Bernie.

Jane turned. "Everything you say is probably true. What it means is, if we stay here, we're dead. If we take the car, we're dead. If we try to make it out on foot before they get here, we have some chance."

Rita looked at Jane, then at Bernie. "What do you think, Bernie?"

Bernie shrugged in irritation. "I'll do what you want. It's nothing to me. I'm old."

"Then leave the suitcases," said Jane. "Take the money and IDs." She stepped to the broom cupboard and opened it. "I'll take the shotgun."

Jane picked up the shotgun and turned the door handle, but Rita's voice said, "Go with her, Bernie."

Rita was pale, her hand quivering as she moved it to the counter for support, but her voice was steady and strong. "The best way is the one you haven't said. I'm the only one they want, and I'm the one who did this. There's no reason for them to know there was anyone else. I'll keep moving, turn lights on and off, play the radio loud—anything I can think of to let them know I'm still here."

Jane stepped closer and stared at Rita for a moment, study-ing her closely. Rita held her head high to show that she was not going to give in this time. Without warning, Jane's right arm shot out, the heel of her hand struck Rita's shoulder and spun her body around, and in the same motion snaked over Rita's right shoulder and clutched her left armpit.

Rita gasped, but the arm wouldn't let her lungs inflate enough to let air out in a cry. In a second she had been jerked backward out the door and onto the porch.

Bernie stepped out and locked the door behind him, and Jane released her grip on Rita.

Rita whispered, "Why—"

But Jane hissed, "Because I don't have time to be persua-sive. Get across this open ground as quickly as you can. After that, there's some cover."

They walked rapidly, their feet crunching on the dry stubble that surrounded the house. The stars were beginning to show in the black sky, but at least the moon wasn't bright. Jane's major worry was Bernie. Rita was a healthy teenager who could walk all night, but Jane sensed that Bernie would be in trouble. He was a bent-over silhouette in the darkness, and his breathing began to sound labored when they were only half-way across the open ground. It occurred to her that he might not be capable of walking the four or five miles to town.

Just as Jane reached the end of the open field, her ears picked up a faint car noise. She hurried on, still listening. The sound was regular and even, but it began to seem a pitch lower than the engine of the usual car. She turned and looked toward the road.

Around the curve she could see the dark shape of a car crawling along with its lights off. When it reached a spot on the far side of the house where the bushes shielded it from the front windows, it stopped. Around the bend came a second car, then a third and a fourth. One by one, they pulled onto the shoulder of the road and stopped.

Jane turned toward Rita and saw that she was staring, wide-eyed, at the cars. Jane pushed her forward, then lingered to keep Bernie moving. She looked over her shoulder, then saw the first two doors open up, and men begin to climb out.

"Is that what you were expecting to see?" she whispered.

"Roughly," said Bernie. "What now?"

"Let yourself get scared," she said. "It helps you move faster."

28

As soon as Jane had hurried the others past the blind, she paused again to look back. There were now several silhouettes making their way toward the doors of the house. Some of them walked with one arm held straight toward the ground, as though they were carrying pistols. Then she saw movement in the foliage near the parked cars and felt a growing alarm. There were men there too, moving into the brush carrying long-barreled weapons. She tried to count them, but the darkness and the bushes near the road made them difficult to make out. One would be visible, but then she would lose sight of him. She would see another movement, but not be sure whether it was a man or the wind.

Finally she saw two men carrying rifles step out of the brush behind the house. When she saw them break into a trot toward the low stubble she had just crossed, she sucked in a breath. They were heading toward the blind.

She spun and trotted to catch up with Rita and Bernie. "We've got to get away from here."

"What does it look like we're doing?" asked Bernie. "Figure eights?"

She took him by the hand and pulled him along. "Once we're away from the blind, we'll be behind them."

Bernie moved more quickly, but Jane could tell that the additional effort was costing him. He was beyond attempting to disguise his heavy breathing now. His jaw hung slack to keep his mouth open, and his breath came out in huffs. His feet seemed to slap the ground, not push off it. Jane knew he was going to have to rest soon, and for the next hundred yards she searched her memory of the trail for places where they could hide. As the minutes went by, she gradually conceded to herself that he wasn't going to make it.

She stopped and held Rita's arm. "Here," she said. "You take this." She held out the shotgun, and Rita accepted it, doubtfully.

Jane squatted. "Help Bernie up on my back."

Bernie was horrified. "What?" He gasped. "You can't carry me."

"I can try," said Jane.

"I'm not dead yet," he puffed. It took a moment for him to get enough breath to say, "I can walk."

"Not fast enough. Do it." Jane's voice was quiet, but Rita could hear in it something hard that reminded her this wasn't a game. She guided Bernie up behind Jane. Bernie brought his arms around Jane's neck and clasped his hands, and Jane slipped her arms under Bernie's knees. Rita pushed Bernie upward to help Jane straighten.

Jane said to Rita, "You lead the way, and I'll follow. Go as fast as you can without tripping or backtracking, and I'll try to keep you in sight."

Jane took a last look back. The two men with rifles were nearly across the burned stubble. As soon as they reached their post at the blind and got their rifles comfortably sighted in, she knew, they would give some kind of signal for the assault to begin.

Jane set off again, making her way through the dry chaparral and spiky plants, threading between rocks and along gravelly inclines, straining to see Rita's shape ahead of her. She could feel the effect of the extra weight on her feet, calves, and knees, but if she kept her hands clasped at her belly and her back straight, she found she could move at a good walking pace.

In ten minutes, her shoulders and neck were tight and painful, and when she heard hard, sharp gasps, they were her own. The sweat had begun to run down into her eyes and sting them, then fall in drops from her nose and chin.

When Jane reached the dry arroyo, Rita was waiting for her, staring at her in horror. Jane stopped, bent her knees, and let Bernie down. Rita whispered, "How can you do that?"

Jane sank to the ground and lay there. She answered in a strained and winded voice, "I kept reminding myself of what would happen if I didn't." After a minute, her voice was stronger. "How do you feel now, Bernie?"

"Better."

"Good," said Jane. "Rita, give me the shotgun. I'll go ahead for a bit. Walk with Bernie at his pace. If there's a problem, run ahead and get me. Don't call out."

"Okay," said Rita.

Jane got to her feet. "Watch your step here. There's a slope." She went down into the arroyo and came up on the other side, then slowly increased her speed to a trot.

Far behind, Jane heard the sound of glass breaking, then a loud creak and bang, as though the front door had just burst inward, the dead bolt wrenching the frame off with it. She kept moving until she thought she heard distant shouts. She glanced over her shoulder.

She could see Bernie and Rita walking toward her. Bernie had his head down, but he seemed to be moving steadily. It looked as though Rita was leaning close to his ear, whispering to him. But far behind them, the lights were going on in the house.

Jane set off again, watching the path ahead and trying to pick out easy, smooth stretches where the others could move quickly. She held the shotgun close to her chest, with her left hand on the foregrip and the right on the stock just behind the trigger guard. A few minutes later, she heard car doors slam, and an engine turn over and start. She turned to see one of the

cars pull up the long driveway to stop beside the lighted rectangle of the kitchen door. A man appeared in the doorway,
blocking some of the light, then moved and was replaced by
another. They appeared to be carrying bulky objects. Were
they loading the computers into the car?

Jane hesitated, feeling the impulse to take the disk drives
out of her pockets and bury them in the dirt, but resisted. She
knew that she couldn't take the time to do it, and she had a
fear that the men would come out here in the daylight and be
able to see the hiding place that had seemed invisible to her in
the darkness. She could hear Bernie's and Rita's footsteps
much closer to her now, so she set off again. She heard Bernie
stumble, but when she took a step back toward him, she
saw he was already coming ahead again, with Rita's hand on
his arm.

Jane went on, and after a time she began to see configurations of plants and rocks that she didn't quite dare feel sure
about, but then she saw distant lights, and she knew that they
were approaching Apodaca Hill Road. She stopped and
turned back.

She could see the faces of Rita and Bernie. Bernie's forehead was wet with sweat, and his neck and cheeks had a
darker shade, which she knew would be red in the light. She
moved closer to look at him.

Bernie saw that she was staring at him, and he rasped,
"What are you looking at?"

Jane said, "Sit down and rest." She turned away from them
and crept closer to the edge of Apodaca Hill Road. She went
to her belly and slithered forward a few more feet to stop between thick bushes, then peered up the road. It was empty
highway as far as she could see. She looked down the road in
the other direction. She could see a car parked a few hundred
feet away, on the other side of the intersection with Canyon
Road. The night was too dark and the car too far away for her
to be certain. She couldn't see people inside, but why else
would anyone park there, where there was no building?

She thought about the men at the house, and tried to repro-
duce their thoughts in sequence. When they had discovered

that the house was empty, and the car was in the garage, they had guessed that the occupants had left on foot. It would have been reasonable to assume that they would head for the city, and to get there, they would have to cross this road.

A big truck appeared on the highway to her left, and Jane pushed her face down into the dirt to be sure its headlights fell on her hair rather than her skin. As soon as she felt the sudden gust of wind from its passing, she lifted her head to watch it go on down the road. When it drew near the parked car, its headlights shone on the windshield and illuminated the heads of four men inside.

Jane began to ease herself backward away from the road, but when she turned to head back, she saw more headlights, this time coming along Canyon Road from the direction of the house. The car appeared, turned right, and drove up to the car that was parked on Apodaca Hill Road, and paused for a moment beside it. Then the car turned around and went back along Canyon Road toward the house. As it turned, she could see heads in the back seat as well as the front.

Jane pondered for a moment. That was eight men so far. They had one car waiting here at the cutoff, and one car driving up and down the road searching. She had begun to move again when she heard another car. She stopped and watched it follow the same routine. When it came to Apodaca Hill Road it paused beside the parked car, turned around and went back out Canyon Road. This one had only two men in it. She waited, and then the fourth car appeared. As it turned, she saw that this one carried two men also.

The empty seats in the last two cars worried her. There could be as many as four men coming on foot across country the way she and Rita and Bernie had. She knew that trying to cross the road in front of the cutoff car would be like jumping into a grave, and it seemed that going back would be no better.

Jane crawled back and lay down beside Bernie in the weeds. "There's a cutoff car with four men in it just down the road, facing this way. The other three cars are driving up and down Canyon Road, one after another."

"Could we stay here and wait them out?" asked Bernie.

"Some of the seats in the cars are empty," said Jane. "I think there might be men following us from the house on foot."

Bernie held out his hand. "Give me the shotgun."

"What for?"

"I'll go down to the cutoff car, blow the windshield out on the driver's side. It'll take them a minute to get over it, and another minute to haul him out of the way so they can drive. By then we could all be in town."

Jane looked at him, trying to make out his features in the darkness. "Tell me, Bernie. Have you done this kind of thing before?"

"Well, no," said Bernie. "But anybody can see it's the sensible thing to do, and anything I get on my conscience now, I'm not going to be burdened with it for long."

"I don't think so," said Jane.

"Why not?"

"Too much noise," said Jane. "I'd rather have the rest of them searching the road and the brush back there than up here in our faces."

"When Frank Delfina is taking the skin off your back with a lemon peeler, I hope you remember that I offered," he snapped. "So what's your idea?"

"Figure out what they know, and make it not true anymore."

"Christ," he muttered. "What do they know?"

"It looks as though they're sure we're here, south of Canyon Road, and the cars going back and forth will keep us here. They just have to wait until the men on foot catch up or it gets light enough to see us."

"How do you know that?"

"The cutoff car is facing this way on the other side of the intersection. All the men are still in their seats, facing this way. If they thought there was a chance we were on the other side, one or two would be out of the car, looking in that direction. They're not. So that's where we go."

"Ever hear of a rearview mirror?"

Jane patted his shoulder and stood. "No plan is perfect."

Bernie raised himself painfully and set off. Rita moved close and put her hand on his arm, but he removed it. "I've had plenty of time to rest," he said. "I'll be fine."

Rita whispered, "I'm not sure I will." Jane was intrigued. She waited to see whether Bernie would overlook the lie and accept the help.

Bernie set Rita's hand on his arm and said, "That's okay, then."

Jane moved ahead, then angled away from Apodaca Hill Road so they would meet Canyon Road five hundred feet from the intersection. When she was fifty feet from Canyon Road, she stopped in the thick brush, sat down, and waited.

"What are you waiting for?" asked Bernie.

"The cars. I want to know where they are."

The first car's headlights appeared to their right a few seconds later, and they lay down to stay out of sight. Jane could see four men in the car. When it had passed and turned to come back, the second car with two men in it came by, then the third. Just after it had passed, Jane tapped Bernie's shoulder. "You first. Get across the road and keep moving. Bear left toward the other road. Don't stop until you're there, then stay out of sight until we catch up."

Jane lifted the shotgun to her shoulder and waited while Bernie hurried across the road and disappeared into the brush on the other side. "Now you."

Rita stood and stepped onto the road. She had taken two steps when she seemed to realize that something was wrong. She stopped, and turned her head to the left.

Jane could see that Rita's features were becoming clearer, brighter, as the distant glow of headlights came closer. Jane glanced in that direction. The car that had been parked on Apodaca Hill Road had come around the corner, and it was moving up Canyon Road toward them.

Jane looked at Rita again. She stared into the bright light as though she were considering waiting for it. Jane saw her chest expand and contract in quick little half breaths: she was going to try to trade her life for Jane's and Bernie's.

"Run!" Jane hissed.

Rita seemed like a sleepwalker awakened. She looked around her anxiously, then decided. She ran back to crouch in the brush beside Jane.

Jane lay still and watched the lights grow brighter until they illuminated the dust above the road and made the air glow. As the car coasted to a stop in front of her, Jane pumped the foregrip of the shotgun to bring a shell into the chamber, and pushed off the safety with her finger.

The passenger door swung open and the two men in the back seat got out. They walked to the edge of the road and looked in the general direction of Jane and Rita, but to Jane it looked as though their heads were both held too high. They were looking into the distance. She remained still and waited.

The two men moved a few paces to the front of the car, craning their necks to see if the headlights revealed anything in the dark fields ahead. She could see them more clearly now with the lighted road beyond them, craning their necks and sidestepping to stare at the field. One man pulled a gun out of his belt at the small of his back and held it at his thigh.

Jane slowly raised the shotgun and gripped it tightly against her shoulder to fight the recoil. She looked down the groove along the top of the receiver, held the bead in the center, and let it settle on the man with the gun. He would be the first, then his companion, before they could dive out of the light. If the driver had the presence of mind to accelerate away, she would put a shot through the back window on his side, and one on the other side before she ran.

The man with the gun raised his free hand above his head and made a quick circular motion. The taillights of the car went dim as the driver took his foot off the brake. Jane lowered the shotgun, pulled Rita to the ground with her and held her there. "Don't move."

The driver pulled to the wrong side of the road and swung the car in a tight half circle, the left tires bumping on the shoulder as the headlights swept across empty brush, over Jane and Rita's hiding place, then settled on the road again. The two men climbed into the back seat, and the car moved up the road the way it had come.

Jane tapped Rita. "There's another way. Come on."

Jane rose and began to trot into the field, making her way farther from the road and back toward the house.

Jane could hear Rita's footsteps behind her, but suddenly they stopped. Rita's voice reached her from twenty feet back. "Wait," she said. "I'm not leaving Bernie out there to die."

Jane stepped close to her. "Keep your voice down," she whispered. "If Bernie did what I told him to, he'll be fine until we catch up with him. If he didn't, nothing we do is going to help him."

"Where are we going?"

"Remember the arroyo?"

"What's an arroyo?"

"That dry streambed where I set Bernie down. It runs north-south. The road runs east-west. Water doesn't stop just because there's a road. It has to cross."

Headlights appeared on the road again, and Jane and Rita had to drop to the ground until the car passed. Then Jane was up and trotting again, and Rita had to trot too, to keep her in sight. Almost as soon as the road went dark, the lights from the next car appeared.

Rita stopped and crouched as they had before, but Jane pulled her on. "They've got their intervals figured out now. There's not enough time between cars to wait for them."

When they reached the arroyo, Jane stepped down into it. When Rita joined her, she said, "See? It's deep. When it rains, there must be a lot of water."

"But which direction does it run?"

"It doesn't matter. It has to cross the road." Jane bent low and hurried along the bottom of the arroyo toward the road.

As they came closer to the road, Rita could see that Jane had been right about the cars. They were moving faster now, and the intervals between them were even.

When they were a hundred feet from the road, Jane stopped and waited. When Rita caught up, Jane pointed at the road. "See?"

Rita strained to see what Jane was pointing at. There was the road. It went across the arroyo, but it didn't dip down and go up again. It was level. From here it looked as though the road had been built on a pile of big rocks. Did the water seep through between the rocks?

The next car approached and Jane turned her face away from the road and said, "Get ready. As soon as it goes past, we move."

The car flashed past; Jane rose to her feet and ran. Rita felt an instant of panic. Jane seemed to be on her way, but Rita had no idea of what she was running to. It wasn't until Jane was at the edge of the road that Rita could see her stop. Jane was below the level of the road on her hands and knees beside a set of low, thick plants. Jane pushed the plants aside and bent lower, then disappeared.

Rita came to the spot and knelt in front of the plants, then fought them aside with her forearms to see. Beyond the plants, she touched something hard and cool like rock, but it was a perfect circle. She reached farther in. It was a big cement pipe. Rita felt relief, and embarrassment at the same time. This was what Jane had meant. Jane had known there would be a big pipe—what did they call it?—a culvert. Otherwise, the arroyo would fill up after a rain and the water would wash out the road. That's why the plants were so thick here. This was where there was the most water.

Rita could hear hollow, echoing scraping sounds from inside the culvert. She felt a swelling in her chest as she dropped to her belly and slithered into the round, dark hole. It was dirty, and the cement scraped her elbows and knees. Moving was hard and painful, but she was crossing the road by going under it, so she ignored the pain and moved.

Jane's echoing sounds ahead of her suddenly stopped. Rita waited, and heard a low hum, then felt a sharp vibration as a car passed over her head. Then Jane began to move again, and Rita struggled to keep close to her.

A moment later, Jane's sounds simply faded and were gone. Rita knew that Jane must have made it to the end. Rita struggled and strained to go faster, and finally she felt a fresh, cool breeze on her cheek. Jane's whisper came from close to her ear. "You did a great job, Rita. Stay still for a second."

This time Rita could see the glow of the headlights on the plants on the left slope of the arroyo twenty feet ahead of her. The lights brightened, and the engine sound got louder and lower. Then there was darkness and the engine sound went up the register until it was a distant whine. "Time to move on," said Jane.

She helped Rita out of the culvert and pulled her to her feet, then set off again. This side of the road seemed to be the same random arrangement of rocks and bushes and plants as the other side, but Jane appeared to know where she wanted to go. After what seemed to be a long run, Rita could see the other road that they had been afraid to cross.

Jane stopped fifty feet from the road, then began to walk along it in a parallel course, staying low and staring at the rocks and bushes ahead of her. Suddenly she turned and hurried toward the road, and knelt down as though to pick something up. When Jane stood up again, Rita could see that what she had bent to grasp was Bernie's arm. She was pulling him to his feet.

Rita trotted to catch up, then watched Jane set the shotgun on the ground and kick dirt over it.

Jane said, "We cross the road here, and make our way two blocks straight ahead before we get back on Canyon. The car is a black Ford Explorer, parked on the right about three blocks farther on."

Jane hurried them to the shoulder of the road. Rita could see the car that had stopped to look for them parked in its spot a few hundred feet away. "You and Bernie go first," Rita said. "If they see you, I can still pick up the—" and Jane's hand grasped her wrist and yanked her onto the road. They ran a few steps and they were across, moving into the shadows of buildings and trees.

They were on a road parallel to Canyon Road, walking fast. After a few minutes of walking, Jane turned to the left, and then right. Jane said, "There. See it?"

They walked on until they came to the black shape Jane had pointed to. Jane swung the door open, climbed up into the driver's seat, and started the engine. Seconds later, Rita had pushed Bernie into the back seat and was beside Jane, closing the passenger door. Jane pulled out, moved up the street, and took the first turn before she switched on the lights.

It seemed to Rita that it took a terribly long time for Jane to drive across town. At each intersection, Jane would look into the mirror over her head before she brought the Explorer to a stop. But then she accelerated, took a turn, and they were moving up the ramp onto the freeway. They passed under a sign that said ALBUQUERQUE.

Jane drove, and they sat in silence for a long time. Finally, Rita spoke. "I'm sorry."

"What?" asked Bernie.

"This was my fault," Rita said, louder. "I did this. Jane made us safe, and I threw it away."

Jane waited for Rita to speak again for a minute, then another minute. Finally she said, "It was not a smart thing to do. It also wasn't an evil thing, or a selfish thing, or a cowardly thing. You made a mistake, you did everything you could to fix it, and it's over. We're all alive, and they don't know where we went."

"Where did we go?" asked Rita.

"Good question," said Jane. "I don't know yet. I guess we'll have to do some thinking. We'll pick a place, and I'll try to start getting you settled: rent a house, buy clothes—"

Bernie interrupted. "Honey, where were you when you found out about Rita's letter and came back for us?"

"Toledo, Ohio," said Jane. "Why?"

"Just at the north end of Albuquerque we meet Interstate 40. Go east on it."

Jane hesitated. "You can't possibly want—"

"It's this truck, or whatever it is. It's full of letters back here. The damned things take up so much space, I can hardly move my arms or legs, lie down, or sit up. Let's go mail them."

"I don't know," said Jane doubtfully. She found herself turning her eyes toward Rita.

The girl was hunched down in her seat, looking very young, thin, and dirty. Her eyes were glistening, and she was staring at Jane. "Please," she said. "Just give us this much. We can hide for the rest of our lives."

29

Frank Delfina liked his Albuquerque bottled-water business because it didn't stink. Flower shops smelled, bakeries smelled. Even supermarkets smelled if you came in the back door, where the food was delivered. There was breakage, and you always found yourself stepping on a spot that made your shoe stick, and then the sole made a little smacking noise for the next few minutes. He looked across the plant at the clean, clear bottles waiting for tomorrow morning's shift to come in and fill them.

He liked everything. He liked it that people were dumb enough to believe that spring water driven down from the mountains in a truck was better than water that came from the same reservoir in a pipe, although they couldn't tell the difference. He knew that, because this plant topped off each bottle with about two inches of tap water.

Delfina didn't like flying into Albuquerque and then waiting like this. He noticed Buccio walking toward him from the distant doorway, and he stared at him in frustration. He had let himself put faith in Buccio and his crew, and it had been a mistake. Buccio had the short-haired, big-shouldered look of a marine officer, always standing up straight and wearing his sleeves rolled up above his big forearms, as though he were about to do something impressive. He always looked like somebody who could pull off just about anything, and to do him credit, he was always eager to try. But that didn't mean things would work. Delfina had almost let Buccio and his guys talk him into letting them pull an attack on a bus carrying the bosses of half the families in the country. At least Delfina had backed away from that one.

Buccio said, "Vanelli's car just pulled up in the lot outside."

"All right," said Delfina. "Get the rest of your guys in here now."

Buccio gave Delfina a puzzled glance, then turned on his heel and strode quickly into the bottling area.

Delfina twisted in his chair to look up at Mike Cirro, then held out his hand. Cirro reached into his sport coat, produced a Smith & Wesson .45 semi-automatic pistol, and placed it in Delfina's palm. Delfina examined it, pulled the slide to cycle a round into the chamber, then slipped it into the back of his belt and adjusted his coat to cover it, and leaned back in the chair.

A few hours ago, Delfina had let Buccio pull one of his commando-raid travesties outside Santa Fe. Buccio had flown a dozen men into Albuquerque, held a rendezvous at the airport, then deployed his troops. He had explained to Delfina how he'd sent snipers in camouflage into the desert to cover the house and the road, then pulled a full-scale assault to kick in all the doors at once and rush in. As Delfina thought about it, he was positive that at some point in the operation, Buccio must have said, "Synchronize your watches."

But Buccio had stormed an empty house. Rita Shelford had been gone. The woman who had been helping her hide had been gone. They had found computers, all set up in the dining room, and lots of different kinds of paper and envelopes. Buccio had had the sense to take the computers. As Delfina thought about it, he could almost forgive Buccio for the childish theatrics. Having the computers was going to be better than having the girl.

Delfina was glad he had listened to Buccio's whole story without interrupting him or shouting, because he had heard about Buccio's mistake. He watched the rest of Buccio's crew coming in from the door to the plant and the outer doors.

They were Buccio's hand-picked protégés, all of them. They all had his close-cropped, overexercised look with thick necks and empty faces.

Delfina heard the distant door to the parking lot open and turned to watch the last four men come in. He recognized Vanelli and Giglia. They were laughing and talking with the other two men, who looked a little more subdued. When they came into the big room and saw Delfina, Vanelli stepped forward and said respectfully, "Frank. I brought some friends of ours to meet you. This is Paul Lomarco." He indicated a tall, dark young man in a pair of jeans and a windbreaker. "This is Pete DiBiaggio." That one was wearing a sweatshirt above his jeans that said, NEW MEXICO, LAND OF ENCHANTMENT.

Both men smiled and nodded timidly at Delfina.

Delfina smiled too, stood up, and shook their hands. "Glad to meet you." He turned to Buccio. "Go get these guys a beer." Buccio prepared to pass the order to one of his crew, but Delfina's stare remained on him until he went toward the office himself. Delfina turned to the two men. "You guys are Cleveland boys, eh? Part of Al Castananza's family?"

Both men nodded. Lomarco said, "Yeah. They sent us here to watch the airport for the two women."

"Yeah, I got guys all over the place on that too." Delfina smiled and shrugged. "The only good part is, I'll bet you've had tougher jobs than that. Probably looked for women when you weren't even getting paid for it. So you guys happened to run into each other at the airport?"

"That's right," said DiBiaggio. "I met Vanelli a couple of years ago, so I went over to talk to him. He remembered me, too."

Delfina nodded. "Ah, here's Buccio with the drinks." Buccio handed each of the two a bottle of beer.

Both men looked increasingly uncomfortable. Lomarco looked around him. "Wow. This is a big place."

Delfina nodded. "Yeah, I figured if you build something, it should be big enough so you don't have to do it again in five years." He looked at the twelve men along the wall to his right. "Come on, you guys. Relax. I didn't mean to leave you out."

The men approached, a little warily. A couple of them nodded at Lomarco and DiBiaggio, who didn't seem to be made more comfortable by the new faces. "Come on, guys. These are friends of ours. Aren't you going to shake their hands?"

A couple of Buccio's men shook hands with Lomarco and DiBiaggio. Delfina stepped back to make room for others. In a moment he was behind the two guests. As Buccio and Vanelli stepped forward and grasped the two men's hands, Delfina reached under his coat to his back, held the pistol behind Lomarco's head, and fired. The noise seemed to make the air in the cavernous building harden and slap the eardrums. Four or five men cringed or ducked their heads, but Delfina already had the pistol at DiBiaggio's head. He fired.

He stepped over the men lying on the floor and walked toward his chair. Buccio, Vanelli, and two others had been spattered by blood. They were looking down at their hands and shirts, and the others seemed to be in the process of awakening from paralysis. They looked at the bodies, then at one another, and then at Delfina, who was shaking his head sadly.

"They seemed to be two pretty good men," said Delfina. "It was a shame to have to do that." He looked up at Buccio's crew. "That was totally unnecessary. Do I have to remind you guys what this is about?"

A few of the men before him looked down at their feet, but Buccio, Vanelli, and a few others stared straight ahead.

"It's everything," said Delfina. "You know what went into this? For weeks, I had people in a Florida prison watching Rita Shelford's mother twenty-four hours a day. Finally, we get a break. The girl writes her a letter. It takes two days to figure out that the place the girl is describing is Santa Fe. It takes a few more to backtrack through old newspaper ads to find out what houses used to be for sale or rent that aren't anymore, then check every single one of them out. When the hard part is all done, I decide 'Okay, these guys are always telling me about their precision and efficiency and all that. I'll give them a shot at this.' "

Delfina held up his hand in wonder. "Did I need to say, Keep it a secret? Don't let guys from other families see twelve of my men fly in at once and meet in an airport that you know is being watched?"

Delfina's glare softened. He held out the pistol and Mike Cirro stepped up, took it from his hand, and slipped it into his coat again. "I know you must have done some of this right, because you didn't get shot or arrested. You got into the house, took what was there, and got home. Fine. But look at these two. I didn't kill them. You did."

He could see the men were sufficiently chastened. "Get them out of here. They depress me."

Several of the men dragged the two bodies out of the room, and others began to swab up the blood with red mechanics' rags from the bottling plant. Delfina returned to his chair and watched the proceedings.

After a half hour or so, he heard the door at the far end of the building open, and saw four men come in carrying big cardboard boxes. He slowly let his excitement build. This was going to be it.

He turned to Mike Cirro. "You're pretty sure you can do this yourself? If you need experts, I can get them. We've got all kinds of people on the payroll in companies all over the country."

Cirro shrugged. "It depends on how hard it is to get around their passwords. If I can't, I won't hurt anything, and we can get the experts."

Delfina watched the men bringing in more boxes. He turned to Buccio. "Give them a hand."

In a moment, Buccio and his men had brought in the boxes and set them at Delfina's feet. Cirro stepped forward and looked into the boxes, then picked one up and walked off toward the wall, with one of Buccio's men. He set it on a workbench, and Buccio's man said, "I'll go find an extension cord."

Delfina watched another man carry a second box toward the workbench, then looked down at the others. "What's in these?"

Buccio knelt beside one. "Here's her suitcase. We went through it, and there's not much in it. Just some clothes. But here's another one, and it might be important."

"Why?"

"It's not for her, or for another woman. It's men's clothes."

Delfina sat up straight. "Open it. Let's take a look." Buccio carried the suitcase out to the floor and opened it. Delfina picked up a pair of pants, a shirt. He set them on the floor and looked at them, then stood and held them in front of his body so Buccio could see. "Look at the size."

The pants reached about halfway down Delfina's shin. "He's not a big guy," said Buccio judiciously.

Delfina tossed the clothes onto the suitcase. "That's because he's not a guy," he said. "He's a disguise for a girl. You didn't, by any chance, see a guy near the house tonight and let him go past, did you?"

"No, Frank," Buccio said hastily. "None of my crew would do that."

"Good," said Delfina. He glanced across the big room toward Cirro, who was connecting cables to the backs of the computers. That was what he was interested in. If this woman who had gotten her hands on Rita Shelford had used them to transfer money, there would be a record of the transactions in those computers. Even if it was too late to reverse them, it wasn't too late to find out exactly where the money had really gone. The rest of the families would spend the next few months trying to trace it from wherever Bernie put it, through fake people and companies and charities that disappeared when you looked at them. Delfina would already have the money.

He saw Buccio's man come back with a long orange extension cord. He said to Buccio, "What else did you find?"

"Nothing we didn't know about before," he said. "There's stationery, envelopes, boxes, labels, all blank. They had a regular office set up."

Delfina glanced across the room at Cirro. He could see that Cirro was turning things on. The screens of the computers lit up, there were beeps and hums. He touched a key as Delfina approached. He pressed others, started clattering away. Delfina's excitement grew. "What have you got?"

Cirro looked back at him. He was frowning. "Something's wrong."

"It's not working?"

Cirro picked up the screwdriver he had been using to tighten the cable connections and opened the side of the computer. He took the big plastic cowling off and set it aside. "Shit," he muttered. "No hard disk."

Disappointment flowed into Delfina's chest and slowly hardened into anger. He watched Cirro open the other computer, but he knew, as Cirro did, that the disk would be gone. He waited for Cirro to confirm it.

"They took the hard disks out before they left," Cirro said. "There's nothing."

Delfina turned and walked back to his chair and stared at the other boxes. His silence and immobility drew his men around him like a magnet. They waited as he stared, growing increasingly anxious. He raised his head.

"Kill the girl's mother," he said. "Call Florida and tell them. If the women we have in there with her aren't up to it, tell them to find somebody." He seemed to sense that his listeners were uncomfortable.

"But if she wrote a letter once, don't you think she might do it again?" asked Buccio. "If her mother's dead . . ."

"Somehow they knew we were coming. I don't know if it was the mother that warned them, or if she could do it again. It's possible this mystery woman got the girl to send the letter just to get us to waste a week finding a place she already left. It doesn't matter. If the mother's dead, I don't have to think about what the next trick will be."

"Okay," said Buccio. "I'll call them in the morning."

"Tonight. By morning I want all this stuff gone so the bottling guys don't see it, and all of you out of New Mexico." He stood up and beckoned to Cirro. "Split up and drive out. I

don't want anybody else seeing you in an airport together."
Cirro arrived at Delfina's side. Delfina said, "Let's get to the
airport, Mike." The two walked toward the door for a few
steps, and Delfina stopped. "The woman in the drawing.
She's the one that's got to be behind all of it. Forget everything except her."

While Cirro drove him to the airport, Delfina thought
about the woman. His people were all looking for her full-
time, and he was pretty sure that most of the soldiers from
the other families were doing the same, but she had not been
spotted since Milwaukee. It was time to make a bigger effort
to get the rest of the world to help with the search. He took
out a pen and a piece of paper and began to compose a new
flyer. She seemed to be into disguises, so it should have her
picture on it, but this time the artist would show other possibilities: long hair, short hair, blond hair, and sunglasses. Instead of just saying she was missing, it would say she was
being sought for questioning. That implied the search was
all legal, but didn't actually say she had committed a crime.

Instead of just alluding to a reward, he would name one. A
hundred thousand? No. It wasn't enough. People got junk
mail from magazine wholesalers every day that offered millions. Make it a half million dollars.

There was another thing, too—the place. People were already looking all over the country, but that haphazard method
didn't seem to be getting anywhere. He had to be selective.
The first thing the woman had done was drag the girl up
from Florida. People had forgotten that. Bernie had lived in
Florida, and the girl had been born there, and that was where
all of this had started. In a day or so, the girl's mother was going to be taken off the count in a Florida prison, and there
would be some kind of burial service. He would put down
that she was believed to be in Florida. That wasn't a sure
thing, though. Where else?

Bernie had been killed in Detroit. There was still the chance
that this whole scheme had been run by the Ogliaro family.
Of course, Vincent Ogliaro was in federal prison, so if she
was communicating with him, she wouldn't go to Detroit to

do it. He looked up at Cirro. "Tell me again. Where's Vincent Ogliaro serving his sentence?"

"Marion, Illinois."

He added that to his flyer: "Believed to be either in Florida or in the vicinity of Marion, Illinois." Then he realized it was wrong. He hadn't been thinking clearly. He should have paid more attention to the way the magazine clearing houses did it. The flyer had to make it sound easy, as though the very next step the person took was going to make him rich. He would do several different flyers. He would send one to Florida that said she was believed to be in Florida. He would send another to the upper Midwest saying she was probably in the Detroit area. He would send one to the lower Midwest saying she was likely to be near Marion, Illinois. Then he could begin to concentrate his men in the strip of the country she was almost sure to pass through at some point, the thin slice that ran from Chicago east along the bottom of the Great Lakes to New York.

30

Phil Langusto sat in the study of his house on Prospect Park and willed himself to believe that things were going the way they should. His brother Joe had the head for finance, and he and Tony Pompi were on top of this. But what they said seemed to him to be impossible to see as anything but a disaster. He glanced at his watch. He had been sitting here listening to them for only five minutes, but it seemed like five hours.

He said, "Joe, can you just let me know when you've got a name and a place? This is like having a sigmoidoscopy, with the doctors pointing out the sights on the television screen while they crank the camera gadget farther and farther up your ass."

Joe said, "No, listen, Phil. I think we're getting somewhere. Tony set up this company. It's in the business of compiling information about charities. We're telling charities we're putting together the ultimate mailing list of big-time donors, and we're going to give it to them if they cooperate. We're using a regular boiler room, fifty guys on phones. The charities think we're helping them, so they're answering. They're even calling us."

"Yeah?" said Phil. "What are they telling you?"

"Big donations are coming in, sure. That's the bad news. They're all coming by mail. We tried a lot of ways of charting the charities that are getting them. Dead end. So we tried tracking the places where they're getting mailed from. We have a pattern. One day, we'll get a whole bunch from the West Coast. That ends. The next day, everything will be from the Deep South—Florida to northern Georgia. After that, there's no mail from there at all."

"This is going to kill me," said Phil. "What good is this?"

"We're making a map."

"A map?"

"Yeah," said Joe. "If we can chart where these people have been, and what direction they're going, we can just draw a line ahead of them to figure out where they'll be tomorrow."

Phil Langusto took his feet off his desk and sat up straight. Maybe Joe finally had something. "Have you got it with you?"

Joe nodded to Tony Pompi, who opened his big envelope, took out a large, white folded sheet, and began to unfold it. Phil Langusto's eyes settled on his brother's face, saw the expression of deranged cunning, and felt a tearing sensation in his chest. Joe had always been the smart one. It was Joe who had gotten the good grades in school, Joe who was supposed to go far. Joe didn't belong in the real world. He was as intelligent as anybody needed to be, but he had been born with no instincts. It was like not getting a joke, or being tone-deaf. There was no cure for it.

The map just kept unfolding, until Joe and Pompi knelt on the big Oriental rug to tug the corners and straighten it. Phil stood and walked to the lower edge of it. The map was seven feet wide and five feet long, showing the whole country. Phil could see red dots sprinkled on the map as though they had been sprayed from a severed artery. The West Coast had been splattered. There were a few drops in Arizona and New Mexico, a big blotch on the upper Plains that ran to the Great Lakes, then a whole line of dots dripping up the East Coast from Florida to Virginia.

"See?" Joe asked expectantly. "We're getting their act."

Phil's jaw tightened so hard that the muscles on the sides of his face hurt. "What the hell are you talking about? San Francisco, Miami, Atlanta, Minneapolis? What am I supposed to do with that?"

"The money is being mailed from those places, and there's an order. We think somebody is driving around mailing the checks." He pointed at the map. "It could be two cars. It doesn't matter, though."

"Joey," said Phil, because calling him that always artificially induced patience: this was still his little brother. "You're a smart man. I love you for it. But what I need you for right now is to find out for me what is going on—the big picture, you know? Somebody is tapping the money that Bernie the Elephant had, right? That much is for sure?"

Joe shrugged. "Of course. We were waiting to see big money moving. This is really big money, and it's bouncing all over the place. We've got hundreds of guys keeping track of it."

Phil said, "But you're not telling me what I want to know. How does the scam work? They pull the money out of wherever Bernie deposited it, or invested it, right? They then donate it to, say, the United Way. No taxes, no questions. That makes sense to me. But how does the money complete the rest of the circle?"

Joe was still staring at his map with pride. "What circle?" he asked.

Tony Pompi said, "He means, how does it then get from the United Way back to these people who stole it. That right, Mr. Langusto?"

"Right," said Phil. "How?"

Joe shrugged again. "We don't know yet."

"Guess!" Phil shouted. "Either of you."

Tony Pompi looked nervously at Joe, who nodded. Pompi said, "We've got people on that, but these are honest-to-God charities. The only way we've thought of that makes sense is that these people have found some way to tap the accounts of the charities. If you send a check to the charity, they endorse it on the back by stamping it with an account number and the words 'For Deposit Only.' Their bank takes it and sends it back to your bank, which sends it to you."

"I've got checking accounts, for Christ's sake," said Phil. "I know that much. So what?"

"You then have their bank branch's location and the number of their account."

"Then what? You cook up a fake check of theirs and write it to yourself?"

Tony Pompi looked at Joe for help, and Joe said, "The short answer is yes. Of course it would be more complicated than that."

Phil closed his eyes. "How?"

"If you write a big check, the bank asks questions before they cover it. So probably it would be done electronically, by a wire transfer of some kind. That way they could do all of the transfers at once by computer. They'd do it after hours, like eight o'clock in the evening, so none of the charities knows anything has happened for at least twelve hours—and maybe not then. And whenever they found out, they would only know it happened to them. They wouldn't know it also happened to anybody else for another twenty-four, when they read the next day's papers."

"Then you're looking for an account somewhere that suddenly gets fat overnight so you can jump on it, right?"

Joe glanced uneasily at Pompi. "What they would probably do is send it to a holding account in a foreign country. The minute the money arrives, they move it again, and the account vanishes."

"So what are you doing to stop it?" asked Phil.

"We don't even know if that's what they're planning," said Joe. "This is all theoretical. If we knew how to do it, we'd be doing it ourselves." He saw the look of despair on his brother's face. "That's why we're trying to stop it before it gets that far."

Phil looked beaten. "And you still don't know who's doing it."

Tony Pompi said inanely, "We're working on that."

Phil gave him a cold stare. Joe saw it and stepped between them before he was deprived of his friend. "The only candidates we've had to choose from are Bernie's bodyguard, his maid, and Vincent Ogliaro. You know Vincent Ogliaro. Was this him?"

Phil sighed. There it was again. Joey knew nothing about people. "If you wanted somebody to go shake down the president of some charity—grab his wife, or something—he wouldn't be a bad choice. But this stuff? It's not him."

Joey said carefully, "What about this bodyguard, Danny Spoleto? Is there a chance he's some kind of genius and we missed it, or that Bernie trained him or something?"

"Joey," said Phil. "You met him. He worked for this family. He might have stolen some list of accounts that Bernie wrote down, but he wouldn't know what to do with it. He could barely read. His idea of a score was stopping over in Tampa when I sent him on errands and screwing Manny Maglione's wife. He didn't think I knew it."

"Then I guess you're right," said Joe. "We don't know who this is. The only one who seems promising is the woman Delfina says was with Bernie's maid."

"She's the only one I'm sure of. She kicked the hell out of Nick Fuletto in the Seattle airport. What I want to know is who she's working for. The only way to find out is to catch her."

"Can I just show you what we've been thinking here?"

"I already heard," said Phil. "You're showing me red dots on a map. I need something people can look at—people like Catania and Molinari and DeLuca—and tell their guys what to do."

"But that's what we've got," insisted Joe. "What we think is that they're spreading everything as thin as they can, so we won't notice. They're mailing stuff from every major city they can get to. Phil, look at the map. Don't look at the red dots. That's where they've already been, and they won't be back. Look at the spaces that are empty. That's where they still have to go."

Phil Langusto stared down at the map for a few seconds, his eyes slowly narrowing until they were slits. Suddenly they widened again, and he hurried to the telephone. He dialed, then stepped as close to the map as his cord would allow. "Bobby? Look, I want you to get the word out as fast as you can. First thing is, we've got to call all the families. Tell them to get everybody off the West Coast."

There was a brief pause while the other man said something.

"Shut up and listen. In fact, move them east of Minneapolis. That was where they saw that woman, right? Milwaukee too? Better not go that far just yet. Tell them to send their guys east, and spread them around between Minneapolis and . . . Buffalo. Major airports are already covered. Put them in rest stops on the big highways, car rentals, hotels. Have you got that?"

The man on the line said something, and it seemed to satisfy Phil. He said, "The second thing is, get everybody off the East Coast south of . . . Washington, D.C., and move them north."

He listened. "Right. I want the area east of the Mississippi and north of Washington, D.C., so full of people that you can't find a hotel room or a parking space. And what I want them all to look for is the woman in the drawing. She's going to be mailing letters."

31

J ane awoke, lying on the back seat of the Explorer. She kept her eyes closed and listened to the steady hum of the engine and the low whistle of the wind blowing in the window above her head to cool her. She heard the voices, and realized that she had been hearing them for a long time.

"I've seen them come and go," Bernie said. "Singers, actresses, whatever. If you try to look like them, then when they go, you'll go too."

"It's just a style. Didn't you have style when you were young?"

"Of course we did. The important thing about styles is that they change. Tattoos don't change." He sighed. "Most men aren't out searching for a woman who matches some particular picture." He noticed she was looking at him skeptically. "Keep your eyes on the road, or you won't have to worry about it."

"I was looking to see if you could say that with a straight face."

"Of course there are exceptions," Bernie admitted. "If one of them happens to pick you out, run like hell."

"I would," she said. "It would have to be because he recognized me and thought I knew where the money was."

"I mean because he's trouble in his own right," said Bernie. "It's just something I've observed over the years, and believe me, my role in the whole issue has been mostly observation, so I got good at it. Poochie Calamato was like that. Ever hear of him? I suppose not. Every time I saw him, he'd have his arm around the waist of a different woman, only they weren't different. It would always be the same type—big and blond, the hair sort of like Marilyn Monroe used to wear it—and each one would be dressed the same as the last one. I don't know if he found them that way, or he got them to change. It's possible he took them to the stores himself and picked the clothes off the rack for them."

"That doesn't sound so bad," said Rita. Jane could hear a little embarrassment in her voice as she added, "It sounds like he looked at them, anyway, and he must have cared about making them feel good."

"You wouldn't have liked him."

"I don't know," she said. "I mean if the clothes weren't—you know—weird or something."

"About once a year, maybe two, he would find another one that he thought was closer to the ideal picture. Then he'd dump the last one. See, when Poochie dumped you, he dumped you. They found one in the Cuyahoga River, and another one in a ditch outside Memphis."

Jane sat up and looked around her. "Where are we now?"

Bernie said, "Still on 40. We just left Shamrock, Texas, next stop Texola, Oklahoma."

"I must have been out a long time," said Jane. "Rita, I'll take over at Texola."

They took the exit at Texola and pulled into a gas station to fill the tank and use the rest rooms. When they came back, Jane took the wheel. Rita climbed in beside her, folding a new stick of gum onto her tongue. "Don't you want to sleep?" Jane asked.

Rita shook her head. "Bernie drove longer than I did."

Bernie climbed into the back seat and lay down. He said, "Keep on 40 until Oklahoma City. There you'll want exit 146, which will take you onto 44 northbound."

"What are the exits just before it comes up?"

"MacArthur Boulevard, then Meridian Avenue. That's 145. If you miss 146, you can pick up 44 a few miles on at exit 153."

"Thanks, Bernie," said Jane.

Rita rolled her eyes. "I'll never get used to that," she whispered.

Jane drove on into Oklahoma, always watching her rear-view mirror for signs of cars that might be following. She matched her speed to the traffic and changed lanes only when she needed to. After a half hour, she could hear Bernie snoring.

Rita asked, "Were you listening to what Bernie said?"

Jane nodded.

"You agree with what he said?"

"I agree with what I heard." She gave Rita a sympathetic look. "He's been around for a long time, and he seems to have had his eyes open through most of it."

"I mean about men."

"The ones he knew probably weren't an appetizing set of specimens, but I think he has the picture." Jane looked at Rita again.

She was slouching now, looking down. "Not that I'll ever know."

Jane sighed. "Right now, we're trying to keep you isolated and invisible, and you're an eighteen-year-old girl who would like to go out and be seen and meet a nice boy and have fun. I'm sorry, but it won't last forever."

"I'm not complaining about that," said Rita. "This is something I wanted to do. But when the money's gone . . ."

"The job isn't just giving away the money," said Jane. "It's surviving afterward. That's the hard part."

"If I had your life, I guess I'd feel better about it." Rita was silent for a moment. "What's your husband's name?"

Jane hesitated. "This is another time I'm going to have to say I'm sorry. You've already found out more about me on your own than I've ever let any runner know." She looked at Rita, her brows knitted. "If those men—say, Frank Delfina—caught you five years from now, then you would have enough in your head to kill me. They already have a picture of me. I can't do anything about that, but I don't think I should make it worse."

Rita shook her head. "I wouldn't tell. I never would."

"I know," said Jane. "I had . . . have a nice, quiet life." She smiled. "That's my secret."

"Huh?"

"Staying invisible is hard. The secret is to find a place in the world where you're surrounded by other people who don't appear to be very different from you, and spend some time working at making yourself happy."

"Why? What does that do?"

"It means you won't take risks because you're restless or bored. You won't move around much. Very soon, people around you get used to you. They don't remember when they first noticed you or how long you've been there. Without knowing it at first, you begin to forget too. Time begins to work for you."

"You told me that in San Diego."

"It was true," said Jane. "You have a lot of advantages, but time is the biggest. The men we have to worry about are career criminals. That means our immediate problems are as bad as they can be—they know what they're doing, and they won't hesitate to kill you. But time will help a lot. Career criminals spend a lot of their lives moving in and out of jails. Some get killed. The reason they became criminals in the first place is that they wanted quick profits without working very hard, so they don't have the patience to keep at something that's not paying off for years."

"You keep talking about years. You mean I have to hide indoors all that time? How long?"

"It's not what I mean at all. What you have to do is make yourself a real life, so that while those men are standing in the rain outside some airport day after day watching for you, you're in some pleasant town having dinner with friends and sleeping in a comfortable bed."

"I don't know how to do those things," said Rita. "I've never done that."

"The good thing about having to give up being the person you've always been is that you get to choose who you'll be next," Jane said. "It's not an impersonation. The new person has your qualities—not your looks, but the things nobody can see. You're a pretty unusual young woman. You took over your own life and began acting like an adult a couple of years ago, at least. You've worked hard and supported yourself and taken care of your own needs. I've been watching you through this whole mess, and you have more courage than is actually good for you. My guess is that all you're going to need is a new town and a good cover story."

"You already did that for me. But I was just hiding. I don't want to be alone, and I don't want my big accomplishment in life to be staying alive."

"What can I do?"

"I want to be with Bernie. And he wants to be with me. Then at least we'll both have somebody to talk to, to do things for."

"We'll work on it. Maybe you'll go to college, if you're interested. I've cooked up some pretty convincing academic records in my time, and I could do it again."

Rita was silent, as though she was considering it.

"That way you wouldn't just be hiding. Of course, there are some simple precautions that you'll always have to take. The Mafia makes most of its money on vices—drugs, gambling, prostitution, and so on. You'll have to stay far away from the places where those things happen. And you can never tell anyone the name you were born with, or anything that's happened to you up to now."

"If I get married, I can't tell my husband?"

Jane shook her head. "The last thing you want to do is to hurt the person you love. There's nothing about this story that will make him any happier, any stronger, any safer. He'll never know it, but part of what you'll bring to the relationship is that you didn't make him afraid."

Jane was silent for a long time, until she felt Rita staring at her with curiosity. Rita asked, "Does your husband know?"

"That's not something I'm going to talk about," said Jane.

Rita lapsed into silence, and before long, Jane saw her take the gum out of her mouth and settle back into the seat to sleep.

It was only one more day before the road swung up into

Missouri and merged into Interstate 70, which took them into Illinois, then Indiana. They slept in shifts, stopping only to eat and buy gas for the Explorer. Jane insisted that they pull off the big interstate and drive into a small town each time. On the second day at two-thirty in the afternoon, they were driving past the hotel where Jane had stayed in Toledo, Ohio.

Jane stopped the van and let Rita out to mail letters at a box a few blocks away, then turned onto Navarre Avenue, stayed on it after it became Route 2, and drove along the south shore of Lake Erie. At four-thirty, they reached Sandusky, where Bernie put some letters into the mailbox beside a newsstand, then drove eastward toward Cleveland while Rita slept and Jane skimmed the newspapers he had bought.

"What are you looking for?" Bernie asked.

"I don't know," she answered. "It could be anything— some sign that Henry was spotted, some sign that people are beginning to notice the big donations, bad weather that could hold us up."

"I heard you tell Rita they had a picture of you."

"It's a drawing. Would you like to see it?"

Bernie held out his hand as he stared ahead at the road. Jane pulled out the flyer she had gotten from the mailbox rental in Chicago. He took it, looked down at it for a second, then handed it back without speaking.

"Well?" said Jane. "What do you think?"

"It explains your hair. Rita said it was a disguise. I was thinking it was just . . . bad hair. I don't know why you have to look in the papers for bad news. The picture ought to be enough bad news for you."

"It doesn't change anything," said Jane.

"I'm sorry, honey," said Bernie. "I wish we hadn't talked you into going on with this."

"You didn't," said Jane. "I would have done things differently—tried to get you and Rita settled before I mailed the rest of the letters, probably—but I wouldn't have given up." She shrugged. "It wouldn't have gotten less dangerous. It would have given the other side more time to figure out what's going on while I was still out. I just wish I knew where the picture came from."

"Niagara Falls," said Bernie. "The day I met you."

"How do you know that?"

"The picture. It's not just your face. It shows the collar of the blouse you were wearing. It was white. But whoever described you to the artist must have noticed there was a faint pattern woven into the cloth, see? The artist put the flowers in, but you could only see them close-up. That's the only time you wore that one."

"It must have been the desk clerk," said Jane. "I'm not surprised you remember, but I didn't think she was in your league."

"Money has a way of getting some people to play over their heads."

Route 2 merged into Interstate 90 at Clearview, and then the traffic moved more quickly until five-thirty, when the cars began to show brake lights and they found themselves in the evening rush hour. Bernie left the interstate at Pearl Road.

"Where are you going?" asked Rita.

"There's a big post office up near the train station," said Jane. "It's on the map."

"What map?"

"The one in his head."

After fifteen minutes of driving, the post office appeared a block ahead. Jane and Rita pulled all of the stacks of Cleveland letters out of the suitcases, and Jane slipped them into a big grocery bag. "Pull up somewhere, I'll jump out and get them into the slots inside," said Jane. "Rita, keep your head down."

Bernie stopped at the curb, but as Jane was about to open the door, Rita grabbed her arm. "Wait," she said. "That man over there."

Jane looked up the steps of the building and saw a tall man standing near the door lighting a cigarette. "Do you know him?"

"I'm not sure," she said. "He looks a little bit like one of the men who came to Bernie's house after he was gone."

Bernie stared out the window. "She's right," he said. "I've seen him."

"Keep going," said Jane.

Bernie pulled back out and merged into the line of cars. "I don't know his name. But he was in a picture I saw once. It was a snapshot of Joe Langusto's son's wedding. He was in the last row, third one from the end."

"Great," said Jane. "There are New York thugs watching a post office in Cleveland."

"There may be," said Bernie. "But he wasn't in the Langusto family. He works for Frank Delfina."

Jane craned her neck to get a better look at the man, but he was only a tiny gray dot in front of the big gray building now. "I guess we'll have to do this differently," she said. "Keep driving until you find a mailbox—any mailbox on a street."

Ten minutes later, Bernie pulled the Explorer over in front of a row of shops. Jane got out and dumped her bag of letters into the box, then hurried back to the car.

When Bernie got the car moving again, he said, "We've got a problem."

"A new one?"

"You've been going all over the country. Henry's been going around the country. But you quit for about five days to go pull us out of New Mexico. I think what happened during that time was that everything you had mailed must have arrived, and made a splash."

"What do you mean?"

"They must know all the places you've been. They don't have enough guys to put one or two in front of every post office in the country, but they've got them here. They know where you haven't been yet."

"You think they've moved all their people into our path?"

"I do."

"Then we'd better change our path. Get us out of town while Rita and I look at the letters we've got left. Head south for now."

Jane and Rita went to work examining the return addresses of the stacks of letters in the back of the Explorer. Rita would read the name of a city, and Jane would put the stack on the floor. After a while, all of the stacks were arranged on the floor.

Jane said, "Okay, I think I know how to do this. They may have enough men to put one at each post office in big cities. So let's skirt the big cities—just pull into the suburbs and back on the road. If we stop even less often than we have been, keep out of the obvious places, and take turns at the wheel, I think we have a chance."

"What do you want me to do?" asked Bernie.

"Head for Akron."

The thirty-nine-mile drive south to the west side of Akron took until nearly seven. Rita mailed some letters there and then climbed into the driver's seat. "Where next?"

"Youngstown," said Jane.

"Switch to the 76 Interstate just ahead," said Bernie. "It's fifty miles. Stop when you get to the Southern Park Mall."

When they reached the mall, Jane mailed the Youngstown letters and took a turn at the wheel. "That was the last of the Ohio letters," she said. She glanced back at the sun as she crossed the line onto the Pennsylvania Turnpike. It was still a few degrees above the horizon, and she was glad. They were still moving, still a little bit ahead of the hunters.

It was nearly nine in the evening when Jane skirted the northern suburbs of Pittsburgh and left the turnpike at Monroeville. On a summer night like this one, the traffic was thin, and the people who were out were mostly young. She thought they walked in a leisurely, languorous way, as though the sights on the other side of her window were in a different universe, where things moved at half speed. Jane's foot was always nudging the gas pedal to keep the needle of the speedometer two or three ticks above the speed limit, and her mind was always on the next city.

The three took turns driving through the night, letting mailboxes and gas stations represent the cities: Harrisburg, York, Lancaster, Reading, Allentown, Bethlehem. Jane awoke in the passenger seat just as they crossed the Delaware into New

Jersey at 3:30 a.m. She was elated. She sat up and looked into the back seat to see Bernie sleeping peacefully. She tried to dissect the feeling as Rita drove. She felt the way she used to in college when she was running on the track team. She remembered being strained, breathless, her mouth set in an unattractive grimace and her nostrils flared like a horse's. But the moment when she had seen her foot touch the fine gravel on the first step at the beginning of the final lap, she had felt a change. Her strides would lengthen and her head go up to straighten the airway, and her limp, tired arms would begin to pump faster. Tonight was like that. She was just coming around the short end of the track, and she would see the last lap ahead of her.

She resisted the urge to take the wheel. It was only about fifty miles across the top of New Jersey to Newark, the weather was clear and the road was fast, and at this hour the traffic was light. She gave Rita's shoulder a friendly pat. "How are you holding up?"

"Fine," said Rita.

"When you get to Newark, find a place to stop, and I'll take over." Jane lay back in her seat and closed her eyes. She had already driven to most of the major cities in about a dozen states and mailed an enormous number of envelopes before she'd gone back for Rita and Bernie. Now, hour by hour, the envelopes were still going out. She had no idea how much money had been mailed since she had taken on her last load in Chicago, but there had been thousands of envelopes. Each time they had emptied a box, she had crushed it flat and laid it on the floor behind the back seat, so now the floor of the cargo bay was littered with them, and there were only five more boxes to go.

Jane sensed another feeling too: a satisfaction that was simple geometry. In another hour, when they reached the Atlantic—no, only forty minutes now—they would cross Henry Ziegler's path. The pattern would be complete.

When Rita reached the edge of Newark, she pulled off Interstate 78 at a gas station. Jane got out and filled the tank.

When she got into the driver's seat, Bernie was in the passenger seat looking alert, and Rita was in the back moving boxes of envelopes into order.

Jane pulled back onto the road. "How are you feeling?" she asked Bernie.

"Like I slept a year," he said. "I took a look at what's left in the boxes a while back, and I thought over the route. What you want to do is get back on 78, and take the bridge over Newark Bay. We'll hit Jersey City and Hoboken next."

Jane drove the route as Bernie dictated it, and Rita hopped out of the Explorer at each stop to drop the letters into the mailbox.

Bernie said, "What time is it?"

"About four-thirty."

"Want to see if we can make it across Manhattan before daylight?"

Jane said, "If we can."

They crossed into Manhattan using the Holland Tunnel, and Bernie gave her directions. When they reached the intersection of Broome and Mott in Little Italy, Bernie said, "Stop here. Rita, give me the box. I want to do this one myself."

Jane watched as Bernie walked to the mailbox and happily slid the letters into it, then deposited the cardboard carton in a public trash receptacle. He climbed back into the Explorer and smiled. "Take Delancey to the Williamsburg Bridge."

She came off the bridge and onto the Queens Expressway, and Bernie said, "Now onto the Long Island Expressway." Jane followed his instructions.

After a few minutes, Bernie said, "Stop in Manhasset." When Jane had stopped the Explorer, Bernie got out and sat in the back seat. He handed Rita the last box. "Put this on your lap. The packets are in order. Just tell Jane what the next one is, and when she stops the car, get out and mail it. I'm going to get some rest."

Within minutes, Jane could hear Bernie snoring again. Rita called out the stops: Great Neck, Port Washington, Glen Cove, Stony Brook, and Port Jefferson. Then Jane moved south across the island to Mastic, Center Moriches, Westhampton, Hampton Bays, Southhampton, East Hampton, and Sag Harbor.

At each stop, Rita would jump out and mail the letters, then announce the next destination. It was late afternoon when she returned to the car with the last empty box. She found Bernie and Jane staring at each other over the seat.

"You don't have to do it," he said.

"It was part of our agreement," Jane answered. "From the first day, this was the plan."

"Things have changed since the first day. They found us in New Mexico, and they've got your picture now. They know what's going on."

"What?" asked Rita. "What are you talking about?"

Jane said, "Look around in the seats and things. Be sure every letter is gone."

"I already did," said Rita. "We did it. It's over."

"Not quite," said Jane. "We'll stop and get something to eat up here, and then see who's up to driving the next leg of the trip while the others sleep."

"Next leg of the trip?"

"We have just one more stop to make."

"Where?"

"Marion, Illinois."

32

Al Castananza sat in his booth at the Villa restaurant and waited for his dinner. He had learned as a child that letting people read on his face the contents of his mind was a bad idea. It had gotten him into so much trouble at school that education had been a brief experience and lingered as an incomprehensible memory after fifty years. After that, he had served the first of his prison terms, and he had learned quickly.

Tonight, he was feeling anxious and confused, but he knew that showing anything except his mask of imperturbability was about the same as putting a gun in his mouth. He sat staring at the poster of the Venice Biennale that hung on the wall across from him, and distracted himself by wondering what it was that happened in Venice every two years. It sounded like a car race, but he couldn't imagine why anybody would have a car race in a city that was half flooded.

Saachi came in from the front dining room and sat beside him on his right, as he always did. Saachi wouldn't end up eating anything until nearly midnight, after Castananza went home. He would sit there protecting Castananza's weak side while Castananza ate. He would make payments from the roll of bills in his pocket and handle all the petty problems that people came in with so Castananza could swallow his food without getting agita.

Castananza always listened while he was eating, but if he didn't have to gulp down a mouthful of unchewed food to say something, then he didn't. If Saachi made a wrong decision, he never told him in front of anyone. He waited until they were alone, so Saachi could fix it himself.

Monday night's special was veal scaloppine, and he felt happy. He could have gone into any restaurant anywhere and ordered the whole menu if he wanted, but he had lived a long life by never doing that. If he had asked Marone, the Villa's owner, for a special meal made of rare and costly ingredients, Marone would have rushed around trying to make it, but the daily specials were what Castananza liked. If half the people in a restaurant were having the same meal, then it would be pretty damned hard to get a spoonful of rat poison on the right plate.

Saachi sat there for a second, then said, "Al, I'm glad I got here before the waiter."

Castananza's hopes fell. Saachi was telling him he wouldn't

want to hear this while he was eating. "Yeah?" he said. "What sort of problem have we got?"

"It's this thing with Bernie."

The owner of the restaurant himself walked toward the table, carrying a tray on which four plates of veal scaloppine were expertly wedged, so the edge of each plate sat on the edge of the next. Castananza gave his head a regretful little shake. Marone saw it and delivered the four plates to other, less distinguished diners without letting them suspect that Castananza had turned them down.

"So tell me."

"I think maybe we should get out of here and talk in the car."

Castananza looked at Saachi. His old friend's face was concerned, the lines over his eyebrows all showing even in the soft light of the Villa, but the eyes weren't scared. That would have required Castananza to behave differently. He had always been alert to signs that Saachi was scared, because that was the way he would look if he ever decided that being Castananza's right hand was the same as being Castananza. He said, "Sure. Should we go out the back?"

"I got my car out there," said Saachi.

The two men slid out of the booth and walked the few steps to the back of the restaurant, past the telephones Castananza's people never used because they were tapped, and out to the little square of asphalt where the waiters parked their cars.

There were two men standing beside Saachi's Continental, and Castananza acknowledged them. "Hi, Mike. Bobby, how are you?" He didn't listen to their respectful mutterings as he got into the passenger seat. They were too much in awe of him to say anything he needed to hear.

Saachi started his car, and the two young men went around the building to another one, and drove up behind them. As Saachi crept down the alley to the street, he sighed to signify that he was ready.

"So?" asked Castananza.

"The two guys we sent to watch Albuquerque airport for

Danny Spoleto and the girl—DiBiaggio and Lomarco. They called the other day and said they saw something strange."

"What was it?"

"They saw some guys in the airport. I guess it was DiBiaggio who knew one of them, really. It was a made guy he remembered from the old Castiglione days. They got to talking, and when they got around to the subject of Spoleto, these two guys don't have anything to say, just look at each other and kind of chuckle."

"How?"

"Like they knew where he was. No, like they had him already. Like the game was over, and they already won. The two of them say, 'Well, so long. Got to go.' Lomarco keeps an eye on them, to see where they're going. Maybe they're changing flights to go someplace else, and he wonders where. But they just go to a restaurant in another part of the airport. Pretty soon a couple of other guys arrive on a different flight, and they all wait."

"This doesn't sound like a big deal," said Castananza. "I would have been curious too, but what's the big deal?"

"Over the next hour or so, they keep arriving. It goes on until there are like twelve of them. Then they leave."

"Is that when Lomarco and DiBiaggio called you?"

"Yeah. I didn't know what to make of it, but it didn't seem like a big thing. I told them guys from a dozen families are all over the place, looking for these people, so you could run into anybody anywhere. We didn't hear from them again, so I let it go. But then we didn't hear from them for a couple more days, so I started to wonder. A couple of hours ago we started making some calls."

"So what did you find out?"

"That's why I thought I had to ruin your dinner, Al. It seems the New Mexico state police found their bodies. They were way the hell out in someplace called Cibola National Forest."

"They weren't supposed to make noise or cause trouble," said Castananza.

"I'm pretty sure they didn't, Al," said Saachi. "When you told me to send guys, I didn't think you wanted walking meat. I sent good, strong hands. Both of these guys were young, but not kids. I was there the night Lomarco made his bones. He went in alone, did this guy with a knife, and walked slow around the corner to the car with a smile on his face. He had a set of stones on him."

"Do their families know?"

"Not yet," said Saachi. "I just found out."

"We'd better make a swing over to their houses tonight, so I can talk to them myself," Castananza said. "You got enough money on you?"

Saachi's look of anxiety returned. "This is just an opinion, Al, but I don't think it's a good idea."

"It doesn't take long, and it's what people expect. If I don't do it, people are going to wonder why. In a little while, their wives are going to be wondering what's going to happen to them and the kids."

"I can go give them some money by myself," offered Saachi. "We don't know how bad this is yet."

Castananza turned his eyes to watch Saachi. He was glancing in the rearview mirror to be sure the two boys were still back there. "You have a theory?"

"I don't know, Al," said Saachi. "Two perfectly capable guys are sitting in an airport, and a few days later, they're dead, a hundred miles away. It makes you think."

"So what does it make you think?"

"Well, what's going on?" asked Saachi. "Nobody killed them in an airport. Maybe they followed those twelve guys into an ambush. Or maybe somebody talked them into leaving the airport. If DiBiaggio remembered one of them from the Castiglione crew, who can they belong to but DeLuca?"

"Could have been Delfina. He got some of those guys when the family split."

"Oh yeah. That's right," said Saachi. "DeLuca got most of them, so I sometimes forget. But Delfina or DeLuca or anybody else, why would they kill our guys?"

"You think our guys found something—like Bernie's money?"

"Or their guys did, and wanted to be sure nobody else knew about it."

"Or maybe it's all been some kind of setup from the beginning," said Castananza.

"You think so?" asked Saachi.

Castananza shrugged. "That's what I've been afraid of. One minute we hear Bernie the Elephant is dead, and we lost a lot of money. Then we hear that we're supposed to send people all over the country. Why? To look for Bernie's bodyguard, who is suddenly missing. Maybe 'missing' means he killed Bernie. But maybe it means somebody else killed both of them."

"It beats me how the hell anybody was going to get the money out of Bernie after he was dead anyway," said Saachi.

Castananza shrugged. "Vincent Ogliaro is in jail, but he was supposed to be smart. And that family has always been tight. Tasso was saying Ogliaro's old man was a tough son of a bitch, and it made me remember him."

"Well, his family ain't tight anymore. It's like somebody lopped off their head, and they're just lying there. I think somebody is going to wait a decent interval and then take over."

"DeLuca?"

Saachi squeezed his face into a doubtful look and cocked his head. "He did put the bomb in Di Titulo's car. And I've been hearing that there are a lot of guys from Chicago hanging around Detroit."

"And everywhere else, too," said Castananza. "There seem to be a few in every airport our guys have been covering."

"What do you want me to do?" asked Saachi.

"I told you. Take me to DiBiaggio's house, and Lomarco's."

"Are you sure?" Saachi turned the car toward DiBiaggio's house.

"We've got no choice, now. When everybody else hears they're dead, they also better hear I already gave their wives a pile of money to tide them over. People have got to feel like this is a tight family if we're going into a war."

"War?" asked Saachi. "With who? DeLuca?"

"Not DeLuca," said Castananza. "It's too big for DeLuca."

"Who, then?"

"Maybe him and somebody else," said Castananza in growing frustration. "DeLuca, at least two of the New York families, and Chi-chi Tasso in New Orleans. I don't know who else, but they're a good bet."

"Chi-chi Tasso?" Saachi's voice revealed his confusion.

"Yeah. He was the one who said this was all a fantasy. He said Bernie took the money himself and gave it to charities. It was a real conversation stopper. He took up half the ride with this nonsensical thing about how Bernie lost his mind and heard voices that told him to do it."

"What do you think they're up to?"

"Just what I said. They got Bernie. They got the rest of us to spread our guys out looking for Bernie's money. Now they'll cut off a few heads and take over. And we can't fight them on that plan. Any one of them is bigger than we are. The best we can do is get our feet out of their trap before they get it all cocked and ready."

"How do we do that?"

"Get everybody home. I mean everybody. I don't want to hear later how one or two guys didn't get the word and suddenly found themselves out there alone. But first take me to DiBiaggio's house, and Lomarco's."

33

Jane kept Bernie and Rita out of sight as she drove west. She bought food at grocery stores, and they ate while they were on the road. They took turns driving, so one person could sleep in the back of the Explorer while the second rested and dozed in the passenger seat.

As they moved across the country, Jane used small ways of bolstering the new identities she had chosen for Bernie and Rita. She bought key chains and wallets and had them monogrammed. When she crossed into Illinois, where the Dailys had come from, she bought souvenirs: T-shirts, caps, jackets with the logos of the Cubs, the White Sox, the Bears, the Bulls, the University of Illinois, and even a couple of sweatshirts that said CHICAGO. She knew that salespeople, banks, and landlords were always watching for people using fake identities to steal money. The ones who did that were not in a long-term business. They simply stole a wallet and used the cards they found in it until it got to be too risky. That took a day or two. They didn't have time to bother with things like monograms, and they didn't wear anything that could advertise where they lived or where they had been.

At Chicago, Jane turned south. Late on the second evening, she stopped the Explorer at a fast-food restaurant outside Urbana. While she waited for the waitress to pack the food she had ordered, she went to the pay telephone in the corner by the ladies' room. She put in coins and dialed the number that Henry Ziegler had given her. She held her breath as the telephone rang. It was long after business hours in Boston, but she knew that it would make no difference to Henry. The phone rang again, and she heard his voice. "Yes?"

Jane said, "I thought you probably wouldn't be home sleeping. I just wanted to know that you made it."

He said, "I've been wanting to call you, too, but nobody answered in New Mexico."

"The last ones went into the mail two days ago," she said. "They'll probably arrive tomorrow."

"We did it?" said Henry.

"We did it," she said. "Now stay safe. And thanks."

"Don't thank me," he said. "If you ever need me again, you know where I am."

Jane laughed. "I should have that kind of money. Got to go." She hung up, paid the waitress for the take-out dinners, and walked to the Explorer. She kept heading south, then turned east.

Jane turned the Explorer off the highway just across the Indiana state line in Terre Haute, and began to search the town. Bernie woke up after a few minutes and rubbed his eyes. "What are we doing?"

"Looking for the right kind of hotel," she said.

"What's the right kind?"

"I'll know it if I see it. There are some hotels that are near airports and big interstate highways. They have the feel of places where people in a big hurry would stop. What I want is the sort of place you would stop if you were on vacation, or maybe the kind where local people go to have dinner."

Jane found the hotel near the Wabash River. It was called the Davis House, and it had the feel of a country inn or a bed-and-breakfast house, but it wasn't small enough to require compromises in privacy or anonymity. She rented three rooms on the second floor, and brought the others in after she had examined the grounds and walked the hallways.

Once they were settled, Jane gathered them in her room. When they came in, she was busy laying out clothes on her bed. "Are you leaving us again?" Rita asked.

"Not exactly," said Jane. "I'm going on an errand in the

morning, but I should be back by nightfall. If everything goes well, we'll stay here tomorrow night too."

"That would be great," said Rita. "The last couple of times I fell asleep, I had dreams about getting a shower and sleeping in a real bed."

Bernie said, "What if it doesn't go so well?"

"I'm sure that the Explorer still hasn't been seen. I'll leave that here for you and take a rental car. If I'm not back tomorrow night, don't get worried. If I'm not back by the next night, start making plans that don't include me."

"You don't have to do this," said Bernie. "You said it yourself in Santa Fe. We've already done the best thing with our lives that we could have done if we'd had the sense to plan it that way. We won."

"It's not enough," said Jane. "We made an agreement. When we've lived up to it, then it will be over."

Jane went out to rent a car and buy a few last items, then made the telephone call to the prison in the name of Elizabeth Moody. Before dawn the next morning she got into the rental car and drove across the state line into Illinois. She took Interstate 70 to Effingham, then 57 south all the way to Marion. She approached the federal prison at Marion in the afternoon.

The high walls and the guard towers were relics of another era, when prisons looked medieval instead of industrial. She reminded herself that what she was about to do was participate in a ritual. The procedures, the movements, were already established.

She walked to the gate at ten minutes before nine and waited with the other visitors. At nine, a guard with a clipboard came to the gate to let the visitors in one at a time. There were a lot of wives, mostly young women with faces they tried to keep expressionless, a few of them with little children who seemed to have no awe or alarm at the horrible place. There were two men in suits carrying briefcases like Jane's, and she listened carefully to what they said. When it was her turn she spoke to the guard in a clear but bored voice. "Attorney here to see a client. The name is Elizabeth Moody."

The guard did a leisurely perusal of the sheet on his clipboard, looking a bit like a maître d' checking restaurant reservations. He made a notation beside one of the lines, and opened the door. Jane went inside to a reception desk, where she was supposed to fill out a form and sign it, then endured more waiting, watched a guard make a cursory search of her briefcase, and passed through a metal detector to another waiting area.

Another guard came in and called for Elizabeth Moody, and ushered her down a long hallway past a couple of barred gates that the guard opened in front of her, then closed behind her as soon as she was past. He put her into a little room with no windows except for a small Plexiglas square on the door with chicken-wire reinforcement between the panes.

She sat in one of the two battered metal chairs at a bare table and waited some more. When the guard returned, he had his hand on the arm of another man, but for a second Jane thought there must have been some mistake. He was much thinner and healthier looking than she had remembered from the newspapers. He was wearing prison jeans and a work shirt, and the general impression he conveyed was odd, until she identified it: he looked too clean. That was the only way of saying it. Priests who wore street clothes sometimes looked like that. His features had not really changed. He appeared to be in his mid-forties—although she knew he was older—with thick, dark, wavy hair that seemed to start a quarter inch too low on his forehead. He was looking at her with eyes that showed little interest.

Jane concentrated on the guard. "Thank you," she said to him. When he stood still, she gazed at him expectantly for a few seconds. He seemed to recollect himself, then turned and went outside.

As soon as the door closed, Jane held out her hand without smiling. "Good afternoon, Mr. Ogliaro. I'm Elizabeth Moody."

Ogliaro leaned forward, grasped her hand and shook it once, then released it unenthusiastically. "Didn't Zabel come with you?"

Jane had studied the Detroit newspapers' articles about the

trial on the Internet while she was in Santa Fe. In the early stages, there was always a partner in the firm Zabel, Dunstreet and Bibberly giving the reporter a denial of each of the charges. Later, Zabel had given the summation. When Jane had made her appointment at the prison, she had said she was an associate in the firm.

"Not today," said Jane. "This isn't about your appeals. I'm not a criminal litigator, I'm a specialist in the firm's financial division. I'm just here to take care of some business."

Ogliaro sat down at the table. He said, "What is it?"

Jane sat across from him and began taking papers out of her briefcase. "A few papers to look over." She handed him the first one.

He glared at it. "Interglobal insurance company? What do they want—to sell me a policy?"

Jane said, "It's something that came to us because our office is listed as your address for business purposes right now. Your mother was Francesca Giannini Ogliaro. Is that correct?"

"Right."

"And she passed away recently?"

He nodded, looking at her warily. "What's this about?"

"In 1948, she apparently purchased a single premium variable lifetime annuity for you from Interglobal Life and Casualty."

"She did?" His eyes seemed to move past Jane and settle on the wall for a moment.

"That's what it says. The premium was a little under three hundred thousand dollars, which was quite a bit at the time, and it's grown." She looked at another sheet, which seemed to be a continuation of the first. "If you were collecting it right now, it would be about forty thousand a month."

"She never said anything."

Jane appeared to feel no interest in whether she had or not. "The annuity is in the form of a trust, and it has some conditions attached."

"What are they?" asked Ogliaro.

"They're a little peculiar," she said. "As an attorney, I can tell you that nobody can make you accept any bequest. All

you have to do is sign off on this other sheet. It says I made
you aware of the conditions and you refused, and I take care
of the rest."

He was impatient. "So tell me what the conditions are."

Jane looked down at the list she had made on the computer
in Santa Fe. "From the moment that you accept the annuity,
you have to meet the following conditions: One. You can
never be convicted of a felony committed after this date."

"How can I guarantee that? I don't have any control over
what some D.A. charges me with."

"It says 'convicted.' Presumably, if you don't commit any
new felonies, you might still be charged, but not convicted."

He rolled his eyes in frustration, then took a deep breath to
control his temper. "What else?"

"Two. You relinquish any control, ownership, management, or profit participation in any business enterprise."

His eyes slowly widened.

"Three. You will not reside within two hundred and fifty
miles of Detroit, Michigan. Nor will you own, rent, lease,
borrow, or otherwise possess real estate within that area."

"But—"

Jane pushed on. "Four. You will no longer use the name
Vincent Ogliaro. You will change your name legally and officially to Michael James Weinstein. All payments from the
trust will be made payable to Michael James Weinstein, with
none due to Vincent Ogliaro."

Jane paused and looked up at him, then down at the paper
again. He was not reacting the way she had expected anymore. He was still frowning, but he was nodding as though he
had lost his capacity for surprise or outrage. She said, "We
can handle the name change for you. All you have to do is
sign this petition, we file it in a court somewhere far away—
say, California—where it won't attract much attention, and
it's done. All it certifies is that you're not doing it to avoid
debts or responsibilities, which you wouldn't be."

He waited in silence, so Jane looked down her list, breezily
alluding to provisions she wasn't reading in their entirety.
"Payments to be deposited directly to the account you open in

the name Weinstein, et cetera, to be terminated upon your death, and so on. The rest is pretty standard stuff for trust funds."

"The first part isn't standard stuff."

She shrugged. "No, it isn't. Basically, if you stop being Vincent Ogliaro, stay away from Detroit, and stay out of trouble, you'll be supported for the rest of your life. Of course, the insurance company can't commence payment while you're in here. I didn't check your file before I left the office. When do you get out?"

"The tenth of August, year after next. Thirteen months and twenty-one days."

"And there's no time off for good behavior in federal sentences, but you don't have parole to worry about either, so that date is firm." She looked at the page with the figures again. "I can't predict exactly, because interest rates will fluctuate a bit, but if you start then, you'll get about . . . half a million dollars a year, round numbers."

Ogliaro's eyes were focused intently on Jane now. "Why do you suppose she would do this?"

Jane shrugged, not merely to show that she didn't know but that she didn't care. She looked around the bare, dismal conference room. "I'd say mothers want their sons living in houses that have windows. Just a guess, though. I don't have maternal instincts, I'm a lawyer."

"It's enough money so that I would never have to do anything at all, and the condition is that I never would do anything. I would just live a nice, safe, comfortable life. It's not enough to give me any power, but it's not enough to attract attention that would kill me, either."

"That's the idea, I guess," said Jane. "We did verify that the trust exists, and that the annuity is real and irrevocable."

Ogliaro sat with his arms folded. "She didn't do this." He waited, but Jane didn't appear inclined to argue with him. "But she's not the only one who just died, is she? Bernie died too."

"Bernie? Who's Bernie?"

Ogliaro's voice dropped to a whisper. "She told me. Bernie

doesn't know that, so you didn't know it either. She came to visit me before she went out to shoot him. She told me how she had set it up, who was handling what part of it. You know why?"

"Why?"

"Because if something went wrong, she wanted me to know who I should hunt down and kill for her."

"And what did you say to her?"

"I tried to talk her out of it."

Jane was silent for a moment. Finally, she said, "Okay. So you know. The single premium wasn't paid in 1948. It was ten million paid a couple of weeks ago."

"He never met me. Why would he do something like this now?"

Jane said, "It's his last chance." She thought for a moment. "Yours too, probably."

He stared at her for a moment, then held out his hand. "Do you have a pen?"

She handed him a pen from inside her briefcase. She watched him sign the papers in some spots, where she had put plastic clips, and initial others. "So you're going to do it?"

He handed the papers back to her and stood up. "Either I signed the papers because I want to be a new person and get a second chance at having a life, or I signed them because I'm Vincent Ogliaro, and I think I can find a way to get the half a million a year without doing anything different. You won't know for a while, will you?"

"No," said Jane.

He turned, walked to the door, and prepared to knock, then held back for a moment. "Tell Bernie thanks for staying away for all those years. If he'd done anything different, I'd be dead." He reached for the door again, then said, "My mother loved him."

"I know," said Jane.

"Tell him." Ogliaro pounded on the door, and the guard opened it. "We're done," he said.

34

As Jane drove back toward Terre Haute, she tried to sort out what had happened. She had spent her life concentrating on the simple goal of not losing. If the other side won, her runner would die. If Jane won, all that happened was that her runner got to keep breathing for one more day, one more week. But this time, she had actually participated in something that felt like victory.

Today, while she had been inside the prison with Vincent Ogliaro, mail carriers all over the country had probably delivered the last of the letters to the offices of charities. Henry Ziegler was home in Boston. Rita and Bernie were sitting comfortably in a nice hotel in Terre Haute, and Jane was driving along a fast, open highway in a clean, untraceable rental car. She had checked her rearview mirror a dozen times in the past five miles, and the road behind her was clear.

Everything had happened as she had hoped it would, and now she had to decide how to accomplish what she needed to make happen next. She was back to doing what she had done so many times for so many people: making them vanish and reappear somewhere else where they would be safe.

Jane was beginning to feel hungry, and as soon as she recognized it, she remembered that she had not eaten today. She looked at her watch. She had hoped to make it back to the hotel in Terre Haute in time to eat with the others, but it was already dinner time. She decided to pull off the highway at Effingham. She would eat dinner and change into comfortable clothes.

* * *

Mary Ellen Tolliver sat uncomfortably in her chair at the Davis House dining room in Terre Haute, and studied her menu for the tenth time. She sat here with the stiffly starched white napkin on her lap, carefully lifted the silver cream pitcher and sugar bowl to see the silversmith's mark on the bottoms, stared out the window at a bird on the crab-apple tree in the garden, and waited for John.

She liked the restaurant. It reminded her of the nice places her parents used to take her when she was a child, with the butter in pats on a little bowl of ice, and silverware that was too big for her hands, and everything heavy—the glasses lead crystal, the tablecloths real linen. She kept wanting to say something about it to John, but he was still out on the telephone.

He came back looking red-faced and excited, and it made Mary Ellen shift her eyes toward the girl. No, she didn't seem to have noticed. She was just sitting there picking at her dinner, the way girls her age always did.

John glanced at her too. "See the other one yet?" he asked.

Mary Ellen shook her head, and her expression was sharp. John had never picked up the knack of whispering. Maybe it was because when he was still working at the car assembly plant, something had happened to his hearing. But he wasn't very good at anything that required subtlety.

He seemed to notice the restaurant only as he put the big napkin on his lap. He said, "I like this place. It reminds me of the way restaurants used to be."

Mary Ellen issued a blanket pardon that forgave him for everything, and settled into the adventure again. Since they had retired, there had been a lot of these trips. That was the way she always said it—since we retired—even though it sometimes made people ask the irritating question of what she had retired from. Both of their lives had been one way, and now both of their lives were another way, and that was that. She and John had started doing things differently.

The enemy in retirement was that nothing you did seemed to cause you to look forward to anything. Weekends were the same as weekdays, and payday was just a notice from your bank that the check had arrived as usual. It was Mary Ellen who had slowly begun to introduce the element of chance. Three years ago for Father's Day, she had bought John a metal detector. They had begun by taking it on a vacation to Florida, and while Mary Ellen had sat on the beach getting sunburned, John had found fourteen dollars in change and a pretty good wristwatch. They had taken it to parks, and even walked along the Mississippi with it now and then. They had never found anything quite as good after that, but Paducah wasn't Miami, either.

Over the past couple of years, a lot of their little adventures had to do with found money. They were adequately provided for, with John's pension from the plant and Social Security. The money itself wasn't the attraction. One time, when the Illinois Lottery had been up to forty million, they had driven over into Illinois and bought tickets. They hadn't won, but they had started driving over for tickets about once a month after that.

That was how they happened to see the flyers saying "Find This Girl" and "Woman Missing." They had driven up from Paducah one day, and when they had stopped for lottery tickets, John had picked up the flyers off the counter. They had decided to keep driving deeper into Illinois, looking hard at the faces of all the women they had seen. They had driven up to Marion, where the prison was. Then they had decided that if the women were somewhere around the prison, the only major routes they had not covered on the way up from Paducah lay to the north. They had ended up here in Terre Haute, Indiana. It had been like a dream. They had come into this hotel to eat dinner, and there was "Find This Girl" sitting at a table overlooking the garden all by herself.

"Did you get through to them?" she asked quietly.

He nodded happily. "I did. They said they'd check it out right away."

"And they took your name and address and everything?"

"You bet," he whispered. "All they've got to do is come and see for themselves that it's the same one, and we're going to get the money."

"If it's the right one," she reminded him.

"Of course it is," he said. "Look for yourself."

Mary Ellen tried to keep the excitement at a low level, the sort of feeling she could manage without getting a fluttery heart or something. She ventured another glance, and she felt her heart quicken a little. There was absolutely no question it was "Find This Girl." Now she let herself hope that "Woman Missing" showed up before the investigators did. That would be twice the money.

As Mary Ellen ate her dinner, she felt a little bit guilty about her good fortune. The flyers had implied that "Find This Girl" was some sort of runaway child. Sometimes what that meant was that there was some terrible story involving abuse. Either that was the reason why they left home, or what everybody feared had happened to them since. It would be a shame to get rich and then find out that her windfall and John's had been based on something like that. She tried to reassure herself with thoughts about "Woman Missing." She looked quite a bit older, and what was said about her implied that she was a criminal, not a victim. Maybe Mary Ellen would be the one who saved the girl and put the criminal in jail.

Mary Ellen was all the way through her dessert—an apple cobbler with vanilla ice cream—and she still could see no sign of policemen or detectives. Maybe John had given them directions that were too vague, or completely wrong. Maybe they had heard his voice and thought he was a nut.

The waiter brought the girl her check in a leather folder. She signed it, got up, and left. Mary Ellen looked at her husband in horror. "She's leaving."

"It doesn't matter," he said.

"But if they don't get here, she'll be gone, and we won't get the reward."

"Sure we will," he said. "Didn't you see the way she signed the bill?"

Mary Ellen was sure her husband had lost his mind. "What was I supposed to see?"

"She didn't give him a credit card. She just signed it, and wrote a room number. She's not leaving. She's staying at the hotel."

35

Jane reached Terre Haute at eleven-thirty at night. She felt a kind of exhaustion that was strangely pleasant. At some point, a week or a month from now, she would think back on all of the driving and the tension and the endless watchfulness, and it would probably be difficult to reconstruct how it had all happened. Right now, she knew that the pleasure of a long, hot bath and a soft bed would be enough.

She drove past the car rental agency, and she could see that it would be possible to leave the car now and drop the key in a lockbox, but she drifted past the entrance and sped up again. It didn't look as though there was anyone on duty to give her a ride to the hotel. She drove toward the hotel, but resisted the temptation to simply park in the lot and step into the lobby. The money was gone, but she, Rita, and Bernie weren't finished yet. Having a car that nobody knew about was not a small advantage if something had gone wrong while she was away. She drove up the street one block west of the hotel and parked.

Jane walked to the end of the block and turned toward the hotel. It was a warm, humid summer night, and even in this commercial part of town, she could hear crickets. She supposed the lawns and gardens of the hotel were part of the reason, but she could hear the sounds coming from a row of low rosebushes along the facade of an insurance agency to her right, then from a patch of azaleas in front of a women's clothing store.

Jane reached the street where the hotel entrance was, but she didn't cross at the intersection. Instead, she turned and walked up the sidewalk across from the hotel. When she had achieved the proper angle, she could see the reflection of the chandelier on the shiny floor of the brightly lit lobby. When she had gone thirty paces farther, she knew that she would be able to see the parking lot.

She knew that it was unlikely that she would see that Rita and Bernie had taken the Explorer and run, but that didn't mean it wasn't worth checking. The Explorer was still there, exactly where she had parked it when they'd arrived. She half-turned to go back to the intersection and cross the street, but something made her stop.

There was a van in the guest parking area. It was nearly midnight, a bit late for deliveries, and this wasn't a van that somebody used as a car, because the back door had printing that said, "How am I driving? Call (800) 555-1100." She kept walking on, trying to achieve the proper angle to read the name of the company on the side. When she had reached the right spot, she could see the name: Mayfair Products. She knew she might be letting weeks of extreme caution overrule her sense of proportion, but she decided to satisfy herself.

Jane kept walking until she found a pay telephone on the front of a discount drugstore a block away. She pulled from her purse the little folder the clerk had handed her at check-in to hold the key cards, read the telephone number, and dialed. When the operator answered, she said, "Room 224, please."

The telephone rang three times before she heard a click and the sound of breathing. She didn't wait for Bernie to speak. "Bernie? It's me."

His voice was hoarse from sleep. "What? Where are you?"

"I'm across the street and down one block at a pay telephone. I was on my way in, but I saw something that worried me. Has anything gone wrong since I left?"

"I haven't seen anything. We haven't left the place. The only time either of us has been out of the room was when Rita went down to eat dinner. She said there was nobody but old codgers. What did you see?"

"There's a delivery van in the parking lot. It might be fine, but it's parked in kind of an odd place—not near a loading zone, but close to the side door where the first-floor rooms are. It says 'Mayfair Products' on it. I remembered Trafalgar Flowers, and—"

"Trafalgar Square Flowers, Parliament Park grocery stores, Belgravia Broadcasting."

"Then it is Delfina?"

"I don't keep track of everything the bastard owns, but do you want to bet it's just some schmuck who misses London?"

"No," said Jane. "Wake Rita up. If they know we're here, then they know the Explorer's ours. I've got the rental car parked on a street parallel to the front of the hotel, one block over. Do you remember what it looks like?"

"Remembering things isn't my problem. White Chevy, license number—"

"Enough," she interrupted. "I'll leave the keys on the ground behind the right front tire. You and Rita come down the stairwell, then out the door by the swimming pool. Go through the garden by the restaurant, and out to the street on that side. Go one block up before you cut over to the street where the car is."

"What about you?"

"I'm going to watch the van and the parking lot and the front entrance to see if they go after you. If they don't, I'll be at the car before you are. If they do, I'll meet you somewhere."

"Where?"

Jane said, "I don't know . . . Evansville, Indiana. I'll be in front of the police station at nine o'clock tomorrow night." She didn't wait for him to raise an objection. "Wake her now," she said, and hung up.

Jane turned away from the hotel and walked another block before she doubled back to the street where she had left the car. She walked briskly to it, bent to slip the keys beside the curb and under the right front tire, and kept going. There was nobody walking on the street, so she was confident that her move had not been seen. The keys would not be picked up by the headlights of a passing car, and the next pedestrian's view would be blocked by the curb.

Jane turned the corner and kept walking until she was directly across from the hotel again. She stepped into the dark space between a small bookstore and a closed restaurant and stared at the van. She couldn't see any heads in the windows, so she turned her attention to the other cars in the lot. There were definitely more of them tonight than there had been last night. She was sure that the hotel kitchen closed at ten, and the small bar off the lobby would not have seated more than a dozen people comfortably.

Then Jane saw the van move. It was a small, subtle motion, just a shifting of weight as someone in the back moved from one spot to another, but she was sure. Then she saw another movement in the shadows near the other end of the parking lot. A man stepped to the back of a parked car and opened the trunk. The light in the trunk didn't go on. It looked like a new car, but the light didn't work. The man took something out and stepped back into the darkness again.

Jane waited, and time seemed to stop. If Bernie and Rita could only slip out of the building without being seen, she could get them out of here. She stared along the front of the hotel, past the facade to the old-fashioned veranda outside the restaurant. She could see no sign of them. She let her eyes go unfocused and stared toward the garden, waiting for the shapes of Bernie and Rita to stand out from the dim tangle of bushes and twining vines to reassure her.

There was movement in the parking lot. Now there were three men standing near the van. Car doors opened across the lot, and three more men stepped out into the light. They seemed to be looking away from the hotel, in the direction of the big drugstore where Jane had made her telephone call. One of the men lifted his hand to his face, and she could see that there was something in it—a black rectangle. He was talking into a radio as he stared up the street.

A moment later, from that direction, she saw a vehicle appear. It was a big Suburban, and it was moving quickly up the street. It turned into the lot, paused for a second beside the group of men, then swung away and parked near the edge of the lot. There was some more discussion between the man with the radio and someone in the Suburban.

Jane looked anxiously toward the other end of the building.

What was taking so long? Where were they? In a moment she detected a moving shadow, then another. They were walking along the outside of the building beside the restaurant.

Jane looked back at the parking lot. The man with the radio in his hand waved his right arm. Three men began to walk toward the side entrance to the hotel, near the Mayfair van. Jane sucked in a breath. In a couple of minutes, they would know the rooms were empty.

She looked at the far end of the building. Rita and Bernie had stopped. They seemed to be standing in the shadow of an arbor, waiting for something. "No," Jane whispered. "Keep moving."

Then Jane saw it was the Suburban. It had moved to the back of the lot, then around the service road toward the other side. It seemed to be parked there, right in Rita and Bernie's path.

Jane turned her attention to the parking lot again. The man with the radio pointed, and the three men he had left began to walk along the outside of the building. Jane realized he must be sending them to watch the other exits. Rita and Bernie were already outside, but they were trapped in the garden. Those men were walking straight toward them.

Jane squeezed her eyes shut and clenched her teeth. She felt a swelling of strong, explosive emotions—anger at these men who had come to shake an old man and a teenaged girl out of their sleep and drag them off, frustration at Bernie and Rita for being too slow, too tentative to survive, shame for not having been smart enough to have avoided this. She felt an overpowering sense of outrage as she pretended to make a decision. But while she was doing it, her hand was in her purse, feeling in the inner pocket for the second ignition key she had gotten when she had bought the Ford Explorer.

She found it, and she moved out from between the two buildings. She stepped across the sidewalk quickly, then off the curb. A strange image floated across her consciousness as she watched the men across the street in the parking lot, staring only at one another and talking into radios.

This was the way hundreds of Senecas had died, the way a Seneca was supposed to die. In the Old Time, raiding parties had consisted of three or four good friends, who had gone quietly and secretly to the territory of their enemies. They would appear out of the forest, do the enemy as much harm as they could, and then disappear into the forest again. They would run along the trail single file, sometimes not stopping for days at a time. But now and then, the strategy would fail. The time would come, somewhere in the wild country hundreds of miles from home, when they would be exhausted, slowing. The enemy warriors assembled to retaliate would be about to catch up. It was then that the strongest and bravest would suddenly stop. He would step back along the trail to a narrow spot, and begin to sing his death song as he waited for the pursuers.

He would fight them, trying to lay as many bodies at his feet as he could. The enemy would fight differently. They would try to wound him with arrows and thrown clubs, attack in waves and retreat, attempt to use up his strength so they could take him down and drag him back alive to be tormented.

Jane's mind was so clear that she could read the minds of the men around the hotel. She knew what they would think before they did. When they noticed the lone woman hurrying across the street toward them, they turned away, hiding the radios and taking a few tentative steps back toward the darkness. She was still just a woman, someone whom they didn't want to see their faces. In a moment she would go into the hotel, and they could resume their hunt. She could feel them looking at her when her foot went up on the curb in front of the parking lot. She moved quickly, knowing that each second gave them more time to sense her fear. She walked purposefully ahead, not letting her eyes turn in their direction. She knew that as soon as she made her move, she would transform herself from a low-level threat into prey.

She relished the few seconds while she prepared, savoring their alarm at her sudden interruption of their plans, and their eagerness to see her gone. She walked close to the Mayfair Products van, as though she was going into the hotel. She took a deep breath as she reached the front of the van, then suddenly slipped to the side, hidden for a moment by the bulk of the van. She took two running steps across the front of it, emerged in the next aisle, stuck the key into the door of the Explorer, swung the door open, leapt into the driver's seat, and pounded the lock button.

She started the Explorer and backed up quickly, then pushed the accelerator nearly to the floor. She saw a man try to step in front of her, but she didn't vary her course at all. He dived to the pavement to escape, and she thought she heard a bump as though the fender might have clipped his foot. She let the van roar out into the road too fast, then had to accelerate out of the wide turn to get out of the opposite lane.

Jane glanced in the rearview mirror to see men running for cars in the lot. She raised her speed, because she knew that if she didn't, the big Suburban would try to block the road ahead of her.

She took one last look at the hotel as she turned right, then left. She searched the picture she carried with her in her mind. There had been men running back along the front of the hotel, away from the restaurant garden toward the parking lot. It had worked. In a few minutes the sound of cars would die in the distance, and Bernie and Rita would be able to stroll down the sidewalk to the car she had left them.

Jane felt a curious sense of freedom as she drove. It was after midnight, and she was on the edge of the city already. Ahead of her were hundreds of miles of flat country with good, fast roads. She looked at the gas gauge. The tank was full. If she did this right, she might be able to keep them following her for a long time. Bernie and Rita would have the new start that she had wanted to give them.

She drove fast, but she had no serious hope of outrunning them. She made four quick turns, then found herself moving south on Route 41. She looked back in her rearview mirror and saw three other cars make the turn after her, then the Suburban. She nudged her speed up some more, but they were still coming.

She saw signs indicating she was passing Farmersburg, Shelburn, Sullivan. The names meant nothing. The world seemed to be a black sky and a slightly lighter line of land below it, as though her life had simplified into two stripes with a road down the middle. Now and then she would see a tiny red glow of taillights ahead, but after a few minutes the car would pull off and the lights would be gone. Then she would see white headlights, and they would slowly grow and brighten. She would hope for a police car, but by the time the lights were close enough to show that it wasn't, they would flash past and be gone.

After a few minutes, she realized that flagging down a single patrol car would do her no good. It would be one rural cop against—what—four carloads of heavily armed men? There was little point in recruiting somebody to die with her. She considered instead trying to make a run for one of the big east-west interstates. Route 64 must be ahead of her. At any hour of the night there would be long-distance truckers and tourists who were pushing themselves, and at each exit there would be lighted gas stations and fast-food places. Maybe these men wouldn't dare to take her in a public place in front of witnesses.

She knew it wasn't true. They had flown here from some-where with the intention of pulling an armed assault on a hotel to kidnap people. She thought about them, and began to grow angrier. There was some special quality about what they were doing that made her feel heat at the back of her neck. It was their arrogance. They felt invincible. They always had everyone overwhelmingly outnumbered. They relied on people being afraid of them. She found herself thinking about the shotgun she had carried in the New Mexico desert. She had reached the edge of the city, dropped it in the dirt, and buried it. She wished she could go back in time, dig it up, and throw it into the back of the Explorer before she drove east.

She was moving as fast as she dared. Whenever she reached the crest of an incline, she would feel the Explorer leave the ground a little, pulling up on the springs, the seat belt tight-ening across her hips to keep her down. Then it would come down, and her arms would seem to grow heavier for a few sec-onds. Each bump in the road threatened to wrench the steering wheel to the side. She glanced back in the mirror, and she could see that she had gained a little ground.

When she returned her eyes to the windshield, she saw the farm. It was enormous, by the standards she had grown up with in western New York, a small cluster of buildings in the middle of a vast expanse of fields. It looked like an oasis in the desert, because big trees had been left around the buildings to provide the only shade for miles, and in front of one of the buildings was a lawn.

There were no lights on in any of the buildings. As she came down the incline toward the place, she could see the fields better. They were filled with corn. It was late July now, so the stalks near the road seemed to her to be higher than the roof of the Explorer.

This was her chance. They might be able to drive long enough and hard enough to catch up with her and bump her off the road, and certainly they could keep her in sight until she had to stop. But she was a runner. She had always run. Every morning since she was twelve, she had gone down to the Niagara River and run along the bank to the Grand Island Bridge and back. She had been on the track team at college, and had won more races than she had lost. The past few weeks had probably left her a little bit out of shape, but she was willing to take the chance.

She watched the fence posts going by, and then forced her eyes ahead. There it was. There was a road that ran from the highway all the way back to the cluster of barns and outbuildings. She took her foot off the gas pedal without touching the brake, so her taillights would not warn the chasers. She coasted as long as she could, then swung to the right onto the side road.

She drove for fifty yards, then wrenched the wheel to the left into the cornfield. She put her front wheels into two ruts and ran up the corn rows, watching the big stalks in front of the windshield looming, then falling in front of her. She drove for a full minute, then stopped the Explorer, got out, and slipped quietly into the vast, dark field of tall cornstalks.

36

Delfina sat in the front seat of the Suburban beside Cirro, moving his head from side to side to get a better view. "Where'd she go?"

Cirro craned his neck as he drove. "I can't tell yet." Then he said, "It looks like she must have turned off somewhere."

Ahead of them, Delfina could see the other cars slowing down, then stopping at the side of the road. Cirro pulled up and stopped. Delfina saw Buccio running along the line of cars, shouting orders into their open windows. As Buccio approached the Suburban, Delfina said, "Now what?"

Buccio leaned in and said, "Frank, she must have turned off at this farm. There's an open gate up here, and a road that leads to the farmhouse and stuff."

"So what are you doing about it?" asked Delfina.

"Waiting to see what you think."

Delfina's eyes went cold. "What do I think?"

"You know. It's a farm. There are sure to be a bunch of people around. It's a big place."

"Christ," Delfina muttered. "Go in after her."

Buccio ran for his car. In a moment, Delfina saw the car pull out onto the road, then turn onto the smaller road. The other three cars pulled out and followed. Delfina nodded to Cirro, who drove up the road to the entrance. He turned, then Delfina said, "Hold it here, Mike."

The cars were stopped just two hundred feet up the road. Delfina climbed down from the Suburban and walked to the line of cars. Other men were getting out and standing on the road. Buccio saw Delfina, and pointed into the cornfield. "It looks like she drove right into the cornfield here."

Delfina took Buccio by the arm and led him a few feet from the others. "Look, Carl. I've been trying to give you every opportunity I can to handle this. But here we are. There's a woman with the key to billions of dollars that belongs to us in that cornfield someplace. I've committed myself now. There's no way I can tell the other families I didn't know where she was, or I was going to cut them in after I got her. Do you understand?"

"Sure, Frank."

"No, I'm not sure you do, even now. When I say I want her, I mean if she isn't going home with us, you won't be going home with us."

He watched Buccio's face and waited while Buccio thought about that, then added, "And don't think that if you lose her, your guys will pop me and say she did it. I already had quiet talks with a few of your crew, and you aren't going to know which ones."

Buccio stood silent for a moment, as though the hand that Delfina had laid lightly on his shoulder weighed hundreds of pounds. Finally, Delfina gave his shoulder a pat. "You're still in charge. Do what you have to do." He turned and walked back to the Suburban.

Buccio's body filled with energy. He knew that Delfina never spoke until he had thoroughly considered his position from every angle. Buccio glanced at the glowing dial of his watch. It was nearly one A.M., and the sun would come up around five-thirty. He had found a kind of clarity that was rare and precious: it was as though his whole life had been compressed into four and a half hours. As long as the night was dark, he would have absolute power to do as he pleased. When the sun came up, he would either have the woman or die.

He took four steps up the dirt road toward his men, making a major decision at each step. By the time he reached them, he had his strategy. He said, "I want two men with rifles to cover the front gate and the north-south fence along the road.

Don't let her slip through and start hitchhiking. If anybody else drives in, kill him."

He looked at the next two. "You two go down to cover the fences on the ends. Move out." He waited for a few seconds while his first four men trotted off to take their positions. He turned to the others. "We have three cars. I want two men to each car. Don't let your car out of your sight. She could be fifty feet away right now, waiting for a chance to sneak in and drive one off. The rest of you, come with me."

"Where are you going?" asked one of the men.

"To secure the farmhouse." He walked up the farm road, and four men followed.

Jane crouched among the cornstalks and watched the five men walk past her up the road. There were six still hanging around the cars, so there was no way to slip into one of them. She crawled closer and looked down the farm road toward the highway. The Suburban was still here, too, and it would be impossible to drive past it to the gate.

Her strategy would have to be dictated by what she couldn't do. She rose to her feet and made her way between the tall cornstalks, following her own trail until she reached the Explorer. She had hoped the men would leave her some way of disabling their cars while they were hunting her on foot, but that was not possible. She had, however, gotten them out of their cars, and some of them had already moved off on foot. Her best strategy now was to try to outrun them.

She climbed into the Explorer, started the engine, and moved ahead. She kept her wheels in the ruts between the rows of corn, and mowed down the stalks as she drove. She couldn't see far ahead, because the corn was too thick and she couldn't turn on her headlights, but it didn't matter. The ruts would keep her straight. She drove for a minute, then another minute, and another. Each time a stalk fell in front of her hood and went under the Explorer, she expected it to be the last. It had seemed to her that she would reach the end of the field by now, but it was much bigger than she had guessed.

She looked into the rearview mirror, and she could see that

she had cut a swath through the field, but it only consisted of the two rows of stalks between her tires. The Explorer rode so high that even those stalks weren't flattened, but tipped toward her at about a forty-degree angle. She could not see anyone following her yet, and she was beginning to be afraid that she wouldn't be able to see them until they were right behind her.

She kept driving. Her best hope was to choose a course and follow it efficiently and deliberately, without the kind of haste that made noise and drew attention, but was quick enough to keep the men from thinking.

She thought she heard a dog barking in the distance. She rolled her window down, but either it had stopped or she had imagined it. She kept going, and now the swishing sound of the Explorer moving through the corn seemed loud. Suddenly she heard a loud metallic creaking, and the Explorer stopped moving and strained against an invisible resistance.

She got out and pushed her way through the cornstalks to the front of the Explorer. She had reached a fence. There were five thick wires stretched across the grille and bowed outward. She followed them with her eyes, and she could see the first fence post on her right. It was being tugged ahead by the five wires, already strained and tilted at an angle by the pressure. She stepped to it and pulled at the wires to see if she could disconnect them, but they were strung in continuous strands from pole to pole, held there by big staples hammered deep into the wood.

She climbed back into the Explorer and gunned the engine. She heard louder creaking, snapping sounds as the vehicle surged forward, but then the wheels began to spin and slip sideways. Jane put the transmission into neutral, then reverse, and tried to back up. She could tell that the tires had already dug into the soft, cultivated soil. She rocked forward, then back again, and felt the Explorer roll up and out. She kept backing up, until she was about fifty or sixty feet from the fence. She put the transmission into drive and gradually built up her speed. She hit the wires fast, heard a loud cracking noise, and the Explorer broke free. As she rolled on, there was a screeching of wires scraping against the front of the

Explorer, and then a loud *bang* that rocked the vehicle. She spun her head to see that the broken fence post had been jerked into the air by the wires and hit the side. She looked around her. She was out of the corn, in another field that was low and grassy, like alfalfa. She stopped for a second to look to her left for the road.

This time the noise was louder, a *bam* as the window behind her head exploded inward and showered the cab with sparkling crystals of safety glass. There was another, and she saw a hole appear in the bare metal of the door ahead of her left knee, a tiny flower of bent steel blooming around it, where the bullet had splashed through. Another, and the windshield seemed to disintegrate, like a falling curtain of water.

Jane rolled between the front seats and hauled herself into the back, then pushed the rear door open and dived into the weeds. As she crawled back toward the cornfield, she heard more rifle shots, but she knew they were not aimed at her. She could hear ringing sounds as pieces of glass and metal were punched off the Explorer and flew against the interior walls.

When she reached the safety of the tall corn, she tried to see the man firing the rifle, but she couldn't. He had to be somewhere near the road. She took a last look at the Explorer. The shooter had adjusted his aim to the engine compartment. She saw the hood vibrate a little as the next shot punched through it, and the next. She slipped farther back into the cornfield, rose to her feet, and began to run.

Jane changed her course to head across the rows of cornstalks. She ran from row to row, then stopped for a moment to listen. She looked to her right in the direction of the farm road, trying to sight along the straight row and detect the approach of men on foot. Then she ran another hundred feet and stopped again. The stalks were tall enough to hide a man or a car, so it was impossible to see precisely where she was going, but she gave herself up to the features of the country. Her feet and legs could tell that she was going up a very gradual slope, and she knew that at the top of it would be the farm buildings.

She kept up her pace, using her ears and her sense of touch instead of her eyes. But slowly, gradually, she began to acknowledge that she heard noises. They seemed at first to be far behind her. They were engine noises, cars driving along, and she told herself that it was just the occasional vehicle moving along the now distant highway. They seemed to be going in both directions, because she would hear one start somewhere behind her right ear, get louder, and then diminish into the range of her left ear. Then, a few seconds later, she would hear the sound again, in reverse.

But then, one of them seemed much louder. She stopped and sighted along the corn row to her right, toward the farm road. She saw nothing. Then she turned around, and the fear gripped her chest so she breathed in quick, shallow gasps. She could see lights.

Only fifty yards behind her, the beams of headlights shone through the tall stalks of corn. They were moving from left to right across the field, the glow of the lights ahead of the engine noises. Then the lights swung around and came back. The three cars were driving back and forth along the rows as she had, flattening the cornstalks so she could not hide. She moved her head, then sidestepped to get a better view. They were halfway up the slope. It was already impossible for her to go back to the highway without being seen.

The headlights were moving quickly. The men had discovered, as she had, that the ruts and mounds of the cornfield were perfectly regular, and that the only obstruction was visual—the tall, frail cornstalks. They seemed to be driving back and forth at twenty or thirty miles an hour. They would reach her in a minute or two.

Jane whirled and began to run. She had to try to make it to the cluster of farm buildings. There would be shelter there, of some sort. There would be a telephone. There might even be a gun. This was a huge farm, after all, in the middle of agricultural country. You could fire a rifle in any direction without much fear of hitting anybody by accident, and there was no neighbor to annoy with the sound of it. There had to be a gun. Please, she thought. Let there be a gun.

The sounds of the cars seemed to her to grow louder. She lengthened her strides and dug into the soft earth to gain speed. She gave up pausing to look along the corn rows. Nothing she could possibly see there would be worse news than what was already behind her, and pausing would just give somebody a chance to aim.

She could tell she was still a long way from the buildings. They had seemed tiny from the highway, like a little village in some remote, forgotten place. But there had been a building shaped like a barn, and she knew that anything as tall as a barn would be visible above the stalks ahead long before she reached it. She ran on, hearing her own breaths now, her mouth open to bring in more air.

But the first thing that Jane saw was a tree. It was a high, old chestnut, and its dark cloud of leaves blocked out the stars. Jane slowed her pace and moved forward between the rows, then stopped at the last line of vertical stalks that stood like a palisade between her and the buildings.

She looked between them. She could see a barn, and it was as big as she had imagined. It had a wide white door that was closed, and she could see that a branch of the farm road ran right into it. This wasn't the kind of farm that raised animals, she decided. The barn must be just a huge garage for all the machinery.

She leaned forward a little and looked at the house. It was a two-story white clapboard structure with a long, roofed-over porch that had several chairs and a table on it, and a wicker love seat. There were no lights glowing behind any of the windows. She looked farther to the left and saw a high, broad shape that she couldn't interpret at first, but then it came into focus. It was an above-ground swimming pool.

Jane waited a few more seconds, trying to interpret each variation in the darkness, attempting to pick out anything that might be a man. She thought she had heard a dog some time ago, but it could not have been here, or it would already have sensed her presence and come to investigate. The place seemed to be deserted. Then the noise of the car engines seemed to grow louder as they passed once again, and Jane stepped forward.

She moved away from the corn onto the edge of a lawn. She stepped quietly and quickly, hoping that if someone she had not seen was nearby, her shape would merge in his vision with the wall of tall stalks behind her. She hurried toward the house.

Jane had no time to formulate even her hopes in any orderly way. She hoped there was a gun, she hoped there was a telephone, another road in the fields beyond the house that led away. She climbed the steps to the porch quietly, but decided that pounding on the door was not the right way to do this.

Jane looked along the porch and saw movement. She froze and looked harder. It was an open window, and the motion had been the curtain inside, swinging a little in the breeze. She stepped to the window, pushed her car key through the screen, unlatched it, slipped inside, and latched it again.

Jane could see that she was in an old-fashioned parlor that had been taken over by someone with modern tastes. There was a new leather couch beside her, and ahead of her a glass-topped coffee table with a stone sculpture as a base. In the far corner of the room was a big-screen television set. She looked down at the floor to see whether it was likely to creak. She couldn't see it very well, but when she knelt to feel it, she could pick up a little of the pattern in the moonlight. It was a new bleached hardwood floor.

She moved away from the window into the room, then found her way to the staircase. Somebody could be asleep up there. She supposed the sound of the rifle dismantling her Explorer could not have been as loud here as it had been to her. It was a half mile away. She began to climb the stairs quickly and quietly, then noticed that something looked odd under her feet. There seemed to be a long black shadow that fell like a stripe on each step—the railing? She waved her hand by the railing, but she could see no difference.

With growing discomfort, Jane reached down and touched a step. It was wet. She raised her fingers in front of her face, and saw that it was dark. It felt a little sticky, as though it were drying. She stared upward, and saw the dog.

He was lying on his side at the top of the stairs, his eyes open and staring with the dull gaze of the dead. She moved closer, and she could see that the blood was his, seeping from a wound in his mouth. She stepped to the top of the stairs and edged past him. She took a step toward the first open door, dreading what she was going to see.

She peered into the room. There was a double bed with a man and a woman lying on it—the woman in a blood-soaked nightgown, and the man in a pair of boxer shorts and a T-shirt that had three holes in the chest. She stepped backward out of the room and went to the next. It was an empty guest room, all made up with a flowered bedspread and lace covers over the dresser and nightstand. She moved along the second-floor hallway looking for more victims, but she found none.

She tried to stop thinking about what she had just seen and concentrate on what she had to do. She forced herself to go back into the master bedroom. There was a telephone on the low table by the woman's side of the bed. She stepped to it and picked it up. There was no dial tone.

She closed her eyes and replaced the receiver. Of course they would have cut the line before they came in. The dog must have met them at the top of the stairs and barked. They had shot the dog, rushed into the master bedroom before the farmer and his wife could get up, and killed them.

Jane moved to the closet on the man's side of the bed. If he had a gun, it would probably be in the closet or in his dresser. She knelt on the floor and ran her hand around the dark closet, feeling for anything that might be a long gun. All she felt were boots and shoes. She reached to the top shelf, but all she could find were hats. She moved to the man's dresser and began with the top drawers, then moved downward. There was no firearm. On the top of the dresser, she could see that the man had left his wallet and his keys. She took the keys and slipped them into her pocket. She had not seen the car yet, but she would probably find it in the barn. She lay on her belly and reached under the bed, but there was nothing hidden there.

Jane got up and walked down the hall toward the stairs. She sidestepped to get past the dog, then walked carefully down the steps to avoid the blood. She walked through the dining room and found the kitchen at the back of the house. She quietly began opening drawers under the counter. She found clean, folded dishtowels, then silverware, then a drawer of miscellaneous things that collected in kitchens—corkscrews, rubber bands, coupons. Finally, she found the drawer she had known must exist. She examined the knives in it. The boning knife was the right one for the purpose she had in mind. She slid the blade of it into the back pocket of her jeans so she could reach the handle, then noticed a second knife that looked right. It was about the same size, with a seven-inch blade, but the edge was serrated, and the handle was flatter. She lifted the right leg of her jeans and slid it into her sock, then lowered the denim to cover it.

Suddenly she became aware of the sound of the cars again. They seemed much louder and closer than they had been before. She realized that she needed to know exactly where they were before she tried to cross the open yard to the barn.

Jane looked out the kitchen window, but all she could see was the field of low alfalfa. She moved to the front of the house and looked out the window where she had entered. The headlights of the three cars were still moving back and forth across the cornfield in a line, flattening about twenty feet of corn at each pass. Beyond the cars, she could just pick out the shapes of several men, a hundred or more feet apart, walking slowly toward the house over the newly flattened corn. She judged the distance and decided that she still had a few more minutes. She was about to turn away from the window and head for the barn when she saw the other set of headlights.

They were higher than the headlights of the cars, and they bounced upward now and then as they came up the farm road toward the house. It was the Suburban. Jane turned and hurried to the side of the house nearest the barn. She opened a window and pushed her right leg over the sill, just as the Suburban came up and turned, its headlights now shining on the barn door. No, she thought. Not in front of the barn. Anywhere but there. The Suburban stopped, blocking the barn door. Its headlights went out.

Jane pulled her leg back inside and ducked down. She saw the doors open, and the interior light went on. There were two men. The driver was young and muscular. The man beside him was a bit older, with a little gray in his dark hair. They both wore sport coats, as though they were dressed for a pleasant visit to the dead family upstairs. They both got out of the Suburban and slammed the doors, then walked toward the house.

Jane heard the older man say, "I'm not saying Buccio and his guys are useless. It just took me a while to figure out what they're thinking—how they see themselves—and try to work with it. They're playing war. He needs to be desperate, like he was a Green Beret behind enemy lines or something. Everything has to be win or die. Look at them out there. They love this, and they're good at it."

"Think they'll find her, Mr. Delfina?"

Jane froze. Delfina. That man was Frank Delfina. She heard the footsteps heading toward the porch.

"If I didn't, they wouldn't be here."

Jane turned and hurried back up the stairs to the second floor. She stepped over the body of the dog and threw herself against the wall just as the front door opened. She heard their footsteps on the hardwood floor.

A light went on. She heard footsteps come close to the staircase. Delfina's voice said, "Mike. Look at that. They even killed the dog."

The younger man's footsteps sounded, then stopped. He said, "It probably barked."

Delfina said, "I suppose. Turn the light off down here, and we'll go up and watch from the window."

"Okay."

Jane looked at the doors on the upstairs corridor. The one with the farmer and his wife in it looked down on the back of the house, where the alfalfa field began. They would want to see the front. She quietly slipped into the room, then hurried to the closet. She crouched in the back of it and pulled the door closed so that only a tiny crack remained. She kept her ear to it and listened to the footsteps.

She heard Delfina say, "The land is practically flat. From up here, we'll be able to see for a mile."

They walked into the guest room. Jane wondered if she could move quickly and quietly enough to slip out and make it across the hall to the stairs.

Delfina said, "I'll watch this one. You go in there and keep your eyes open."

The younger man appeared in the doorway to the master bedroom. Jane held her breath as he moved to the window beside the bed. His voice startled her. "Mr. Delfina?"

"Yeah?"

"You can't see the cornfield from out here. This is the wrong side of the house."

"That's right," he called. "If she's in the cornfield, they'll see her, or I will. I want you to cover the field where she hasn't been yet. If you see her, try and drop her from the window. Even if you miss, Buccio's guys will hear the shot and come running."

"Okay." Jane watched the younger man reach into his coat and pull out a pistol. He stood watching for a few minutes, while Jane's mind ran frantically through everything she knew. Each time she thought of a way out of this, something stopped her. Maybe she could wait in this closet until daylight came. Maybe Delfina would have to pull his men out and leave. But the others were all moving methodically through the fields, destroying the cover, and when they were through, they would arrive at this house. They would be here in ten or fifteen minutes. They would probably realize that if she had not turned up outside, she had to be in the building. Even if they gave up, they might decide to burn the house to cover the murders.

Jane waited. Any small change would improve her chance of getting out. She watched impatiently. The young man sighed in boredom. He seemed tired of staring out the window at the empty, unchanging field. He let his eyes drift a bit. He looked at the two bodies on the bed. Jane detected no horror at the sight, and not even any visible distaste. He looked out the window again. The next time, he looked around the room. His eye happened to land on the top of the man's dresser, where his wallet was visible.

The young man turned and looked in the direction of the door. No, Delfina wasn't watching him. He put his gun away, walked around the bed, picked up the wallet, and examined it. Jane saw him pull the bills out of it and stuff them into his pocket. He glanced at the door again. Then he began to look in the dresser drawers. He seemed to find nothing that interested him, so he moved to the woman's dresser. There was a jewelry box, but when he opened it, she heard him snort in contempt. He walked back to look out the window again.

A minute later, Jane saw his eyes begin to wander. He turned completely around. She tried to guess what it was, and she decided that it must be the woman's purse. He had found the man's wallet, but no purse. He turned away from the window, and she expected him to search the far side of the room, but he didn't. He walked directly to Jane's closet and opened the door.

Jane sprang toward him, the boning knife in her hand. She stabbed it into his torso above his belly and pushed upward, toward the rib cage, hoping to reach the heart. His right arm swung hard, and knocked her away from him. The knife was still stuck in the front of his shirt, but he didn't seem to be aware of it. He reached across it into his coat to grasp his pistol. Jane threw herself on him, her arms around him to hug his arms to his body, her face within two inches of his. He reacted instinctively, charging forward to push her into the wall.

The impact pounded the wind from Jane's chest, but she clung to him. She opened her eyes and saw the shocked, empty look on his face. His lunge had pushed the knife in farther. His knees gave way, and suddenly his weight was on Jane. She could not hold him up, and as he slumped toward her, she slid down the wall to the floor with his torso resting on hers. Jane brushed his right hand away from his coat, reached to the spot where it had been, and grasped the hand-grip of the pistol.

She looked up and saw Frank Delfina in the doorway. He stepped forward into the dim room. "Great, Mikey! You got her!"

Jane drew in a breath and waited.

Delfina stepped up to the entangled pair, looked down, and said, "I wouldn't waste too much energy wrestling, babe. He can bench-press twice what you weigh. Get up."

Delfina's grin slowly turned to a look of puzzlement. Mike Cirro didn't look right. Then he saw Jane's right hand appear, and there was a gun in it.

Jane freed herself from Cirro's corpse and stood up. "Find the keys to the Suburban."

He stood motionless, both his hands held out in a pleading gesture. "Hey, I just wanted to talk to you. There was no reason to kill anybody."

"Get the keys." Jane stepped along the wall away from Delfina. She watched while he knelt down and patted Cirro's pockets. Then she saw him reach into the front pocket of Cirro's pants. He seemed to have the keys. She could hear jingling as he extracted his hand.

Jane watched his other hand. When she saw it close around the handle of the knife, she straightened her arm so the gun was aimed at his chest. "Leave the knife."

He stood up slowly, holding out the keys so she could reach for them.

Jane said, "Hold on to them. Head for the stairs."

He walked toward the doorway. "You think I'll make a good hostage or something?"

"We're going to drive off the farm together," said Jane. She reached to the top shelf of the closet without looking and found a baseball cap. "Then I'll let you off on the road and be on my way."

When Delfina got through the doorway, Jane prepared to see him dive to the side, trying to surprise her in the hallway.

He seemed to sense that she was ready for it, so he simply walked into the hall and down the stairs. Jane kept him eight feet away from her, so she would have time if he tried to lunge for the gun.

When they reached the front door, Jane said, "All right. Drop the keys on the floor and step away."

He dropped the keys, but moved off only about a yard.

"Farther."

Delfina obeyed. Jane picked them up and said, "Okay. Out the door and down the steps. If anybody calls to you, answer him. No matter what happens, keep walking at a normal speed. Go right to the passenger door of the Suburban, open it, get inside, and close it." When he began to move, Jane put the baseball cap on her head and pushed her hair up under it, then followed.

Delfina walked down the front steps ahead of her. She watched him walk straight across the yard, up the little driveway in front of the barn, and get into the car. Jane came around to the driver's side watching through the rear windows, never taking her aim off the back of his head.

She swung the door open and saw the gun in his hand. He was smiling. She could see it was already aimed at her chest.

He said, "Mike left a spare under the seat. So here we are."

Several thoughts competed for Jane's attention. No matter what this man said, it would be a lie. He would torment her until he learned that Bernie's money was gone, and then kill her. He had a gun aimed at her chest, and she had one aimed at his. If one of them fired, the other would too. Another thing she knew was that the human nervous system could do several things at one time, but it didn't always do them with the same speed. One action always had priority. She wanted Delfina to talk. If she moved, it would take an extra fraction of a second for him to change priorities and shoot. He would never fire while he was in the middle of a word. "What do you want?"

"I need you to get my money back, and you need me to get off the farm. Let's see if we can reach an agr—"

Jane fired four times, the bullets piercing his chest. She pulled the gun out of his lifeless hand and tossed it into the

back seat, then slid into the driver's seat and started the Suburban. It took an immense effort to overcome her revulsion
and push him up to a sitting position. She reached across him,
tugged the seat belt across his chest, and secured it.

She turned on the lights, backed the Suburban up, and then
drove slowly along the road. Suddenly, she saw the three cars
coming through the field toward the road, just ahead and on
her right. As they came, the stalks fell before them. They had
heard the shots. She thought of speeding up, trying to get past
before they got too close, but she remembered the men with
rifles coming along behind.

She drove even more slowly. She put her right hand on Delfina's chest under his chin, holding his head still and keeping
it from bouncing on the bumpy ride. Ahead of her, the three
cars were pushing over the last few rows of corn before them.
They were nearly at the edge of the road. The drivers saw the
Suburban coming, so they paused there. Their headlights
glared on the side of the Suburban, illuminating the face, head,
and shoulders of Frank Delfina as his driver coasted by, taking
him past the acres of flattened corn to the main highway.

37

At nine o'clock the following night, the rental car from
Terre Haute pulled up on the street across from the
Evansville police department and stopped. The old man at the
wheel looked nervously at the wide front doors as a pair of
uniformed policemen walked down the steps, then at the
young girl beside him.

"After everything that's happened, being this close to them
still gives me the creeps."

"You're not a criminal anymore, Bernie. They're here to protect people like us. Well, maybe not people like us, exactly, but the kind of people we'd be if we hadn't done anything."

Bernie looked at his watch, then at Rita. "You know, I was hoping that I wasn't going to have to say this. But the chance that she's going to show up isn't very good."

"I know," said Rita. "But she'll be here."

"I know she'd want to be here," he said gently. "And I know she's smart. But sometimes smart isn't enough."

"What are you saying—that you want to leave without her?"

"No," said Bernie. "Not at all. I haven't got any pressing engagements. I figured we could wait here a while without attracting those cops. Then we could get some sleep and come back tomorrow night at the same time. It's just that . . . well, she's used up a lot of chances. If things had gone the way she wanted, I think she would have been here, waiting for us. That means things didn't go the way she wanted. So I think maybe we ought to figure out what's going to happen next—what we do if she doesn't show up."

"I don't know," said Rita. "Do you?"

"Well, she's a specialist, and she seems to have been good at it. I think that we probably ought to do what she told us to. We'll go someplace, use the identification she gave us, get settled, and try to take care of each other." Bernie was silent for a few seconds. "Is that okay with you?"

Rita turned, leaned toward him, and gave him a small kiss on the cheek, then looked straight ahead. Bernie could see that there were tears in her eyes.

There was a sharp rap on the window that made Bernie jump. He turned, and Jane was opening the door. "Let me drive," she said.

Bernie got into the back seat, and Jane took his place and drove up the street.

"What happened?" asked Rita. "Are you all right?"

Jane looked at her, then said quietly, "I'm terrific." She drove a few more blocks, then said, "Bernie?"

"What, honey?"

"Coos Bay, Oregon."

Bernie said thoughtfully, "It's a hell of a long drive, but on the other hand, it's not much like Florida, and I'm sick of Florida. Come to think of it, I'm sick of the Midwest, too. And Coos Bay is right on the Pacific, so Rita would have a chance to go to the beach. Don't care much for the beach myself, but—"

"I wasn't asking your opinion."

"Oh," he said. "Well, Interstate 64 across to St. Louis, then switch to 70. The junction comes right after you cross the Mississippi River, so it's hard to miss. If you cross Seventh Street, you've gone too far. Then you drive a couple of days, take a jog up 15 to 84 in Utah. You get off at Route 20, go across Oregon, and turn left at the ocean."

It took four days to drive across the country once more. Jane found a house on a hill overlooking the ocean and entered into a lease-to-buy arrangement with the owner in the name of Michael Daily.

When Rita saw the papers, she said, "What about me? Who am I supposed to be?"

"You're his only living relative: his granddaughter."

Rita looked embarrassed. "Bernie, if you don't like that, I can just be your housekeeper again."

"No, you can't," said Jane.

"Why not?"

Jane sighed. "In the first place, the identification I made for you has the same last name. The reason I did so is that in the long run, your best chance is if you protect each other. If something happens to one of you, the only one who can even go into the hospital room is a relative. Bernie is pretty spry, but he's already over seventy. If he's suddenly out of the picture, a housekeeper isn't going to be allowed to live in his house. A granddaughter will inherit it, if we get around to making a will. If you get arrested, they'll release you into a grandfather's custody, but not the custody of an elderly employer. I could go on this way for a long time, if you had the patience to hear it."

"I'm sorry," said Rita. "I just didn't want to be a lot of trouble."

"Let her do it her way, kid," said Bernie. "After it's done, I don't think I want to call her back to do it again."

Jane bought a car for Michael Daily and his grand-daughter, Karen, then spent a week teaching them how to make themselves look a bit different from Bernie "the Elephant" Lupus and Rita Shelford, and how to use their new environment to keep hidden rather than draw attention to themselves. She took them to the stores they could patronize safely, and drilled them in the different ways of getting away from the area if they were recognized. She helped them open joint bank accounts. The last thing she did was take them to a lawyer. Bernie made out a will, leaving all of Michael Daily's worldly goods to his granddaughter.

When Rita awoke the next morning, Jane was packing a bag. She noticed Rita standing in the doorway watching her. Rita said, "I'm going to be sorry to see you leave."

Jane smiled. "It's time." She hesitated, then said, "You were at my house the day we met. This is your new life, and that's mine. The one thing I ask is that you remember your promise. Never mention anything about it to anyone."

"I understand," said Rita.

"And one more thing," Jane said gently. "I know you miss your mother. But please, give it a couple of years. Wait until she's out of prison and has had time to lose whoever is watching her. Then don't write a letter. Go there at night, pick her up, and talk while you drive."

She noticed that Rita had begun shaking her head before she had gotten through the first sentence. "What?" she asked.

"My mother's dead."

"How do you know?"

"I've known a long time. Practically since it happened. I started checking the Florida newspapers every chance I got since Albuquerque. One day it was in there. She got killed in prison."

"Why didn't you tell me?"

"I didn't want you to know." After a moment, she added,

"Don't ever tell Bernie. It would make him feel sorry for me. Nobody is ever going to feel sorry for me again."

Jane took Rita into her arms and held her for a moment. "I won't tell him," she said.

Jane picked up her bag and walked outside to the car. Bernie was waiting for her. "I brought your purse out," he said. "It's on the front seat. I knew you'd probably forget it, and we'd have to take some big chance to get it back to you."

"Thanks," said Jane.

She opened the car door, but Bernie stopped her. "One last thing. Don't worry. Right now it looks like they all got together for the sole purpose of hunting us down. It won't last. I know them. They get distracted. If they're looking for a pile of hundred-dollar bills and happen to see a kid with a nickel in his hand on the street, they'll stop to get the nickel. Then they'll fight over the nickel."

Jane shrugged. "I hope you're right."

"Of course I am," snapped Bernie. "I'm B . . . Michael Daily." He turned and walked toward the house, then stopped. "Thanks for the ride."

Jane waved, then hugged Rita. "I'll think about you."

Jane drove all day and into the evening before she stopped to make a call at a pay telephone under a street lamp in Provo, Utah. She dialed the number of the house in Amherst, and heard the answering machine.

Jane said, "I'm on my way home. It will take a few days. I love you."

She hung up, and reached into her purse to put her extra change back. In the corner of her purse she detected something unfamiliar. It felt like tissue paper. Could she have left that in since she had bought this purse? She pulled it out, but it felt heavier than it should have. She squeezed it between her fingers. There was something hard and round in it, like pebbles. As she took it out, carefully pulled apart the folds of tissue paper, and looked down, she remembered Bernie handing her the purse. The light from the street lamp glinted off the facets of the diamonds, and made them look like small, cold stars.

38

Molinari sat on the bench beside the enormous fake adobe building and stared at the scrubby cactus plants across the walkway. The sun was low, and no matter how he turned his head, the sparse, dry Arizona trees didn't cast enough shade to keep the glare out of his eyes.

"Mitch, stand over here in front of me." He pointed at a spot on the bricks and watched his nephew step into it, shuffle his feet sideways until his body blocked the sun, and then stand still. Molinari crouched in the cool shadow and felt the temperature of his skin begin to drop.

"You okay?" asked his other nephew, Steve.

"It's like being on another fucking planet," muttered Molinari.

"Why would anybody like him come here to live?" whispered Steve.

Mitch leaned forward confidentially, and an explosion of sunlight flashed in Molinari's face. "Maybe it's for his lungs."

"Yeah," said Molinari. "He wanted to make sure air only came in at the tops."

"Oh, yeah," said Mitch. "I meant here, instead of someplace else." Even they knew that Castiglione had been the architect of the conspiracy of 1987. The other two bosses had been executed after the attempt, but the Commission had accepted Castiglione's offer to go quietly into exile.

"Come in," said a woman's voice.

Molinari walked to the shaded porch with the two nephews flanking him, as usual, but the young woman in the white

346

dress who was waiting in the doorway lowered her eyes and shook her head. Molinari said to his nephews, "Wait here."

He followed the woman across a tiled foyer the size of a hotel lobby. Molinari was conscious of the tapping of his leather soles on the tiles, and looked down to notice that the woman's feet were bare. He had wondered about her since he had first seen her. He didn't remember hearing that Castiglione had any daughters. She seemed to be some kind of employee. Maybe she had a weapon hidden under the embroidered apron.

He found Castiglione sitting at a wooden table that looked as though it had been made by splitting logs into two-inch boards with an axe, then pounding ten-penny nails into them. The old man was thinner than the last time Molinari had seen him, but his skin had a healthy brown sheen that he didn't remember.

Molinari bent his head in a little bow of respect. "Don Paolo, I see you're looking good. This must be a healthy place."

Castiglione smiled at his clumsiness. "It's not as bad as you think it is. Sit down."

Molinari sat. The young woman padded up behind Castiglione's shoulder with a bottle of wine in one hand and two glasses in the other. Molinari watched her set them down, pour two glasses, and disappear through the rounded doorway. Castiglione lifted one of the glasses, said, "Salut'," then sipped.

Molinari imitated him. "Salut'."

"What are you here for, kid?"

Molinari was taken aback. After a moment he remembered that when the old man had last seen him, he had been a kid, not much older than his two nephews outside. "It's a long story."

"I know most of it," said Castiglione. "All the families that gave Bernie Lupus money are trying to get it back. Forget it. Bernie died intestate."

"What?"

"It doesn't mean no balls, it means no will—nothing written down about where the hell the money is. All this stuff about him telling somebody before he died is a fantasy. Out here there's a persistent old story about some prospector. He found a vein of gold as wide as Main Street in a mountain. He died. But every few years, a new bunch of suckers still get convinced he left a map. Why the hell would he make a map? You think a guy with a mountain of gold is going to want to show other people where it is? Do you think he's going to forget how he got there?"

"I guess not."

"Well, Bernie the Elephant lived by his memory. What the hell would have made him write anything down? That he wanted all his very good friends to get their money back? His friends would have taken the paper and dropped him in a Dumpster, and he knew it."

Castiglione took a drink of his wine, then set it down. "Don't get me wrong. I liked Bernie. It was always a pleasant experience to talk to a man who knew things, and Bernie couldn't help knowing everything he ever saw or heard. I would have gone to his funeral, but there are people who would have considered that breaking my word."

Molinari said, "I wouldn't have."

Castiglione gave a quiet chuckle. His head turned to look out at the garden, but his bright eyes were still watching Molinari from the side. "You should listen to your elders. Funerals are where a lot of deals get made."

Molinari hesitated. "You've been thinking about coming back?"

Castiglione waved a hand lazily to dismiss the idea. "There are still too many people alive who remember. They have to, because they know I do, and that I think about them every day." The way he said it made Molinari feel a chill in his spine.

Molinari said, "I came to talk to you because a lot of things are happening that I can't figure out. I need advice. After Bernie died, we all agreed to get together and watch to see if big money started moving."

Castiglione nodded. "I can't blame you. It's hard to lose that much money."

"We made a deal, and we all watched. All of a sudden, about a week ago, money starts showing up from no place. It's like a buried pipe broke under the street, and it starts gushing up from the manholes and the cracks in the sidewalks. Only it looks like it's all going to charities."

"I heard that."

Molinari kept his face from revealing that he had noticed the response. Castiglione knew things that he had no obvious means of knowing. Molinari went on. "So we all send our people out to find out what's going on. We pull every string, pressure every banker or broker or anybody we've got on the hook to trace the money back from the charities to where it came from. Finding out does zero, because the givers are made up. So we decide to find the people who might have had something to do with Bernie's death. There's Vincent Ogliaro. Bernie was killed in Detroit, and it's his city, even if he's in jail. But there's not much chance he could be doing the rest of it."

Castiglione nodded.

Molinari knitted his brows as though he had trouble reconstructing the list. "There's one of Bernie's bodyguards. He got scarce about the same time Bernie died. There's this girl who cleaned Bernie's house. And there's this woman." He shrugged. "Nobody knows anything about her, but somebody saw her with Bernie's housekeeper. They made a drawing of her, like the cops do."

Castiglione's eyes shone with amusement as he watched Molinari.

"We sent people everywhere with pictures, offered rewards. We watched airports, hotels, car rental places, everything. The only one who gets seen is the woman, and it may not even be the same woman."

Castiglione listened, his eyes gazing down into the deep, dark wine in his glass, letting the sunlight shine into it and turn it blood-red.

"Yesterday, my people start to look over their shoulders, and something has changed," said Molinari. "Castananza's guys are gone. Okay, I figure, he's got a small family, and he just decided he's lost enough on this. Next thing, it's a few of Catania's guys—not all, but some. This morning, my guys start seeing Delfina's guys leaving for home."

"So what did you come to me for? You think I got Bernie's money?"

Molinari made the face of surprise that Castiglione expected. "I'll be open with you, Don Paolo. I'm nervous. I want to know what you think."

Castiglione sighed. "I'll be open with you too. The money we all stashed with Bernie in the old days was big from the start. That was when a million dollars was still a million dollars. It's billions by now."

"That's what we all figured."

Castiglione spat toward the tile floor. "Kiss it good-bye. It died with him."

"But somebody is moving it."

"Maybe somebody in the FBI watching Bernie figured out where it was, and they're washing it because they're sick of asking Congress for money. Maybe Bernie confessed to his priest where it was, and now there's a crew of Jesuit accountants secretly slipping it to the lame, the halt, and the blind. Who gives a shit? If you can't find it and grip it with your hands, it's gone." He glared at Molinari. "The only question is, who was the first one to figure that out?"

"I don't know . . . Castananza pulled his guys out first."

"I'm sorry, kid," said Castiglione gently. "But you're way behind on this. Somebody used this to see what he could take that was worth more than Bernie's money. When you had this sit-down and decided everything, who was the one that arranged it? Where was it held?"

"John Augustino got everybody down to Pennsylvania. We met in this bus he has."

"It figures."

"Why? The Langustos seemed to do all the talking, and they were the ones who brought Bernie into the city in the first place. Or their father was."

"I'm talking about way before that. Bernie was from Pittsburgh. There was a meeting in the forties in Miami. The one who brought Bernie in and sold him to all of us was Sal Augustino, John's father. The Langustos just had the job of keeping Bernie fed and protected because in those days we wanted him in New York. I'd say that the one you want to watch out for isn't the one who's doing the talking. It's the one who's sitting behind him and watching everybody's faces. If Phil and Joe Langusto did all the talking, forget them. The one who's getting ready to cut your throat is John Augustino."

"I never would have thought of it that way," said Molinari. He stared at Castiglione for a few seconds. "I know that when you came here, you didn't get out of the life. I can see you still have money coming in, and somebody is telling you things."

Castiglione's face was empty of expression.

Molinari said, "I think maybe you still have people who work for you but don't say they work for you. I think maybe, if you said the word, all of a sudden you would have some soldiers."

Castiglione stared into his glass of wine. The time was here. "That's a dangerous thing to talk about. If anybody thought there was a chance you wanted that, they'd get together and come for your head."

Molinari shrugged. "If I get through this and they don't, it won't matter what they would have done."

Castiglione lifted his wine glass, held the stem between his thumb and forefinger and twirled it, watching the wine try to catch up. "I've been here for a long time. The soldiers I had, they're still where they always were. Their bosses probably don't remember what family these guys belonged to before."

"I want you to come back with me."

Castiglione pretended to think about it. He had known that this day would come. After all these years sitting in the desert and waiting, it was all coming together. Molinari had no idea who he was asking for help. He was too young to remember. In a month or a year, all of the capos who had forced Castiglione to come here would be dead. Then it would just be

Castiglione and Molinari, then just Castiglione. "I'll try to help you," he said.

"How many of these guys from the old days will come if you call? How many are you sure of?"

Castiglione pursed his lips. "Not many. Two hundred."

Molinari's heart began to thump. He had been right all along, but this was beyond his expectations. Let Augustino come; let all of them come. It just could be that when they did, the guys they had come to trust, the middle-aged, reliable ones who had worked for them for a dozen years, and before that had been part of the old Castiglione organization, would put the shotgun to the backs of their heads.

39

Phil Langusto stared at his brother, then at Tony Pompi. Their faces were expressionless. They didn't want to come in and tell him anything that required them to draw a conclusion. They just wanted to pretend they were technicians, showing him facts and figures because facts and figures weren't their fault. He waited impatiently while Pompi extracted the folded map from its envelope and laboriously unfolded it. His brother Joe took the other end of it, and they held it like a blanket and set it on the floor.

Phil walked to the edge of the map and looked down. It made him sick. The country looked like the body of a dead hippopotamus, lying there on its side with blood-red dots all over it. The spatters of red that had been concentrated on both coasts now overlapped into huge streams that ran down from Canada to Mexico in the west, and from New England to Florida in the east. But the part that had changed most was the midsection. There were dots on most of the major cities from Minneapolis to New York, and from the Great Lakes south to the Mason-Dixon line.

Phil said quietly, "This is what you wanted to show me?"

Joe nodded. "It was pretty much what we thought. They were on their way into the Midwest to mail the rest of the donations."

Phil glared at Joe, then at Pompi. "What is it? Did you come in just to tell me that you were right and get a pat on the head? Do you have some new theory, some new plan?"

Joe stared down at the map regretfully. "Not exactly. We just thought it was time to show you what we were seeing."

"I see a few thousand bright red dots. What do you see?"

Joe cleared his throat, nervously. "The map hasn't changed in a few days."

"What do you mean? It looks terrible."

"Yeah," said Joe. "It does. But what worries us is that it isn't any more terrible than it was about a week ago." He waited for Phil to catch on, but his brother's eyes just burned into his. "We think they're through mailing letters."

Phil stared down at the map. "But there are still a few empty spots. Nothing down in here at all." He pointed at the bottom of the map with the toe of his shoe, vaguely indicating Mississippi, Arkansas, Louisiana.

Tony Pompi said, "We noticed that too. But the letters have stopped. Either they weren't going down there in the first place, or . . ." He shrugged.

"Or somebody stopped them?"

Joe Langusto said, "Well, it's a possibility."

Phil walked to his desk and dialed the telephone. "Bobby?" he said. "Phil. Have you found him yet?" He listened for a few seconds. "What? Are you sure?" He stared at the floor for a moment and frowned. "Bobby, stay right where you are. I'll call you back in a few minutes." He hung up.

"What's that?" asked Joe.

"While you two have been playing with your map, a lot of stuff has been happening," said Phil. "Things I don't like."

"What kind of stuff?"

"To start with, guys are getting pulled out. One minute they're in an airport watching the baggage claim, and then next minute they're upstairs buying a ticket out. Our own guys have been calling in from everywhere. They want to know what's up."

"What is up?" asked Joe.

Phil stared at him with an expression that was almost hatred. After an effort, the look softened, as though he had momentarily forgotten Joe's face, then recognized it. "First it's Castananza. All of his guys went in the middle of the night. Then it's Catania: a few here, a few there, sneaking off. Then Delfina. None of them said a word to anybody."

"Why would they do that?"

Phil backed to the chair by the phone, let his knees buckle, and sat down hard. He scowled into space, and then his eyes cleared. "They must have found it."

"Found what?"

"What the hell are we talking about? Bernie the Elephant's money."

Joe shrugged. "I don't see how you can—"

Phil sighed, then spoke to his brother patiently. "Joey, listen carefully, and think. Every family has been out searching for Danny Spoleto, for Rita Shelford, and for this woman who was mailing letters. Why would anybody stop looking?"

Light seemed to enter Tony Pompi's eyes. "If they caught one of them!"

Phil nodded. "Or all of them. Anyway, they found the one who could give back the money." He began again. "Now, we have another strange happening. Frank Delfina has disappeared."

"When was he anything but disappeared? He travels all the time, like a salesman."

"Since the minute the first of his guys started to leave, I've been calling, trying to reach him. His guys in L.A. say he's in Omaha. His guys in Niagara Falls say he's in Albuquerque. The ones in Oakland say he's in L.A. They'll make sure he gets back to me. They're all nervous, they don't know when he left or when he'll be back."

"I don't get it," said Joe.

"Why would he drop out of sight right now? He's the one who has the money," said Phil. "You just said they're not mailing money out anymore. Well, I know why. Because Delfina caught them. He's got them, and he's spent the last week getting the money collected. By now he's got enough of it back to start buying himself the support of a few other families. Castananza, Catania. There will be others soon."

"I can hardly believe it," said Joe.

Phil stared at the carpet. His look of understanding deepened, then turned sour. "This is why the families have never been able to get anywhere. You make a deal that whoever finds the money will share it, and . . . here we are again. These people, their word is worth shit."

Joe cocked his head. He and his brother had spent hours discussing ways to keep most of the money themselves, but there was no reason to distract him now with unwelcome reminders. "And you think they won't share it?"

"If they were going to share, would they do it this way—call their guys home with no warning, no explanation?"

"I guess it makes sense that if they found it, they wouldn't leave their guys standing around in airports forever." He thought for a moment. "And if Delfina is the one behind all of it, I suppose he would want to be hard to find."

Phil reached for the telephone and pushed a few numbers. "Bobby? Yeah. Here's what I want you to do. Call in all our guys except the ones in Chicago, Cleveland, New Orleans, Pittsburgh, Boston, Philadelphia. In those places, leave a few guys. Have everybody else home tonight. The ones who are left, tell them to stay put, but make themselves invisible. I want them to slip out of sight, rent a room someplace, and sit tight by the phone."

He listened for a few seconds. "Right. Get enough home to protect our territory, and leave a few out there that nobody knows about. If somebody decides to surprise us, they'll find out my arm is longer than theirs. Somebody hits, I want soldiers right under his nose to hit back."

His brother Joe watched him, and he could feel that something was on his mind. "What?" he snapped.

"It sounds like you're getting ready to retaliate in all directions at once. Wouldn't it be better to figure out who's doing what, and then pick who you're going to hit?"

Phil winced. The man knew absolutely nothing. He had grown up in this house watching their father run the family, then watched Phil do it, and he had learned no more than if he had been the family dog. "Don't you think that if our guys noticed all these soldiers were being pulled back, somebody else noticed too? Do you think we're the only ones in the country who know that Frank Delfina has dropped off the radar screen?"

Joe said, "I imagine other people wouldn't have missed that."

"Well, nobody called me. I've known about it for a week, and not one person bothered to pick up the phone and tell me."

40

It was nearly morning, and Tommy DeLuca was getting worried. "Why don't they call? They should have found Delfina by now." He had begun the evening by drinking single-malt scotch to keep his excited anticipation from growing too great to bear. A little after midnight, he had changed to coffee, because he had begun to lose the feeling of jovial confidence and had descended into a slow, lazy feeling of defeat. Now he was edgy and irritable.

"They'll call," Guarino said. DeLuca could hear that

Guarino's voice had a different tone. That wasn't the way he wanted to hear Guarino's voice. Guarino was just saying what he was supposed to say.

"We should have brought in the other families before we started looking," announced DeLuca. "Then it wouldn't have been sneaking around, three guys here and five guys there. We could have gone into every one of his businesses with an army. We could have surrounded each building, set fire to it, and shot anybody that came out."

Guarino sighed. "It might not have been that easy. They're sitting in their houses with the gates closed and the lights out."

"That's just the little guys: Castananza, maybe a couple of others. The Langustos still have their guys out there looking, and Tasso and Molinari and Augustino."

"It's better we didn't call in everybody until we know for sure," Guarino said. "I'm telling you, everybody's tense. What if we got them in on it and a few of their guys got killed? It wouldn't take much to set these people off right now. We could see that army of guys, only they'd be coming up Michigan Avenue to drag us out and hack our heads off."

"We all agreed to cooperate."

"Sure," said Guarino. "But it's going to be a hell of a lot easier if we already took all the risks, and did all the work, and then bring them in on it. Then it's you handing out the money, and not Phil Langusto. And as soon as we find Delfina, we're ninety percent there. If you do it this way, there's no risk."

"There's a risk, all right," said DeLuca. "You ever thought about what happens if somebody finds out we grabbed Delfina and got Bernie's money back before we tell them ourselves?"

"Like who?"

"I don't know. The New York families. With all five of them, they must have two thousand made guys, and they've been fighting each other every few years since the Stone Age. These people like Molinari . . . they worry me."

"That's why this is the best way. You let them in on it,

and what was to guarantee they wouldn't cut a side deal, dust our guys, and take all the money? Molinari is capable of that . . . Catania's crazy, and Phil Langusto is the fucking Prince of Darkness."

The ring of the telephone in the stillness made DeLuca jump. He lifted it with his fingertips, as though it might be hot. "Yeah?"

Guarino watched Tommy DeLuca's face. DeLuca squeezed his eyes closed as though they stung, and rubbed his forehead with his fingertips. "All right," said DeLuca. "Bring everybody home now." He hung up, and turned to Guarino. "They're pulling their guys home."

Guarino stood up. "Who is?"

DeLuca said, "The big guys. Langusto, Tasso, Molinari, Augustino, Catania . . ." He squeezed his eyes closed again, then took a deep breath and let it out in despair. "When Castananza pulled his people out, I should have known. He's been around for a long time, and he figured out he didn't belong in this. It's all been some kind of trap. It's probably Catania. When we had that sit-down, he kept trying to make everybody think we imagined the whole thing. He and Delfina probably had our money all the time."

"If they've got the money, why would they do anything else? What else do they want?"

"Delfina always thought he got screwed when Castiglione left and the Commission divided up the family. He got nothing, and I got Chicago. So what do you suppose he wants?"

"What about Catania?"

"Catania wants to take over the world," DeLuca said. "We've got to get ready to protect ourselves. . . . We'll make it really obvious, make it clear that Chicago isn't going to be easy, so he'll try to gobble up somebody else first."

Guarino was silent for a moment, then said, "I don't know, Tommy. Are you sure it's a good idea to look like we've got something in mind? People are nervous. All it would take right now is one little thing. A car backfires near one of those guys, and we're going to have bodies dropping from one end of the country to the other."

"There's nothing else we can do," pronounced DeLuca.

Guarino said, "I'd better get started, then. First thing is to get the word to people in all our businesses this morning, so nobody gets surprised."

Guarino walked to the front door, then was startled to hear DeLuca's voice right at his shoulder. He didn't remember DeLuca ever walking him out before. "One more thing. Before this starts, I want a promise."

"Sure, Tommy. What is it?"

"If anything happens to me, I want you to get Catania."

Guarino shrugged. "He's dead." He opened the door and went outside. As he walked toward his car, he contemplated the strange observation he had made years ago. He had just seen another demonstration of it, but he still did not fully understand it. He remembered Tommy DeLuca from not that many years ago, when he was just the head of a crew on the South Side. He had been hard and audacious. When things had gotten ugly during the attempted coup in '87, he had walked the street in a kind of strut, his overcoat open, his hands in the pockets, where he could reach through the lining for the little machine gun he carried. He had been alert and watching—not looking for something he was going to run away from, but something he was going to open up on with that gun.

Guarino had worked for four bosses in his life, and he had seen this happen before. For some reason, after a year or two in power, they began to change. They stopped going out and having fun with the guys, and they stopped smiling. But the less pleasure they got out of life, the more attached to it they seemed to get. It was as though they had won and kept so much money that they couldn't bear the thought that they might ever die. He had noticed Tommy getting timid a couple of years ago. The few times he had seen Catania, he was always popping vitamins and drinking orange juice or bottled water, and that was a sign too. He wanted to live forever, like some Egyptian pharaoh.

The only exception that Guarino had ever seen had been

Paul Castiglione. That was a man who had kept his edge. Even when his try at empire building had been betrayed and his allies killed, he had gone into exile the right way. He had done it like a crocodile backing out of a house. There was no question he was going: the Commission had said he was out. But they knew they had to be satisfied with that, and not kill him, because as long as he was going anyway, there was no reason to get any closer to those teeth.

If Castiglione ever disappeared from Arizona, there would be a number of people in New York, Chicago, New Orleans, Pittsburgh, and a few other places who would find themselves rethinking some of their decisions from those days. There would be a lot of others who would be glad to see those days come back, and Guarino was one of them.

He got into his car and drove off toward the bookmaking service he ran on Fifty-fifth Street. It was the only place he could be absolutely positive had a phone line or two that he could use without being overheard or taped. It had always been one of his favorite places. He supposed that, with a war coming, he would probably have to shut it down in a few days, even though it supplied ten percent of his income. It was going to put a dent in his plan to save for the kids' colleges, but it was the only thing to do. He wasn't going to put twenty-seven people, half of them women, in front of a fire-bomb, at least not for ten percent.

As Guarino drove, he pondered all the calls he would have to make this morning. DeLuca had sent about two hundred and fifty guys out, and each had some people of his own. That had been far too many to have away from home for any reason, and now it just might cost something. He was going to have to make about fifty calls before the sun came up.

Tommy DeLuca sat inside his big brick house, wondering what he should be doing. By noon he was going to be surrounded by soldiers, but now he was in this peaceful, quiet room with nobody to talk to. This was when he could think, and he would have to think. In a few hours, when the guys started gathering around him, they were going to want to hear something that sounded like a sensible order of battle, and a strategy for defending the South Side of the city from . . . whom?

From Delfina and Catania, certainly, but Delfina was too devious to act without having the numbers on his side. DeLuca thought of the possibilities and felt his chest shrinking inward away from his shirt. Catania had probably brought a few other families with him from the beginning. The only ones that made sense would be a couple of other New York families. He wouldn't want anyone at his doorstep waiting for a chance to take him out.

DeLuca thought of a few preliminary precautions. He would keep guys at O'Hare. There would be a few people in the arrival areas to spot the invaders, but the real meat of the crew would be outside, where they could do something about it. They would need some way of communicating, so spotters could alert the shooters to targets. Radios? He had a strong suspicion that it was a bad idea. There were so many radios already at work in an airport that somebody would end up telling an American Airlines pilot to shoot the man with the yellow tie, and everybody would go to jail. Cell phones, maybe.

There should be teams along the last stretches of the big highways—Interstate 90, certainly, and maybe one or two others. People should be placed in windows near all of his businesses. He would give them binoculars. There would be a few heavily armed defenders inside to hold off the assault.

That was the anvil. He would have to prepare a hammer for it. He would need to institute a flying squad. Every time the defenders got hit, a ready, massive force would sweep in and smash the invaders from behind. He would probably need two or three squads. Chicago was too big for one group to cross whenever there was trouble.

DeLuca glanced toward the window, and things looked different. After a second, he realized that the pair of security lights on the eaves above the window that went on at night and off at dawn weren't illuminating the yard. He walked to the window and looked up. Both bulbs had burned out. He sighed in frustration.

He would have liked to have one of the soldiers who came later replace the bulbs. But he couldn't call in his people for a fight to the death and give them chores like handymen. Besides, by then it might be dangerous. Once he called everyone in, the enemy would know he was on to them. These might be the last few hours when a man going up on a ladder in front of the house would be entirely safe. He decided to forget the bulbs.

He looked out the window at the light fixture in hatred. He couldn't just forget it. That light was the one that illuminated the thick shrubbery along the house, and the middle section of the driveway. Leaving those areas dark wasn't safe. They were the spots where a hit team could sneak up to the house.

DeLuca went to the basement and returned with a stepladder, then went to the cupboard in the laundry room and found two new bulbs. He went out the kitchen door with the two bulbs under his left arm and the aluminum ladder banging his knee at each step, and came around to the front of the house.

He set the bulb box on top of the thick hedge, opened the ladder and planted it firmly in the dirt under the eaves, then climbed up to reach the dead bulbs. He began to unscrew the first one, but it came too easily. On a hunch, he turned it clockwise.

The light came on. DeLuca's heart began to pound. He whirled, and the shot pierced his left eye. He was dead, but more shots came rapidly, punching into his chest, his belly, his arm as he fell, then pounding into the side of the house where he had been, and through the window.

When Di Titulo heard the gun's *click-click-click*, he opened his eyes. DeLuca was gone, but Di Titulo dimly understood that he must have been hit. There was blood on the side of the house where he had been. Di Titulo sprang to his feet and crashed through the hedge. He hurried across the lawn to the street as the car pulled up.

As Di Titulo ducked through the open door to the back seat, he realized he still had the gun in his hand. The car moved off so fast that the door swung shut, then rattled all the

way to the corner. When the car bobbed in a half stop before
the turn, Di Titulo put the gun in his left hand and slammed
the door shut. He felt the gun being taken from his left hand,
and turned to look at Saachi.

The thin, cadaverous face was close to his, and the odor of
cigarettes was overpowering. The pointed teeth were bared
all the way to the gums, and Di Titulo sensed it must be a
smile. "You okay?"

Di Titulo felt pressed with claustrophobia. He wanted to
open the window, to push the door open and get outside. He
wanted the car to stop, and he wanted it to reach the speed of
light. He hadn't understood what Saachi had said, but he
knew what it must have been. "That was . . . awful."

Saachi nodded. "Don't worry. It gets easier."

Di Titulo's eyes widened. "I thought . . . I'm not a . . . I
thought it was just this one, because of the bomb in my car."
Saachi looked at him, but his face showed no sign that he had
heard. Di Titulo tried again. "I'm a businessman."

Saachi looked ahead over the driver's shoulder. "As of two
minutes ago, we're at war. Everybody's a soldier." He turned
suddenly to hold Di Titulo with his eyes. "This is your job
now. Get good at it."

41

Jane looked up at the second-floor window beside the big
maple tree. The bedroom light was off, but she had seen a
glow in the casement windows at the front, and now she could
see that the kitchen lights were on. She stepped to the back
door and reached for the knob, but it swung open and Carey
took a stride toward her and gathered her into his long arms,

holding her gently and rocking her a little. It felt warm and safe and restful.

After a long time she said, "I guess you do remember me."

He kept her in his arms. "Sure. You're the reason I never felt the urge to get a cat. I already have something sleek and beautiful that never comes when I call it, just drops in when it feels like it and goes away again."

She burrowed deeper into his arms, then leaned back and lifted her face to kiss him. The kiss was soft and leisurely and perfect. "Can I come in?"

They walked through the little entry into the big old kitchen, where Jane could hear the watery chugging of the dishwasher. She stepped into the dining room and ran her hand along the smooth surface of the table.

"Checking for dust?" he asked.

"No," she said. "I don't need any dust right now, thanks. This feels more like one of those occasions for champagne, and I can't remember if we have any."

"Of course we do," he said. "I've always kept some in case somebody spills something on the carpet." He pulled a bottle from the refrigerator and peeled off the foil.

"Champagne doesn't do that. You're thinking of club soda."

"Oh?" He popped the cork. "This isn't any good, then." He stared at it sadly. "Might as well drink it or something."

Jane reached into the cupboard for a pair of tulip glasses. "I think we have to. Otherwise, when we put a note in the bottle, it'll get wet."

They sipped their champagne and walked into the living room. She turned and faced him. "Have you seen these nice clothes I bought?"

"Very fetching, as my grandmother would have said."

She began unbuttoning the blouse with her left hand, then glanced at him. "Have you been sufficiently fetched?"

"More than enough," he said. "I wouldn't need to see them again for a long time."

"Good." The blouse slipped off her shoulders. She undid the clasp of her slacks and stepped out of them, and Carey's arms enveloped her again. There was the gentle touch of his fingers that gave her chills, then the warm, firm feeling of the palms of his hands, smoothing her skin, defining the shape of her body, always moving as though he needed to touch her everywhere at once. She needed it too, as she had needed to take off her clothes in the first minutes after she saw him.

It wasn't just because she felt she couldn't wait, but because part of it was showing him that this was what she wanted. And she wanted to see and feel his joy at knowing that she did. Her own hands were nimbly, urgently undoing buttons and buckle and slipping off his clothes. They made love where they had stopped in the living room, then went upstairs to their bedroom and lay in the dark on the cool, clean sheets with the warm summer breeze pushing in the curtains to direct itself across their bodies. After that they lingered over each moment, letting the night reach its dark, unchanging no-time, pretending that night was permanent and they could stay like this forever. Hours later, Jane caught sight of the glowing red digits of the clock on the nightstand, and wasted a second hoping she had read them wrong.

She said, "It's nearly three A.M.," but his lips pressed against her mouth to silence her, then stayed. His hand moved gently along her throat, and already her feelings were building again.

When she was able to look at the clock again, she heard the first tentative chirps of a sparrow in a tree across the back yard. She turned away from it to look beside her at Carey, and she could see that he had fallen asleep. She very softly placed her hands under his heavy forearm and held it while she slipped out from under it, then set it down on the bed where she had been.

She kept her eyes on him as she walked quietly toward the door. She let herself adore his long legs and his big feet and the peaceful little-boy look his face acquired when he was dreaming. I had this, she thought. If I die now, at least I recognized and accepted the best thing that life offered to me.

She looked down to be sure her bare foot touched the two pieces of hardwood floor closest to the hinge of the door, where it never creaked, then slipped down the long second-floor hallway to the best of the spare bedrooms. She showered in the bathroom there, then put on an old sweatshirt and jeans and went downstairs to start making her husband's breakfast.

When Jane had let Carey sleep as long as she dared, she went back up to the bedroom and kissed his cheek. He didn't move. She kissed his neck, then kept her lips pressed to his cheek and watched his eyelids. "Hypocrite," she said. "You're awake already."

"I'm playing dead," he said. "Waiting to see just how far you're willing to go."

She stood up. "Mother was right. Men are too dumb to do anything but keep going until you tell them to stop." She dropped her pillow on his head. "The good ones, anyway."

He swung his feet to the floor and stood up. She pretended not to look at his long, lean body, and ached to hear him say she had made a mistake, that it was Saturday. He said, "I smell something good."

"That's right. I want you to have time to taste it and wake up before you go to the hospital and try to cut something out of somebody."

"Very responsible of you," he said.

She put her arms around him and held him. He stood still, facing away. He said, "I was afraid I'd wake up and you would be gone."

"I'm sorry," she said. "I'm home now, and I'm going to be the wife of your dreams."

He turned, his face intrigued. "Oh?"

She nodded. "It's because you didn't say anything about my hair. You hate it, but you didn't say it. That means you're too smart to just throw away."

She went downstairs and waited for him, then sat at the table with him and pretended to eat so she could be close to him. After a few minutes, he asked quietly, "Are you going to tell me what happened?"

"Yes," she said. "But there's too much to tell now. It's over and I'm home."

"Why didn't you call again?"

Here it was, so soon. No, this wasn't soon. It seemed abrupt, because it was something that she should have said in the first seconds, and hadn't. "Things turned out to be much . . . stranger than I expected. There wasn't anything I could have said that would have made you less worried."

He stared at her for a second, then went back to his breakfast. She could sense what he wasn't saying. She put her hand on his. "I love you," she said. But that was just what people said when there was nothing else to say—like a dog nuzzling up to lick his face. "You know why I went. Somebody needed help. I felt I had to help her."

"Just like Richard Dahlman," Carey said. "That wasn't what you were going to say, because we both know it. I understand. I made you promise never to do this again, and then, when it was somebody I cared about, I asked you to save him."

Jane shook her head. "You're wrong. We have to get this story straight right now, or it will be between us forever. You didn't make me promise. I just promised. It wasn't hard. I wasn't giving up something. It was just part of being married to you, and I made it to myself before you ever thought of it—before you knew that there was going to be a need to ask for it."

"It doesn't matter," he said. "What matters is what you want now. Today."

Jane took a deep, painful breath, and kept the tears out of her voice. "I want more than anything to stay here with you. I want to call Joy at your office and have her cancel your surgery and your afternoon appointments and maybe never let you out of my sight again. We're thirty-four years old, and we might have forty or fifty years left. I want every day of that so much that I don't want to let any of them slip by when I don't reach out and touch you at night before I close my eyes."

"But this girl came along, and you heard her story, and off you went."

"The promises we made to ourselves about the nice life we were going to have were in place. They just had to be forgotten until I had done what was required to keep my self-respect."

"That's what we said when we decided to help Richard Dahlman."

"I guess it is. They're both proof that when you make rules about what's going to happen in the future, the universe doesn't always hear what you say."

"So a promise is like a wish," he said. He stood up.

Jane had tears in her eyes now. "No. Or I guess it's yes. What I'm trying to say is that this isn't fair. I did something good. I can't forget what I know, or who I am. If the same thing happened in the same way tomorrow, I would do it again. Just because I risked my life a year ago to save Dahlman, I shouldn't lose the kind of closeness to my husband that I had." The tears came, and she stood to face him. "Don't you see? I don't want you to shut up and stand aside. I want you to say what you think—that your breakfast tastes like soap, or my haircut looks funny, or—"

"You'd drop me like a twelve-point buck on the first day of hunting season."

"No." She threw her arms around his neck and held him. "No, I wouldn't. Especially if it was that you loved me and would rather I didn't go out and get killed. Maybe we'll get to choose what will happen, and maybe we won't. I told you what I wanted if I get to choose."

Carey pulled her closer and gave her a long, tender kiss. Suddenly, she put her hands on his chest and held him farther away. "Now get your hands off my ass and go to work. Honestly."

Carey smiled. "Sorry. I'm just a romantic at heart."

"More like that twelve-point buck," she said. She hugged him again, then spun him around. "It's twenty minutes to seven. Get going."

He took three long steps into the back entry, stopped, and looked at her once more. Then he was out the door. Jane walked through the dining room listening to the car engine, then watched through the living room window as he backed his black BMW out the driveway and drove off toward the hospital.

Jane made her proprietary tour of the house. When she was not here, Carey seemed not even to pass through the rooms that weren't in his way during his routine movements. He came in the back entrance near the garage, used the kitchen, climbed the stairs to the master bedroom, and went to sleep. He was not an especially neat person, but his profession had given him a cold-eyed view of microbes, so the kitchen was spotless. All she had to do was keep an eye out for the pots, pans, and utensils that he had put in the wrong places, and move them back where they belonged while she put away the dinner dishes and washed the new batch.

An hour later she backed the rental car out of the long driveway. She drove west to the Niagara, turned and headed north looking at the river until she reached the house where she had grown up in Deganawida.

Jane pulled the car all the way into the garage so it wouldn't attract attention, then stepped to the front porch, un-locked the door, and used the next few seconds to scan the neighborhood for any sight she had not seen a thousand times before.

She swung the door open and stepped inside to punch the code on her keypad to turn off the alarm. Then she lingered in the doorway for a few seconds. There was no sound. The air was still and a little stale because the house had been tightly sealed. She closed the door and lifted the telephone beside the couch off the hook to hear the dial tone reassure her that the wires had not been cut. She relaxed her muscles. Nobody had been here while she had been away.

Jane walked the first floor of the house, glancing at each door and each window, then went upstairs. The house always seemed tiny after she'd spent a night in the McKinnon house. Jane stopped at the answering machine in her bedroom. The red glowing display said zero. Until she had looked at it, she had dreaded the possibility that there would be another call.

She went to the vanity. She picked up the large perfume bottle on the end, unscrewed the little gold cap, and sniffed. It was still fresh enough. The juice of water hemlock and may-apple would still kill quickly. She set the bottle on the vanity with the others, and left the room.

She went downstairs, through the kitchen to the cellar. Down here was the only place where the real age of the house was visible. The cellar had been dug with a shovel and built of blocks of stone, and the beams were just logs that had been cut near here. A few of the square-headed, hand-forged nails that held the floorboards could be seen here, pounded into the beams near the wall so somebody long ago could hang something there.

Jane walked to the far end of the cellar, where the coal bin had once stood, and moved the stepladder under one of the old round heating ducts that led along the ceiling to a point where it had once curved upward to a big floor register. The coal furnace had been replaced long before Jane was born.

She pulled apart two sections of the duct and reached inside for the metal box she kept there. She placed it on the top of the ladder and looked inside. There was the supply of identities she had grown for runners but never used—credit cards, birth certificates, licenses.

Jane began to unload her purse. She put all of the false identities she had brought from Chicago into the box. Then she put the few thousand dollars she had not spent inside. She dug deeper into the purse and found the tissue paper Bernie had put there. She opened it once more, looked at the collection of sparkling stones, and hesitated. Mrs. Carey McKinnon could probably afford to have a few of those diamonds set, and even get away with wearing them. But Mrs. McKinnon couldn't afford to forget that she was still Jane Whitefield. And Jane Whitefield lived in a world where the only practical use for diamonds was to transport a great deal of flight money in a small space. Jane folded the paper and put it into the bottom of the box, under the money, where she kept a special set of identities that nobody else knew existed.

These were particularly good ones, grown in pairs and carefully renewed and tended so that all of the licenses, passports, and credit cards were kept current. The pictures on them were hers and Carey's.

Jane pushed the metal box into the dark duct, closed the two sides, and moved the ladder across the cellar to its space beside her father's old workbench. She climbed the stairs. Before she turned off the light, she took a last look at the heating duct to reassure herself that the two sections had come together tightly to keep her hiding place secure and invisible.

THE JANE WHITEFIELD NOVELS
BY THOMAS PERRY

She will help you disappear, if it helps you stay alive . . .

Jane Whitefield is in the one-woman business of helping desperate people disappear. Thanks to her membership in the Wolf Clan of the Seneca tribe, she can fool any pursuer, cover any trail, and then provide her clients with new identities, complete with authentic paperwork.

VANISHING ACT

Jane opens a door to another world for an attractive fugitive named John Felker, and walks into a trap that will take all her heritage and cunning to escape.

DANCE FOR THE DEAD

A calculating killer stalks an innocent eight-year-old boy, and Jane faces dangerous obstacles that will put her powers—and her life—to a terrifying test.

NIGHTLIFE

A Novel

THOMAS PERRY

Nationally bestselling author of *Pursuit* and *Dead Aim*

As Portland detective Catherine Hobbes follows the evidence in a puzzling murder investigation, she finds herself matched with an unpredictable adversary capable of changing her appearance and identity at will. Catherine must use everything she knows as a homicide detective and as a woman to stop a beautiful serial killer who acts on impulse and with ease, and who becomes more efficient and elusive with each crime.

www.ballantinebooks.com